Marry Me

by

Kristin Wallace

Marry Me
by Kristin Wallace
Published by Astraea Press
www.astraeapress.com

ISBN 13: 978-1494298159
ISBN: 1494298155
Cover Art Designed by Book Beautiful

Thank you to my family, who never stopped encouraging this crazy impulse to be a writer. I would not be the writer I am today without the friendship, encouragement and advice from everyone at Florida Romance Writers. Thank you for helping to make this dream come true.

Chapter One

The past is like a revolving door, and if people aren't careful it'll come back and whop them in the backside. Hard.

Like Julia Richardson's just did.

"Julia, we... Sarah needs you. It's the baby."

Two sentences, barely audible, as her former stepsister's husband fought to get the words out. Those two sentences had Julia behind the wheel in the dead of night, headed back to the small Southern town — and the family — she'd successfully avoided for fifteen years.

She looked in the rearview mirror and spotted an errant, titian-colored curl sticking straight up. With a stifled groan, she mashed it down. Ah, humidity, such a lovely thing. The farther south she got, the more it curled. By the time she reached her destination she expected to look like a dead ringer for a certain redheaded, singing orphan. If said orphan was a full-figured Amazon with a bad attitude.

By the time Julia drove past the quaintly painted sign, which proclaimed she was entering Covington Falls, Georgia — *Covington* for the founding family, *Falls* for the trickle of water which emptied into Lake Rice, the name of the other founding family — the sun was blazing. Surprisingly, she knew exactly where to go. Or maybe not so surprising since it didn't look like much had changed in fifteen years. It still looked like a small and dainty cousin of Savannah.

She turned down a tree-lined lane that could have doubled for a 50s television show and a moment later pulled into the driveway of Grace's house. A white, two-story Colonial number with a wrap-around porch, complete with a swing. Rounding out this picture of all-American perfection was an honest to goodness white picket fence. Julia stared at the house, wondering what in the world she was doing here. She so didn't belong in a place like this.

Before she could back out of the driveway, the front door opened, and a woman stepped out onto the porch.

Grace. Ex-stepmother #3. Mother of Sarah and the reason for the midnight run.

Julia got out of the car unsure what kind of reception to expect. Before she knew it, Grace flew down the stairs with arms outstretched.

A familiar scent of cookies and violets invaded her senses. Exactly the way an angel might smell, she imagined. When she 'd been thirteen, and angry at the world, she hadn't been able to hug Grace back. Now Julia did. Then didn't want to let go.

Grace pulled back, taking Julia's face in her warm hands. "How I've missed you."

"You have?"

She smiled. "You have no idea."

"I've missed you, too."

"Let me look at you," Grace said, stepping back to get the full view. "Why, you're gorgeous. I always knew you would be, but my goodness you're stunning."

"You look good yourself."

And she did, Julia thought. There were a few more lines, and a lot more grey hairs, but the sparkle was still there. Only now there was a deeper contentment in those blue eyes Julia didn't remember from before.

"I can't believe how quickly you got here," Grace said.

"Well, it's not like I had to bother getting off work. Getting fired sort of opens up your day."

"I got your e-mail. Your boss had some kind of heart condition, and he had to sell the business?"

Julia nodded. "Right, and the new owner brought in his own marketing people."

"The poor man. It must have been difficult for him."

"I'm sure. The fantastic thing is I can't even be mad at him, because how can you blame the guy for wanting to live a while longer?"

Grace chuckled a little. "I'm sure you'll find something else. Maybe even sooner than you think."

Julia spun around at the odd statement. "What do you mean?"

For a second Grace almost looked guilty, but in the next moment she clapped her hands. "Look at me, letting you stand here when you're probably dead on your feet! Let me help you get your bags inside. Are you hungry?"

"I'd rather go see Sarah."

"Okay, but bags first, and I need to tell my husband where we're going."

Julia took a tentative step inside the house. "I got your letter about him having a stroke. How is he doing?"

"He has his days, though he's much better. His speech is getting clearer, and he's regained some strength on his bad side. We're taking it one day at a time. Letting God handle all the big stuff."

Julia bit her tongue. She'd just arrived, and now wasn't the time to get into the topic of her skepticism about God and faith.

Grace smiled.

"What?"

"Still have the same doubts about God I see."

Julia looked at the floor.

Grace tilted Julia's chin back up. "You have to come to it in your own way."

She walked away before Julia could respond. On the second floor, Grace stopped in front of the second bedroom on the right and opened the door. Julia's breath seized, and she came to an abrupt halt. It was the same one she'd occupied as a teenager. She was swamped with an instant flashback of the first time she'd stepped into this room. She'd been carting an enormous designer suitcase her mother had bought for the "trip". Of course, Julia had known it was more like an "exile", away from her mother and stepfather #2.

Julia had dragged the blasted thing up the stairs herself, having refused to let her father touch either her or her belongings. She'd glanced down to contemplate a spot on her thigh where a bruise would surely form, and then looked up. Into a fairy room. Fairies on the wallpaper, on a gorgeous poster, and even on the white shag throw rug.

Somehow, Julia had known the woman who'd become her father's third wife had done it. For her.

Grace turned. "Are you all right?"

Julia snapped back to the present. "Sure."

"I can put you in another room," Grace said. "Sarah's old room, if you like."

"No, this is fine." At least the fairies were gone now, replaced with light blue paint. She stepped over the threshold and put her bag down on the bed.

"For the longest time, I didn't even know if you read my letters," Grace said.

"It was pretty hard to ignore those scented, handwritten letters." Julia could hear the bite in her voice, but couldn't help it.

Grace winced. "It was too much. I told myself I should leave you alone. You'd been hurt enough, but I didn't want you to think we'd forgotten you. I wanted you to know what was going on in our lives. When you eventually started answering them, I hoped—"

"I'd come back?"

Grace flushed. "It was silly of me, I know."

Great, in the house five minutes, and she'd already hurt Grace's feelings. Julia tried to be nice.

She drifted to the window, which looked down onto the street. "So, you married Mr. Graham from next door?"

If Grace looked surprised by the olive branch, it was only for a moment. "Yes, but then I've known John all my life. He has a son Seth. He's your age. Do you remember him?"

"Vaguely. He didn't talk much."

Grace smiled. "He's a minister, so he has to talk more now. Of course, I told you about his poor wife Beth."

Julia nodded. The letter telling her about Seth's wife's battle with cancer coming to an end had broken her heart, even though she'd never met the woman.

Julia turned, arms folded. "How could you do it?"

"Do what?"

"Get married again? Your first husband died, and the second one dumped you. How in the world do you get to a place where you can trust your heart to someone else?"

Grace's face crumpled. "Oh, Julia. Maybe if you'd come to the wedding, or Sarah's, you would have seen—"

"Seen what? That there is such a thing as a happy ending? I was cured of such romantic notions by the time I was ten. I guess I should have sucked it up and come to Sarah's wedding. I know she was hurt because I didn't, but I made a vow to myself I wouldn't attend another wedding as long as I live, and it's one I intend never to break."

Grace reared back a little, and Julia was immediately ashamed of her outburst. She was the world's biggest jerk. "I'm sorry."

"No, no. It's fine," she murmured. "I'll go tell John we're

leaving, and I'll meet you downstairs."

The door closed with a soft click, and Julia sank onto the bed. This had been such a bad idea. She should grab her suitcase and get out of here right now. The only thing stopping her was the memory of Eric's choked voice on the other end of the phone.

A few minutes after finally returning downstairs, they were on their way to the hospital.

Julia finally broke the stilted silence. "What's going on with Sarah? Eric didn't say much on the phone."

Grace concentrated on the road. "There were some contractions. The doctor managed to get them to stop, but it was touch and go for a while. We spent the night praying, I can tell you."

"Is the baby going to be all right? And Sarah?"

"She has to be careful right now, but I'm sure she'll give you all the details when we get there."

"Why did Eric ask me to come down here, anyway?"

Grace glanced over. "I think they're hoping you'll be the answer to their prayers."

"What do you mean?"

"I'll let them fill you in."

"Why can't you fill me in?"

Another flick of the eyes in Julia's direction. "They made me promise."

A prickle of unease worked its way down her spine. "What aren't you telling me?"

Grace patted Julia's hand. "Don't worry. You can always say no."

The queasy feeling escalated. "Why do I feel like I should get right back in my car and escape before it's too late?"

Grace chuckled, and for the first time Julia realized the angel act *was* completely an act.

Why had she never noticed Grace was evil?

****

"She's changed a bit," Grace said, as they looked into the hospital room where Sarah was sleeping.

Julia couldn't speak over the lump in her throat. The volleyball size bulge in Sarah's middle was the least of the changes. There was nothing of the little pipsqueak who'd followed her around like a frisky puppy for two years. Sarah's honey-blond hair, which used to hang past her waist in thick braids, had been cut short. The baby fat was gone, and now she looked like a young Grace. Her former stepsister had grown into a beautiful woman.

As if sensing a presence in the room, Sarah stirred and opened her eyes. She spotted Grace first. "Mom, I thought I told you to go home and rest."

"I know, honey, but there's someone who wanted to see you."

Sarah turned and looked at the tall redhead standing next to her mother. For a moment, her brows furrowed in confusion, then her eyes widened in delight. "Julia!"

"I'll give you guys a few minutes," Grace said, as she slipped out of the room.

Julia laughed as Sarah tried to lever herself up in the bed. "Don't get up," she said, leaning down to hug her stepsister. She took a deep breath. One thing hadn't changed. Sarah still smelled like sunshine, albeit with a hint of the wonderful antiseptic hospitals loved to use.

Sarah looked her over and grumbled. "Look at you! All your glorious hair, and a figure to die for. I think I hate you!"

Julia perched on the side of the bed and rubbed Sarah's extended belly. "This is just as beautiful."

"This is Mary."

She touched her lips to Sarah's stomach. "Hi, Mary."

"Eric told me you were coming, but I was afraid to believe it. The Prodigal Daughter has come home at last."

Julia held on to her smile and rolled her eyes. "Two seconds in the room, and I'm already getting Bible analogies. Please don't go killing any farm animals to welcome me home."

Sarah's eyes twinkled with humor. "I'm impressed you even know the story of the Prodigal Son. You weren't exactly open to religion when you lived with us."

"It was hard not to absorb some of it, but you know I didn't drive through the night to trade Bible stories. What's going on? I've been scared out of my mind, and Grace has been no help whatsoever."

"I started having contractions. We almost lost the baby," Sarah said in a shaky voice.

"Oh, honey," Julia said, rubbing Sarah's belly again, as if willing the tiny life to stay in there longer.

"They gave me medication and finally got them to stop."

"Will it happen again?"

"It's possible. They think I'll be able to carry the baby to term, but I have to be careful. They want me on almost total bed rest for the next couple months."

"Sounds sensible."

Sarah took a deep breath and reached for Julia's hand. "I need your help."

Julia squeezed Sarah's cold fingers, rubbing them to restore some warmth. "You know I'll do whatever I can."

"I need you to run Marry Me."

"What's that?"

"It's my wedding planning business."

Julia burst out laughing. Only Sarah didn't join in. A tight, queasy feeling returned. "You're not serious?"

"You must think I'm terribly selfish to have you come all this way and spring this on you, but I wouldn't ask if it wasn't so important."

Julia jumped up and started pacing. "Has this pregnancy made you a touch crazy? Or have hormones replaced your common sense? I know we haven't seen each other in fifteen years, but surely you remember my feelings about marriage and especially weddings. They were pretty firmly established even when I was a teenager."

Sarah calmly watched Julia pace. "You still have hang-ups about love and weddings?"

"You try dealing with your parents' divorce and then gaining two stepmothers and two stepfathers by the time you're thirteen, and see how well adjusted you turn out. How willing to believe in true love and soul mates."

"You don't think love exists?"

"Love is the excuse we use to do whatever we want, no matter who it hurts."

Sarah's eyes widened. "I knew you were cynical, but seriously that's—"

"Realistic?"

"I was going to say sad."

"Which is precisely why you should get someone else to do this. I'm liable to tell your couples they should run for the hills."

"You wouldn't. Especially not when you know why Marry Me needs to stay open. I won't be able to handle the business for the next several months, and if it closes it would affect a lot more than my clients."

Julia came to a stop. "What?"

"My husband, Eric, runs a community center and shelter for at-risk kids."

"You have those here?" Julia asked, arching a brow.

"Big cities haven't cornered the market on kids in crisis, you know."

"Sadly. What does your husband's center have to do with your wedding planning business?"

"The income from my business allows him to work while taking a minimum salary, so most of the donations go directly back to the Center."

"So, you're essentially supporting your family through Marry Me?"

"Yes, it's what we agreed on when Eric decided to open the Center. If my business were to close, even for a few months, we'd lose the income, and with the baby coming—"

"In other words, you're in a mess," Julia said, sinking into a chair next to the bed.

Sarah winced. "It's our own fault for not planning better, I know, but frankly we never thought it would become an issue. We'd given up hope of ever having a baby. We tried for so many years and—" she broke off, overcome by emotion.

Julia reached over and stroked Sarah's hair. "I know. Grace told me."

"I wish you'd have been here. I could have used a big sister. There were so many times I wanted to call, but I never knew if you'd welcome it."

Julia could hear the hurt in Sarah's voice, the same as with Grace. "Let's not get into old history right now. You're under enough stress. Why don't we get back to the subject of me running a wedding planning business? Are you sure there isn't someone better suited for this? Someone who might have a clue what to do? I don't know a garter from a garden hose."

"You'd learn. You're so smart, and you do have business experience."

"I'm in marketing. I tell people who's buying what and when, which is not at all the same thing as planning somebody's nuptials."

Sarah held up her hand and started ticking off a lightning-fast rebuttal on her fingers. "You're organized. You know how to create budgets and stick to them. You know how to research. You understand what makes people tick better than anyone I've ever met. You've been a manager, so you're used to delegating. You're a born leader. And best of all, you won't let anyone push you around, be it a spoiled bride, a demanding mother, or an unscrupulous vendor out to pad his bill."

"Impressive qualities, indeed," Julia drawled. If she'd realized she was such a crack businesswoman she could have made a better case to her new boss and not been canned.

She was amazed, and flattered, despite knowing she was on the receiving end of a world-class snow job.

"Don't you need someone who actually likes weddings?" Julia tried again. "I'm allergic to them."

"No one is allergic to weddings."

"I am. I broke out in a rash once at a wedding. Well, it might have been the flowers they were using, but it's the principle of the thing. I made a vow after my dad's last wedding to bride #4. No more weddings. Ever."

"Your dad has been married four times?"

"Five. I missed the last one, and again, we're off the subject. Are you sure there's no one you know who can do this? What about Grace?"

"Mom has her hands full already. Her husband still hasn't fully recovered from his stroke."

"Don't you have assistants or something?" Julia asked, knowing she sounded desperate.

"I have an assistant, but she's young. The women who help out during the weddings all have families."

Julia slumped back in the chair. "Unlike me who has no one. I suppose Grace informed you I got fired, too?"

"Yes, she did." Sarah tried to look sympathetic without much success. "I'm sorry, and I'm sure it must have been awful, but maybe this is—"

"If you say this is God's will, I swear I'll start throwing things," Julia warned.

Sarah sat up straighter. "Maybe it *is* His will."

"Right. He had my boss develop a heart condition so he had to sell the business, which resulted in me getting canned. All so I could be free to come back here and run your wedding planning business?"

"God works in mysterious ways," Sarah said, with a shrug.

"God must have been up to a lot of chess playing."

"We don't know God's plans. Maybe all this is happening so Mary can be born healthy and strong because she's going to cure cancer someday, thereby saving millions of people. Maybe even you."

Julia blinked and stared at her former stepsister, wondering how she'd never noticed Sarah had evil tendencies, too. Grace had passed on the stealth, manipulator gene to her daughter.

"Low blow," Julia said in defeat, visions of white, frothy dresses and weepy brides filling her days.

So, this is what comes of caring for someone, she thought. *You get roped into doing crazy things like planning weddings, when you'd rather have a root canal than attend one.*

"Have you girls finished your little talk?"

Both women looked up as Grace walked back in the room. "Oh, yeah. We talked, and I caved," Julia said.

"I told Sarah not to guilt you into it."

Julia pointed to Sarah's extended stomach. "Don't you know God had me fired, leaving me free to run Marry Me, so that baby in there could one day cure me of cancer?"

Grace gasped. "Oh, my goodness… Sarah! You should be ashamed of yourself."

Laughter tinged with both exasperation and admiration at Sarah's rather astounding manipulative abilities escaped Julia's lips. "She's not ashamed. She's evil. You're both evil. You knew what she wanted."

"I told you earlier you could always say no," Grace pointed out, trying to look innocent.

Oh no, Julia was on to them now. Their act wouldn't wash.

"Say no to what?" a deep male voice asked.

Julia turned again as a tall, athletic man entered the room.

His sandy-brown hair flopped into his eyes as he went to the bed and kissed Sarah.

"Eric, this is Julia," Sarah said.

He held out a hand. "It's nice to finally meet you, Julia. You got here pretty quick."

"It seemed urgent," Julia said. "I didn't know I'd be drafted into service."

Eric looked at Sarah. "You asked her already?"

"She said yes."

His eyes closed for a moment, and he released a deep sigh. "Thank you. You don't know what this means to us."

"Hey, I'm only doing this so I don't die of cancer."

"Excuse me?"

She waved her hand. "Inside joke."

"Eric, maybe Julia would like to see who else she's going to be helping by running Marry Me," Sarah said.

It was Julia's turn to be confused. "Hmm?"

"The softball game this afternoon."

"A softball game?"

"I organized a game for the kids at the center," Eric answered. "We put together teams, and they're playing this afternoon. We'll barbecue afterward. It's going to be a real party, and there should be a big turnout."

"Plus, Julia will have a chance to meet people," Grace said. "Seth will be there, too."

Sarah clapped her hands together, looking like a ten-year-old again. "Oh, you have to see Seth. You remember him, right? I can't wait to hear about his reaction when he sees you."

"I doubt he'll even remember me. It's not like we hung out much."

"Well, you're going to now. You're going to be living with him for the next several months, after all."

A flash warning went off inside Julia's head. *Excuse me?*

"Sarah," Grace admonished. "You're going to start some

unpleasant rumors if you're not careful."

Julia waved her hands. "Hold on. Hold on. Can we back up a minute? I didn't realize I'd have to negotiate living arrangements in this deal. I thought I'd be living with you, Sarah. I'm going to need all the help I can get, and it would be so much easier if we're in close proximity."

"Everything's in close proximity in Covington Falls."

Sarah wasn't getting around this one. Julia gently tapped her on the head. "The living arrangements?"

Sarah actually pouted. "Eric and I live in a one-bedroom apartment right now. You'd have to sleep on the couch if you stayed with us, which doesn't seem right. At Mom's you'll have a nice bedroom, a garden, and a big kitchen where you can cook to your heart's content."

"I don't cook, and the last time I went digging in the ground, I was searching for my hide-a-key rock after a storm."

Sarah made a little *tsk* sound, which meant this was a minor detail. "Whatever. You'll be so much more comfortable at Mom's. Trust me."

Julia was incredulous. "A one-bedroom apartment?"

"We chose it because we were trying to save money," Sarah said, color rising in her cheeks. "It was all we needed at the time."

"Where are you planning to put the baby? In the sock drawer?"

Sarah turned indignant. "No, we have a perfectly nice cradle, and the baby can sleep in our room for the first few months. Then we're going to look for a small house."

"You all missed out on the family planning classes, didn't you? Financial planning as well."

"I told you, we never thought—"

Julia smiled. She couldn't help it. Sarah was so cute when she got embarrassed. "I know. You weren't expecting your little miracle. I understand. Maybe you should take up this issue with God. At least he gave Abraham advanced warning he was about to become a father at age one hundred."

Sarah paused. "Again, I'm impressed."

Julia rolled her eyes. "Please. Adam and Eve. Cain and Abel. Abraham. Virgin Birth. Those are staples. I'd have been deaf and blind not to absorb them. We're getting off point here. Again. Can we get back to me and Seth living in the same house?"

Grace stepped in to explain. "Seth doesn't actually live in the house. We converted the storage area above the garage into an apartment and office."

"Why?"

"He moved in after his wife died. Some people weren't comfortable going to a single minister's house. This way, I can act as hostess if I'm needed."

"Oh," Julia said, though she still didn't get it.

"In any case, it's not like you're going to be stumbling over each other," Grace continued. "Seth's rarely home. He's usually off on church business."

"Fine. When is this game? Do I have to time to take a nap and maybe grab a shower?"

****

The nap and the shower should have done wonders. Unfortunately, sleeping in the same bedroom she'd lived in as a teenager was a bit disconcerting. She felt as edgy and unsure as she had at thirteen. Everywhere she looked brought back unsettling memories. By the time Eric arrived to drive her to the game, Julia was practically frothing at the mouth to get out of the house.

She was waiting in the foyer when Eric pulled up in an SUV, which had seen better days. Much better. Julia raced out before he could honk the horn, and if he was surprised by the speed at which she leaped into the car, he was polite enough not to comment on it. She watched the passing scenery as he started down the street. Summer had taken over this part of the world and the trees had an intense green color she'd never seen anywhere else.

As they turned the corner she spotted an ice cream truck. A real one, that played a tune. She hadn't known those existed anymore. Grace used to give Julia and Sarah fifty cents to buy a treat. Sarah had always taken forever to make up her mind, which had driven Julia crazy. A skill her former stepsister still possessed in abundance. The knowledge made her chuckle.

At the sound, Eric turned his head. "You look tired. Beautiful, but anxious," he was quick to add.

"You're so diplomatic," Julia said, a grin pulling up the corner of her mouth. "I feel like I spent a week in the car with two bratty kids."

Eric's voice remained gentle, as if he didn't want to spook her. "Why so anxious?"

"Being here. It's hard."

"Why?" Again, he was extremely gentle.

"I don't know. Lots of ghosts."

"What kind of ghosts?"

"The ghost of stepmothers past," she said, scowling at him. "I can see why you set out to help troubled kids. You're pretty good at getting people to spill their guts without them realizing it."

He chuckled. "Guilty. I only got the briefest of sketches about your history from Sarah. I can imagine it is unsettling being back in a place where you spent some pretty turbulent years."

"The years *here* were fairly calm. All the other years surrounding them were turbulent."

"Yes, but your emotions weren't as engaged as they were here, with this family. With Grace and Sarah."

Julia folded her arms over her chest. "Nice trick, reading people's minds. Do you see dead people, too?"

He laughed again. "No, I'm just observant."

Eric's eyes crinkled up when he laughed. Julia liked him. She was coming to realize Sarah had done well for herself in the husband department, even if he was a terrible financial planner. In fact, she thought Eric was much too good for Sarah, the evil little manipulator.

"I can tell you care about Grace and Sarah," he said. "Maybe more than you want to, or think you should, but it's there."

Julia looked out the window at the passing trees again. "The first time I met Grace, I remember thinking she was what a mother was supposed to be like. She even smelled like a mother. I spent the whole time here loving her, and hating her."

"What did you love?"

"I loved that she gave me chocolate chip cookies right out of the oven," Julia said, with a smile. "I loved that she sang while she cooked. I loved that she asked me about my day and actually listened when I told her, and she never let a day go by without giving me a hug, even though I never responded."

"And the hate part?"

"I hated her because she wasn't my mother, and because by then, I already knew how the story would end. I knew my father would end up leaving her, and then I would lose her, too."

"Is he why you never came back?"

She nodded. "Because they're not mine."

Yes, she was whining, but she couldn't help it.

Eric's tone got sharper. "I've got news for you, Julia. They most certainly are yours. You may not be related by blood or have been in the same room with them in fifteen years, but you share a connection with them. The sooner you accept it, and embrace it, the happier you'll be."

There was nothing she could say, so they drove the rest of the way in silence. Once at the park, Julia quickly put distance between Eric and herself. Sure, she might have decided she liked him, but he'd come unbearably close to hitting the truth, and she had no desire to deal with more self-awareness on no sleep.

The park was indeed crowded. There were kids all over the place, as well as adult volunteers, and from the looks of it, a good number of observers. The kids spotted Eric right away, and they swarmed around him like ants to a drop of honey, until they saw Julia. The younger ones looked at her with suspicion, while the older ones took on all the finer characteristics of your average construction workers. The whistles, 'yeah baby's', and outright leers were nothing Julia hadn't seen or heard since she'd started wearing a bra in the fourth grade.

"Young men do not make catcalls at a lady," Eric said.

"Sorry, ma'am!" erupted all around.

"The only thing worse than whistling at a woman is calling her 'ma'am'," she said, matching Eric's stern tone. "It's Julia."

"Come on, Seth is around here somewhere," Eric said. "Let me introduce you. Oh, wait... I forgot. You two know each other, don't you?"

"Yeah, but we weren't exactly friends."

Julia followed Eric, and in the distance she spotted a group of men helping to set up the field. She searched for a geeky-looking beanpole, but her eyes stopped on a beautifully built, dark-haired man. All she could see was the back of him. He was tall, with shoulders a mile wide, and long, powerful legs.

Who knew they grew such delicious specimens down here in Covington Falls?

"Hey, Seth!" Eric called out. "Look who I found."

All the men turned, including the delicious one. Oh, yeah. Mr. Tall Guy was wonderful from the front, too. Nicely crafted masculine features. Julia couldn't quite make out the eye color, but she had a feeling they were spectacular as well.

Their eyes met, and she felt a little jolt. *"This one,"* a voice reflected in her head. His eyes widened, and Julia knew he felt it, too. If they were in a movie this would be the moment when violins swept into a chorus and drums started pounding.

Then he frowned, and his expression became shuttered. He broke away from the group and started over in her direction. That's when it dawned on her exactly who she'd been drooling over.

The drums turned to clanging bells.

Oh... my...

The breath lodged in her throat. There was no way the geeky boy she'd known had grown into... him! But somehow he had. She stiffened even more when she recalled this gorgeous man was also a minister.

Can you get struck by lightning for thinking impure thoughts about a minister? Isn't lust one of the seven deadly sins?

Oh, this was not good. Not good at all.

****

It's not good for a woman to look so amazing in a pair of denim shorts, Seth Graham thought. Not good at all.

How was it possible? Fifteen years and she still made him feel like... well... like he was fifteen. He'd grown up, answered the call to the ministry, and married and buried a wife. Yet somehow prickly, bitter, keep-your-distance Julia Richardson still scared the life out of him. Because prickly, bitter, keep-your-distance Julia Richardson was also still the sexiest female he'd ever met. A sexy woman who was now his stepmother's ex-stepdaughter, making her his... well... he didn't quite know what it made her. He only knew it was bizarre and twisted.

His mouth went dry like he'd swallowed a box of chalk sticks, and he could swear drums were pounding somewhere. As he walked toward her, he concentrated on not tripping over his feet or otherwise reminding her he used to be a huge putz. Their eyes locked. The drumbeat intensified. He knew the moment she figured out who he was because her eyes suddenly widened, and she drew in a shocked breath.

Yeah, Julia, the putz you remember did grow into this.

He stopped in front of her.

Eric did the honors. "Julia, this is Seth Graham. John's son. Seth, you remember Julia, right?"

"Hey, Julia," he said, with almost no inflection. If he was careful and kept his tone even maybe she wouldn't notice his voice was shaking.

Her eyes made a visual track up and down again. "Hey yourself. You've changed a bit."

He had to admit, it was nice she seemed so rattled by his changed appearance. It made his mouth twitch as he fought back a smile. "A bit. How've you been?"

"Fine."

"Good."

"And you?"

"Fine."

"Wow, you two, don't go overboard on the effusive greetings," Eric teased.

At this, Seth and Julia both laughed, and it seemed to lighten the moment.

"Are we almost set up here?" Eric asked, gesturing to the field.

Seth swiveled his head around, grateful for any excuse to look away from Julia and try to regain his sanity. "Almost. We'll be ready to go in a few minutes."

"I'll go check with the guys."

Seth started to go after him, to escape, but Eric waved him off. "No, no, I can go. You two catch up. I'll be right back."

Seth fought back a surge of panic. Now what? Was he supposed to talk to Julia? Like they were long-lost friends? He barely knew her anymore. Plus, he couldn't look at her without swallowing his tongue, which made conversation pretty difficult.

Julia was the one who tried to break the ice. "I saw Sarah."

"Good. I'm sure she was thrilled to see you."

"Not half as thrilled as I was to see her."

The comment finally broke through the haze of attraction. He swiveled his head and stared in amazement. Julia was pretending to care about Sarah now? "Surprising, considering you haven't bothered to come back in fifteen years."

She reared back a little. "Well, I'm here now, and I'm going to be here awhile. I'm going to help Sarah with Marry Me."

The surprises kept coming. Seth would have laid odds the prospect of planning weddings would make Julia run away fast enough to leave skid marks. "She talked you into it?"

Julia's mouth pinched into a straight line. "I'm happy to do it."

"I thought you weren't a big believer in love and marriage."

"You barely know me," she said, through gritted teeth. "Where'd you get such an idea?"

"Remember when we had to read *Romeo & Juliet* in school? You said Juliet was an idiot for killing herself over Romeo. If she'd given it a few weeks the feelings would have gone away."

Julia didn't have anything to say.

Having made his point, Seth changed the subject. He didn't want to get into an argument with her. "I assume you saw Grace, too?"

"Of course," Julia said. "I didn't realize how much I'd missed her, until I saw her come out of the house."

Again, astonishment made him curt. "It would have been

nice if you could have shown you missed her, by maybe coming to see her."

Julia turned on him, blue eyes flashing, her glorious red hair practically standing on end like the mutant who could control the weather. "Look, I'm having a hard enough time dealing with my own guilt about Grace and Sarah without you heaping on a big helping of it. So, why don't you back off? Aren't you supposed to be this compassionate minister? Isn't it in your job description to show mercy and forgiveness? If so, you missed a few classes."

Seth's jaw dropped.

She swiped a hand across her face and seemed to deflate before his eyes. "I'm sorry I lashed out. My only excuse is I drove all night, and I've been worried sick about Sarah and the baby. Plus, I haven't had any decent sleep since I lost my job."

Regret lanced through him. He cleared his throat. "No, I'm sorry. You're right. I am supposed to show mercy and forgiveness. *My* excuse is I've become protective of Grace and Sarah. I know your relationship with them is complicated, and it means a lot you would put your life on hold to help them."

You're such a liar, Seth Graham. You lashed out because prickly, bitter, keep-your-distance Julia Richardson made you remember you're still alive.

His apology seemed to knock the wind out of her sails. "All right then. Umm, I see Eric waving for you. It must be time to start."

Seth started to open his mouth and try to explain, but what could he say? I've lusted after you since the ninth grade, and it's made me insane? In the end, he gave her a weak smile and walked away, the image of mile-long legs stretching endlessly from body-hugging denim burned into his brain.

God? You know what? The testing? I think I've had enough now.

Chapter Two

Amazing what a good night's sleep would do to convince yourself all is right with the world again. For instance, eight hours of sleep had Julia convinced she could run a wedding planning business. It was only flowers, food, and a dress, right? Couldn't be too hard.

She was also convinced her bizarre reaction to Seth yesterday could be chalked up to the effects of a twelve-hour car trip and anxiety over Sarah and baby Mary, the future cancer genius. Right. It wasn't an attraction. It was sleep deprivation. Julia wasn't even sure she liked Seth, though he did have fantastic eyes. Light, clear blue like a husky's. Edged with a circle of navy and framed by thick black lashes. Endless, piercing, simmering—

Ugh! Stop it, Julia.

Not to mention it was weird seeing as how he was Grace's stepson and she was… whatever she was. A little too kissin' cousins for her. Then there was the whole issue of his life calling. Never in a million years could she see herself with a minister.

Though, if all ministers looked as good in a pair of jeans,

she imagined there'd be more of a following—

Julia! Quit it!

So, wouldn't you know the object of her intense internal dialogue would be in the kitchen when she went down to breakfast? She rounded the corner, and there he was, at the table. Julia wasn't expecting him to be there, so she let out a little, girly yelp.

One dark brow quirked in amusement. "Good morning."

Julia decided to go with attitude. "Are you supposed to be here?"

"I live here."

Hmm, seemed he was going with attitude, too.

"I thought you lived over the garage and rarely came to the main house," she said.

"Sort of like a relative the family keeps hidden away in the attic?" he asked, with a nice touch of sarcasm she had to admire.

In spite of her own unease, Julia couldn't help a slight smile. "Grace seemed to imply you were gone a lot on church business. Although, maybe she said that so I wouldn't bolt. I've come to realize both she and Sarah have devious minds."

The brow quirked again. "This is news to you? I've known since I was a kid. Especially Sarah. She looks so sweet and innocent—"

"So you don't realize you've been bamboozled until after the fact."

They both chuckled, and it seemed to ease the tension.

Seth pointed to the counter behind her. "If you're hungry, Grace left a plate warming in the oven. There's coffee, too."

Julia pivoted and walked over to the oven. The smell wafting out of the oven when she opened the door nearly brought her to her knees. Even though she'd only been planning on grabbing a cup of coffee, she was suddenly famished. She took the plate out of the oven and peeled back the foil. Eggs, bacon, and a fluffy biscuit. Her mouth watered.

She carried the plate over to the table along with a cup of the coffee. She reached for the biscuit first.

The first bite had her groaning in pleasure. "Mm, I'd forgotten about the biscuits."

A grin tugged up the corner of his mouth. "They are pretty amazing. You strike me as a grab-a-cup-of-coffee-on-the-way-out-the-door kind of girl."

She conceded his point. "Or a bagel. So, was Grace playing me? Am I going to be running into you all the time?"

"Actually, she wasn't far off," he said, as he took a sip of his coffee. "I am busy. We sometimes go all week without seeing each other, but I stop in for breakfast when I can. Today, I'm here to help look after my dad while she does some shopping."

"Oh. Does he still need full-time care?"

"He did at first. He's made a lot of improvement though. Have you seen him yet?"

Julia nodded, even as she took a bite of eggs. "Briefly, last night. Grace seems happy with him."

"I know I'm prejudiced, but I think my dad is the best thing that could have ever happened to Grace. Especially after what she went through with—" He broke off, as if realizing what he'd been about to say.

"With my father," she finished for him.

Seth flushed and cleared his throat.

Julia shrugged. "It's all right. It's not like what my father did is a secret. I'm certainly happy for Grace. Believe me, I know firsthand the destruction my father leaves in his wake when he decides to head for greener pastures."

"I suppose you do."

"Is it weird? Your dad married to another woman, I mean?"

It was his turn to shrug. "My mom died when I was in college. It was rough for both of us. I was still away at school when Grace and Dad went from neighbors to a couple. It was kind of strange at first, but if he's happy, I'm happy."

Julia looked down at her plate and realized she'd scraped it clean. "Wow."

"There are more biscuits."

"No way," she said, patting her full stomach. "If I eat like this all the time, I'll be huge."

"You've got a great figure. I wouldn't worry."

As if realizing what he'd said, he looked away. Not appropriate for a minister to comment on a woman's figure? Probably not.

"I should get going," Julia said, trying to be nonchalant. "I'll clean up if you need to look in on your dad."

"The nurse is here right now. I'll go visit with him after she leaves. I can help you clean up. Grace would kill me if I left you alone with the dishes on your first morning. You rinse, and I'll load the dishwasher."

They stood side-by-side. The silence wasn't as awkward as Julia might have expected. In fact, it was easy enough she felt emboldened to probe a little more.

"What made you move in here?" she asked, handing him a plate. "Grace told me it was because people felt awkward going to a single pastor's home."

Seth didn't answer right away. "She's partly right," he said, as he fit the plate into the dishwasher. "In the end, it wasn't the main reason though."

They continued with the mindless ritual of rinsing and passing plates, glasses, and silverware. "What was it?"

The answer, when it came, was so soft she barely heard it over the running water. "I couldn't stand living in our house by myself."

"Because of your wife?"

"We moved in there when I came back to take over the church. Beth was…" he hesitated and took a deep breath. "She was healthy then. The cancer was diagnosed a year later."

"And all your hopes and dreams were replaced with

memories of her sick. There were lots of ghosts there, I suspect."

He looked at her, and Julia could see he was surprised she had enough insight to guess anything about him. She was a little amazed by it herself, considering they didn't know each other. Although, perhaps since she was a stranger she could see things someone closer to the situation might not.

Of course, the other option was he was so stunned by her sympathy he didn't know how to react.

She gave him a small smile. "I'm not always an acid-tongued shrew. Sometimes I'm even capable of saying a comforting word or — dare I say — being nice. It's so much work, though. Takes a lot out of me, you know."

Laughter shook his shoulders. "Some people were uncomfortable at a single man's house, so it was a good cover. As it turned out, I was here when Dad had the stroke, so I've been able to help out. I believe it worked out the way it was supposed to."

"More chess playing from God? He's been rather busy lately."

Seth grumbled something which sounded suspiciously like "God forgive her" as he closed the dishwasher, but when she pinned him with a look, all she saw was an innocent smile.

Okay, now she understood. The whole family was sneaky and evil, even the ones who weren't blood-related.

Julia picked up a pretty flowered dishtowel to dry her hands. "Well, I should be going. Gotta herd some brides."

"Good luck."

"Thanks. I'll need it."

"Can I offer a small insight of my own?" he called out as she turned to leave.

Pausing, Julia glanced over her shoulder. "I suppose."

"I don't think you're half as tough as you pretend to be," He leaned back against the counter. "In fact, I think you're genuinely a nice person. You turned your whole life upside down to help Sarah."

"I kind of had my life jerked out from under me when I lost my job. It wasn't like I had much to do back home. The soap operas and talk shows were starting to get annoying."

"You can't fool me, Julia Richardson. You put on a good act, but I think deep down you're actually a sweetheart."

Julia gave him her best evil eye. "If you ever tell anyone else, I'll have to kill you. I have a reputation to consider, you know."

Then the most amazing thing happened. He winked at her. "Your secret's safe with me."

****

Seth knew he'd gotten a glimpse of the softer side of Julia Richardson. An intriguing side, which hinted at depths beyond sarcasm and prickliness. He still couldn't believe how easily she'd decoded his reasons for escaping the house he and Beth had shared. Not many people took the time to ask why he'd moved into the tiny apartment above the garage. Fewer still had the courage to ask about his wife and listen without showing pity or horror.

Which didn't explain why he'd ended up flirting with her. Had he winked at her? That had to stop, because no matter how perceptive she was, he couldn't forget her cynicism carried over to every aspect of her life, especially the faith part. It wasn't exactly unusual. In fact, it was pretty common for people to deny God, but coming from Julia it cut deeper.

Exactly why, he didn't want to examine.

Fighting back a groan of frustration, Seth went to visit with his dad. His father's presence was always soothing, even if the conversation was halting. Once Grace returned from her shopping, Seth went back to the garage apartment to grab his keys. As he scooped them up off the dresser, his eyes fell on the framed picture of Beth. Sometimes when he looked at the photo the grief seemed to swallow him whole. Other days it was a dull ache. Lately, he'd even been able to manage a smile as he recalled a sweet memory.

Today, the grief seemed fresher, and it tore a new hole in his gut.

He touched the frame. "Miss you, BG," he whispered, using the pet name he'd given her on their wedding night. The name he'd never tired of saying, Beth Graham.

Taking a deep breath, he turned and walked away. He had things to do. A church to run. People to save. Literally.

Seth got in the car and headed to the hospital. There were several people he needed to see. Hospital visits were one of his favorite duties as a minister. Some people might find it depressing, especially if the person in question was dying, but more often than not the visits turned out to be the sweetest and most uplifting time of his day.

Because when they — or a loved one — were ill, people allowed God to enter. On most other occasions people could pretend they had control of their lives. Illness had a way of reminding them life was not so easily managed. Many found God in those times, others became angry, blamed Him for the suffering, but either way it was Seth's joy to minister to all of them.

His last stop was someone who'd become one of the most special people in his life.

"Hey, young lady," he called from the doorway.

Sarah's eyes drifted open, and she smiled. "Hi."

He walked over to the bed and took her hand. "How are you?"

"I'm all right."

"And how's this little lady?" he asked, touching Sarah's swollen belly.

"The doctor says she's doing all right, too."

"Good."

Despite the brave smile, tears filled Sarah's eyes. The minister in him felt it was about time.

The newly appointed big brother in him wanted to smash something, but all he could do was squeeze her hand. "It's okay. Let it out."

"I'm so scared," Sarah sobbed. "How could this happen? We waited all this time. We gave up hope. This was supposed to be a miracle."

Seth leaned down and stroked her hair. "It *is* a miracle. Mary's still here. Still in there fighting."

"I don't know what to do."

"You pray."

"I don't want to pray," Sarah said, her lips turning down in a pout. "I want this to go away. I want to walk out of here and get back to my life. My job. My husband."

"*This* is your job right now," Seth said, rubbing her stomach again. "And your husband isn't going anywhere. It's his turn to take care of you now. Let him do it."

The bracing words seemed to have a good effect. She took a deep breath, and the sobs started to subside. "Okay."

Seth chuckled at her quicksilver emotions. *Pregnancy hormones*, he thought. Although, Sarah had always been one to switch from storm clouds to a sunburst in the blink of an eye, so it could be her natural personality.

He snatched a Kleenex from the box on the side table and handed it to her as he sat down. "I don't think you need to worry about Marry Me either. You called in Julia as backup, remember? Though how you talked someone so cynical into running a wedding planning business I don't know."

Sarah wiped her eyes. "She's just been hurt, so she acts cynical to keep people at a distance."

Seth held back the snort of derision. "I always thought she was simply cold and unfeeling."

The last of the tears dried up, as outrage replaced terror. "Seth, what a horrible thing to say."

Yes, it was, especially since he'd been introduced to the nice Julia earlier this morning. "You're right. Sorry. She gets under my skin."

A little glimmer of a smile tugged up the corner of Sarah's mouth. "Oh? Like she used to?"

"Don't go there," he said, giving her a stern look.

Sarah put a finger to the corner of her chin. "What was it you drew in the school book you dropped at the bus stop?"

"I don't remember."

"Julia's quite the bombshell now, isn't she?" she asked, refusing to give up.

"Sarah, cut it out," he said. "I know exactly what you're thinking, and it's not gonna' fly. We'll be lucky if we don't kill each other while she's here. Besides, I'm not ready—"

The teasing light went out of her eyes. "You're not over losing Beth. All right, I won't tease you anymore. It was a silly thought."

"It's twisted anyway," he said, standing up to leave. "I have to get to the church."

She reached for his hand again. "Thank you for coming, Seth. And for letting me bawl on your shoulder."

"It's what I'm here for."

"I can't break down in front of my mother or Eric. They'd only freak out."

He leaned down and kissed her forehead. "I've got news for you. I nearly *did* freak out. I can't be Pastor Graham around you. You're like my little sister now."

Sarah smiled. "Cool. Now I've got a pseudo big brother and big sister."

"A rather twisted family."

She laughed. "Listen, do me a favor."

"Anything."

"Would you keep an eye on Julia? Help her out if she needs it?"

His shoulders stiffened. "I don't know what I can do."

"Just help her with whatever. You're so good with people. I'm sure she'll need an ally."

Seth knew it was a bad idea to have anything to do with Julia, but he nodded anyway. "I'll do what I can."

And he'd do what he could to preserve his sanity as well.

****

Sarah had given Julia directions to Marry Me the day before. The boutique was located in downtown Covington Falls. The not-quite-bustling town center consisted of Main Street, which ran north-south, while 1st Avenue ran east-west.

Framing the four corners of town were four churches. On the north end of Main Street was Covington Falls Community Church, where Seth was the pastor. On the southern end was Christ Memorial. The eastern sentinel was Good News Gospel Church, and the western front was guarded by St. Mark's. Covington Falls was an equal opportunity town so there was also a Jewish Temple, though it wasn't on the main downtown strips.

At the intersection of Main and 1st Avenue was Rice Circle, which surrounded a picturesque park. On one side of the park was City Hall and opposite was the Main Library. The wide sidewalks were lined with old-fashioned street lamps. Colored awnings swayed in the breeze, and each store window was decked out to the nines. It was as though someone had conjured up the image of what the perfect small town should look like and plopped it down right here.

It was downright creepy.

Julia found Marry Me and pulled into a parking space. The shop was framed by a dress boutique on one side and a baby store on the other. She wondered if anyone had ever noticed the irony in the order of the stores. Boutique where you buy the dress for the date, which leads to the wedding, which leads to the requisite babies. True one-stop-shopping right here in downtown Covington Falls.

She was about to go in when she happened to glance at the window display. The centerpiece of the window featured a beaded wedding gown hanging from one of those Oriental silk dressing screens. A lovely antique vanity, loaded with a collection of makeup brushes, a silver brush and comb set, perfume atomizer, silk hose, and even a blue garter, sat next to the screen. Hooked on the corner of the mirror was a long, filmy veil.

Julia stared in fascination. The scene seemed to be a slice in time, and she half expected the bride to appear and commence getting ready for her wedding.

The bleat-bleat of a car horn brought her back to earth. She spun around as a red compact car pulled into the empty space next to hers. Out popped a tiny blonde with cornflower-blue eyes and the widest grin Julia had ever seen. The woman was wearing a lavender suit with matching pumps. Her wispy, chin-length bob was held back with a lavender headband, and she was carrying a lavender handbag.

Good grief! A pixie in a business suit.

The pixie bounded up onto the sidewalk, her grin getting even wider if possible. "Hi. I'm Betsy. Sarah called and told me you'd be starting today. This is so *exciting,* you coming back like this. It's going to be so much *fun.*"

Julia opened her mouth to respond, but Betsy was off again.

"You probably don't remember me. Well, of *course* you wouldn't. I was only like *five*_when you lived here before. Truthfully, I didn't remember you, either. I don't think I even knew Sarah *had* a sister. Wow, you're a tall one, aren't you? Love the red hair."

Betsy floated by on a cloud of flowery-scented perfume and unlocked the front door. Feeling a bit like she'd been run over by a lavender eighteen-wheeler, Julia followed.

She looked around her new workplace. The inside was

much like the display window. Against the far wall sat an antique oak desk. The main room had plush, cream-colored carpet, which made her want to take off her shoes and walk barefoot. The wallpaper had the barest hint of a cream stripe, which was at once elegant and soothing. Black and white photographs of impossibly beautiful couples in wedding attire lined the walls, and small antique display tables were placed strategically around the room. One had samples of lace, and another a pile of wedding invitations. Still another had photographs of different venues from gardens, to lakeside parks, to churches.

Julia sighed in relief. She could work with this. She'd been expecting something nauseatingly romantic or cheesy, like a Vegas wedding chapel, and though the place was definitely romantic, it was a tasteful romantic. Her estimation of Sarah was growing by leaps and bounds.

Betsy was talking again, and Julia brought herself back to earth. She had a feeling she was only ever going to catch every fifth word out of the woman's mouth, so she'd better pay attention.

"This is where we meet with clients," Betsy said.

"It's beautiful."

Betsy gave her a pleased smile. "It is, isn't it? Sarah did it all *herself.* Well, she had *lots* of help, of course. Her husband and some of the kids from the Center. Plus, Seth and other church members. It was a regular *barn raising* I tell you. Come on to the back, and I'll show you the office."

"I thought this was the office."

She giggled. "Oh no, this is where we meet with clients. The back isn't quite as neat."

Julia's first instinct when Betsy opened the door was to make a run for it. Not quite as neat? It looked like a tornado had gone through the room. Twice. There were piles of books on every wedding-related subject imaginable all over the place. Complementing the books were stacks of magazines.

Julia was sure every bridal magazine published in the last century had wound up here. There were four or five stacks on wedding attire alone.

Crammed in amongst the books and magazines were file cabinets, which clearly weren't being used properly because there seemed to be more files lying around the room than were actually *in* them.

Betsy took in Julia's horrified expression. "It's quite a shock at first, isn't it?"

Julia waved her hand around the room, unable to comprehend the madness. "Are you telling me you two work in here? What is all this anyway?"

"Reference material, mostly. Planning a wedding is sort of like trying to maneuver an army. All the little pieces have to come together on "D-Day" or "W-Day" in this case."

"This is unbelievable. How on earth am I supposed to know where things are located? Sarah might know, but she's not here."

"Well, all you have to know the location of is *the bible*."

"Huh?"

A Bible was going to help her plan weddings? Was flower arranging part of the Ten Commandments?

Betsy delicately made her way past an ugly green couch, a couple of wooden chairs and a scarred, wooden desk and lifted a huge binder off a shelf. The resounding thud of the book landing on the desk made Julia wince.

"This is *the bible*," Betsy said. "Or Sarah's bible. It's got all the information you need. Lists of vendors, bridal boutiques and men's formal wear stores, caterers, cake makers, florists, musicians, photographers, and printers for invitations. Local hotels, inns, and B&B's. The churches in the area. Different venues. Plus, contact numbers of people from the country club manager to the wedding coordinators at the churches in town."

"All in this book?" Julia asked, sure her head was going

to explode.

"Mm, hmm. A lot of the vendors aren't local, of course. Often we end up having to order from the bigger cities. We're planning the mayor's daughter's wedding right now, and she won't have anything local in her wedding."

"So you order from out-of-town?"

"It depends on how fancy the client wants to go. We do have some great local talent. The owner of the boutique next door is also a designer, and she makes the most amazing wedding gowns you've ever seen. She's even starting to get quite a reputation, with clients coming from as far away as Atlanta for her gowns."

"Good to know."

"And the local florist is a genius floral designer. She usually takes care of ordering anything from out-of-town, too. Then there's our local caterer—"

Julia understood the gist of it now. "Let me guess, she's the finest chef in the South."

Betsy nodded and flashed her sunny grin. "Amazing. She's not truly a local though. She only moved to town about three years ago. Used to work for some fancy restaurant in Chicago. We've also got fabulous local talent in the music department, too. Meredith Vining is the Music Director at Pastor Graham's church, but she also has a band and they perform at weddings. She has the voice of an angel. She had a budding music career, but gave it up to come back home."

"So, you're telling me Covington Falls is populated by a bunch of wedding prodigies?"

Betsy giggled. "Sort of. Sarah originally decided to open Marry Me to help tie all the town's resources together."

"When opportunity knocks."

"You are the *funniest* thing," Betsy said, giggling again. "I can tell I'm going to *love* working with you."

Betsy started toward the door.

"Where are you going?"

"I have to go pick up some invitations at the printers. The client is coming by this afternoon to look them over."

"What?"

"I'll only be gone a few minutes."

This was not reassuring. "But you're leaving me here. Alone."

Betsy smiled. "You'll be fine. It's been pretty quiet around here. Everyone knows Sarah's been in the hospital, and it'll take at least a few days before word gets out you've stepped in."

"What do I do while you're gone?" she asked, desperate to keep Betsy in the office.

"Start reading *the bible*." Betsy rifled through the mess on the desk and retrieved an appointment book. "Or if you feel too overwhelmed, you can look through this. It has the upcoming appointments and schedule of weddings. It takes months to plan a wedding, and the ones we have now have been in the works for a while. Mostly you'll be making sure things get done on time."

Betsy left. Julia was still staring at the empty doorway when she heard the little bell above the door jingle. No doubt the bell was laughing at her. With a deep sigh, she sank into the battered office chair and opened Sarah's bible. At least it had an index of sorts. Unfortunately, it was mostly a bunch of symbols and numbers.

Julia was about to get a headache looking at it, so she snapped the cover shut and reached for the appointment book. These things she understood. Hopefully. Who knew what kind of hieroglyphics Sarah used for appointment making?

Fortunately, this book was in English. She glanced at the week's appointments. As Betsy said, it was pretty quiet. In fact, a couple appointments looked as though they'd been rescheduled. Probably after Sarah had the scare with the baby. Under the Saturday column there was a notation. "Ashley Wedding".

Wait a minute!

Julia stared at the two words with a dawning horror. Looked at the date on the top of the page and then at the calendar.

Betsy breezed back in with a cheery hello. "I'm back. Good, you're getting settled."

"Betsy," Julia said, trying hard not to panic. "What does this note here mean?"

She trotted over and glanced down. "Oh, Maureen Ashley's wedding."

"Did you happen to notice the date?"

Betsy looked closer. "Oh, dear."

I'm going to throw up. "Oh dear, is right. Get Sarah on the phone."

It only took a minute to get through to Sarah's room. Julia grabbed the phone. "Sarah? How are you feeling?"

"Ready to get out of here," Sarah said, with a put-upon sigh.

"You're sure you're doing all right? No more scares? Baby's fine?"

"Nothing in the last forty-eight hours."

"Good. Can I ask you a question?"

Sarah must have sensed something was wrong because she hesitated. "Sure."

"Does the name Maureen Ashley mean anything to you?"

There was a brief silence. "Oh, my goodness."

"Oh my goodness is right," Julia said. "Now, tell me what I'm supposed to do when there's a wedding scheduled for this Saturday?"

Chapter Three

Julia couldn't remember the last time she'd prayed, but she figured now was as good as any to start. After taking a deep breath, Sarah had somehow convinced Julia she could handle Maureen Ashley's wedding. Everything was already in place, and all Julia needed to do was direct traffic.

So here she was, sitting in the parking lot of the Covington Falls Country Club at 11:00 a.m., wondering how on earth she ever let herself get talked into such madness.

In her lap was a bulging folder outlining every detail of Maureen Ashley's wedding. Sarah had insisted the affair was simple, but looking at the file Julia felt as though she was about to march an army across Europe. The battle plans included a schedule of activities which seemed to account for every second of the day. 11:10... meet with country club manager, 11:15... begin setting up tables, 11:17... inventory glasses, 11:25... call Bride to ensure she's at hairdresser.

This was insane. What happened if she was a minute off with one of these things? Julia was terrified she was going to miss a crucial step and spin the whole wedding into chaos. She stared at a hand-drawn diagram that explained where everything should go. It looked like a ninth grade geometry book. Squares for tables, circles for chairs, triangles for—

Actually, she had no idea what the triangles were supposed to be.

Worst of all Betsy was at the church setting everything else up, so Julia was completely on her own.

Well, one thing was for sure, she couldn't spend any more time in the car doing deep-breathing exercises.

All right, Julia. You can do this. Stick with the schedule, and you'll be fine. You're good at schedules.

Taking a deep breath, she got out of the car. First order of business was to find the country club manager. As it turned out, she didn't have to find him because he was waiting right inside the door. Dressed in unrelieved black, he looked exactly like the poor sap who'd been chased by the evil Headless Horseman.

Julia smiled. "Hello. You must be the manager. I'm Jul—"

"You're late."

She reared back. "Excuse me?"

Ichabod looked down over his long, hawkish nose. "I realize you undoubtedly feel it's acceptable to make people wait where you come from, but here in Covington Falls we have the courtesy to keep our appointments in a timely manner."

Oh, now this was too much! She was getting etiquette lessons from a guy who looked as though he belonged in a funeral parlor?

"Listen, Ichy, I've been literally thrown into this in the last week, so you can take your scowls and lectures and shove 'em up your—"

"Hello there!"

They both turned as a tall, slender young woman hurried toward them. Her cap of chin-length, ink-black hair bounced as she approached. As she got closer, Julia could see violet eyes shining out of a heart-shaped face. Wow, she was gorgeous. Like a runway model. Moved like one, too.

Ichabod apparently agreed because he visibly softened. "Devon," he said.

"Roger, you old sweetheart, you're not giving the new girl a hard time, are you?" Devon drawled in a perfectly genteel Southern accent.

He flushed. "I was explaining about the importance of keeping to the schedule. As you know, the slightest delay can throw off the entire day."

This last part was directed at Julia with the looking-down-his-nose move he seemed to have perfected.

"Roger, stop teasing her. She's here helping our dear Sarah, after all," Devon said, sending a discreet wink Julia's way.

Roger cleared his throat. "Yes, of course, you're right."

Model girl turned to Julia. "I'm Devon, the caterer. You must be Julia. Sarah called me last night and told me you'd be on your own here. Said I was to make sure you didn't drown in the sea of chaos."

Feeling as though she was reaching for a life preserver, Julia took the outstretched hand. "I think I love you."

Devon laughed. "Oh, I can tell I'm going to like you. Come on. Let's get this shindig up and running. My people are waiting to bring everything in."

"Your people?"

"It's only four people," Devon said, with a chuckle. "But this is Covington Falls, after all."

"Thanks for helping with Ichabod back there," Julia said as they walked away.

"Ichabod?" Devon asked, her nose wrinkling in confusion.

"*Sleepy Hollow?* Headless horseman?"

Devon threw back her head and laughed. "It certainly fits."

"I wasn't getting off to a very good start with him."

"Well, I know what it's like to be the new girl in town. The outsider."

Julia stopped. "Wait a minute. Betsy was telling me about you. You're the wunderkind chef from Chicago."

"I don't know about wunderkind, but I am from Chicago."

"You were using a Southern accent back there. A good one."

"I found it helped me get further in this town if I went all Southern Belle on them," Devon said, violet eyes flashing. "Sugar works down here. They dump it in their tea and smother each other with it in their conversation."

Devon's people were indeed waiting at the loading dock out back. Two men and two women. The guys looked to be around mid-twenties. The women were older, probably mid-forties.

"Okay, everyone, this is Julia," Devon said. "She's going to be in charge today. Julia, this is my team. George, Kevin, Maria, and Sandra. Guys, Julia is new in town, so help her out if she starts to look lost." She turned to Julia once more. "I have to get to the kitchen. Will you be okay now?"

"Absolutely," Julia said, with a big fake smile. Maybe if she said it enough times it might be true.

Devon shook her head and touched Julia's shoulder. "Holler if you need anything."

Julia resisted the urge to chase her newfound friend down, but she didn't even get a chance to breathe before Roger approached. Trailing in his wake was a severe-looking woman in a navy business suit.

"This is Ellen Simmons, our Events Coordinator," Roger intoned. "She'll be in charge of the staff and setup in the room."

She held out her hand. "Hi. I'm Jul—"

"I know who you are," Ellen responded.

Roger spun on his heels and glided away, leaving Julia

with the ever-so-cheerful Ellen Simmons. Ellen gave an impression of a smile as she turned.

Julia smiled right back. She opened the folder and pulled out the diagram with all the squares and circles. "I'm guessing this will make more sense to you than it does to me."

Ellen barely glanced at the paper. "I met with Sarah last week, and we finalized the setup. I wrote everything down, so there's no need for your little paper. My staff has already been briefed on their duties today."

"How convenient."

"We are most efficient here at the Covington Falls Country Club."

"Too bad they forgot to teach you how to smile at whatever boot camp they sent you to," Julia muttered under her breath.

"I'm sorry?"

Julia held the big, fake smile for all she was worth. "I said, we'd best be getting on with this. Why don't you get started in here? Then I need to go call a bride about a hairdo."

The Master Plan indicated Julia was supposed to call the hairdressers to confirm Maureen Ashley had made it to her appointment. Julia tried to call on her cell, but for some reason couldn't get any reception. Typical. So, she went off in search of a landline. Locating said landline meant she had to ask Roger. He gave a long-suffering sigh before leading her to his office. She'd have to look into a satellite phone, since cell reception was proving to be spotty in Covington Falls.

Julia dialed the number and then waited. And waited. And waited. Finally, someone picked up. "Cut & Dye Salon. This is Melinda-Sue."

The voice dripped with Southern charm. In the background Julia could hear what sounded like three dozen women squealing and chattering like black birds on a telephone line.

"I'm working with Marry Me. My name is Jul—"

"Oh, my goodness, you're the sweet girl who's helpin' our dear Sarah! She called me last night to let me know you'd be in charge."

Would no one let her say her whole name? At this point everyone in town was going to think her name was *"Jul—"*.

"Sarah sure does get around for a hospital-bound lady," Julia said.

Melinda-Sue laughed. "She sure does. What a firecracker. We love her to pieces. Such a sweet girl. Now, you're the daughter of that Yankee scoundrel, am I right? The one poor Grace took up with in her grief over losing her dear Samuel? Who could've blamed her, though? Your daddy was a handsome devil, but anyone with a lick of sense could tell he was nothin' but trouble."

Julia had no idea how to respond to such a statement.

"Now, what can I do for you, honey?" Melinda-Sue crooned.

"I'm supposed to make sure Maureen is there—"

"Oh, sure, she and the entire bridal party arrived right on time. We're fixin' her hair right this minute, and she is going to be just lovely, so don't you worry about a thing."

"Great, thanks. I need to be getting back to the preparations."

"Don't say another word. You go on and do what you have to do. Bye now!"

Julia hung up the phone in a bit of a daze. Good grief. It seemed everyone in this town talked like Betsy, on high octane Southern. She thought things were supposed to move slower down here.

Chuckling to herself, she headed back to the reception room. The country club staff had made good progress. The tables were set up and linen tablecloths were being whisked onto each one. Then the service doors opened, revealing a troupe of people bearing flower arrangements. The head flower-bearer approached her.

"I'm Carole," she said. "Donna's at the church setting up there. I'm in charge of setup on this end."

"I have no idea who Donna is, but I'll take your word for it."

The woman softened a little. "I've got your table arrangements and planters, plus some ivy for the trellis."

This meant nothing to her. "Okay."

Carole grinned this time. "We'll get to work."

"Sounds good to me."

She strode away, and Julia sighed. She was so in over her head.

****

After what seemed like days, the arrangements at the country club were coming together, no thanks to Julia. By now she had a splitting headache. People kept asking her questions, and she had no idea how to answer any of them. She glanced at her schedule, then at her watch. According to the timeline she was supposed to have left for the church ten minutes ago. Her headache intensified. As gut churning as it was trying to play Ring Master for this circus, the prospect of hanging out at the church for the next couple hours was even worse. Julia could feel hives forming already.

Betsy had provided directions to Covington Falls Community Church, but Julia didn't need them. It was the same church Grace had gone to, and she'd managed to drag Julia and her father to services as often as possible. Except now Seth was the pastor. How could the geeky kid Julia had known be trying to lead his flock on the path toward righteousness?

Julia pulled into the parking lot and turned off the ignition. Then stared. Dark, red bricks, aged with time, contrasted with the arched, stained-glass windows which marched down the sides. The windows sparkled in the sunlight. A tall steeple with a bell tower reached up into the sky, and at the very top was a white cross. Four stone steps led up to arched, double doors made of oak. She knew this because Grace had once related the story of how the church had been built in 1902 and how the doors had been shipped from England.

Taking a deep breath, Julia got out of the car and headed inside. Once inside the foyer, she paused to let her eyes adjust to the dim light. Directly ahead was the sanctuary. She could hear voices, so she headed toward them. Peeking inside, she saw there was a lot of work going on here, too. There was a group of people setting up flower arrangements and another placing tall candelabras next to the pews. One of the women looked up.

"I'm looking for Betsy," Julia said.

The woman started up the aisle. She was short, but curvy, with wavy, brown hair and brown eyes. "You must be Sarah's stepsister."

"Everyone seems to know who I am."

Chuckling, the woman held out a hand. "I'm Donna, the florist."

"Oh, right, you're another one of the wedding gurus."

A brow shot up. "I'm a guru? I had no idea. I should put that on my business cards."

Okay, Julia liked her, too. "Betsy was telling me about the local talent. She mentioned you, the chef, and the boutique owner."

"We do our best. We're almost done setting up in here. How's my crew doing at the country club?"

"Better than I am."

Donna laughed again. "Good to hear. As soon as I'm done, I'll head over there to double check everything is ready. In the meantime, you can find Betsy in the bride's room. Turn around and go back out the way you came. It's at the end of the hall to the left."

"Thanks."

As it turned out the directions were unnecessary because as soon as Julia got back out to the foyer, she saw Betsy and another woman dash out of a room. Betsy stopped in mid-stride, but the woman behind her didn't have such quick reflexes because she almost mowed Betsy down.

"Julia!" Betsy called out. "Thank goodness you're here. I was about to call you. We've got a big problem."

"What's wrong?" Julia asked.

Betsy indicated the woman with her. "This is Nancy, the church wedding coordinator. Nancy, this is Julia, Sarah's sister. She's the one I was telling you about."

Julia waved off the introduction. "It's nice to meet you, Nancy, but we can become friends later. What's wrong?"

"You'll see," Betsy said.

All three women raced back to the bride's room. There were at least two dozen women running around. Most of them were wearing the same yellow dress. Julia assumed they were bridesmaids, unless there'd been a run on yellow fabric around town. There was also an older woman in a powder-blue dress and another in a pale-green number. Mom and future mother-in-law, she guessed.

In the middle of it all stood Maureen Ashley in her billowing wedding gown. She was of average height and nicely rounded, with generous hips and chest. Her brown hair was arranged in an artful French twist, with a pearl-encrusted headband as the centerpiece. She'd obviously been crying. Everyone in the room seemed to be fussing over her dress, but Julia couldn't understand what they were saying over all the caterwauling.

She stuck two fingers her mouth and let loose with a loud, shrill whistle. Everyone froze.

"Hi. I'm Julia, Sarah's sister. Of sorts. As she may have told you I'm taking over while she concentrates on having a healthy baby. What seems to be the trouble?"

They all started talking at the same time. Julia did the

two-finger whistle again, and they groaned and covered their ears.

"Why don't we try having one person tell me?" Julia suggested. "Slowly?"

The older woman in the blue dress stepped forward. "We're having a problem with the dress."

"It looks okay to me."

She sighed. "Turn around, Maureen."

A fat tear slid down the younger woman's cheek as she turned. Julia noticed the bride's gown hadn't been fastened at the top, leaving a gaping hole.

The woman in blue gestured to the buttons. "It won't close."

Chills raced down Julia's back. "Why not?"

"Because I'm too fat!" Maureen wailed.

"Well, dear, I told you to watch what you were eating," her mother said. "You know where sugar goes. Just like me, to your hips and bosom."

"Mother!"

"I'm sorry, but it's the truth. It's the curse all the women in our family have to bear."

"Wait, wait, wait!" Julia cried, holding up her hands. "Are you saying you can't get her in the dress?"

"Yes," Mrs. Ashley confirmed.

Maureen's eyes welled up again. "I knew I was overeating, but I couldn't help it. I've been so nervous about the wedding and all, ya' know? It's what I always do when I get nervous. I eat. And now I'm a fat slob! What man would want to marry me looking like this?"

"Most men are more interested in what you've got underneath the dress," Julia said. "I think they also like some curves on a woman."

Maureen blinked in bemusement. "Huh?"

Oops, forgot where I was for a minute. "Sorry," Julia said. "Didn't you have a final fitting or something?"

Maureen nodded. "Three weeks ago, and it was okay then. It was a little snug, but I figured I'd be all right."

Julia looked around the room. "So, what do we do?"

Two dozen women gave her a blank stare.

"We were hoping you could think of something," Betsy said.

Panic clenched Julia's lungs, cutting off her air supply. "Me? What do I know about dresses?"

"You're a wedding planner, aren't you?" Mrs. Ashley asked.

"Only since Wednesday."

A horrified look passed over Mrs. Ashley's face. "Oh, dear, we all assumed you had experience in these matters."

Maureen started to cry again. "This is awful."

Julia approached the weepy bride and shook her a bit. "You've got to stop or you're going to wind up looking like a raccoon. We'll figure something out before you have to go down the aisle."

"We've got pictures in twenty minutes," the wedding coordinator said helpfully.

Julia scowled. "So we'll figure something out in *twenty minutes*. Let me think."

"Well, think quickly," Maureen's mother said.

"Did you call the dressmaker?" Julia asked.

Betsy nodded. "She's out of town doing a fitting for one of her clients."

"Perfect."

Julia stared at the half-dressed bride. What a nightmare! She actually felt sorry for Maureen, poor kid. Standing there in her puffy, white gown, she looked like a chubby china doll.

Wait a minute. Puffy. White. Gown. Julia started lifting layers to see what was underneath.

"What are you doing?" Maureen asked, swatting Julia's hands away.

"I'm solving your gaping problem. Look at all this

material."

"What about it?"

Julia looked at Mrs. Ashley. "Can you sew?"

The woman looked at the dress. Her eyes widened as understanding dawned. "Yes."

"Anyone else?"

Nancy held up her hand. "I can sew."

"Okay, we're going to play hide and seek here," Julia said. "Take a little from underneath and then you two will sew her right into the dress and fill in the gap."

"But if I'm sewn into the dress, how do I get out of it later?" Maureen asked.

"Why don't you let your new husband take care of it?" Julia said, with a wink. "He might like the idea of cutting your clothes off."

Maureen blinked in confusion again. "Huh?"

Yeah, lost track of where I was again. "Never mind. We're going to need scissors, needles, and thread."

Betsy raced to the corner and picked up what looked like a giant tackle box. She flipped the lid up and unearthed the needed items.

Julia stared at the treasure box. "Where did this come from?"

"Sarah put it together. It's got everything we need in case of an emergency."

"Good to know."

"Do you think this will work?" Betsy asked as she handed over the requested materials.

"Do you have a better idea?"

Betsy let out deep sigh. "No."

****

Seth didn't remember every moment of his wedding day. He'd been too nervous to fully comprehend everything going on around him. Most of it was stored in his mind as a series of hazy pictures, like yellowed photographs in an old album. There were several crystal clear moments, however. Brief, vivid flashes of sights, sounds, and smells. Beth's father lifting the veil from her face to reveal a gentle smile. Her hand as he slipped the ring on her finger. Her soft voice as she recited vows. The smell of the candles as the wax melted.

Those vivid images always came back to haunt him when it came time to invite a bride and groom to recite their vows. When he watched young couples gaze into each other's eyes with joy and trepidation. Seth wondered if he would ever be able to officiate a wedding without feeling like he'd scraped open an old scab. He always had to catch himself from admonishing said couple to make sure they remembered every single detail because they never knew when a tiny cell would mutate and go on the attack.

He'd made it through this one, though. The bride and groom had left a few minutes ago, and most of the guests had soon followed. Unable to face his empty, garage apartment yet, he'd volunteered to help with the cleanup.

"Hey, Rev, congratulations on another successful ceremony."

Seth shoved the last of the trash in a plastic bag and turned as a tall, blond man approached. He smiled. Ethan Thomas was someone Seth had gotten to know after he returned to Covington Falls. A former high school quarterback, Ethan had been the town golden boy back when Seth was still tripping over his own feet in middle school. A college injury had ended Ethan's hopes of a professional football career, and now he was the principal of the high school.

Sadly, a shared tragedy had forged their friendship. Ethan's wife had died suddenly only a few months after Beth lost her battle with cancer. Seth imagined weddings were just as much torture for Ethan, but since Maureen Ashley was a teacher at his school, he was duty-bound to attend.

"Thanks," Seth said. "I didn't know you were still around."

Ethan pulled off his tie and shoved it in his pocket. "I had to give the bride and groom a proper send off. How would it look if the boss skipped out before the throwing of the rice?"

"I don't think they throw rice anymore. Something about birds."

Ethan shrugged. "Whatever."

Seth eyed his friend. "How'd you hold up today?"

"How did *you*?" Ethan asked, shooting the question right back.

Seth's mouth quirked. "Same as always."

"Right," Ethan said, a knowing smile curving his lips. "Don't know how you stand doing this all the time."

"I pray. Give a sermon. Say hello to people… pick up trash."

"You stay busy."

"I suppose."

Ethan clapped him on the back. "I'm off. You should do the same."

He held up the full trash bag. "This is the last one."

Ethan nodded and ambled across the room. Seth took the bag of trash and headed toward the kitchen. He halted when he saw Julia hunched over the table, her head balanced in one hand. A full plate of food sat in front of her, but unless she'd learned to eat with her eyes closed he doubted she'd touched it.

He'd been aware of her most of the day. Annoyingly aware. She and Betsy had been shadowy figures threading in and out among the guests as they ensured everything came together. All the activity had meant he hadn't spoken to her yet.

Seth took a moment to drink in the sight of her. She was wearing a simple, black dress. Correction. On anyone else it would have been simple. On Julia it screamed danger.

He must have been feeling brave or stupid, because rather than drop the bag and run, he cleared his throat. "Hey there, sleepyhead."

Her eyes popped open. For one sweet moment, she smiled as if she were actually glad to see him. Then the Julia he knew and lov… well… the one he *knew* returned.

"Hi yourself," she said. "I thought you'd gone home."

"I was helping with the cleanup. Taking out the trash."

Her mouth quirked. "A man of many talents, I see. Minister by day, garbage man by night."

"You look beat," he said, venturing further into the room.

"I feel like I've been beaten," she said, with a bone-deep sigh.

"You did a great job under the circumstances."

"I did all right."

Drop the garbage and go, Seth. Do it now.

Rather than obey the inner warning, Seth leaned against the counter. "So, I keep hearing rumors about the bride's dress."

Her eyes widened. "You know?"

"One of the bridesmaids blabbed. Everyone's been talking about it. Ingenious of you."

"It's called desperation. I still can't believe it worked."

"I only wish I could've seen the look on Maureen's face when you suggested cutting her wedding gown," he said, with a soft chuckle.

She waggled her eyebrows. "You should have seen her face when I suggested her husband might like cutting her out of it later."

He tilted his head. "Cutting her out of it?"

"Yeah, you know, on their honeymoon," Julia said, with a wink.

Seth started thinking about scissors and a dress… and her. His eyes darkened, and he cleared his throat.

They stared at each other. Julia shifted, and for the first time Seth could recall, she blushed. He watched the pale, reddish tone rise in her cheeks, and a corresponding heat rose in him.

Next time… run.

Chapter Four

Morning came much too early. Bright sunlight pierced through the window as Julia pried open one eye. She immediately slapped a hand over her face.

Did it ever get cloudy in Covington Falls?

Peering between her fingers, she glanced at the clock on the bedside table. She'd slept later than she could ever remember. Who knew playing cruise director for a wedding would turn out to be so exhausting? Julia got up and looked out the window. What she needed was a good run. Back home she'd been fanatical about getting in her daily three miles, and she'd been shamefully neglectful about it here.

Within minutes she was pounding down the pavement, enjoying the stretch and pull of muscles. At the end of the block she turned right. Downtown was to the left, but right now she needed open space. Within minutes she was jogging past Lake Rice. The sun glittered off the water like a million diamonds. It wasn't a big lake, but it was certainly picturesque. Surrounding the lake were trees of all varieties from ancient oaks and tall pines to graceful magnolias.

Rounding the curve of the lake, Julia came upon the very

falls that gave the town its name. Rising over six feet high, the water tumbled over black slate rocks and gushed down into a shallow reservoir. Lush foliage and flowering plants surrounded the pool of water. She paused a moment to drink in the sight, then continued on around the lake.

By the time she turned back onto the street leading to Grace's house, Julia felt much more relaxed. She bypassed the front porch, in favor of the kitchen door at the back of the house.

"Hello."

She yelped and spun around to find Grace's husband, John, sitting at the kitchen table.

"Sorry," he said, with deliberate emphasis. "Did not mean… to scare… you."

His speech was clear, but halting, as if he had to search for the right words. He smiled, and one corner of his mouth curled up while the other side drooped down, giving the impression of a tilted question mark. Julia's encounters with Grace's husband had been brief so far, as he spent a lot of time in his room. This was the first time Julia had seen him in the kitchen.

There was no way for Julia to escape and not seem rude, so she conjured up an answering smile. "Hi."

With his good hand, John Graham gestured to a chair across from him. "Join me?"

Okay, not getting out of the room without a confrontation. Julia sidled closer and perched on the edge of the chair, her mind skittering over possible topics of conversation. What could she say to him anyway?

"Grace is so… happy… to have you here," John said, solving the dilemma.

She relaxed. John's crystal blue eyes, which he'd passed on to his son, still twinkled with gentleness and good humor despite his physical and verbal limitations.

"You think so?" Julia asked. She couldn't get over the

feeling Grace was only being polite. How happy could she be having the living reminder of a disastrous marriage living in her house again?

John nodded. "She likes... having all her... children... close."

"I'm not her real daughter."

"In her heart you are."

"I think sometimes her heart is too easily won," Julia said, thinking of her father. How in the world had he managed to fool someone as discerning as Grace?

John rubbed a finger across the plain gold band adorning his left hand. "Not always."

Julia watched the gesture, her interest in a man she barely remembered growing. "She gave you a fight? How did the two of you happen anyway? You lived next door for years, and then one day you looked over here and decided you wanted to marry Grace?"

"I've known Grace since... we were five. We were all friends."

"All?"

"Grace, Sam, me, and Susan. My wife. Susan passed, and I couldn't—" For a moment the light in his eyes dimmed.

Julia could almost see decades' worth of memories flash across his face. She reached for his hand, seeking to bring him back to the present. "Couldn't what?"

"I couldn't be... in the house. I would sit... on the porch. All day."

Father and son were so much alike, Julia thought. Both trying to escape places containing endless *could-have-beens*. "I'm sorry."

"Grace would come and sit with me," John continued. "We talked. I fell in love with her. I wasn't sure she would ever... take a chance. After everything."

"With my father, you mean?"

John nodded. "He hurt her... She was not... the same.

Sad. Lonely."

"But you wore her down and convinced her?"

A dry chuckle rumbled through his chest. "I did."

Julia sat back and rested her chin in her hand, regarding him with a smile. She wished now she'd paid more attention to the man across the street, back in the day. She had few memories of John as a solid, healthy, and vital man. "If it means anything, I think you make Grace very happy."

The lopsided question mark that made up his smile returned. "Thank you." He glanced at the clock on the wall. "Church will be over soon."

John struggled to stand, and she jumped up to help him to his feet. "Are you running away?" Julia asked.

"People will… come for lunch. It is… hard… with so many people talking. Wears me out."

"No kidding."

He gestured to her clothes. "You should go… get ready. People will not just come… for lunch. Come to… see you."

Julia looked down. Her jogging outfit was sweaty and gross. She had a feeling greeting visitors smelling like a wet, odorous dog wouldn't make the best impression. "Right. I'll go shower and change."

"Do not let them scare you," he said, with a wink.

"I don't scare easily."

He patted her cheek. "Just remember… most of them… mean no harm."

Her mind latched on to the most important word. "Most of them? What about the rest?"

"They have… nothing better to do than… get in your business."

Forty minutes later Julia was showered, dressed, and ready to do battle with anyone not included in the "most" category. For the past fifteen minutes she'd heard a chorus of car doors slamming. A glance out the window revealed a packed driveway, along with more cars parked down the street.

Julia heard voices as soon as she left her room. She didn't get halfway down the stairs before being spotted. The lookout was a short, round woman with snow-white hair. Dressed in a navy, polka dot dress she looked like the grandmother from *Little Red Riding Hood*. Julia wondered if Granny had big teeth to eat her with.

"There you are," Grandma Riding Hood said as Julia approached. "Grace told me to be on the lookout for you."

"Was she afraid I might get lost?"

"I think she was worried you might take one look at the horde in the living room and run right back up the stairs," the other woman said.

Grace wasn't far off. Julia's hands felt clammy, and sweat had started to form on her brow.

Get a grip, Julia. They're church members, not hit men.

"I'm Edith Austin," the older woman said.

"Austin? Are you related to Sarah's husband?"

"I'm his mother," she said, weaving a hand through Julia's elbow and heading toward the living room. "I'm so grateful you agreed to help out my son and daughter-in-law. It's an incredible thing you're doing, especially considering everything."

Julia glanced over, wondering if this was where she caught it for being related to the no-good scoundrel who broke poor Grace's heart. "What do you mean?"

"I can't imagine it's easy to come back here after what happened between your father and Grace."

"It is a bit awkward."

"Plus, it's been such a long time since you lived here. You barely kept in touch all these years, and yet you agreed to put your life on hold for Sarah and Eric. It's amazing."

"Grace was good to me. It's the least I can do."

Edith smiled. "You're a good girl."

Julia was still gaping at Edith's last comment when they

reached the living room and were instantly surrounded by a ring of people. Edith made the introductions and then started to walk away.

"Where are you going?" Julia called after her.

"I have to finish the potato salad."

"But—"

Just then Betsy bounded up. "Hi, Julia."

Julia had never been so glad to see a familiar face in her life. She even allowed her assistant to drag her around the room making introductions.

"Do you remember Mary-Ellen Carter?" Betsy asked, as they stopped in front of a stout, grey-haired woman. "She lives across the street."

Julia did actually. "Hello. You're looking well."

"Thank you," Mrs. Carter said. "You've turned into a beautiful woman. Of course, you were lovely even as a girl, so it's no surprise."

"Thank you," she said, caught off guard by the effusive greeting.

Julia definitely remembered the next woman in the circle. She'd been her ninth grade English teacher. The woman had been in her early twenties then and had been one of the few teachers to make her feel truly welcome.

"Mrs. Shannon," Julia said, giving her a hug.

"You do remember," her former teacher said, looking pleased.

"Of course. Are you still teaching?"

"Oh, yes. I hope you'll stop by for a visit."

Or maybe not. Julia swallowed. "Mm—"

Betsy gestured to a young woman about Julia's age. She looked familiar, but Julia couldn't recall the name.

"This is Nicole Rivers," Betsy said.

"You might remember me as Nicole Coleman," she said, holding out her hand.

A light dawned. "Oh. Nicole. We had chemistry together,

right?"

"Right. We also used to go to The Old Diner after school."

How could Julia have forgotten her? Nicole was the closest thing she'd had to a friend in those days. Of course, Nicole had been skinny as a rail with hair half way down her back then. Now, she was rounder, and the hair was cut in a short bob.

Nicole grinned, as if reading Julia's mind. "I know, I look a little different, but what can I say? I've had four kids. Figure goes to pot, and who has time to deal with long hair?"

Julia goggled in amazement. "Four? Wow."

"Two sets of twins. You'll have to stop by one day and meet my family."

"Mm—"

Julia and Betsy slowly made their way around the room, stopping to greet people. Some of them Julia remembered, but the majority she had no clue about. Most seemed to remember her, though. She didn't know if everyone had come to an agreement, but surprisingly not one person mentioned her father.

Although, what could anyone say without sounding rude or awkward?

Finally, they made it to the kitchen. The place was a regular beehive of activity. Several women were serving up food. The countertops were overflowing with dishes. There was a ham, roast beef, green beans, mashed potatoes, potato salad, and several different kinds of pies and cakes for dessert.

Grace was right in the middle of the chaos, directing traffic. She spotted Julia and rushed over. "There you are. I was worried you'd escaped after Edith left you."

"Betsy made sure I didn't bolt."

She smiled at Betsy. "Thank you for looking out for her."

"I'm happy to help," Betsy said.

Grace looked around the kitchen. "I think everything is

ready. Betsy, could you find Seth so he can pray before we eat?"

Seth was summarily fetched, prayer commenced, and serving began. As the kitchen started to empty out, Julia stepped up to the line to fill her plate.

"Hi."

Julia looked over her shoulder. Another delicate-looking blonde was standing behind her. Was no one over 5′2″ in this town? And where had they put the dark-haired people? Aside from Seth, she hadn't seen more than a handful since she'd arrived. This particular dainty blonde looked like she'd stepped out of a 50s-inspired window display. She was wearing a pink, flowery dress, complete with a little, white collar, and matching, three-inch pink pumps. Her honey-blond hair fell in soft waves to her shoulders.

"You're Julia," the woman said.

"How'd you guess?"

The young woman didn't answer. Instead, her eyes drifted down and then back up. Julia had the odd feeling the strange woman was cataloging every detail. When the inspection was over Julia was quite certain she'd come up wanting, and this somehow pleased the newcomer.

"So, you're the long-lost daughter."

This was the strangest conversation Julia had ever had. "Long-lost stepdaughter if you want to get technical about it. Who are you?"

"Oh, I do declare," she said, oozing sugar out of her pores. "I am bein' so rude. I'm Amy Vining."

Julia didn't know people actually said "I do declare" anymore.

"When I heard you were livin' here, I got a touch jealous," Amy said.

"Jealous? Of what?"

Amy leaned in closer as if she was about to impart a state secret. "The truth is, I've had my eye on a certain preacher since I was a little girl."

"You mean Seth?"

Amy nodded, and her expression turned dreamy. Good grief, Julia hoped she didn't turn into such a sop when she saw Seth in a pair of jeans.

Hey, weren't you going to stop thinking about him?

"I know he loved his wife very much, but a man still needs a companion," Amy said. "When I heard you were going to be living with Grace, I did worry. After all, you're not his sister, and I had heard several people remark on how stunning you are."

"I can assure you there is nothing going on between Seth and I."

And nothing is ever going to go on between us. Right, Julia?

Amy giggled. "I realized how silly the whole idea was the moment I saw you."

Had she just been insulted?

Apparently, her expression indicated she had because Amy giggled again. "I'm sorry. I didn't mean to offend you. You are beautiful, of course, but Seth's wife was such a delicate creature. Ethereal and so spiritual. Why, the love of Christ shone all around her."

Oh, now Julia understood where this little inquisition was going. "A little bit like you perhaps?"

Amy bowed her head, making a believable attempt to look modest. "I could only hope to share some of Beth's finer qualities."

I've landed in another universe populated by little blonde people who talk in riddles, Julia thought.

"I see you two have met," a male voice said from behind them.

It was Seth. Even if Julia hadn't recognized the voice, Amy's gushing smile would have been a tip off. It was truly a thing to behold.

Seth didn't seem to notice. "I was planning on

introducing you two, but I see Amy beat me to it."

Amy was still in full gushing mode. "I simply had to come and welcome your… um… Julia."

Julia smothered a smile as Amy stumbled over the title. Actually, she couldn't be faulted there. Julia didn't even know how to describe her relationship to this family.

"It's amazing Julia would be so generous as to come here and help Sarah like this," Amy continued.

"Yes, we're all grateful," Seth said, oblivious to Amy's adoration. He focused on Julia. "I understand you had an interesting conversation with my dad."

"How did you know?"

"I stopped in to visit with him when I got here. He told me you'd had breakfast together. I think he was impressed with you."

"I like him, too."

Seth chuckled. "He thought you were sweet."

Julia crossed her arms and huffed. "I'm starting to think I need to work harder to maintain my image."

"Maybe a little softness is a good thing."

"Softness is just another word for vulnerable."

He took a step closer, his expression serious. "When we allow ourselves to be vulnerable we often discover the sweetest treasures to be had in life."

"You mean like love?" Julia asked, with a brittle laugh.

"Among other things. I've always believed God speaks to me when I'm vulnerable enough to admit I can't do it on my own."

"I haven't done too bad on my own."

His mouth twisted in a wry grin. "So, you've got a perfectly full life?"

"Yes."

For a moment their gazes locked, then those violins she'd first heard at the softball game started up again. So annoying. How was she supposed to fight with someone when her brain kept running an endless love story soundtrack?

Apparently, Amy had heard enough because she stepped fully into Seth's vision. "Seth, I wanted to talk to you about ordering the curriculum for next year's Sunday school."

Seth blinked in bemusement. "Sunday school?"

Amy's head bobbed up and down. "Yes. I know it's early, but it takes so long to decide and then wait for the order." She turned to Julia. "I'm the Christian Education Director at Seth's church."

Julia decided to escape before she had to endure any further interrogation. She needed to get her brain functioning again anyway. "No problem. You two go on and discuss your curriculum. I'm dying to sample some of this food."

Amy didn't need any more prompting. She hooked an arm through Seth's elbow and led him away before he could protest. Julia resisted the urge to watch them. Let Amy have him. Julia had no idea what a Christian Education Director did, but she knew about Sunday school, and if Amy was in charge, she would make a much better minister's wife.

Not that Julia was considering becoming a minister's wife. Or that he was considering making her one. If only they could stop having these Hallmark moments. So unnerving. And they were going to stop.

Right now.

****

What had just happened? Seth fought the urge to watch Julia as she walked away. Amy continued to babble something about workbooks and the theological implications of one choice over another. He tried to concentrate, but his mind wouldn't let him. How had their conversation gotten so deep so fast? One minute he'd been teasing her about being nice, the next they were engaged in a philosophical debate. What's more, Julia was clearly as perplexed by their odd connection as he was. He'd seen it in the depths of her blue eyes, along with annoyance. She didn't like it when he challenged her beliefs.

Well, too bad. After the night he'd spent tossing and turning she deserved to be uncomfortable. For the wedding dress comment alone, she deserved retribution. Dreams of scissors and threads coming undone had undone him. He'd woken up in a state he hadn't experienced since Beth became too sick to do more than cuddle in the bed. So, now not only was he alive, he was kicking.

And it was all Julia's fault.

"Seth, did you hear what I just said?" Amy asked.

He blinked away the image of revealed skin. "Of course, Amy."

"So what do you think?"

Huh? "I think you'll make the right decision."

She smiled, so he must have said something right. Meanwhile, he was losing his mind.

And it was all Julia's fault.

Chapter Five

The day after Sarah was released from the hospital, Julia showed up at the apartment bearing gifts. She knocked and heard Sarah call out.

"Come in!"

She twisted the handle, and the door swung open. "I know this is a small town, but is an unlocked door a good idea?" Julia asked, as soon as she spotted Sarah on the couch.

"I asked Eric to leave it unlocked because our neighbor is supposed to come by to check on me every hour or so."

Julia sat on the end of the couch. Dropping her gift on the floor, she took Sarah's hand. "How are you?"

Sarah squeezed back. "I feel fine. Mary is kicking up a storm and not letting me sleep."

"Well, you certainly look better. The color is back in your cheeks. Where is your husband, by the way? Isn't he supposed to be making sure you don't get up? What about when you want to fix lunch? Or need to go to the bathroom?"

"My neighbor is coming over. Between my husband, my mother, Seth, my mother-in-law, and nearly everyone in this building, someone should be here twenty-four-seven to make sure I don't move from this spot without supervision."

Julia nodded in satisfaction. "Good."

Sarah smiled. "So, I hear you came through in the Ashley wedding. Betsy called and told me everything. I can't believe you sewed Maureen into her dress."

"I think Maureen's mother about had a heart attack when I suggested cutting the dress," Julia said, with a grimace.

"Be glad her mother was one of the reasonable sorts. You wouldn't believe how crazy some of them get when it comes to weddings. Speaking of Maureen's mother, she called and told me to relay a message to you."

"What?"

"Maureen says you were right about her husband cutting off the dress. Then she thanked you for suggesting it."

Julia laughed.

Sarah gave her a quizzical look. "I guess you know what she's talking about?"

"I think you had to be there," Julia said, still chuckling.

"All right, changing the subject. How is everything going at the house? Eric told me your first meeting with Seth was pretty tense."

Julia glanced away. "I think he takes his role as surrogate big brother very seriously, and I'm not sure he trusts me. We're managing not to kill each other, though."

"I was hoping you'd get along better."

"I don't think we'll ever be best friends. We have nothing in common."

"I wanted things to be different, so we could all be a family of sorts. Only a better one this time because—"

"My father isn't around to muck it up?"

Sarah gave her a stern look. "You should work at getting past your anger at him. Your dad wasn't perfect, but then none of us are. He did have good qualities."

"Sure, he was charming when it suited him or got him what he wanted."

She rapped Julia's hand like a prim schoolteacher. "He was also kind to me. He knew how much I wanted a daddy, and he obliged. He never brushed me off when I wanted attention or treated me like I was an annoying kid. Was he different with you?"

Kind? Yes, her father had been kind. He'd also been charming, funny, and sweet. He'd had a way of looking at you like you were the only person on the planet. When she'd been a little girl Julia had adored him.

She supposed it wasn't uncommon for girls to adore their fathers, but she'd had a serious case of hero worship. She'd always sensed a distance with her mother. Even as early as the toddler years Julia had understood that her mother didn't like to be mussed. "Mussed" as in hugged, which led to wrinkles in skirts, stains on blouses, or a hair out of place. Thomas Richardson had always been a hugger, a toucher, and a *look-into-my-eyes-and-tell-me-your-deepest-desires* kind of guy.

Julia still had vivid memories of Sunday mornings. She used to wake up early and pad into his study to sit on his lap while he read the paper. Most of the time they didn't speak, but sometimes he'd comment on an article he was reading. Julia hadn't understood what he was talking about, but it hadn't mattered. She was with him.

He'd been her prince. Her hero. Her friend.

Then he went away. Left her with the pretty woman who smiled vaguely and patted her head on occasion as she wafted out the door on a cloud of expensive perfume en route to her next date. There hadn't been any more Sunday mornings.

Julia swallowed the sudden lump in her throat. "No, he was affectionate, but he always sent me away when it suited him, too. He simply never cared enough to stick."

Sarah reached over and turned Julia's head back. "Like I said, not perfect, but not a monster either. For your own sake, you need to come to terms with him."

The statement pulled Julia back from the abyss of her

own maudlin memories. Thank goodness. She stared in amazement. "Good grief, when did you morph into your mother?"

Sarah rolled her eyes. "I've caught myself spouting my mother's words lately, and it's unsettling. I think some "wise momma" gene must get mixed in with all those pregnancy hormones."

"Do they tell you that in those pregnancy books? Because I think women should be forewarned they're about to turn into their mothers."

Sarah laughed outright. "I guess I don't mind becoming more like my mother. She's a pretty good example to follow."

"True." Julia stood up. "Well, I have an appointment with a client and a singer."

"Oh, with Meredith?"

"I'm supposed to help the couple pick out music, though what I can contribute I can't imagine."

"You'll do fine. Let Meredith handle everything. She's a dream to work with. Wait till you hear her sing. She's incredible. She was on her way to a big time music career, but she gave it up."

"Why?"

"I probably shouldn't tell her secrets, but if she's comfortable enough, maybe she'll tell you herself. It's a fascinating story. I think you'd relate to her."

"If I get around to it, I'll ask. Before I go, I have something for you," Julia said, reaching for her gift. "Call it a welcome to the twenty-first century."

Sarah's face lit up. "A present?"

Julia put the box in Sarah's lap. Her mouth formed an "oh" as she realized what was inside. "You got me a tablet?"

"Yes, a good one which includes the ability to do video calls so I can see you face to face when disaster is about to strike. I called and someone should be here to set up your wireless connection tomorrow."

"Julia, this is too much," Sarah said, even as she took out her new toy.

"There is no such thing as too much. After the last wedding, I knew you needed to be with me all the time, even if it wasn't physically. Plus, you can use it to order movies and books to ward off the boredom."

Sarah beamed. "Or I could use it to order a pizza without getting up off the couch."

Trust a pregnant woman to think of food. "I'm sure there's an app for pizza ordering, too."

"I feel so modern."

She leaned down and kissed the top of Sarah's head. "I really do have to go now."

"Hey, don't be a stranger!" Sarah called out as Julia started to leave. "I've only been home one day, and already I know I'm gonna go crazy cooped up here all by myself."

"Don't worry. I plan to pester you as often as possible. Now, take care of my little Mary. Gotta protect the woman who's destined to save my life someday."

"I will."

Julia's appointment was at Seth's church, where the singing phenomenon was also the Music Director. She'd spent too much time at Sarah's and was already running late. Betsy had helpfully written down directions on how to find the choir room, otherwise Julia would have ended up having to leave bread crumbs to find her way back out. At the foyer, she hung a left and circled around behind the sanctuary, then hurried down a flight of stairs. Someone was playing a piano as she rounded the corner. Then the singing stopped her cold.

The voice was smoky and rich. Part siren, part angel. Julia had never heard anyone express so much emotion through music. It was almost enough to make her believe in true love and happy endings after all.

"Wow, that's the most beautiful thing I've ever heard," a young woman said, in a sad, wistful voice. "My dad used to hum that song to my mom."

"Then it looks like we found the song for your first dance," the owner of smoky voice replied.

Julia slipped through the doorway. The choir room was more like a cave, with white walls and no windows. Padded chairs were arranged in rows on three elevated steps. The woman with the amazing voice was seated at the piano.

The couple consisted of yet another tiny blonde and a strapping, brown-haired young man. They looked up as Julia entered, which caused the piano player to turn around.

"Hi, I'm Julia. I'm sure Sarah already called to let you know I'm going to be handling things until her baby is born."

The owner of the spectacular voice stood up. Julia was thrilled to see the other woman was tall and willowy, with auburn hair and green eyes. Finally, she'd found someone who'd gotten left out of the blond, pixie gene pool.

"Yes, Sarah did call. I'm Meredith Vining, and I'm doing the music for the wedding," she said. "This is Stacey and Carl, our bride and groom."

Julia shook hands with both of them. "I see you've already gotten started."

"I met with them two weeks ago, and we chose music for the ceremony," Meredith said. "Now, we're picking special numbers for the reception. We just found the song for their first dance. Stacey's father passed away a year ago, so it will be a tribute to him.

"I'm so sorry about your father," Julia said. "It must be difficult for you."

Stacey's smile was sweet, but a little forlorn. "It is sad, but he's in a much better place now. He was ill for a long time. Now, he's at peace in the presence of the Lord."

Julia blinked. She'd never heard death described in such a way.

Meredith put an arm around Stacey's shoulder. "I'm sure he'll be here in spirit, though. He would never miss his little girl's big day. Julia, why don't you have a seat, and we'll get these two settled?"

Meredith was so good Julia didn't have to do anything except nod her approval occasionally. The more she listened, the more impressed she became. Meredith was amazing. Everything she sang, whether a ballad or a dance tune, was flawless. Julia could picture her on any radio station in the country or on stage entertaining thousands. She wondered what had caused Meredith to give up her career and come back to conduct a church choir in a sleepy little nowhere town.

Once all the selections were made, Stacey and Carl thanked Meredith and left.

"You're amazing," Julia said, once they'd gone.

"You're very kind."

"I'm not being kind. What in the world are you doing stuck here in Covington Falls?" Julia asked, then winced at how rude she'd sounded. "Sorry. I probably shouldn't have been so blunt."

"It's all right," Meredith said, with a dismissive wave. "I'm used to it. I know it's difficult for most people to understand."

"Impossible. Why would you walk away from your career? You were obviously born for it."

"I was born to do exactly what I'm doing now," Meredith said, with a decisive shake of her head. "I know to the outside world it seems crazy."

Yeah, it did seem crazy. "But why?"

Meredith looked at her watch. "I'd tell you about it, but right now I've got music lessons, and I have to prepare for choir practice. Why don't I call you, and we can meet for dinner sometime?"

"All right."

"Great," Meredith said. "It was nice to meet you."

"You, too."

Julia made her way back upstairs. She needed to get back

to Marry Me to do… something… she was sure. She was passing through an empty hallway when she heard voices coming from one of the offices.

"Seth, I'm only letting you know what some of the members are saying about Miss Vining."

The door was partially open, and Julia peeked in. Seth was seated at a large oak desk. His hands were folded on top of it, and she could tell he was trying to control his temper. She recognized his steely gaze. It was the same one he'd directed her way at the softball game. An older, white-haired man was seated across from him. Julia knew it was wrong to eavesdrop, but couldn't help herself.

"I'm well aware of the attitude of some members," Seth said. "Don't think I haven't heard the same things myself from the bolder ones. I know not everyone approves of Meredith."

"With her past, can you blame them?"

His eyes turned frosty. "Actually, I can, Paul. We're the Church. We're supposed to rejoice when one of God's children finds their way back to the Lord. Meredith has changed her life, which is something to celebrate, not condemn."

The man held up his hands in surrender. "Seth, I'm not the enemy here. I understand your support of her, and I even applaud it. I'm only warning you to be careful. There are some here who will use any excuse to make trouble for you."

"I know. Thank you for your concern."

They stood up and shook hands.

****

Seth waited for Paul to walk away before venting his frustration. He felt like cursing. Instead he let out a sigh mixed with a groan.

"It sounds like you've got a mutiny on your hands."

His head shot up. Familiar flashing blue eyes regarded him with curiosity. "Julia?"

"You know how to make enemies, I see," she said.

A small chuckle escaped. "In the Church, there are always enemies to be made."

"I thought it would be all sweetness and light over here."

If she only knew.

She wandered further in the room and started poking around the office. He wondered what she thought. He'd wanted his office to feel comfortable. The room consisted of dark wood wainscoting, with honey-colored walls, a sage-green carpet, floor-to-ceiling bookshelves, an antique brass desk lamp, and two cushy sage-green armchairs. A big picture window looked out on to a pretty interior courtyard. He loved to write his sermons here.

"I thought everyone would be wandering around with angelic smiles on their faces all day long," she said.

She'd made her way over to the bookshelves and was scanning the titles, an eclectic collection containing everything from Billy Graham to Charles Shultz to Shakespeare.

"Like a bunch of simpletons, I gather," he drawled. "What are you doing?"

"Being nosy," she replied, with a cheeky grin. "So, tell me about these enemies?"

"Well, in my opinion the real enemy isn't a person."

"Who is it?"

"As someone more famous than me would say... Satan?"

Julia laughed at his spot on impersonation. "Satan is the reason you've got a bunch of judgmental biddies snapping at your heels trying to get rid of your Music Director?"

"You overheard?"

"I did eavesdrop, though I didn't mean to. I just met Meredith, and she's amazing."

"That's why I hired her."

Julia moved on from the shelves to the side table by his desk. There was a framed picture of a child's drawing depicting the church. Standing in front of it was a male figure with dark hair.

"This is supposed to be you, I assume," she said, picking up the frame.

"So I'm told."

Her eyes darted up to meet his, amusement evident. "Cute. So, what makes you think Satan is the problem?"

Seth leaned back in his chair. "Because he wants nothing more than to create problems in God's church, divide His people, and lead them astray. What better way to discourage people from embracing God than for them to see infighting."

A brow shot up. "You actually believe there's a malevolent spirit out there trying to take over the universe?"

"Of course. If I believe in the ultimate good, God, then it makes sense there is an ultimate evil, Satan. I sense it everyday. Sometimes I feel like I'm under siege."

"I guess that makes sense," she said. "You're trying to do God's work, and if Satan can take you out he wins."

Seth regarded her with a new respect. "For someone who claims to know nothing about God or religion, you understand better than most."

"I understand people," she said, with an annoyed little huff. "I know they can be selfish. If I were Satan, I'd play on their weaknesses. So, why are you getting flack for hiring Meredith?"

He dragged a hand through his hair. "Truthfully, she does have a bit of a past. Meredith went through a wild phase in her teen years. Her stint in the music business draws some ire as well. There are a lot of people who don't much like what the popular culture and its music represents."

"You could tell them to get over themselves. What's the big deal?"

"It's not so simple." He reached into a drawer and pulled out a CD, and then tossed it across his desk.

Julia snatched up the case. A low whistle blew past her lips. "That's Meredith?" she asked, opening the cover and pulling out the insert to look at the rest of the pictures.

Seth nodded. He didn't need to see the photographs again. Glossy shots of Meredith Vining, or Mika Vine as she'd been called then, in various states of undress, cavorting with a barely-clothed man. "There's a video, too. Wound up going viral. Meredith managed to get it taken down, but the CD won't go away. Cousins and friends and sisters-in-law of people in town love to mail them here when they find one."

"Did she tell you about this scandalous photo shoot before you hired her?" she asked.

"Would it matter?"

"If you were blindsided with this little gem, then maybe she doesn't deserve the all-is-forgiven award," she said. "Part of Meredith being this reformed citizen you claim she is, would include coming clean about her past. At least to you, since you're the one sitting out on the shaky limb."

"She gave me the CD when she came in for her interview. And I saw the video long before it wound up on the Internet. She played it for me."

"I knew I liked her. Good to know I didn't misjudge her." Julia sat on the edge of his desk. "So, even after seeing the risqué antics of Mika Vine you still hired her? Why?"

"Meredith came back a changed person," he said. "Her desire was to serve the Lord through her music. I gave her the opportunity. I've been trying to move this church — and the town — to a place where we can stop sitting in judgment of others. It doesn't mean we condone sinful behavior, but if we ever hope to change hearts, we have to approach people with compassion and mercy."

She looked at him for a long time. Finally, her head swiveled back and forth. "Who knew you'd turn out to be a maverick?"

Heat crept up his cheeks. "I'm only serving the Lord as I hope He'd want."

"You must get so overwhelmed. Doing the Lord's work

while fighting off the forces of evil." She said the last part with a little boxing duck and dodge move.

Another jolt of surprise ricocheted through his body, and he went still. "How is it you get me better than people who've known me my whole life?"

And why does it have to be a woman who scorns everything I believe?

"I'm sure you have people in your life who understand," she said, taking a deep breath.

"Beth was the only one who seemed to really get it, but her father was a minister so perhaps she had special insight."

At the mention of his wife, Julia's gaze went to the framed photograph on Seth's desk. This picture was older than the one in his apartment.

Julia leaned forward. "Is this Beth?"

"Yes. It was taken—" He stopped. Memories assaulted him. This photo had been taken when they'd bought their first house in Memphis after he'd graduated from Seminary. The one in his bedroom had been taken here in Covington Falls. Beth had looked completely healthy, but in truth she'd already started to die. The injustice of it hit him again. A wave of anger and grief threatened to take him under.

"Before she got sick," Julia said. "She was beautiful."

The softly spoken words snapped Seth back to the here and now. Julia was looking at him, and in some odd way he had the feeling she was trying to give him strength. And a chance to recover.

He cleared his throat. "She was."

Seth was about to say something else when a sprightly, middle-aged woman joined them.

"Pastor Graham—" She broke off when she saw Julia. "Oh, I'm so sorry. I didn't realize you were with someone."

Seth stood up and walked around the desk. "It's all right, Clarice. Have you met Grace's stepdaughter?"

The woman blinked. "No, I haven't had the pleasure."

"This is Julia. Julia, Clarice Johnson, one of our members."

"Nice to meet you," Julia said.

Mrs. Johnson's head swiveled back and forth between them. "Likewise. I hope I'm not intruding."

"Not at all," Julia said. "I came by to meet with Meredith Vining about a wedding, and I couldn't resist stopping in to see where Seth works."

"Of course," Mrs. Johnson said, before turning to Seth again. "Pastor Graham, I came by to invite you to dinner tomorrow night. My niece is visiting. She's just back from the mission field in Venezuela, and I know you two would have so much in common."

Oh, not again! He forced a smile. "I'd be honored to meet her and enjoy your splendid hospitality."

Mrs. Johnson looked delighted. "Wonderful! We'll see you at seven tomorrow then?"

"I look forward to it."

Julia turned, brow arched as Mrs. Johnson bustled from the room. "She wants you to meet her niece?"

"Mrs. Johnson has no children of her own, but she comes from a big family and so does her husband. I think she must have about twenty nieces."

"Do people try to fix you up a lot?"

Seth shifted, uncomfortable with the topic. "It started about eight months ago. The fix-ups anyway. At first it was only dinner. I guess they thought I'd starve on my own, even though Grace fed me well. Then eventually eligible women started to get thrown into the mix. Seems everyone in town has a sister, daughter, granddaughter, or niece of marriageable age whom I need to meet."

"Any interesting prospects?" she asked, picking up the letter opener on his desk and twirling it between her fingers.

Seth looked down at Beth's picture. Sadness reached out to swallow him whole. "No."

"She wouldn't want you to live your life alone."

Something in her tone brought his head back up. Their eyes met. Hers were flat and guarded. Seth realized the question hadn't been idle curiosity and knew his answer had hurt her. He wished he could make her understand.

"I know. I just can't—" he tried to explain. "I'm not sure anyone will ever take her place."

"You're not ready yet, I get it." She stood up, looking anywhere but at Seth. "I need to go."

Yeah, she was hurt all right, but there wasn't anything he could say to undo it. He ran a hand through his hair. "Julia—"

She did look up then, but keep-your-distance Julia Richardson was firmly back in place. "Seth, I *know.* I'll see you around."

What had happened here?

He blew out a deep. "Right. See you."

Chapter Six

Some women feel they don't exist unless they're with a man. Julia's mother was one of those women. She simply could not be alone. In between marriages Brooke Richardson kept time with a professional tennis player, a congressman, a doctor, a lawyer, a real estate developer, a CEO, an investment banker, a minor league baseball player, a chef, and a violin player for a symphony orchestra.

Each relationship followed a predictable pattern. She'd fall madly in love and spend every waking moment with her new man. Until he did something completely offensive like leaving his dirty coffee cup on the kitchen counter all day, causing her to kick him out, or she became so jealous and possessive she turned into one of those crazed stalker women and the man headed for the hills.

Living in the house had been like an endless soap opera, filled with angst and pity. She was angst. Julia was pity.

Julia had decided back then her life would never revolve around a man. Ironic, since her life now consisted of helping other women revolve their lives around a man.

Something else twisted? Having an outdoor wedding in

the middle of summer. Slipping on a fifty-pound wedding dress and standing around in one-hundred-plus degree weather all day was not Julia's idea of a good time. At least she'd had a week to prepare for the outdoor extravaganza, as opposed to a couple days.

The wedding and reception was taking place at the Botanical Gardens on the outskirts of town. It hadn't taken long for Julia to realize dealing with the country club staff was a piece of cake compared to transforming a patch of nature's glory into a suitable setting for the grand nuptials.

Since the crack of dawn she and Betsy had been directing a dozen workers in the set up. Well, Betsy had been directing, Julia had mostly been pointing in a vague direction whenever anyone asked her where something was supposed to go.

The ceremony was to be held in the rose garden. In front of a semicircle of rose bushes was a white trellis festooned with ivy. Six rows of dainty white folding chairs were arranged in front of the trellis. About a hundred feet away, a giant tent with filmy white drapery and a temporary parquet dance floor had been erected for the reception. Chef Devon was catering the wedding, and she and her staff had been busy underneath the tent for hours now.

Speaking of the ceremony, according to Julia's schedule it was nearly time to start. Most of the guests were already seated. She went in search of Betsy. As she walked, Julia pulled her sticky blouse from her skin and fanned herself. After hours of running around in the Georgia soup, her hair had turned into a giant frizz ball. Plus, her deodorant had thrown up its hands in defeat some time ago, so now she was a *smelly*, giant frizzy ball.

Beautiful.

Julia spotted a white limousine in the parking lot so at least she knew the wedding party had arrived. The employee's lounge doubled as a bride's room for weddings. Julia burst into the room and was confronted with a half-dozen young women giggling and chattering like a bunch of chipmunks in hot pink dresses.

Betsy turned as the door shut. "Hi, Julia. Is everyone here?"

"Looks like it. Please tell me everything fits this time."

Betsy gestured to a young woman in white who was fully dressed, thank goodness.

Lisa Evans, the bride, shot her a worried look. "Are there any clouds?"

Julia shook her head. "No."

"You're sure? Because I thought I saw one when we came in. I would die if it rained on my wedding."

"I don't think you have to worry about any freak thunderstorms today. Heat exhaustion, maybe, but not rain."

"And the roses? The dresses match, right? I specifically told my dressmaker I wanted the bridesmaids' dresses to match the roses in the garden. I even brought her out here so she could see the color."

"Of course they match," Julia said. She had no idea if it was true, but at this point she'd say anything to get Lisa up and out of the room in time for the ceremony.

Lisa was satisfied because she nodded. She and the bridesmaids started to file out of the room.

"Ugh, it's hot," one of the bridesmaids said. "Remind me not to have my wedding here. My makeup is already melting."

My everything is melting, Pinky.

Julia ran ahead to signal the string quartet to start the processional music. With relative ease, she and Betsy got the attendants and the bride down the aisle. Julia turned to her tiny cohort, and they gave each other a little high five.

"Not bad for only our second wedding," Julia said.

Betsy grinned. "Piece of cake."

Seth was performing this ceremony, too, and he stepped forward. "Dearly beloved, we are gathered here today, in the sight of these witnesses to celebrate the union of Lisa Anne Evans and Scott Edward Thompson…"

Julia surveyed the wedding party and had to admit Lisa and Scott made a lovely picture. She noticed the bridesmaid's dresses did indeed match the roses.

"I'm going to head over to the reception tent and make sure everything is in order there," Betsy said. "You stay here."

Since she was feeling invincible, Julia nodded. "Okay."

She turned back as Seth was getting to the vows. "Lisa, repeat after me. I, Lisa Anne Evans…"

"I Lisa Anne… *Ah!*"

Julia jumped as the bride started screaming and slapping her arms. Julia rushed forward, along with most of the guests.

"It's a bee! Get it off me! Get it off!" Lisa screamed.

Julia pushed through the crowd, in time to see the bride drop to the ground in a heap of white crinoline.

"Lisa!" Scott cried.

Julia knelt over the prostrate girl. Her face was flushed, and she looked like she was struggling to breathe. So, not just a panic attack.

"Someone call an ambulance!" Julia shouted.

Julia was pretty sure she'd seen this reaction before in movies. This was not good.

"Is Lisa allergic to bees?" Julia asked.

Lisa's mother looked panic-stricken. "Yes. We never should have let her talk us in to an outdoor wedding."

Julia cursed under her breath. "Is the ambulance coming?"

"They're on the way," Betsy said, pushing through the crowd.

She dropped down to the ground. The giant tackle box was with her again. Betsy reached in and pulled out a long, thin wand and handed it over.

"Where did you get this?" Julia asked, staring at the instrument in confusion.

"Lisa gave it to me when we met last week," Betsy said. "Just in case, she said."

"What am I supposed to do with it?"

"She's in anaphylactic shock. You need to give her a shot of epinephrine."

Julia goggled at her assistant. "I have to do *what*?"

"Pull the cap off, stick it in her thigh, and give her a shot. Lisa said we're supposed to hold it for ten seconds and then rub."

"Why don't you do it?"

"I hate needles."

"Are you kidding me?"

"Julia, just do it!" Betsy said. "Remember to keep it in for ten seconds."

Man, she hoped these people weren't prone to lawsuits. Taking a deep breath, she whipped off the cap, flipped up yards of ruffles and lace, and plunged the needle in Lisa's thigh. Julia had just reached ten when the wail of a siren cut through the buzz of panicked conversation. The paramedics pushed everyone out of the way, and within minutes, Lisa was being driven away. Most of the members of the wedding party headed to the hospital, too. The rest of the guests were left standing around in shock.

"I feel like *I* need a shot," Julia said. "Is every wedding you guys do this exciting?"

Betsy's hand shook as she brushed a strand of hair from her face. "No, this is a first."

"Betsy, I have to say, you're a good woman to have around in a crisis," Julia said, giving the younger woman a grin.

Betsy giggled. "So are you."

Just then, Chef Devon approached. "Good save, ladies."

"Thank you," Julia said.

"I've got one more little problem though."

Julia's chest tightened. "Little problems" were usually

full-scale disasters with this business. "What?"

"Well, I'm all set for a reception," Devon said. "Unfortunately, most of the wedding party is at the hospital."

"Can't they postpone?" Julia asked. "It's obvious there won't be a wedding today."

Devon shook her head. "Most of the food has to be eaten today. It'll spoil. They've already paid for everything, too."

Julia ran a frustrated hand through her frizzed-out hair. "I think I might kill Sarah."

"I'm sorry to heap more troubles on you, but someone has to make a decision," Devon said.

Julia looked at her assistant. "Is there anyone from either family still here?"

"I think one of the groom's cousins is still around."

She nodded. "Go fetch him. He's just been appointed family representative."

Okay, now they were about to have a reception without a wedding, which was par for the course for her life lately. She felt like someone should go to the hospital and wait for word on the allergic bride, and Betsy volunteered to stay and oversee the party.

Julia reached the hospital in minutes. Rushing into the Emergency Room, she encountered the family members milling about the waiting room.

All fifty million of them. She'd never known someone could be related to so many people.

The mother-of-the-bride spotted her first. "There she is! The woman who saved my baby!"

Julia was immediately enveloped in a bear hug.

"How is Lisa?" Julia asked.

"We're still waiting for word."

With a shuddering sigh, Julia sank into a plastic chair to wait.

****

Julia was sitting in one of the chairs in the waiting room when Seth finally tracked her down. Actually it was more of a reclining position than a sitting one. Her eyes were closed, and she looked utterly exhausted. A grin kicked up the corner of his mouth as he slipped into the chair next to her.

"It's the hero of the hour," he said.

She rotated her head on the chair back and peeled her eyes open. "Shouldn't you be off praying somewhere, Reverend?"

"I've been praying with the family members," he said.

"First wardrobe malfunctions, now killer bees," she said, letting out a soft groan as she sat up. "I thought things would be dull and uninteresting around here."

"You're lucky I guess. Seriously, that was amazing. You might have saved her life."

For the first time Seth could recall, Julia Richardson actually blushed. He watched the dusky, pink color rise in her cheeks with fascination.

"Betsy was the one who had the medicine," she said. "I only stuck the needle in."

"Something she was too afraid to do. You did a good job today, Julia."

"Thank you."

She looked down, which drew Seth's gaze in the same direction. At some point he'd taken her hand. He drew away with a start, unnerved by how natural touching her felt.

Before either of them could say anything else, the doors to the waiting room opened and the doctor walked in. Everyone came to full attention.

"Lisa should be fine," the doctor announced. "She's awake now and has a pretty bad breakout of hives, but she should recover fully in a couple days."

"Oh, thank goodness," Lisa's mother said. "Can we see her?

"Yes, of course, but keep the visitors to a minimum for

now."

Scott and Lisa's parents hurried off after the doctor. The rest of the extended family started to gather their things to leave.

"If any of you are interested, the party is still on at the gardens," Julia said.

Most of them looked too weary to go anywhere but home, though some actually perked up. Before long, Julia and Seth were the only ones left.

"You could probably go home now, as well," Seth said.

"I feel like I should make sure our client is all right before I leave," Julia said.

"You heard the doctor."

"I know, but I still—"

The doors opened again, and Lisa's father hurried in. "Reverend, Lisa and Scott would like to speak with you."

"All right." He turned to Julia. "Why don't you come with me so you can look in on Lisa yourself?"

Julia glanced at Lisa's dad, who nodded his okay. They trailed the older man up to Lisa's room. The almost bride was sitting up in bed. Her wedding dress was gone; replaced with a blue, cotton hospital gown. Her arms were covered in red welts, and her face looked a bit swollen. Scott was sitting on the edge of the bed. They both looked up eagerly as Julia and Seth entered the room.

"Lisa, you're looking well," Seth said, going over to kiss her cheek. "You had us all pretty scared for a while. I'm glad you're all right."

"Thank you. Reverend, Scott and I were talking, and we still want to get married."

"Of course. Let me know what day, and we'll do it."

Lisa giggled. "No, we'd like to get married today."

He looked at them with surprise. "What, now?"

"Yes."

Julia stepped forward. "Are you sure? You had that big

wedding planned and everything. It can be rescheduled."

Lisa shook her head. "What matters is that Scott and I love each other, and I don't care if we get married in a garden or in this hospital room. All I want is to be Scott's wife."

A grin lit up Seth's face. "It's unusual, but I'd be glad to marry you. Why don't I pick up where we left off? Repeat after me. I, Lisa Anne Evans..."

"I, Lisa Anne Evans..."

****

By the time Julia made it back to the house, the sun had long departed. After the impromptu ceremony, she'd gone back to the Botanical Gardens to help Betsy oversee the not-really-a-reception and the cleanup afterward. At this point she'd surpassed tired and was approaching catatonic. As she trudged up the steps, every cell in her body protested the latest injustice. Her mind drifted back to the ceremony she'd witnessed.

After her father and Grace had divorced, Julia had ended up in a weird parental limbo. Her father was single again, and a teenaged daughter had not been conducive to his swinging bachelor lifestyle. Her mother was still on husband #3, and Julia's presence had not conducive to *his* lifestyle. So, Julia had wound up at an exclusive, all-girls prep school in Connecticut. The change had turned out to be a blessing, as it served to shield her from the drama surrounding her parents' lives.

It also brought her into contact with girls of means, or to put it bluntly, girls whose families were loaded. Julia had made a lot of friends, which meant she'd spent the years after prep school and college attending nearly two dozen society weddings. Lavish, overblown affairs where the brides wore $20,000 designer wedding gowns, and guests dined on lobster tail and $400 per ounce caviar.

Of course, of those two dozen girls, sixteen of them were

now divorced. They'd had the fairytale wedding but never bothered to think about what happened after the clock struck midnight.

Julia couldn't help but compare those affairs to the wedding in Lisa's hospital room. What should have been an awkward occasion had turned out to be one of the most touching things Julia had ever witnessed. The bride had glowed, despite the highly unflattering hospital gown and red, splotchy skin. The groom had teared up when Seth got to the "till death do us part" line. Everyone else got misty, too. Even Julia had fought back a few tears.

Lisa and Scott understood, Julia thought. They realized an expensive gown — and rose-colored bridesmaid's dresses — didn't lead to a successful marriage. Their relationship counted, not a ceremony.

Darkness enveloped her as she slipped in the front door. All she wanted was a hot bath and a bed.

"Julia?"

She jumped and then realized the disembodied voice was coming from the back of the house. She made her way to the kitchen.

Grace was standing at the stove stirring something in a pot. "I thought you might be hungry after the day you had."

Julia's mouth watered, but she forced herself to focus on Grace. "You heard about the bees obviously."

"I was at the wedding."

"I didn't see you."

"You were a little busy," Grace said with a wry grin. "I saw what you did for Lisa. Is she going to be okay?"

"Yes. They'll have to wait a few days for the honeymoon, but otherwise—"

"Honeymoon?" Grace queried in bemusement, as she filled a bowl with soup.

"They had Seth do the vows in the hospital."

She chuckled. "Oh, how sweet."

"It was actually."

"Sit, sit!" Grace ordered, setting the bowl down on the table.

"You didn't have to cook for me," Julia protested, even as she dug into the soup.

"It's from a can," Grace said in a pseudo-whisper. "If my mother were still alive, she'd be horrified."

"Why would she care?" Julia asked as Grace walked over to the refrigerator and grabbed the ever-present pitcher of iced tea.

"My mother always made hers from scratch."

"But you're going to be a grandmother yourself soon."

"I don't think we ever outgrow the need to please our parents."

Well, here was the opening Julia needed, but how did she go about asking Grace why she had been dumb enough to hook up with a jerk? "Speaking of parents, can I ask you something personal?"

"You want to know why I married your father," Grace said as she sank into a chair.

Julia blinked. "What… How?"

"I can see it in your eyes every time you look at me. What in the world did my sophisticated father see in that little church mouse?"

Julia winced at knowing Grace would think that. "No, mostly I wonder how a wise, sensible woman like you wound up with a no-good playboy like my father."

"Sometimes we're all fools, especially when it comes to our hearts," Grace said. "When my first husband died, I went into a tailspin. I was devastated and felt so alone. I was angry at God for taking my gentle, loving husband, and frightened about raising a child on my own."

Julia took a sip of tea. "I can understand."

"Unfortunately, emptiness and anger left me vulnerable to someone who offered an escape. Someone like your father."

"Did you love him?"

Grace seemed to consider the question for a moment. "I did, though it was different from what I felt with my Samuel. Your father was handsome and charming. He made me laugh. When I was with him, I felt like the most beautiful woman on earth."

"He was good at making women feel special."

Grace nodded. "Yes, he was. The combination was intoxicating, let me tell you. I couldn't believe a man like him would even look at me, let alone profess to love me. Before I knew it, we were getting married."

"How much did you know about him? Did he tell you about his previous marriages?"

"I knew about your mother, and you, of course," Grace said, with a grimace. "I didn't know about the others until after we were married. I'm afraid I didn't ask too many questions."

"Were you happy with him?"

Grace rested her hand in her chin. "For a while. I soon realized his charm was mostly surface. Of course by then I'd already fallen in love with his daughter."

Julia choked on the soup. "Me?"

"Yes, you," she said, with an indulgent smile. "I wanted to make our marriage work for your sake as much as mine. I knew you'd been shuffled around most of your life, and I wanted to give you a stable, loving home."

"I was horrible to you."

Grace laughed again. "You were a teenager. You were also a young girl who'd been hurt, which made me want to protect you even more."

"Is that why you kept writing and calling, even after my father and I were gone?"

The answer was slow in coming, and when Grace finally did speak her voice was husky and filled with sadness. "It nearly broke my heart when you left. It felt like someone had ripped my body apart. For weeks I'd go into your room and just look at it."

Julia drew in a sharp breath. "I didn't know—"

Grace took Julia's hand. "I couldn't put an added burden on you. I couldn't bear to lose you entirely, so I started writing. I tried not to push too much because I was afraid you'd bolt. You'd learned not to trust love, and you were so skittish. So, I contented myself with whatever snippet of your life you'd allow me to have, and I prayed someday I'd get the chance to teach you what love is."

"It only took Sarah nearly losing her baby to do it."

"Well, everything happens for a reason."

Right. God, the ultimate chess player. "Everything? Even your marriage to my worthless father?"

Grace winced. "You shouldn't talk about your father that way, but yes, of course God had a plan. You came into our lives because of my marriage, and you are worth any disappointment I suffered."

"Great, now all the pieces fit," Julia said, with a cynical laugh. "God allowed you to marry my father so you'd meet me, so some day I could come back here and run Marry Me, so baby Mary can be born healthy and some day keep me from dying of cancer. It's all coming together."

No response.

"I was kidding," Julia said, starting to get a little unnerved.

Grace wasn't laughing. Rather, she looked thoughtful.

"Grace, I'm joking."

She smiled. "Of course, dear, I know."

Chapter Seven

Since she'd arrived in Covington Falls, Julia always seemed to be running late. In her previous life as a business executive, she'd prided herself on being punctual. Had been rather fanatical about it, in fact. Like her career, those days seemed to be over.

It was only 8:30, but already Julia was behind schedule. Tires squealing, she pulled into a parking spot in front of The Old Diner where she was supposed to have met Meredith Vining for breakfast twenty minutes ago. Every establishment in town must have one of those annoyingly cute bells over the door because the one at the restaurant heralded her entrance loud and clear. Heads turned, and two dozen pairs of eyes sized her up. She gulped, feeling like the new kid in school.

As its name implied, the restaurant was designed like an old-time 50s diner. Black-and-white checkerboard tile set off walls displaying photographs of silver screen icons. A long counter with swivel seats ran down the length of the dining area, along with a row of red vinyl booths against the windows.

Meredith was already seated in one near the back. As

soon as Julia slid into her seat, a plump blonde in a pink, polyester dress and white apron sidled up to the table. She looked pointedly at Julia.

Meredith took the obvious hint. "Sally-Anne, this is Grace's stepdaughter, Julia."

"Why, aren't you the prettiest thing?" Sally-Anne said. "I already know Meredith is getting the French Toast Special. What can I get you?"

"A couple of fried eggs and toast would be good," Julia said. "Some coffee, too. Make it strong, please. I had a long weekend."

Meredith grinned as Sally-Anne left to put in the order. "I heard about your bee encounter on Saturday."

"I'm not surprised," Julia said. "Grace told me the news was all over church yesterday."

"No one could talk about anything else. Especially the impromptu wedding ceremony at Lisa's bedside, which is the sweetest thing I've ever heard."

"Even I cried a little, and I'm a committed cynic."

Meredith took a sip of her coffee. "I also heard you turned into an emergency room doc."

"Please. All I did was stick a needle in Lisa's leg," Julia said, rolling her eyes.

"So you didn't whip out a portable defibrillator and restart her heart?"

"What? Give me a break."

Meredith placed her cup back on the table and leaned back in the booth. "I didn't think the CPR part was true, but it made for a great story."

"Good grief," Julia muttered. "Pretty soon they'll have me performing open-heart surgery right there in front of the rose bushes."

They chatted more about the wedding and Meredith's job as the Music Director.

A few minutes later, Sally-Anne arrived with breakfast.

"Two eggs, fried with toast, and the FT Special."

Sally-Anne filled Julia's coffee cup and turned to leave, only to pause and turn back. "That was a real brave thing you did yesterday, Miss Julia. Real brave."

"Thank you."

The waitress hustled away, and Julia turned back to her companion. "Not to change the subject, but I'm still rather curious as to why you're here instead of making records?"

Meredith shook her head. "You're someone who likes to get right down to business."

"I can't help it. I've been wondering about it ever since we met."

"My whole life, all I ever wanted was to be a singer," Meredith said after a long pause. "I wanted to be on stage in front of thousands of screaming fans."

"I saw you in a musical back in high school. Even then you were good. Special."

"Perhaps. My parents were horrified at the prospect of having a daughter in the rock music business, which in hindsight was probably part of the lure. You see, for all the so-called talent, it was always my younger sister who got the attention. Especially from my mother. Amy was her entire world."

Julia paused with her fork in the air. "I met an Amy at Grace's house. Tiny blonde with matching everything?"

A small grin played around the corner of Meredith's mouth. "Right."

"She cornered me in the kitchen and gave me the third degree about living so close to Seth. I got the feeling she thought I wasn't above sneaking over to the garage apartment and seducing him."

Meredith was taking a sip of coffee, and she nearly spit it out. "Yep, definitely Amy. She's had a crush on him since she was about six."

"I had no idea she was your sister. You two look nothing

alike."

"A fact which was pointed out to me by my mother on a daily basis," Meredith said, cutting through her French toast with a bit more force. "Anyway, music became my way of trying to stand out. Then it became my dream, and when I was seventeen the opportunity to escape moved in right across the street."

Julia jabbed a piece of toast at Meredith. "A boy, no doubt."

"Got it in one." Meredith dipped her head. "Nick came to live with his aunt and uncle when I was a senior in high school. He'd gotten into some trouble, and I guess his parents hoped some time here would straighten him out."

"I'm guessing it didn't work."

"Of course not. Nick was brooding and gorgeous, and best of all he was a rock musician. Before long, he became my whole world. I dumped my boyfriend. Rebelled against everything my parents stood for, including God. The day I turned eighteen, I ran away with him to New York."

"Pretty brave of you... leaving everything behind to pursue your dreams."

"It was stupid, but all I cared about was making it big. I didn't need God in my life. I could do it all on my own."

Julia nodded. "That's always been my philosophy."

A long look from Meredith followed before she continued. "Anyway, for a while it seemed like everything was working out. I got a manager. Scored some good gigs. Unfortunately, Nick wasn't so lucky."

"Was he jealous of your success?"

"Yes, but there were other problems. He was possessive in every way. If I so much as looked at another guy, he exploded in a fit of rage."

Something in her eyes made Julia queasy. "Did he hit you?"

Meredith didn't answer, but looked down and fiddled

with her napkin.

"Why would you stay with someone who abused you?" Julia asked in horror.

"I loved him." She dropped the napkin. "At least I thought I did. I'd turned my back on everything for him."

"How long did this go on?"

"About two years."

"Two years!"

"I know, I know," Meredith said, holding up a hand in surrender. "I did leave eventually, but I didn't come to my senses. Then I drifted through one meaningless relationship after another."

"So, what finally changed? Something dramatic must have happened to make you come back here."

Meredith waved her fork. "Actually, it wasn't so dramatic. I was sitting in bed one night — next to the latest meaningless relationship — and I looked at him and started sobbing."

"Why?"

"I didn't know at first. I only knew I felt like I was dying inside. I had let myself drift so far from everything I'd believed in, and I was so empty. I'd tried to fill the emptiness with everything else. My music, with men, with fame, but none of it worked."

"So you came home?"

"Let's not forget how stubborn I am," Meredith said, with wry humor. "It still took me a long time to acknowledge God knocking on my heart. Then one night I was walking home and passed this little church. The doors were open, and I could hear the choir practicing, so I went in. It had been so long since I'd heard gospel music, let alone sang it. I sat there for the entire hour, weeping and praying. Then I went home and started packing."

"Just like that?"

"Well, "just like that" plus ten years."

"What was your reception like when you came back?"

"No one rolled out the red carpet, I can tell you," Meredith said, with a grimace. "Not much had changed. My mother was still obsessed with Amy. My father, before he passed away, chose to stay out of it. I had changed though, and I knew I'd made the right decision. Other things had changed. Seth had moved back to town and offered me the job as the Music Director. I even reconnected with my ex-boyfriend, and we're engaged now."

"He forgave you for breaking his heart?"

A smile lit up Meredith's face. "He did. I wasn't sure he'd ever speak to me again."

"And you're happy, even though you gave up your dream?"

"No, this is my dream. Where I'm supposed to be. Where God wants me to be."

Hmm, there seemed to be a theme going here, Julia thought. If she wasn't so stubborn she might start to listen.

****

Meredith was still very much on Julia's mind as she walked down the block to Marry Me. She still couldn't get over Meredith giving up a promising career. Julia sensed a peace in her new friend, which intrigued her.

When she stepped inside, three heads swiveled around in unison. She only recognized one of them. Betsy was sitting at the desk, with two other women. One older and one younger. The older woman had brown hair, while the younger had strawberry blond.

Julia froze. "Hi…"

Betsy immediately sprang up from her chair. "Julia. Right on time. Marsha and Patricia got here a few minutes ago."

Since Julia hadn't known they were supposed to be here, it was a good thing she'd arrived at all. She had to get a better handle on the schedule.

She gave the two women a bright, confident smile. "Hi. I'm Julia, Sarah's stepsister. Hopefully, Betsy has already explained about the family emergency, and you know I'm filling in for Sarah for a while."

"I did tell them," Betsy said, with a matching we've-got-it-covered grin. "Julia, this is Patricia Amonds and her mother Marsha."

"Nice to meet you, ma'am. Patricia."

"Oh, please call me Patty," the younger woman said.

Mrs. Amonds gave Julia a long, searching look. "Of course I already knew about dear Sarah's predicament. It surely did give us pause when we heard someone new was going to be taking over, though I've heard good things about you. Everyone is still talking about the near tragedy at Lisa's wedding and how you saved the day. Maureen Ashley's mother has done nothing but sing your praises at Bible Study, too."

"Nice to hear."

"We're in the planning stages of Patty's wedding right now," Betsy added. "We're trying to pick out her color palette for the wedding."

Julia knew she should understand what picking a color palette meant. "Great."

She glanced down. Fabric swatches in all colors were spread across the desk. She stared at the pile and gulped.

Please tell me no one expects me to know what to do with those.

"Most weddings have color themes," Betsy said. "This helps in the choosing of bridesmaid dresses, flowers and decorations, table linens. Often we'll have a mix of colors. Maybe different shades of the same color or complementing colors. I was showing Patty these swatches so we can narrow down our choices."

Betsy directed all this explanation to the clients, but Julia knew it was more for her benefit. She adored Betsy.

In any case, choosing a color palette seemed simple enough to handle. "Sounds like a good plan," she said. "How are we doing?"

"Well, Patty keeps gravitating toward pink," Mrs. Amonds said, with a pointed look at her daughter. "But I keep telling her it will clash horribly with her hair."

Patty heaved the long-suffering sigh of a thoroughly put-upon daughter. "But I like pink."

Julia looked at all the little swatches. "Any other choices?"

"The greens are awfully pretty and they'd go beautifully with Patty's coloring," Betsy suggested.

Mrs. Amonds wrinkled her nose. "Green washes me out completely."

Julia thought the day was supposed to be about the bride and not her mother.

"What about this one?" Julia asked, pointing to a royal-blue square.

Mrs. Amonds' shrill objection made the hair stand up on Julia's arm. "Oh, no! Blue is so depressing."

"Yellow?" Julia asked, waiting to hear why yellow wouldn't do either. She didn't have to wait more than half a second.

"Do you want Patty to look like she's got jaundice?"

Julia folded her arms. "Orange."

"*I'll* look like the one with jaundice."

"Red."

"If this was a Christmas wedding, I might agree, but then we're running into the issue of Patty's hair again."

"What about your basic black? I read an article the other day that said it's actually quite a trend in weddings now."

Julia had no idea if such an article existed, but at this point, she didn't care.

Mrs. Amonds' face turned red with horror. "Like a funeral? My dear, maybe in the big city they like to go *avent garden—"*

"Avant-garde."

"I'm sorry?"

"It's *avant-garde,*" Julia repeated.

"Yes, that's what I said. As I was pointing out, we like tradition here in Covington Falls."

Julia turned to Betsy, who responded with a helpless shrug. The bride, meanwhile, looked ready to sink right through the floor. Julia decided it was time to get the Color Police out of the room.

"Mrs. Amonds, have you started looking for your dress?" Julia asked.

"I've drawn up what I want, of course, but I haven't spoken to Karen yet," Mrs. Amonds said after a confused blink.

"Karen is the one next door, right?" Julia asked, directing the question to her assistant.

Betsy nodded.

"Well, why don't I let Betsy take you over there right now, and you can make arrangements with her?" Julia said. "I'll stay here, and Patty and I will hash out this whole color business."

Mrs. Amonds hesitated. "Oh, but I should help Patty—"

Betsy, being a smart girl, sprang out of her chair. "What a perfect idea. Come with me, and we'll have you looking like the best mother-of-the-bride this town has ever seen."

Betsy managed to pull the woman out the door. Julia turned back to Patty, who promptly bursts into tears.

Oh great. Now what?

"Patty, it's not so bad," Julia said, hoping she didn't sound too desperate. "We'll find the right colors."

"It's not the colors," Patty said, through a shimmer of tears.

"What is it then? I can tell your mother is a bit difficult, but—"

"She's not the problem either."

"Then what's wrong?"

Patty let out a deep sigh. "I'm not sure I want to get married."

Julia dropped into the chair with a thud. "What?"

"I know. Talk about bad timing," Patty said, wiping her eyes.

"If you don't want to get married, why are you going through all this?"

Patty's eyes filled again. "I'm just so confused. Jim and I dated for two years. Everyone assumed we'd be getting married. I even assumed we'd get married. So, when he asked I was thrilled, but lately I've started to panic. What if I'm getting married because it's expected?"

Great, Julia thought. She was so not the person to handle this.

"Have you talked to anyone about this?" Julia asked. "Maybe your friends or parents? Your fiancé?"

"Are you kidding?" Patty asked in an incredulous voice. "Tell my mother this might all be a mistake? She'd have a heart attack."

"Well, if you want out, don't you think it's best to do it now?"

"I don't *know* if I want out or not. What do you think I should do? How do I know if I'm truly in love?"

Julia wondered again how she kept getting into these situations. Oh right, she'd agreed to run a wedding planning business.

"Patty, I'm the last person you should be asking about this."

"But you're a wedding planner. Love is your business."

"To tell you truth, I've never worked as a wedding planner before."

Patty's eyes widened. "You're kidding."

"Sadly, I'm not. I'm probably the least romantic person

you're ever likely to meet. I'm a cynic through and through."

"You're *kidding*."

"I should probably tell you it's cold feet, and that it's natural to be nervous when you're making such a big change in your life, but the truth is I'm not sure I believe in true love."

By this time Patty's eyes were about to bug out of her head. "Wow, are you in the wrong profession."

Julia's laughter was tinged with bitterness. "No kidding."

"You don't believe in love?" Patty asked, tilting her head like a curious puppy.

"I don't know."

"How can you live without even the hope of love?"

"I've been doing pretty well."

Patty sighed.

Julia echoed the exhalation. "Listen, here's the only advice I can give. Take my personal feelings out of this. In fact, take everyone's personal feelings out of this, and decide what's going to make you happy. Don't get married because it's expected or because you're too afraid to back out of it. I do know too many people treat marriage lightly. They decide they're bored, or there's someone better out there, or they don't love the person the way they used to. The ending of a marriage hurts everyone involved. If you go into this with doubts, you'll only end up in a disaster."

"You think I should call off the wedding?"

"No, I'm only saying, be sure," Julia said. "Try and imagine yourself ten years from now. Will you regret settling for someone everyone expected you to marry, or will you regret walking away from the best thing that ever happened to you?"

Patty stared in amazement. "Thank you."

"For what?"

"Whether you know it or not, you're pretty good at this advice thing. I was picturing myself ten years from now, and I automatically saw Jim and I, and it felt right."

"You mean I helped?"

Patty nodded.

Julia looked down at the desk and the multi-colored fabric swatches. "Does that mean we *do* need to sort out this color situation?"

"Preferably before my mother comes back."

"I'm up for it if you are," Julia said, with a grin.

I think I might be able to handle this wedding business after all.

Chapter Eight

So now Julia had turned into some kind of therapist. She hadn't realized counseling would be part of the job description. Her next challenge? Planning a wedding from the beginning. The bride and groom were Annie Truman and Todd Baldwin. Julia didn't even have the luxury of her assistant running backup during the first meeting because Betsy had to take another client to look at venues.

"It's only an initial interview to find out what they're thinking," Betsy had explained earlier. "Just don't stare at the scar."

Scar?

Julia picked up the phone and dialed her stepsister.

"Hello?"

"Sarah? Baby all right?"

Julia could hear the smile in Sarah's voice. "She's restless actually."

"Sounds normal. Listen, I need the scoop on Annie Truman and Todd Baldwin. They're going to be here in fifteen minutes, and all Betsy said was don't stare at the scar, which as usual makes no sense."

"Oh, I'd forgotten about Annie and Todd's wedding," Sarah said. "What a beautiful story. They're like one of those Hallmark movies."

"Can you give me the shortened version of this beautiful story? I don't have much time."

"Annie and Todd were engaged a year ago, but then they were in a terrible car accident. Annie was fine, but Todd was badly injured. He was in a coma for nearly a week, and they weren't sure if he would survive. When he did come to, they realized he'd lost parts of his memory. The Annie parts."

"Sounds awful."

"I know, but Annie wouldn't let go. They've had to relive their courtship, and now they're planning their wedding again."

The little bell over the door jangled, and Julia looked up. A young woman with wispy, light-brown hair and a tall, unnaturally thin man came through the door.

"Listen Sarah, I have to go. They're here."

"Okay, but call me if you have any questions. I'm sitting here going out of my mind anyway."

"Will do."

Julia stood as the couple approached. Despite the admonition, she looked for a scar right off. It wasn't hard to spot. A jagged, pink line ran from the top of his cheekbone to the temple and up into his hairline. Julia gulped. Todd was lucky all he'd lost was part of his memory.

"You must be Annie and Todd," she said, holding out a hand.

"It's the scar. Gives me away every time," he said, with a self-deprecating chuckle.

Annie smacked his arm. "Maybe you should wait until we know her a little better before you bless her with your comedic wit." She turned to Julia. "Yes, I'm Annie, and this is my fiancé Todd. And you're Julia."

"This hair gives me away every time."

Julia looked at Todd, and they shared a little moment of understanding. He grinned, and Julia suddenly understood why a woman would stay with him even if he did lose his memory and had a scar.

"Please have a seat," Julia said, gesturing to the chairs in front of the desk.

Betsy had helped start a file for the wedding earlier, and now Julia opened it with a feeling of dread.

"I'm supposed to find out what kind of wedding you want," Julia said after studying the first page. "Something small and intimate, or a large celebration. Traditional, or modern? A theme you'd like to have, or a place in mind where you want to get married."

"We'd like to get married out by Lake Rice," Annie said after a quick glance at her fiancé.

"Sounds good," Julia said, relieved that something finally made sense. "By the waterfall would be lovely."

Annie shook her head. "No, not by the waterfall. Next to the road."

"The road?"

"Where the accident happened," Annie said, with a gentle smile.

"You want to have your wedding in the same spot where you both nearly died?" Julia asked, shock flooding through her.

"We're not crazy," Annie said, the smile still playing on her lips. "The site of the accident is sort of where our relationship began. Again. We think it's fitting to pledge the rest of our lives together there."

Julia looked at the two of them and marveled at their closeness. The way Annie gazed at Todd. The softening in his voice when he spoke to her. The way their hands naturally gravitated toward each other. Julia's breath caught as she realized what she was seeing.

Love...

A smile bloomed on her lips. "Sounds perfect."

****

That evening, Julia arrived at the house only to find several cars parked out front. Avoiding the front, she slipped in the kitchen door. Voices drifted out from the living room. Women's voices. Curious, she drifted down the hall and peeked around the corner.

She'd barely gotten a chance to eavesdrop when a baritone voice whispered in her ear.

"What are you doing?"

Julia nearly jumped out of her skin. Even as she spun around, a hand clamped over her mouth. Seth's blue eyes twinkled down at her. Julia glared with all the fury she could muster. He dipped his head back toward the kitchen and proceeded to drag her down the hall. Once they were safely in the kitchen, Julia punched him in the arm. It felt good, so she did it a couple more times.

"Ouch," Seth complained over his laughter, even as he held up his arms in an attempt to protect himself.

"You scared me to death."

"I couldn't resist," he said. "I came in to check out the leftovers, and I saw you skulking around at the living room door."

"I wasn't skulking."

"What were you doing then?"

"It's not like they were passing state secrets," she said, drawing herself up to full height. "I was curious."

He arched a single brow. "About Grace's Bible study? I didn't think you were interested in religion."

"I'm not."

"Just interested enough to listen in at the door?"

Julia glared at him again. "Maybe, but I'm still not buying into the whole God thing."

"I know, I know," he said, holding up his hand in surrender. "You're much too logical to believe in things like faith and love."

She ignored the sarcasm. "Love is a nice concept, but I'm not sure it exists outside of movies and novels. I've certainly never seen proof of it."

"Never?"

"No."

Even as she said it, a picture of Todd and Annie flashed through her mind.

Seth must have noticed the change in her expression because his own gaze sharpened. "Something come to mind?"

"Do you know Annie Truman and Todd Baldwin?" she asked, looking away.

"Sure. They're members. I've counseled them since the accident. They're an extraordinary couple."

"I'm planning their wedding."

"They certainly do represent the picture of true love. Makes you rethink your "love doesn't exist" motto, doesn't it?"

Julia sputtered, trying to think of a cutting remark, but even she couldn't deny Annie and Todd had something rare.

"It's all right to let yourself believe in something, Julia," Seth said, in an extremely gentle voice, like an animal rescue activist trying to calm a wild bird.

"What is it you think I should believe in?"

"You could believe Grace and Sarah love you, and always have. You could believe there is a God who loves you, too. You could believe you're an amazing woman who deserves His love."

He'd drawn closer during his speech until he was standing directly in front of her, and just like at the park that first day, their blasted soundtrack started up again. He must have heard the music too because she saw, rather than heard, his quick, indrawn breath. As if in a trance, he reached out and twined a lock of her hair around his fingers. The touch seemed to transfer from his hand right to her scalp.

Voices cut through the stillness. The Bible study had finished. In an instant, Seth moved across the room. All four women came to an abrupt halt when they realized the kitchen was already occupied. So abrupt they ended up banging into one another like characters in a slapstick comedy. Varying degrees of the same curious stare flashed across their faces.

Julia recognized Sarah's mother-in-law, who looked interested if a bit puzzled. Grace's neighbor, Mary-Ellen Carter, was among the group, and she was definitely on the scent of gossip. Julia could see the woman's nose twitch as she sniffed for a tidbit.

Julia's gaze switched to the last member of the group. This one was a stranger. A hostile stranger. Then she realized the beady-eyed, edge of insanity stare seemed familiar. She absolutely recognized the store window display get-up. De-age the woman by about thirty years, and she'd be looking at Amy Vining.

Which explained why the woman looked as though she wanted to plunge a knife in Julia's back. No doubt Mrs. Vining knew about her daughter's obsession and figured Julia was the competition.

"Well, hello," Grace said. "I didn't know you two were home."

Seth leaned against the counter. "I came to scrounge in your refrigerator and found Julia already here."

Grace smiled. "I'm glad you got a chance to visit. Julia, I think you know everyone here, except for Sylvia Vining. I believe you met her daughters, Meredith and Amy."

Hunch confirmed, Julia held out her hand. "Yes, I have met them."

Mrs. Vining's glare was worthy of a queen, but deeply engrained Southern manners compelled her to take the offered hand.

Man, the woman sure knew how to drop the temperature in a room, Julia thought. No wonder Meredith had been so anxious to get away.

"I wasn't aware you had met Meredith," Mrs. Vining said.

"She's planning the music for a wedding we're doing. We hit it off, and I met her for breakfast the other day. You must be so proud of all she's accomplished. Such a rare talent."

Mrs. Vining practically quivered with rage. "Of course I'm proud of Meredith. Both of my daughters are accomplished. Amy is going to be an example in the community one day."

"How nice for her."

"Young people like my daughter and Seth will be the beacons of leadership for the next generation."

Julia glanced at Seth, who looked a little dazed at the prospect of being a "beacon of leadership". Her gaze flitted back to the Bible brigade, in time to see the other women roll their eyes in unison. Something told her Mrs. Vining had made such grandiose statements before.

Grace broke into the awkward silence. "Well, ladies, it was delightful as always."

The women took this as their cue and filed out the back door.

"Sorry about Sylvia," Grace said, once her friends were gone. "She's always been a bit too involved in Amy's life."

"From what Meredith said it's more like an obsession. I'm sure it's a big reason why she left in the first place."

"It's unfortunate when a parent favors one child so heavily over another," Grace said, not bothering to deny the assertion. "Anyway, I left plates for you both in the refrigerator. All you have to do is heat them up. I'm off to check on John, then I'm going to bed. You two carry on with whatever you were doing."

The last line was delivered with a little wink, which made

Julia shudder. Surely Grace didn't know what was going on in here before she came in.

Grace paused for a moment. "And Julia?"

"Hmm?"

"Next time, come on in and join us in the Bible study," she said as she slipped through the doorway.

On second thought, Grace probably did know.

Julia glanced at Seth, but he wouldn't look at her. Instead, he went to the refrigerator and pulled out the two prepared plates. He shoved one in the microwave and punched out numbers in a quick staccato motion. Then he stood there with his arms folded across his chest watching the revolving dish.

The microwave dinged and he repeated the same procedure with the second plate. He still didn't pull his gaze away from the appliance.

"What's gotten into you?" Julia asked.

"Nothing." His voice was as blunt as his fingers.

"Are you mad at me?"

"No."

"Are you mad at yourself then?"

His head swung around, and she reared back a little at his harsh expression. "I think it's probably best if we don't talk about this right now." He picked up the first plate and headed for the back door. "Your dinner will be ready in a minute."

"Where are you going?"

"My apartment. Tell Grace I'll bring her plate back in the morning."

"Wait—"

The only sound was the crack of the screen door as it slammed shut.

Chapter Nine

Seth's goal for the day. Avoid Julia Richardson at all cost. Whatever had possessed him to touch her last night? It may have only been a lock of hair, but he'd crossed a line. Now he knew what it felt like to feel the silky strands curl around his fingers. Dangerous knowledge for a man who'd been alone as long as he had. He had a sneaking suspicion all those people who kept trying to fix him up knew something he hadn't even wanted to acknowledge.

Being attracted to Julia wasn't the problem. No, the real problem was he liked her. Even the sarcasm had begun to grow on him. She was smart, funny, and in her own way, caring. Not to mention perceptive. He couldn't forget her uncanny ability to see right into his soul.

There was a primordial soup of guilt and frustration, along with an unhealthy dose of overactive hormones, swimming around inside him at this point. Guilt because he somehow felt as if he were betraying Beth, and frustration that the person responsible for the hormone surge was wrong for him in every conceivable way. All of which had sparked a killer rage.

As he drove to the park the next morning, he fought to contain the tide. He hoped the weekly basketball game with the guys would help take the edge off. He figured any type of physical activity at this point might help.

He was the last to arrive. Ethan Thomas and Eric were already warming up, and Meredith's fiancé, Brian Lawson, was stretching out.

"Late again, Rev," Ethan called out, as he leaped into the air and dunked the basketball with ease.

"You know the Devil doesn't follow an exact schedule," he retorted.

Ethan launched the ball at Seth's chest. Seth caught it. Barely.

"Whose soul were you saving this time?" Brian asked, as he straightened.

Seth propelled the ball toward his friend. Brian didn't miss a beat, turning to make a shot, which bounced off the rim and rolled away. Watching him chase after it gave Seth enormous satisfaction.

"I bet I know why he was late," Eric said. "Probably dreaming about his enticing new neighbor."

Everyone shut up.

"What enticing new neighbor?" Ethan asked.

You know, friends were highly overrated, Seth thought. In-laws, too.

Eric used his telepathic power and somehow seemed to sense the joke wasn't a joke. "Sarah's stepsister. She's helping out with Marry Me until the baby comes."

"Oh, Julia," Brian said, with a nod of recognition. "Meredith told me about meeting her. They hit it off."

"And she's hot?" Ethan asked, directing the question at Seth.

Seth kept his lips shut.

Ethan turned to Eric. "How hot?"

"If this were World War II you'd probably hang a poster

of her on the wall."

"Right next door?" Brian said, with a teasing grin. "You're not lucky. You're blessed."

"You shouldn't even be looking at other women," Seth said, scowling at Sarah's husband.

Eric shrugged. "I've still got eyes."

"Well, keep them to yourself. Can we play now? I don't know about you clowns, but I have important things to do today."

All three of them shared knowing looks.

"He's going down," Ethan said.

Eric chuckled. "Like a sinker."

"Welcome back, my friend," Brian said.

If Seth had known he was going to get this kind of grief he'd have gone straight to the church where there was always someone willing to take him to task. "Did any of you consider it might not be a good thing to get tangled up with her?"

Brian's eyes danced. "It can never be a bad thing to get tangled up with a good woman."

"I say tangle away," Ethan said.

"Even if she's not staying and doesn't believe in anything I do? Even if she's difficult and troubled and so afraid of commitment she'd run the other way screaming before tying herself down to anyone? Even if she's nothing like Beth?"

"Beth is gone," Eric said, using the voice he practiced with the troubled kids he helped. The same tone Seth himself used when counseling *other* people.

"I know," Seth said, his voice sharp and tight. "I'm aware she's gone, every second of my life."

Seth looked at Ethan for help. Surely the other widower in the group would understand. Ethan knew what it was like to lie in bed alone at night, looking at an empty space.

Except Ethan was nodding like the rest of them. "I know, but maybe it's time. It doesn't have to be Julia, but perhaps it's time for someone." He paused and then smiled. "Although

God did put a gorgeous woman fifty feet away for a reason, so I wouldn't ignore that."

Was it time? Or was he simply having an early midlife crisis? Either option promised a lot more sleepless nights.

Chapter Ten

Julia didn't see Seth again over the next several days. Not at breakfast, and certainly not at night. He even managed to always be on the other side of the room during her next wedding, which he officiated.

Thankfully, she had someone to distract her. Two someone's to be precise, though *one* would most certainly prove to be the biggest challenge of Julia's short career in wedding planning.

The challenge was named Catherine Manning.

Julia supposed every small town had its ordinary citizens and local royalty. In Covington Falls, the reigning monarchs were the Mannings. Edward Manning III was the current mayor. Covington Falls didn't have term limits so The Third had held the office for the last ten years. He was also the fourth Manning to be elected mayor, making the family a political dynasty.

Catherine was the mayor's wife, and rounding out the royal family was their only daughter, Laurel. Laurel was the reason Julia would most likely have a nervous breakdown in the near future. Princess Manning was getting married, and since Sarah was ensconced in bed, Julia now had to plan the wedding of the century.

The assignment for the day was to pick a venue for the ceremony. Julia actually didn't have much to say in the matter, as Catherine Manning had already decided nothing would do but Hadden Acres. The Antebellum plantation home sat on two fabulously lush acres outside of town. Julia had to admit the mansion was certainly worthy of the occasion, with its white marble façade, majestic columns, and wide verandah.

As she walked the grounds with the Mannings, Julia reflected she might enjoy planning a wedding here if it weren't for the client. She could deal with Laurel. Not only was she a living, breathing fairytale character, she was also quiet, sweet, and slightly dim. Of course, she didn't need to do much talking when her mother was around.

Oh yeah, Mamma was going to be a big problem. The mayor's wife could give Sylvia Vining lessons in how to deliver the how-is-it-possible-you're-breathing-the-same-air-as-me stare.

La Manning was delivering said stare now, as a matter of fact.

"I do hope you realize how important this day is to Laurel," Mrs. Manning said, coming to a stop in front of the fountain in the English-inspired north garden. "I had my misgivings about choosing Sarah Austin's establishment in the first place. Laurel had her heart set on obtaining the services of Victoria Wasserman-Smith in Atlanta, the most sought-after wedding planner in the South, but Edward insisted we needed to do our part to support Covington Falls' local talent, such as it is."

Julia wondered if a speechwriter had penned that little bit of condescension.

"What a nice gesture," Julia said, staring at the woman's perfectly arranged chignon. Julia didn't think a single hair had moved all morning. Same with the forehead. Seemed freezing facial nerves had made its way to Covington Falls, too.

Catherine nodded. "I am not above making sacrifices in order to benefit our town. However, I have to tell you, I am troubled by this latest turn of events. Even though Sarah is certainly not a sophisticate, she is most accomplished in this arena. This trouble with her baby is most inconvenient."

Julia gripped her clipboard tight, fighting the urge to whack Mrs. Manning over the head with it. Julia deliberately took a deep, calming breath. It wouldn't do to physically assault Sarah's biggest client.

"It's a trying time for all of us," she said, through clenched teeth.

"Yes, it's so difficult on my nerves."

On the other hand, Sarah would probably be relieved not to have to deal with this woman ever again, Julia thought.

"Still, the most important thing is Sarah's baby," Julia said, a kill-her-with-kindness smile firmly in place. "I'm here to ensure Laurel's wedding goes off as planned."

"I'm glad we understand each other. There is nothing more important to me than my daughter. I want her wedding to be perfect. I will tolerate nothing less."

"I understand, Mrs. Manning."

For a moment, their eyes met. Then Mrs. Manning offered a satisfied smile. "Good. Now, have you had any luck finding doves?"

****

The question of the day: Where was one supposed to find white doves? Julia had heard movies used animal wranglers. She wondered if there was such a thing as a dove wrangler?

Julia trudged home, utterly exhausted from a day spent with the Mannings. As usual, she went around to the back door. She was reaching for the handle when she heard music coming from somewhere above her head. She walked around the side of the house until she could see the garage. The apartment above it had a small, narrow balcony, and Seth was standing there.

Julia stepped off the porch. For a moment neither of them spoke.

"Feels like we're reenacting a famous tragedy," she called out.

"Except we've got it backward," Seth said, with a grin. "Juliet was the one on the balcony."

She shrugged. "Pretty fitting, considering the screwed up nature of our relationship."

"Do we have a relationship now?"

"A weird one for sure."

Another awkward silence. The charged moment in Grace's kitchen and his week's worth of avoidance was heavy between them.

Oh, forget it, she thought and started to turn. "If you want to be alone, I can go back—"

"No, it's all right. Come on up."

There was no way she should be doing this, but Julia started up the stairs anyway. "You're not going to leap off the balcony if I get too close, are you?"

"No, I'm not that much of a chicken," he said, even as he backed up a step.

She reached the landing. "But you are a bit of one?"

"Where you're concerned, absolutely."

"Why?"

"You know why," he said. "You felt it, too."

Seemed she was a chicken, too. She broke eye contact and looked out across the yard. It was too dark to see anything, but she could picture the rose bushes out by the fence and the huge trees that provided welcome shade. Years ago there'd been a makeshift fort out by the fence, which she'd built with Sarah.

"You're smiling," Seth said. "What are you thinking

about?"

"I was thinking that Sarah always managed to get her way, even when she was little. She talked me into helping her make a fort one time. Followed me around for days begging me to help her until I finally relented."

"I remember that fort."

"You do?"

An odd look swept over his face, one she couldn't quite read. "I helped you and Sarah build it. You couldn't carry the plywood by yourself, and you weren't too handy with a hammer."

"You did?"

A hand went to his heart, and he staggered back like he'd been shot. "Ouch. Nice to know I made an impression on you on all those years ago."

"Like you remember me any better," she said, fighting a grin.

"You'd be surprised."

"What?" Something in his tone had the hairs standing up on the back of her neck.

He cleared his throat. "Nothing."

Julia looked past him into the apartment. Curious, she stepped over the threshold. The small space consisted of a single room. On one side sat an old leather couch and a battered coffee table. Against the opposite wall was a double bed with a beautifully patterned quilt featuring two interwoven rings. A television was set up so it could be seen from the bed or the couch. A kitchenette with a mini refrigerator, sink and a two-burner stove stretched across the back of the room.

Seth leaned against the doorframe. "Home sweet home."

She drifted toward the bed and sat down. "What a gorgeous quilt."

"It was a wedding gift from my grandmother."

"She made it?" she asked, running her hands along the

stitches.

"Beth used to wrap it around her shoulders when she had her chemo," he said. "She was always freezing afterward."

Since he'd brought up the subject, Julia felt brave enough to venture further into dangerous waters. "Is that why you ran the other night?" she asked. "Because of Beth?"

"Not entirely," he said, refusing to look her in the eye.

"But partly?"

He shifted and looked over his shoulder. "Listen, I think maybe you should come back outside. You sitting on my bed is—"

Julia reached the balcony in seconds. "Tell me about her."

Seth hesitated a moment, but then leaned over to rest his arms on the railing. "We met my sophomore year of college. We had American History together, and she sat two rows in front of me. I took one look at her, and I was a goner."

"I bet she was sweet and cheerful."

The words came out with a tinge of bitterness she couldn't help.

Seth's arched brow told her he hadn't missed the acid. "You say that like those qualities are defects."

"I didn't mean it like that."

"Yeah, you probably did," he said, with a shake of his head. "The truth is, Beth *was* sweet and cheerful for the most part, but she was no pushover. I asked her out, and on that first date, I knew."

"That you would marry her?"

"That she would be my life," he whispered into the night.

He seemed to be struggling with his emotions, so she gave him time to compose himself. "Did she inspire you to become a minister?" she asked after a moment. "I have to tell you I never saw you as the ministerial type when we were kids."

"Trust me, neither did I. I wanted to be a lawyer. I'd even

gotten accepted into law school. The summer before I was supposed to start we went to visit Beth's parents. Her father was a minister, and when I heard him preach I was blown away. I knew I had to do that."

"You said earlier that she understood you like no one else because of her father."

"She was aware of the frustration that goes along with this calling. She always seemed to know the right words to say to keep me from drowning in my own self-doubt."

Julia couldn't be bitter about that. "She knew how to keep the devil at bay."

"That's certainly an interesting way to put it," he said, laughing at the description. "Beth probably could've taken on the devil and won. I didn't realize how much I relied on her strength until it started to disappear."

"I know she was sick for a long time."

"The longest two years of my life," Seth said, his voice catching a little. "Every day she got a little weaker, a little frailer, and I couldn't do a thing to stop it. She was in a lot of pain in the end, and I couldn't do a thing to stop that either."

Julia's bitterness disappeared, replaced only with sadness over the terrible loss he'd suffered. She hated the despair in his voice. Julia wished she could comfort him, but didn't know how. She folded her arms across her chest to keep from reaching for him.

"I can't imagine," she said. "It must have been a nightmare."

"Only I couldn't wake up. After she was gone I could barely function. I don't remember a thing I said the first six months. I have no idea how I managed to even keep my job."

"It's no wonder you moved in here," she said, indicating the little apartment. "It's a cozy little refuge, isn't it? A place to escape and try to heal."

"How do you do that?" he asked in amazement.

"What?"

"Manage to read my mind?"

Julia squirmed, uncomfortable with the thought. "It's only an observation."

"Then you've got a great gift for observation."

"Comes from a lifetime of watching other people screw up their lives," she said.

"Stop doing that."

She blinked at his harsh tone. "Doing what?"

"Dismissing the things that make you special."

"Getting a read on people is special?"

"Absolutely. You have a way of seeing through all the layers people put up to protect themselves, and that's so rare," he said, turning toward her. "So few people take the time to look below the surface in others. To see their pain and anger. Their joy. But you see it, and you respond."

Why did she feel like crying? "Thank you. I think that's the nicest thing anyone has ever said to me."

He gave a frustrated groan.

"What now?"

"You are a dangerous lady."

"Me?"

"God, she doesn't even see it!" he called out to the heavens.

"Are you praying?" she asked in bemusement.

"For strength. You tempt me, and it's making me crazy."

"Are you talking about the other night in the kitchen?"

"It goes way beyond last night," he said, hands gripping the railing. "Did you know I had a wild crush on you when you used to live here?"

Julia's mouth dropped open. "What?"

"I helped you build a fort."

"You pounded nails so you could be near me?" she asked, batting her eyelashes at him. "What a way to court a girl."

"It wasn't like I could talk to you," Seth said, shuffling his feet. "Not without sounding like an idiot."

"I didn't think you even liked me."

A dry chuckle escaped from his chest. "Like and lust are two different things. You were every teenage boy's fantasy. Everything about you fascinated me. The way you walked, the way you tossed your hair, even the way you smelled. It drove me nuts for two years."

"I was your fantasy?"

"The problem is now you're back, standing there looking like some kind of screen goddess, and you get me like no one ever has," he said, as if she hadn't spoken.

Her skin started tingling. "You think I'm beautiful?"

"You're so much *more* than beautiful."

Jumping him right now would be bad... Right? "This is a little complicated."

"You think?" he asked, drifting closer. "You're a guest in Grace's house and living about a hundred feet away. Plus, I am a minister, and it wouldn't look good if I grabbed you right now and kissed you senseless."

"Not in the job description?"

"Definitely not."

"So, bad idea," she said, taking the last step to close the gap between them.

"I'm sure it is."

"Terrible," she said, staring at her hand, which had somehow made its way to his chest.

Julia didn't know who made the final move, but suddenly she was in his arms, and he was doing a pretty good job of kissing her senseless.

Who knew a preacher could kiss like this?

Somewhere down the block, a car door slammed, and they sprang apart as if a gun had been fired. Before her eyes, Julia watched Seth's walls go back up.

"I should go back," she said. "It might be Grace or some other nosy neighbor. Don't want to start any bad rumors."

"I'm sor—"

"Don't you dare apologize," Julia said, holding on to her jumbled emotions by a thread. "You're finally learning to live again, and obviously dealing with crazy brides has rubbed off on me. So, let's consider this a team effort and try to move on."

"Julia—"

"I'll see you around."

You are the stupidest woman on earth.

Chapter Eleven

After spending the night tossing and turning, Julia realized her current situation could all be laid at Sarah's door. If Julia hadn't been guilt-tripped into taking over Marry Me, she would still be unaware Seth could make her toes curl with a simple kiss.

Life would be so much easier then because despite the unsettling attraction — and some pretty combustible chemistry — the same roadblocks to a relationship still existed.

Namely, his life calling and her lack of belief.

So, at 7:30 the next morning, Julia showed up at Sarah's apartment.

A bleary-eyed Eric answered the door. He blinked in surprise. "What are you doing here?"

"I'm here about some doves."

Another blink. "Doves?"

"Believe me, I'm just as confused," she said, pushing past him. "Is Sarah up?"

At that moment Sarah called out from the bedroom. "Julia? Is that you?"

Julia followed the sound, and found that Sarah was

indeed awake. The bedroom looked to be about the size of a shoebox. A queen-size bed took up most of the space. An ancient, faux-wood dresser had been shoved against one wall and a closet with sliding doors took up the other.

Good grief, Julia thought. They *might* have to put the baby in the sock drawer. There might not even be enough room for a bassinet.

Sarah sat up in the bed, a breakfast tray balanced over her legs. "Please tell me you're going to stay awhile."

"Are you kidding?" Julia held up a file folder. "I met with Catherine Manning yesterday, and there's no way I'm planning anything without you."

Eric came in and took the tray. "You girls have fun, but don't overdo it."

Sarah reached for the file. "I'll be careful."

"Thanks for coming," Eric said as he passed. "Sarah's been getting cranky staring at the walls all day."

"Hey, it's as much for my sanity as hers," Julia said.

Once they were alone, Julia sat down on the bed. "The first item on the agenda is doves."

"Doves?"

Julia laughed at Sarah's confused expression. "Yes, I know. Your husband gave me the exact same look. Mrs. Manning wants three dozen white doves to be released the moment — and I emphasize *the moment* — the minister says "you may now kiss the bride". So, do you rent them? Do they come through mail order? What?"

"Before we tackle the dove issue, why don't you tell me what's going on?" Sarah put the file down on the bed.

"Besides the Manning wedding?"

"You show up at my door at the crack of dawn all twitchy and agitated, and I don't think it has anything to do with a wedding."

"I'm not *twitchy*. I'm exhausted."

"You're also a bad liar."

Julia bit her lip. "I think I'm going crazy."

"Because of the business?"

"No, it's Covington Falls. Sleeping in my old room. I spent fifteen years running from everything this town represented. Everything I couldn't have. I learned to be happy with my life."

"Were you happy?

"I don't know." Julia stood and started pacing the small room. "Before I came back here, I knew who I was. Where I was going. I was a career woman on my own. Now, everything is a mess, and it's all your fault."

"My fault?" Sarah echoed.

"Yes, you and that miracle baby. Not to mention your disastrous financial planning skills. I'm confused, and it's making me do stupid things."

"What kind of stupid things?"

"Oh, things like kissing totally inappropriate people."

Sarah's eyes widened. "Who have you been kissing?"

"Seth—"

Shoot, had she said that out loud?

Judging by the silence from the bed, she had.

"Come again?" Sarah said.

Julia flounced down onto the bed. "You heard me the first time," she said, waiting for the outrage.

Instead, Sarah laughed in delight. "This is so cool."

"That's totally not the reaction I expected," Julia said in stunned amazement. "I thought you'd be upset. His father is married to your mother. We're practically related."

"You're not practically anything. Besides, I was hoping this would happen."

"Hoping what would happen?"

"That you'd fall for each other," Sarah said, her expression smug.

An awful thought seized her. "Wait a minute. Is Seth the reason you asked me to run Marry Me?" Julia eyed her stepsister with deep suspicion. "Did you have some kind of weird fix-up in mind?"

Sarah shook her head. "No, I did need you to run the business for me, but once I saw you, I couldn't help thinking about it. You're so beautiful. You were back then, but now you make me sick," she said, with a teasing glint. "Seth would have to be blind not to notice. And I may be married, but I've certainly noticed he's gorgeous."

"Are you crazy? Did you think we'd take one look at each other, swoon into each other's arms, and ride off into the sunset together?"

"I know it's a bit unorthodox—"

"Unorthodox?" Julia parroted. She jumped up again and resumed pacing. "You're describing an episode on one of those terrible shock shows."

"Oh, shoot, it's not like you had a baby and didn't know who the father was," Sarah quipped.

Julia halted in mid-pace and glared. "Stop it. I'm freaking out here."

"I'm sorry," Sarah said, smothering a grin. "I'm trying to figure out what's so terrible."

Pacing resumed. "I can't believe you don't see it."

"What is there to see, except that you're both single, both in need of love, and obviously attracted to each other?"

"I see so many obstacles, I can't even begin to count them."

"I think the only obstacles are the ones you're putting up."

Sarah's room didn't allow for proper pacing, and dizziness had set in. Instead, Julia leaned back against the battered dresser.

"Why would you want me with Seth anyway?" she asked. "I assume you like him. Maybe even feel brotherly toward him. Why would you want anyone you care about to become involved with someone like me?"

"You're not as mixed up as you think. You have such a fire. You're also fiercely protective, like one of those Amazon warriors going into battle. Seth needs someone like you. Someone who won't be intimidated by the harpies at the church."

"Don't you think he also needs someone who shares his faith? I should think that would be up there at the top of the requirements for a minister's wife. And I am absolutely not what his congregation would accept."

"Why not?"

"Well, there's the aforementioned lack of faith. I'm also an outsider with a fuzzy past in this town, thanks to my father. Plus, I don't have the gentle spirit or the moral code they'd expect. I mean, look at the way they treat Meredith, and she was born here."

"I think you're strong enough to take it. Like Seth's wife."

"Like she had to take anything." Julia held up her thumb and index finger an inch apart. "Beth Graham was this close to being named a saint as far as I can tell."

"She didn't have it so easy at first. She had to earn the trust of the people in this town."

"I don't think I could compete with someone so good."

"Julia, there are no good people. Not if we compare ourselves to God. We're all sinners, and our so-called good deeds aren't what get us in to heaven. Only Christ can do that. Beth was human. She was a sinner, like I am, like Seth. Even my mother," Sarah added.

Julia was startled into laughter. "Insane. You're completely insane."

"All I want is for Seth to be happy again. He's been through so much. You can't imagine what it was like watching him."

"That's what I mean. Thinking I could make him happy. There's too much baggage there," she said, going over to the bed to kiss Sarah on the top of the head. "Besides, you know how I feel about marriage. I'm not interested in going down that path."

Sarah heaved a put-upon sigh. "Someday, Julia, you'll have to stop running. I only hope it's not too late when you finally realize it."

Chapter Twelve

It was a Saturday, which meant Julia was thoroughly confused and bewildered as she stared at another one of Sarah's wedding blueprints. She needed to figure out what the little triangles on the diagrams meant.

Today's venue… the Good News Gospel church. The couple… Angela Jerome and Eddy Carmichael. Points in Julia's favor…. the ceremony and reception were being held in the same place. After the vows, the guests would walk across the courtyard to the reception hall. Best idea Julia had ever heard. She could supervise both venues and didn't have to worry about the stray killer bee.

Good News Gospel epitomized the small-town, shining-beacon-in-the-middle-of-the-postcard church with its white façade and silver steeple reaching into the sky. Arched windows marched down the west and east sides of the building, reflecting the rays of the sun.

Julia almost expected a ray of heavenly light to shoot down from the sky while a chorus of angels sang *"Hallelujah"*.

Despite her ongoing inability to figure out the triangles, she managed to get the church and reception hall decorated.

Or rather the church wedding coordinator managed to get everything done. The woman and her crew were dynamos. Meanwhile, Betsy had been on wedding party duty.

Julia glanced at her watch. According to the master schedule, everyone needed to be in their proper places now because people should be arriving any minute. A massive collection of bridesmaids had arrived an hour ago. Julia knew they were here because she'd heard the high-pitched squeals all the way across the courtyard. The groom's party made a similar, though not quite as high-pitched, entry soon after.

Leaving the reception hall in the more than capable hands of the wedding coordinator, Julia went in search of Betsy and the wedding party.

Please, God, let's make sure we don't have any wardrobe malfunctions, okay? And no insects.

Julia didn't know when she'd started praying, but she figured divine intervention couldn't hurt. She entered the church and hurried to the bride's room. Even before she reached her destination she heard a host of high-pitched voices. Only now they seemed edged with panic instead of excitement, which couldn't be good.

Dashing around the corner, Julia encountered the entire wedding party congregating in the hallway outside the bride's room. There were dozens of women dressed in a bilious-yellow, halter dresses with big hoop skirts. So attractive. They looked like the before images from one of those makeover shows.

There were an equal number of groomsmen. The lucky guys got to wear a pretty normal tux, save for the matching bilious-yellow cummerbund. Everyone stood near the door with similar looks of bewilderment on their faces. The only person Julia *didn't* see was the bride. However, she could hear said bride screeching from the other side of the door.

"Hi." Julia called out.

Everyone turned to look at her, even as the screeching

continued at an ear-splitting decibel.

"What seems to be the problem?" Julia asked.

Betsy emerged from the middle of the pack, with a look of intense relief. "Julia, thank goodness. I was about to look for you. Angela won't come out."

"Why not?"

"Apparently, one of the groomsmen missed his flight this morning so we're one short today."

"Didn't we have a rehearsal last night?" Julia asked in bemusement. "They weren't all here then?"

"No, we were short one last night, too."

Typical. No doubt the number of groomsmen resided in the file somewhere.

The groom stepped forward. "My friend from college had an emergency at work yesterday so he was going to catch a flight this morning. Only the airline overbooked, and he didn't get on. He's stuck in D.C."

"That's the crisis?" Julia asked, still trying to understand. "She's screaming like a banshee because we're missing a groomsman?"

"Did Eddy tell you he waited until now to let me know?" Angela yelled from the other side of the door.

Julia cringed. *Man, talk about a voice made to shatter glass.*

"Angela, it would be much easier to handle this if I could see you face-to-face," Julia said. "Can you come out here?"

"No! Eddy can't see me before the wedding. It's bad luck."

Well, this ought to be fun.

"We didn't find out about the missing groomsman until about ten minutes ago," Betsy explained. "One of the bridesmaids asked about Drew, and before I knew it, Angela had locked herself in."

To Julia's left, a bridesmaid with curly brown hair looked ready to sink through the floor. So apparently Eddy had decided to bamboozle his bride about the AWOL groomsman.

"Why didn't you tell me he wasn't here hours ago?" Angela screeched again.

"Because I knew you'd react this way!" Eddy yelled back. "I'd hoped we could avoid this sort of drama."

Julia had to admit the strategy had some merit, considering the hysterics. Unfortunately, they were still left with a bride who wouldn't come out.

She maneuvered herself through the pile of yellow halter dresses to the door. "Angela, it's Julia."

"Who?" the disembodied voice responded.

"Your wedding planner."

"I thought your name was Sarah."

"I'm filling in for Sarah."

"Were you at the rehearsal last night?"

"Yes, of course I was there," Julia said, glaring at the door. "The giant redhead."

"Oh, right! Love your hair!"

There had to be cameras somewhere, right? They had to be secretly filming this grand drama for some stupid prank-style TV show.

"Thanks," Julia said. "Listen, we don't have much time. Your guests will be arriving soon, and we need to get this show on the road. Can't we go ahead without the missing groomsman? What's important is that you and Eddy are here. Besides, who's going to notice? You've got about eighteen bridesmaids and as many groomsmen."

"There are only fourteen."

Right. Only fourteen women in the bilious-yellow get up.

"And I can't have my wedding with uneven numbers," Angela said. "It's bad luck. My whole marriage will be cursed!"

"Because you'll have thirteen groomsmen, instead of fourteen?"

"*Thirteen!*" Angela gasped. "I hadn't even thought of that. Now I know we'll be cursed."

Julia contemplated banging her head against the wood. The resulting concussion couldn't hurt any less.

Eddy stepped into the doorframe. "Angie, we won't be cursed. This is stupid."

Oh, Dude, totally wrong thing to say. Julia screamed silently.

She socked him in the arm.

"I don't think you're supposed to be assaulting your clients," he said, rubbing his arm and acting offended.

"Stop trying to help, and I won't have to."

The damage had already been done, however. The voice on the other side of door reached a pitch only dogs could hear.

"Stupid? Stupid?" Angela cried. "If you think I'm so stupid maybe we shouldn't even be getting married!"

"Whoa, whoa, whoa." Julia said. "Let's take a step back and calm down. Much longer and we're going to be worrying about how to cancel a wedding, instead of the vacancy in the wedding party."

Angela's sobs increased in volume. "I'm sorry, Eddy. I know I'm overreacting, but I want everything to be perfect."

"It will be perfect," he said. "We'll think of something."

They all looked in Julia's direction.

Oh, great. They were leaving this up to her? Talk about a bad plan. Except they had no other plan. Someone had to talk the bride off the ledge.

"Angela, I can't have a conversation through the door," Julia said after taking a deep breath. "Can you please come out?"

"I told you, Eddy can't see me before the wedding."

"Eddy, go stand over there," Julia said, pushing him back so he was out of the line of sight. "All right, he can't see you. Now, open up."

The door cracked open, and one dark eye peeked out. "Where's Eddy?"

"I'm over here," he called out from his place in the

corner.

The door swung open wider. Dark hair and a puffy cloud of white were revealed. Angela looked like a delicate china doll. Unfortunately, the dolly's hysterics were holding up everything.

"We're running out of time," Julia said. "Can't you go on without the fourteenth groomsmen?"

"I guess if I had to," Angela whispered, looking like the kid who'd had to shoot his dog in that old movie.

Yeah, Angela would go through with it, but she'd be miserable, Julia realized. So how did one go about finding a substitute groomsman anyway? Could you rent one the way you did the tuxedo?

Speaking of tuxedos. "If we could find someone else to fill in, would he even have anything to wear?" Julia asked.

"Drew's tuxedo is at my house," Eddy said. "We thought it would be easier to arrange that here. The groomsmen sent their measurements, and the altering was done in town."

"So all we need is a body. How tall is your friend?"

"My height."

"Got any spare relatives or friends about your height?"

Eddy's face flushed. "We had fourteen bridesmaids. Everyone I know is already in the wedding."

"Anyone else know someone who could fill in?"

Betsy raised her hand. "My brother is Eddy's height."

Julia laughed. Of course the dynamo with the tackle box would have a spare relative. "Okay. Go pick up the tux from Eddy's place, and then get your brother here ASAP."

****

Unbelievably, the replacement groomsman worked out fine, and the ceremony went off without another hitch. The reception was now well underway. The guests had dined on their choice of chicken or salmon, and the band, which looked an awful lot like a group of high school kids, had kicked it into gear.

Julia surveyed the reception hall, observing the guests as they gyrated on the dance floor. Well, the younger ones were dancing anyway. The older folks were sitting along the sidelines with perplexed expressions on their faces.

As she continued her visual trek around the room, her gaze fell on a balding, middle-aged man. His tie was askew, and his hair stood up in wild disarray. If she wasn't mistaken, he was drunk. Though how he'd managed to become inebriated was beyond her as there was no alcohol being served. Instinctively, Julia started in his direction, but before she reached him, he lurched up from the table and started toward the dance floor.

Yeah, definitely three sheets to the wind. He wasn't so much walking as bobbing and weaving. She picked up her pace, hoping to reach him before anyone noticed. She managed to catch up to him as he bobbed two steps away from the parquet surface.

"Hi, I'm Julia." She gently slid an arm through his.

"Walter," he said, after a moment's confusion.

"Walter, how about we take a walk around the courtyard?" she asked, already guiding him toward an exit. Thank goodness he waddled along beside her without protest. They slipped through a pair of double doors.

"I'm drunk," he announced, as they walked along the path.

"A bit."

"Never drink. S'bad for you."

"Where did you get the alcohol anyway?"

He reached into his suit pocket and removed a silver flask. He shook it. "S'gone," he said. "Like my wife."

"Where did she go?"

"Nashville. Our baby went off to college, and the next day she said our marriage was over. She wanted to live her life. Twenty-five years and *poof.*" He tried to snap his fingers only they weren't working, so it looked more like he was trying to swat a fly.

Ah, alcohol as pain reliever, Julia thought. She should have guessed.

"I'm sorry."

A door opened behind her, and Seth appeared. Her whole body went on alert. She hadn't seen him since "the kiss". He must have been uncomfortable, too, because he kept his gaze focused on Walter.

"Hi, Walter," he said.

"Hi, Reverend," Walter said. "D'ya know Julia... uh... what's your last name?"

Amazing. Drunk as a skunk and yet his inbred Southern manners still abounded. "Richardson. Julia Richardson."

He turned back to Seth. "D'ya know Julia Richardson?"

"We've met," Seth said, flashing a brief smile in her direction. "I saw you two leave and thought I'd better make sure everything was all right."

"We were getting some fresh air," Julia said.

"I'm drunk," Walter declared again.

"I know," Seth said, his gaze filled with compassion. "I've told you, a bottle isn't going to help."

Walter sighed. "I know. Been doing better, but then the wedding. Niece's wedding. Couldn't miss it. S'just sad. Still remember how pretty Janet looked."

"Well, you've done your duty," Seth said. "Why don't I call you a cab?"

Walter's shoulders bobbed up and down. "'Kay—"

Seth glanced at Julia over his shoulder as he led Walter away. "Wait here. I'll be back in a minute."

****

It took only minutes for a cab to arrive. Seth instructed

the driver to make sure Walter got inside. He waited until the cab turned the corner and disappeared out of sight before venturing back toward Julia.

He should bolt in the opposite direction, but his feet didn't want to cooperate. Their kiss a few days ago had replayed in his mind a million times. He'd gotten a few more sleepless nights out of it, too. At this point he'd probably end up in a funny farm after he went crazy due to sleep deprivation.

A funny farm might be worth it if it meant experiencing one more kiss, though. Even the one might be worth it.

Julia stood waiting in the courtyard. He'd expected her to take off the minute he walked out of sight. He'd half hoped she would. Trust her to listen to instructions at the worst time. Why couldn't she be contrary as usual?

"I could have handled Walter," she said as he approached. "You didn't have to come save the day."

"I'm know, but he's a friend."

She sighed. "Poor guy."

"Yeah, he's had it rough. Sent shock waves through the town when Walter and Janet split up. They were a staple around here."

"Guess the real world has finally made its way to Covington Falls."

"I hope we never get so jaded that we look at divorce as commonplace," Seth said, with a shake of his head.

"You keep on hoping," she said, her voice dripping with sarcasm.

Oh, a challenge. He loved these. "Is it only your parents who made you so cynical?"

"Remember the keen eye for observation you find so endearing?"

The corner of his mouth quirked up in spite of himself. "Did I say it was endearing?"

"It's my most attractive quality apparently," she said,

batting her lashes.

His eyes drifted over her face. Then down. "I'm not sure I'd go that far." Seth heard the words come out of his mouth and couldn't believe he'd just uttered them. "I shouldn't be saying things like that."

A choked sound escaped as her eyes went wide. "*Anyway*. That observant quality means I don't look at the world through rose-colored glasses. Walter and Janet aren't the exception. They're the rule. I simply realized it early in life."

Embarrassment turned to anger, though for once his ire stemmed from another source. "Your parents have a lot to answer for. How many times have they both been married anyway?"

"Dad's on number five, or maybe six. I lost count. He married a twenty-three year old fitness instructor named Tiffany about a year ago. Seems the older he gets, the younger they get. My mom is on her third husband. She's actually been with him for ten years, so maybe she can make it work. I'm just glad to be out of the whole mess."

"It must have been traumatic for you growing up."

"I didn't live in a war-torn nation," she said, her voice once again dripping with sarcasm. "They didn't lock me in a closet and give me only bread and water. I was mostly an afterthought in their lives."

"Did you live with your mother?"

Wariness crowded out her annoyance. "Why are you so interested in the soap opera that was my life?"

"I guess I'm trying to understand why you're so skeptical about love."

"Why? So you can fix me? Make it all better with your wise counsel?"

How could he have the urge to kiss her and throttle her at the same time? "No. I want to know you."

She drew herself up, as if readying for a battle. "You

want to know what makes me tick, Rev? Fine. Might as well start at the beginning. My father left my mother for a lounge singer named Vanessa when I was five."

"A lounge singer?"

"I know, not very original," she said, wrinkling her nose. "Vanessa wasn't crazy about kids, so I rarely saw my father for the next couple years. Then my mother married a Frenchman named Henri. He hated kids even more than Vanessa, so I got shipped off to my father's."

An image of a little redheaded girl filled his mind, and Seth's heart broke for her. "How old were you by then?"

"Ten. Vanessa was replaced by a corporate lawyer named Brooke when I was thirteen. Can you guess her feelings about kids?"

"She didn't like them."

"Ding, ding ding! Got it in one. Give the man a prize," she said. "Off to Mom's I went, who by this time was re-divorced and re-married to Charles Winthrop, an English aristocrat who claimed he was 211th in line for the throne of England."

Despite the horrifying story, he smiled. "211th? That close?"

"I'm not even sure if it was true or something he made up to impress everyone," she said, grinning back.

"Then why not pick a number a little closer? Like 114th?"

"I love how you're making light of my traumatic childhood." Her mouth turned down in a mock pout. "Here I am spilling my guts, and you're not taking it seriously at all."

In an instant, his amusement vanished again. "Believe me, I'm taking your story seriously. I'd like to get your parents alone in a room."

"Why? So you can defend my honor?"

"I'd do it in a heartbeat."

Julia held his gaze for a long while, as if seeking an answer. Finally, she took a deep breath. "What if I told you that Charles didn't mind having a teenaged stepdaughter around? That he might have liked it a little too much?"

"What do you mean?"

She lowered her head, and he noticed her hands were clenched tight enough to turn her fingers white. His pulse kicked up. He had a feeling he wasn't going to like her next confession.

"He liked to look at me," Julia said, with barely any expression at all.

No, he wasn't going to like this. At. All. "Look at you?"

"I developed early, you know? By the time I was thirteen, I looked like one of those college coeds you see on those awful videos. You said it yourself. I was every teenage boy's fantasy."

Seth's skin suddenly seemed too tight. "He wasn't a teenager."

A thin, high-pitched laugh escaped. "I know. Creepy, right?"

No!

The shout lodged somewhere in his throat. Seth finally understood what a killing rage felt like. Blood pumped through his body with such force he thought he would explode. He paced a few steps away, trying to get hold of himself, and then whirled around to face her.

"Did he touch you?"

"I—" She shrank back, as if sensing the menace rising up inside him.

Even then, Seth couldn't stop. He stalked across the short expanse and leaned down, until his face was only inches from hers. "Did your stepfather *touch* you?"

"No, no! He never laid a finger on me," she said, head shaking back and forth.

The primordial scream in his mind eased. A little. "Never?"

"He only looked." She searched his face. "Are you all

right? You're not going to pass out, are you?"

Seth straightened up and swiped a hand across his face. "I'm sorry, but the thought of someone hurting you like that makes me crazy."

"You'd probably feel the same way if you found out any child had been abused."

"Of course I'd be angry, but thinking of it happening to you—" He swallowed the bile in his throat. Thinking of someone abusing Julia undid him.

"You'd like to get Charles in a room alone, too?"

"I think I'd kill him with my bare hands."

Even as the words left his mouth, Seth winced. He wasn't some medieval warrior haring out from the castle into battle, but a minister.

Her eyes filled. "Oh…"

"Are you crying?" he asked, heart stopping at the sight of the tears. "You're probably traumatized, and I made you relive everything. I'm so sorry."

She reached out a hand. "No, I'm not upset over Charles. I'm not used to anyone caring. It's pretty sweet, actually. Caveman-like, but romantic in a weird way."

"You think it's romantic that I want to hunt down your mother's husband?"

"She's not married to him anymore. She's with some Australian named James. I told you, she's been with him for a long time by her standards, so maybe he'll stick."

The laughter that bubbled up from his chest startled them both.

"What?" she said.

God, are you kidding me? "She finds it romantic."

"Are you talking to the sky again?"

"You might find my caveman tendencies are cute, but they scare me to death." He was still trying to shake off the effects of a near implosion.

"Why?"

"I'm a man of God," he explained. "A man of peace and forgiveness. I'm not supposed to want to tear a guy limb from limb."

"Would you rather get him in a room alone and counsel him?" she asked, tilting her head and sending him a teasing smile. "Tell him it's creepy to look at young girls?"

"I think my fists would be doing most of the counseling."

Julia took a deep breath. "You say the most romantic things."

Wow, caveman does work on girls. "Better than flowers, huh?"

"Oh, yeah," she whispered, her eyes dark and inviting.

Since Julia enjoyed his caveman-like transformation, he took advantage and leaned forward. So did she.

"Seth—"

They jolted apart. Amy Vining stood about ten feet away. She seemed annoyed, though he couldn't fathom why.

Seth straightened and slipped his hands into his pockets. "Amy. Lovely evening."

"It certainly is," Amy said. "Enjoying a walk in the courtyard?"

"Julia and I were talking."

"Of course," Amy said, flashing a bright, almost manic, smile. "I hate to interrupt, but actually I'm here to fetch Julia."

"Me?" Julia squeaked.

Amy's gaze shifted toward Julia. For some reason Seth felt like he'd been caught with the innocent Victorian lady. Would he have to meet Amy with pistols at dawn now, he wondered?

"Betsy asked me to find you," Amy said. "They're about to cut the cake."

"Okay, I'll be there in a second."

Amy didn't move. "I think she wants you to come now."

Julia glanced at him.

"Go ahead," Seth said.

Julia slipped past him and disappeared inside without looking back. Feeling like he'd run a marathon, Seth sank down onto a bench.

And started to pray.

Chapter Thirteen

There should be a law about having to deal with difficult people before 9:00 a.m. Especially if said difficult person's last name happened to be Manning. As in Catherine Manning, mayor's wife and all around pain in the… neck.

Today's mission involved cake. They were meeting with Chef Devon and her baker-slash-cake designer, Audrey Samson, a robust, brown-haired woman with rosy cheeks and twinkling blue eyes. Think Mrs. Claus without the white hair.

Julia and the Mannings were all seated in the empty dining room of Devon's restaurant as she and Audrey brought out plates filled with different flavors of cake for tasting.

Getting paid to eat cake… Best idea Julia had ever heard. No doubt she'd actually enjoy the experience if Mrs. Manning weren't such a pain in the… *neck*. No question as to who had a say in the wedding planning process, either. Poor Laurel, the bride, had done little more than take bird-like bites of each cake and then turn to her mother before giving anything resembling an opinion.

Mrs. Manning puffed out her considerable chest and eyed the delicacies as if they were live grenades. "The butter cake is too common," she announced. "Everyone has that."

"The angel food is too sweet."

"Lemon? No, too overpowering."

"Mocha? We'll serve the coffee in a silver urn, not in the cake."

"Golden vanilla? We might as well serve the butter cake."

"Mousse? We're serving mousse as the dessert for the dress rehearsal. We can't have it twice."

"Chocolate? A chocolate wedding cake? Oh, no dear. Now, for a groom's cake…"

"Orange? Oh, my goodness, no."

By the fifteenth cake Julia had gone way past the novelty of sampling. In fact, she might never eat cake again, a crime against nature she could lay right at La Manning's feet.

Enough. "Mrs. Manning?"

Julia fought a shiver as the mayor's wife turned her perfectly smooth, unwrinkled face in her direction. "My boss was the president of a Fortune 500 company, and his daughter had a white chocolate wedding cake."

Julia did not consider her statement an outright lie. There had been a white chocolate wedding cake. Her old firm in no way approached a Fortune 500 status, however.

Mrs. Manning didn't need to know the whole truth, especially as she seemed intrigued. "White chocolate?"

"It's all the rage, apparently," Julia said, perfectly comfortable with her subterfuge if it meant she could leave this restaurant within the next century. "Everyone who's anyone in the northeast has one. The cake was square with four tiers and had little, hot pink roses cascading down the sides."

Mrs. Manning turned to Devon and Audrey. "Can you do something like that? Of course Laurel's would need five tiers, and her colors are violet and white."

Audrey Samson was no fool. "Five tiers it is," she said without missing a beat. "I'll draw up some sketches for the decorations, and you can choose the one you'd like. I can have it ready by Monday morning."

Mrs. Manning bent her head forward in a regal nod to her serfs.

Julia nearly sank to the floor in relief. She'd started to have visions of dancing wedding cakes invading her dreams. Everyone stood up. Mrs. Manning took the lead out the door, and like any good servant Julia followed ten paces behind.

As she was about to slip out the door, Julia looked over her shoulder. Devon and Audrey Sampson stood by the table. Audrey winked, while Devon grinned and mouthed, *"You're my hero."*

Julia stifled a laugh as she slipped out the door, only to stop short when she realized Mrs. Manning had also turned back.

"Is there a problem, Miss Richardson?" Mrs. Manning asked, regarding Julia with a hawk-eyed glare.

Julia swallowed. "None whatsoever, Mrs. Manning."

The little *hmph* said La Manning didn't buy the quick save, but she must have decided to delay the execution because the Grande Dame swiveled on her elegant pumps and led the way down the street. Once they reached the shop, Mrs. Manning came to an abrupt halt. So abrupt, Julia almost knocked over everyone like a bowling ball. She stumbled and opened her mouth to ask what was wrong. Then she realized Her Majesty stood waiting for the door to be opened for her.

Clipboard is not a weapon, Julia. Not! A! Weapon!

Julia reached around and pulled the door open, allowing Mrs. Manning and Laurel to pass through. They hadn't gone more than two steps before coming to yet another halt. This time Julia did barrel into someone, and thankfully Laurel took the brunt of the collision with grace.

"Sorry," Julia whispered. "Is there a problem?"

Yes, there was a problem, in the form of Amy Vining, who sat at the desk.

"What are you—" Julia began, but didn't get to finish the thought as Mrs. Manning glided forward with her arms outstretched.

"Amy, dear. Don't you look lovely?"

Julia's mouth dropped open. She hadn't known the woman possessed the muscles required to form a smile. Amy rose from her seat, and the two met in the middle of the shop. They exchanged a French two-cheek kiss, while Julia continued gaping at the transformed mayor's wife.

Amy flashed a smile in Julia's direction. "I hope you don't mind that I let myself in. I waited outside for a while, but I declare, a girl could melt in this heat."

There went the "I declare" nonsense again. Did Amy think she was on the set of a Civil War movie or something? Julia half expected curtains would be pulled down soon so Amy could sew her own dress.

Julia tried her question again. "What are you doing here?"

"I came to help."

"With what?"

Amy giggled. "With the wedding planning, of course. I visited dear Sarah this morning, and she told me how hard ya'll have been working over here. I've been feeling so sad about her situation, but I didn't know how to help."

"You want to help run Marry Me?" Julia asked, her blood going cold.

"I do," Amy said, giggling at her own little joke.

Oh, please no! "I couldn't ask you to do that."

"It's no trouble. Sarah mentioned sweet Laurel's wedding, and I'm sure you're completely overwhelmed with the preparations. I know quite a bit about Covington Falls. I did grow up here after all, and I've been told I have quite the flair for planning and decorating."

"That is so sweet of you, dear," Mrs. Manning said. "I'm sure Miss Richardson would be grateful for your assistance."

A cold sweat broke out all over Julia's body. She could not work with Amy Vining. Talk about a nightmare.

Only one thing stopped Julia from tossing Little Miss Sunshine out the door. Amy probably did know more about Covington Falls than anyone on the face of the earth. So, Julia silenced the shrieking voice inside, and nodded as Amy beamed and Mrs. Manning signaled her approval.

Oh, Sarah, you are so going to be punished.

Chapter Fourteen

Julia stepped inside the house late that evening and stumbled upon a gaggle of women in the dining room. They were gathered around a dozen or so baskets, along with piles of food spread out across the table. Some of the women were filling the baskets, while others were shuttling back and forth to the kitchen. The noise level was deafening as they chattered and laughed. Julia felt as if she'd walked into a human ant pile. A noisy, giggling, gossiping, ant pile.

She tried to escape upstairs, but before she'd taken more than two steps, Sarah's mother-in-law spotted her.

"Julia. Hello, dear."

A dozen heads swiveled in her direction. Julia froze, having a sudden notion of what an animal must feel like while staring into the glare of oncoming headlights.

"Hi," Julia said, giving them a weak beauty pageant wave.

Grace emerged from the kitchen, and a smile broke out on her face. "Hi. The ladies are here helping to put together baskets for some of our members who've been ill, or in need of a good, home-cooked meal."

"Sarah and Eric are on the list," Mrs. Austin said.

Julia nodded, even as she eyed the door. "How nice. Everything smells wonderful."

"Are you hungry?" Grace asked. "There's plenty of food."

Julia would have refused, but her stomach suddenly took the time to remind her she hadn't eaten anything except sample wedding cake since breakfast.

Stupid stomach.

Grace chuckled. "Go help yourself."

Well, why not? A body needed food. With a smile of thanks, she headed toward the kitchen. Then nearly whirled right back around when she realized who had cooking duty.

Mrs. Vining nodded, but there was no welcome in the gesture.

"Umm. Grace told me to… ah… help myself," Julia said, fighting the urge to squirm like a kid sent to the principal's office.

"There's roast beef on the counter," Mrs. Vining said after a long, tense silence. "It should still be hot."

Julia crossed the room and grabbed a plate. She dished out some of the tender meat, along with some green beans and potatoes, keeping her back to the woman at the stove.

Another ice-filled silence fell.

"I understand Amy came by your shop today," Mrs. Vining said.

Julia held back a sigh and braced for the punch line. She didn't know when the blow would come, or what form the roundhouse would take, but she expected an assault. "Yes, she did. She volunteered to help with Marry Me."

"My Amy has always been a generous girl. So kind and helpful. So nurturing. She'll make a wonderful wife and mother some day."

Uh, huh. Start with a game of my-daughter-is-the-bestest-thing-in-the-world. Julia understood the rules of this challenge and decided to play along. She leaned back against the counter and forked a piece of meat into her mouth. "With you as her guide, how could she not?"

As Julia hadn't bothered to disguise the bite in her voice, Mrs. Vining didn't miss the sarcasm. "Amy is also a woman of virtue and grace," she said, eyes narrowed in challenge.

"Again a credit to you, no doubt."

Mrs. Vining's nostrils flared. "I pride myself on knowing I raised a daughter who understands the right way. A woman of faith. She is, in fact, the model of a good, Christian woman."

"I know my experience is rather limited in these matters, but I understood we're all on a level playing field in God's eyes. We're all supposed to be sinners, right?"

"Of course we are."

Mrs. Vining's face went red and splotchy as she fought to hold on to her temper. Julia watched the build up with a touch of glee. Even so, she didn't want to fight so she reached for a glass from the cabinet.

Mrs. Vining apparently had no intention of letting the round end, however. "Reverend Graham has even commented on Amy's lovely qualities."

Well, now at least they were getting down to the reason for the interrogation. Seth. Julia had no idea why the old bat would bother to warn her off, though. Surely no one knew about "the kiss".

"Seth is kind that way," Julia said.

"Sometimes too kind. He often doesn't see things that could hurt him."

The pointed words carried enough venom to make the hair on the back of her neck stand up. "What do you mean?"

"There has been some talk."

"About what?"

Mrs. Vining hesitated. "The… uh… living arrangements here. You know?"

Oh, Julia understood, but if the harpy planned on making

ugly accusations, she'd have to come right out and say them.

"No, I don't know," Julia said, daring the woman to step across the line in the sand. "You'll have to explain these accusations to me."

"You have to admit, it is unconventional for you to be living here while he's in that apartment," Mrs. Vining said, cheeks flushing as if knowing she'd gone too far.

"Are you implying Seth would act in an inappropriate manner toward me?" Julia asked.

"I would never— "

"Or perhaps you think Grace would condone improper behavior under her own roof?"

"Of course not." Mrs. Vining said, looking aghast.

"Or maybe it's me you're worried about? The heathen outsider? The daughter of the man who betrayed Covington Falls' resident angel?"

Mrs. Vining blanched and pulled herself up straight. "I hope you know I would never insult you that way."

"Not to my face, anyway."

"I was only trying to help." Mrs. Vining said. "I know how much Grace and Sarah mean to you."

"They all mean a lot to me."

"I know, dear, and that's why I wanted to warn you. There are people who will think the worst. We're human after all, and we're prone to the same harmful thoughts as any other."

"You mean you're apt to think the worst, especially of someone you don't know or particularly trust?"

Mrs. Vining huffed in exasperation. "I wanted to tell you, for Reverend Graham's sake. I'm sure you wouldn't want— "

Julia held up a hand. Any more kind warnings and she might resort to violence, and she didn't want blood all over Grace's kitchen. "I get it. You're only acting from a loving heart."

"Exactly," Mrs. Vining said, missing the irony in Julia's

words.

"Thanks for letting me know."

Mrs. Vining beamed, as if they'd come to an understanding. And maybe they had.

"Well, I'm done here," Mrs. Vining said, wiping her hands on a dishtowel. "I'm going to help the ladies with the baskets. You enjoy your meal now."

The roast beef suddenly tasted like sawdust. Leaving the plate in the sink, Julia escaped upstairs. A half hour later there was a knock at her bedroom door.

Grace stuck her head in. "How tired are you?"

"I guess that depends on what you're about to ask me to do."

"Nothing torturous, I promise," Grace said, holding her fingers up in a scout salute. "We've finished up with the baskets, and I have to deliver them. Would you like to come?"

"You have to deliver all of them yourself?"

"No, we divide them up. I only have three stops."

"Sure, why not?"

The first stop was two blocks over. Christina and Stuart Franklin. The door swung open, and a harried-looking young man peered out. In the background Julia heard a baby crying. A chorus of babies crying, actually.

Stuart's shoulders slumped, but he managed a tired smile. "Hello, Grace. Excuse... *everything*," he said, as he stepped aside to let them in.

A cyclone had upended the house. Stuart as well. He'd missed a button on his shirt so the plaid pattern was askew. Giant yellow stains adorned both shoulders and his jeans. His hair looked like he'd taken a weed whacker to it, and several days' growth of beard covered his jaw. He led them back to the kitchen, where Julia deposited the basket of food on the counter. Meanwhile, baby cries had reached Defcon 1.

"Excuse me," he said again, rushing off down the hall.

A couple minutes later, he returned carrying a tiny baby.

The tyke looked to be no more than a couple weeks old. A young woman toting two more babies trailed behind him.

"Wow," Julia said. "Triplets?"

A corner of the young woman's mouth pulled up, which was all she seemed to be able to manage. "Triple the fun."

As Grace reached over to take one of the babies, the younger woman looked at Julia with curiosity.

"This is my stepdaughter Julia," Grace said. "She's visiting for a while."

"You're the one running Sarah's business," Christina said. "It's nice to finally meet you. Actually, it's nice to see anyone over twenty inches tall. I'm Christina, by the way, and this is my husband Stuart. The crew here is Jacob, Jeremiah, and Joel."

"Julia is helping me deliver meals tonight," Grace explained.

"You have no idea how wonderful this is," the young mother said, already poking around in the basket.

"Right," Stuart said, with good-natured laughter. "Especially since we've been relying on my cooking lately."

"It's not so bad," Christina said, patting him on his shoulder. "He only burned two things today. He's pretty handy with the bottle warming, though."

"Are you two doing all right?" Grace asked.

"Oh, my yes. The church has been amazing." Christina turned to Julia. "Grace and her angels organized a schedule during the day so there's always someone here to help out while Stuart's at work. My parents both passed away, and Stuart's folks moved to Florida last year, so we're on our own. It's been such a blessing having our church family."

Grace rocked the baby in her arms and kissed his tiny head. "Well, we've sort of adopted these little guys. Believe me, we enjoy our time here."

Christina laughed again. "How's Sarah doing?"

"She's fine," Grace answered, managing a confident

smile. "Restless, of course."

"Don't I know it? I had to spend the last few months of my pregnancy in bed, too. You tell her we're praying for her."

"I will." Grace handed the baby back to Christina. "Well, we've got more meals to deliver. You call if you need anything."

Christina managed to kiss Grace's cheek despite the squiggling babies between them. "We will. Thank you so much."

The second house was Ruth Boyle, who'd fallen and broken her ankle. Finally, they reached the third house, Olivia and David Connor.

A stout, balding man answered the door. He smiled in sincere welcome. "Evening, Grace."

"Hello, David. How is Olivia doing tonight?"

"She's better today. Come on in."

They followed him into the living room. Sitting on the couch was a tiny, bird-like woman. Once Julia took in the baby-soft tufts of hair on the top of the woman's head the reason for the basket became apparent.

Olivia Connor's face might be tired and drawn, but her smile was glorious. "Visitors! And you've brought goodies."

"Olivia you look wonderful. Much better than last week," Grace walked across the room to kiss the woman's pale cheek.

"Shoot, I look like a cancer patient."

Grace chuckled. "Olivia, you might remember Julia."

"Thomas's girl, huh? You've turned into quite a stunner." Her eyes lowered to Julia's ample chest. "I do miss those."

David Connor choked on the piece of cheese he'd pulled from the basket. "Olivia!"

Her eyes twinkled. "I love to tease him."

Julia felt like she'd tuned in to a television show in the middle of the season.

Olivia must have sensed Julia's confusion. "Breast cancer, dear. They had to take them both. I know it's vain, but I miss them."

"Of course you do," Grace said. "They were part of your body. Part of what made you a woman."

Olivia looked sad, but resigned. "I suppose in the end, I'd rather have my life than my breasts."

David looked at his wife with such tenderness Julia almost felt she should leave the room. "I know I'd rather have you," he said.

"Isn't he sweet?" Olivia asked, blushing like a schoolgirl. "Anyway, it's all in God's hands now. And my oncologist's, of course."

Grace touched her hand. "I don't want to keep you. I'm sure you must be tired."

"I am a bit worn out," Olivia acknowledged. "Thank you for the food, though. Even if I feel too nauseous to eat, David will enjoy it at least. Before you go, there is one thing I'd like."

"Anything," Grace said.

"Could you pray for us?"

Grace squeezed her hand. "Oh, Olivia, of course I will."

With some help, Olivia managed to stand up. Her husband took one hand and Grace the other. Right before they all bowed their heads, Grace reached out her other hand toward Julia.

"I don't think—" Julia began, already backing up.

"Yes, please do join us," Olivia said.

There was no way Julia could refuse without being rude. With a resigned shrug, she clasped Grace's outstretched hand.

Grace closed her eyes and bowed her head. "Father Almighty, I lift my prayer tonight for my dear friend, Olivia. Father, you are the great physician, and I ask that You put Your healing hand on this dear woman and eradicate this cancer that has invaded her body. And I ask that You envelope her with Your love in this time. Give her courage to deal with whatever lies ahead.

"Father, I also pray for David. Hold him up and give him

strength when he is tempted to fall. We know that Your will is perfect. We don't know why this has happened, but I ask that You give David and Olivia the peace that only You can bring. That they may know they are in Your hands, now and forever more. I pray this in Your name. Amen."

"Amen," Olivia and David echoed.

With a shaky sigh, Julia lifted her head. Glancing over she saw both Olivia and David wipe tears from their eyes. Then he put his arm around his wife and kissed her soft, downy head. For a moment Olivia leaned into her husband's body and brought her hand up to his cheek.

Julia's breath seized like a vice was squeezing her chest, and with a sudden burst of panic, she raced out the door. When she reached the front porch, she stopped and took a few deep breaths. The tears that had threatened to fall from the moment Grace started to pray finally came. She couldn't even explain why she felt like sobbing. It wasn't sadness exactly. She didn't even know the woman.

No, it was something more. Something in that room. Something powerful and terrifying at the same time

Grace appeared, and wrapped strong arms around Julia's waist.

"Sorry I ran out," Julia whispered.

"It's all right."

"How can they be so happy?" Julia asked, on the verge of sobbing. "She might be dying."

"Trust me, they're frightened. They have faith, though, even if they don't understand."

"I don't think I understand anything. I don't know what's happening to me."

"Julia, I think you know exactly what's happening, and it's why you're so panicked. It's frightening to open up and care about people. To question everything you've always believed. Especially when you've spent most of your life keeping others at arm's length."

Julia released a deep sigh. "Do we have any more deliveries?"

"No, that was the last one."

"Good. I think I need to call it a night."

"All right, we'll go, but Julia?"

She avoided looking at Grace. "What?"

"At some point you're going to have to face your fears, otherwise you'll be running for the rest of your life."

"You and your daughter," Julia said, letting out a shaky laugh. "You should write a book for the emotionally crippled."

"You're not crippled, Julia. Just scared. I have faith in you, though. You'll find your way."

Chapter Fifteen

God save him from petty people.

Seriously, God, Seth prayed, *save me from petty people who have time to write a letter complaining about the color of soap dishes in the bathroom.*

"Seth, you still with me?"

Seth mentally shook his head and looked over at the building maintenance supervisor. Frank Zeeman regarded him with bleary brown eyes. Frank sported a potbelly and a graying buzz cut left over from his days in the Air Force. At the moment Frank looked ready to fling said soap dishes across the room.

"I heard you," Seth said, stifling the biting comment that sprang to his lips. "Axe the soap dishes."

Seth tried to remain focused. Tried not to care that so much of his job entailed placating the grumblings of perpetually dissatisfied individuals and playing ringleader to warring factions within the church. Tried to remember why he'd felt called to be a minister. Where had his enthusiasm gone? He used to be so gung ho. He was going to save the world.

Ha! Save the world? He couldn't manage to save his own sanity. Sometimes, all the infighting made him want to throw his hands up and walk away.

Which had to be the most insidious threat of all. The work of the devil, for sure. *"You're not good enough. Not strong enough. They don't appreciate you, so why should you stay?"* the dark one whispered at night, or during his weekly staff meetings.

Days like this made him feel Beth's absence more than ever. The twisting ache lodged in his chest again, radiating through his whole body. Would he ever be rid of the emptiness? Was he destined to spend the rest of his life feeling like half a person? He'd heard amputees talk about feeling their missing limbs, but what could a guy do about an amputated heart? There was no prosthesis for his malady.

Beth had been more than someone to warm the other side of the bed. She'd been his anchor, and now he felt adrift. He wondered if all those kind-hearted people who kept trying to set him up knew it wasn't just physical intimacy he craved. He needed a sounding board, someone he could unload on before all the frustrations caused him to implode.

Maybe he should listen to everyone's advice and consider dating again.

A vision of Julia floated through his mind. Her face pinched with sadness as she related the awful story of her youth. Her laughing blue eyes as she teased him about sewn up wedding gowns. By some miracle the tension eased… a bit. Enough so he could breathe again. Enough so he could tell Satan to take a swim in a flame-licked lake. For now anyway.

Except the knowledge that Julia, of all people, was able to bring comfort to his soul, seemed almost as unsettling as the devil's false words. There had to be something wrong with him to think *she* could be the answer to his problems.

The meeting concluded and Seth hoped no one would ask him a question about the day's agenda. He wouldn't have an answer.

He made it back to his office without being stopped. His secretary, Gladys, hopped up from her desk as soon as he came around the corner.

"You have a visitor," she whispered.

Seth lowered his head and matched her tone. "Who is it?"

Gladys seemed to grasp the absurdity of the situation and straightened to her not inconsiderable height. "It's Reverend Markham."

"James? Is that all?" he asked. "Why are we so furtive?"

James Markham was the former minister of Covington Falls Community Church and Seth's mentor. James had been the one who'd convinced Seth to put in his application when the older man had retired.

"He looked serious," Gladys said, her expression still dark.

"James is always serious," Seth said, stepping around his secretary to reach for the door.

"And my left knee hurts."

He paused. "I thought your right hip bothered you."

"Right hip is for rain. Left knee means bad things are coming."

Seth held back a sigh. Like he needed a chorus of naysayers right now. "Gladys, go see an orthopedist."

He opened the door and stepped into the office. James Markham rose from the leather chair with much more grace than a man of his size should be capable of. Standing at 6'6", with the build of a linebacker, James commanded a room not with fire and brimstone, but with a quiet, gentle assurance. As his build implied, he'd once played football. Had a chance to play in the pros, but chose to be a minister instead. As a child, Seth had looked at the big man with awe. James had literally filled the pulpit with his bulk and especially his presence. Now the two shared a bond only ministers could.

James held out his hand. "Seth, good to see you again."

He grasped the offered palm and gestured for his old friend to sit. "You, too. How's Betty?"

The older man's wizened face softened at the mention of his wife. "She's well. We just got back from visiting the grandkids."

"I bet they're getting big now."

"The oldest starts college next year," James said, with a disbelieving shake of his head.

"What brings you by?" Seth asked, sinking into his chair. "It's a little late for lunch."

James hesitated long enough to make Seth tense again.

"There was a letter waiting for me when we got back," James said.

Tension gripped the back of Seth's skull. James looked worried, and if he looked worried, Seth knew trouble was coming. "What kind of letter?"

"From a member — I can't say who. He'd hit the roof if he knew I'd come to warn you. He and several others are planning to go to the Session."

"Over what?" Seth asked, wishing he didn't have to know.

"Your music director. They want her removed."

"Meredith again." Seth exploded from his seat. "How many times do we need to go over this issue? She hasn't done anything to warrant being fired. She's brought more life into this church than we've had in years."

James nodded in his calm manner. "I know. I've visited, and seen and heard her. I think you've made a good choice."

"I knew some people weren't happy with her, but I thought we could move past this attitude."

"Long-held attitudes are hard to break, Seth, you know that."

Sudden weariness flooded through his body like a wet sandbag, and he rubbed his eyes. "I don't know why I'm surprised. I've heard enough grumbling. I just hoped — well, never mind what I hoped. Thank you for the heads up."

James tilted his head and regarded him with deep compassion. "Are you doing all right, Seth? You look troubled, and not just because of the controversy with Meredith Vining."

Seth didn't have the strength to pretend. "I'm beginning to realize why everyone's so nervous about single pastors. I feel like I'm losing my mind."

"You're waking up," James pronounced.

The odd statement caught Seth's attention. "Waking up?"

"You've been in a kind of deep sleep since losing Beth. A safe place you had to be in while you mourned," James said. "Coming out of that cocoon isn't easy. It can even be painful. The final letting go. Facing the fact that you want and need someone else."

"Yeah, except the one I want is completely wrong for me," Seth said before he could stop himself.

"Ah, so it is a woman." James sat back and hooked his ankle across his leg.

"No... well... yes... in a way. She's a mess. Or she's making me a mess."

"The best women often do. Betty still makes me crazy," James said, with an indulgent chuckle wrapped in miles of love. "What's so messy about this woman?"

"I don't have time to list all the reasons."

"Then it's serious?"

"I didn't say that," Seth said. Everything in him seized up at the notion of anything serious with Julia. "It's nothing. Like you said. I'm waking up, and you're right, I don't like it. I'll be fine. Just need to get a handle on things. Maybe take the hints all the busybody matchmakers have been making and get out there again. Even if it kills me. I haven't been out on a date in... well, I can't even remember."

"Take your time, Seth. You've been down a dark path."

"Yeah, and who knew the end of it would be so jagged?"

His mentor left then, but Seth's strange funk stayed with him the rest of the day. He couldn't seem to shake the restlessness and the anger. Only he didn't know who he was angrier at… his congregants or God. He wasn't ready to face his solitary apartment, so he pulled into a spot along Main Street and took a walk to clear his head.

At this time of day, a cool breeze had kicked up, and he sucked in the air, filling his lungs as well as his mind. His footsteps eventually took him past Marry Me, and he stopped to look at the window display.

The bedroom scene with the wedding gown hanging from the screen had disappeared, replaced with a different one. The white gown remained, only now the dress had been pinned to the wall, with the long veil stretched out behind it. Next to the gown were four fuchsia bridesmaids' dresses, skirts billowing out so the material seemed to be in motion. It looked like the bridesmaids' dresses were chasing down the wedding gown. Only one person would think to have the wedding party depicted as an angry mob about the tackle the hapless bride.

Julia *really* didn't like weddings.

He chuckled, and before his brain could yell stop, he went inside. Sarah's assistant, Betsy, sat at the desk in the main room. She popped up like a Jack-in-the-box when she saw him.

"Reverend Graham?" she said, hurrying over to his side.

"Hi, Betsy."

"What are you doing here?" Betsy asked, her expression equal parts welcoming and panic-stricken. "Did you need something?"

At the moment, Seth had no idea why he was there. There couldn't be anything he needed in this shop. Betsy still appeared petrified, though, so he had to come up with a plausible excuse. "I… uh… thought I should check in and see how things were going. You know, for Sarah. I promised I would keep an eye out."

Betsy gave him a blinding smile. "Well, aren't you the *sweetest* thing. We are just doin' fine here. You can tell Sarah that Marry Me is in *excellent* hands… though we sure do miss her, of course."

"I can see that." He tilted his head toward the door. "I like your new display outside."

A furrow appeared between Betsy's eyes. "Julia did it when she came back from meeting with Catherine Manning the other day. I think she's using the window as some sort of therapy."

He'd had dealings with the esteemed mayor's wife, and he couldn't blame Julia for seeking an outlet.

They grinned at the shared secret.

"Is… umm… Julia here?" he asked, halfway hoping she'd left. If God had decided to stop messing with him, she'd be gone.

"Oh sure, she's in the office. You can go on back," Betsy said, with a cheerful grin.

Nope, God wasn't ready to let him off the hook. "Right. I'll do that."

Betsy opened her mouth, and for perhaps the first time, she stopped before speaking. Her eyes looked thoughtful as she gazed at him. "You doin' all right, Pastor? You look…" She trailed off.

Did he look that bad? Maybe he needed to take up running again.

"You look sad," Betsy said. "You know, my cousin lives just over in Allenhurst. She's finished law school and is looking to set up a practice nearby. She's real active in her church, and I know for a fact she wants kids. She might be your type."

Seth fought back the shudder at the thought of another fix-up. "Thanks, but no thanks. I'll go and look in on Julia."

"All right, Pastor. You let me know if you change your

mind. Her name's Theresa."

Seth hurried by before Betsy could come up with any more relatives for him to date. He took another deep breath once he stepped into the quiet hallway. Quiet, except for the angry muttering coming from the office. He tiptoed in that direction and peeked inside.

Julia slammed a heavy bound book on the desk with enough force to leave a dent. "Purple daffodils. Where in blazes am I supposed to find purple daffodils?"

Seth leaned against the doorframe. "Have you tried the Yellow Pages?"

Julia screamed and whirled around, her hands up in a defensive gesture. When she saw who had invaded her office, she pressed a hand to her chest and blew out a gust of exasperated air. "Seth, don't do that! You're going to start the heart attack I already feel coming on."

The corner of his mouth lifted. "Sorry. I should have knocked."

"Yes, you should have," she said, dropping into the cracked leather chair. "What are you doing here anyway?" Her eyes widened, and she looked on the edge of panic. "Did we have a meeting? Please tell me I didn't miss another one."

"No, we didn't have an appointment," Seth said. "I was wandering around town and thought I'd stop in to see how things were going."

"Wandering?" she echoed, one cinnamon-colored brow arching in sardonic amusement. "Your church isn't keeping you busy enough?"

"Oh, I've got plenty to do. Just needed a break."

"Yeah? Are the natives restless?"

"You wouldn't believe. I spent an hour discussing the theological implications of red soap dishes in the women's bathroom."

"Seriously?" she asked, eyeing him with extreme doubt.

"Uh huh." As if he could make up something so

ridiculous.

"Wow, I think your job might actually be worse than mine," Julia said, letting out a whistle.

"No, I love my job."

"Doesn't look like it right now. In fact, you look terrible."

Seth threw up his hands. "What? Am I pale and sickly all of the sudden?"

Julia's gaze traveled over his face and down to the tips of his toes. He tried not to react to the slow journey.

"No, more like melancholy." She propped her chin in her hand. "Your eyes are hooded, and your clothes look like you took them out of the dryer and left them in a heap on the floor. Plus, your hair is sticking up a hundred different ways like you took an air blower to your head. So, what gives?"

"I'm fine."

"Seth. You might as well tell me," Julia said, wagging a finger like he was a naughty kid.

Perhaps there had been a reason he'd ended up here. "I do love being a minister, but I get frustrated, too." He dragged a hand through his hair, demonstrating how all the tufts had come to look like they did. "Sometimes I wish I could unload on someone."

"All right. I can handle that." She gestured to the chair in front of the desk. "Have a seat, Rev. You've listened to me gripe enough. Guess it's my turn to return the favor."

As said chair was piled with books, magazines, and several fabric pieces, Seth approached with obvious misgivings.

"Just throw everything on the floor. It's not like you could make the mess any worse," she said, her voice as dry as the Sahara.

He shoved the junk aside and perched on the seat while he contemplated what to say, or whether he should say anything at all. He *shouldn't* be here. Shouldn't be inviting a new kind of intimacy between them.

Julia cut through his inner struggle when she reached across the desk and took his hand. "Seth? What's wrong?" she asked, all traces of amusement gone.

"Some members of the congregation are trying to get rid of Meredith Vining."

"Because of her past. You told me that before."

"They've made a more formal protest now," Seth explained. "A group of them are bringing the matter up before the Session."

"What's that?" she asked, her eyes clouded with confusion.

"They're kind of like the rulers of the church. I'm only an employee. The Session has ultimate say over what goes on."

"So they could force her out? Or force you out if you won't?"

"Possibly. I'm not sure what to do."

Anger replaced confusion. Her blue eyes sparked like a firecracker. "I'll tell you what you should do. Go into that meeting and knock some heads together."

"What?"

"You heard me. Tell those old ladies they can take their pious judgment and stick it where the sun don't shine."

Despite the seriousness of the situation, Seth couldn't help but chuckle. "I don't think I can tell the Elders to shove off."

"Maybe you should." She held up a hand to forestall an argument. "Okay, maybe not literally. You're capable of being more diplomatic than I am. I'm talking about holding up a mirror in front of their faces and reminding them they haven't always made the right choices either. What's that verse about the stone throwing?"

"Let he who is without sin cast the first stone."

"Yeah, definitely that one," she said, pointing in her enthusiasm. "I'm sure you know more."

"A few," he allowed, with a smile.

"Of course. So, go in there with guns blazing, and save the girl. You talked Meredith into taking the job, now you've got to fight for her. And please stop feeling sorry for yourself. You think you're the only one who's ever had trouble with people on the job? I've dealt with backstabbing coworkers. People who will do anything to get ahead. You can't let them win. You know you're right… You *do* know you're right?"

"Yes."

"Then don't give up. You know, chances are there are even more people who love Meredith. I bet they'd support you, and her. You're not alone."

No, he wasn't. He had been feeling sorry for himself, and it was time to stop wallowing. He rose to his feet. "Stand up."

"Why?" she asked, eyeing him with extreme wariness.

"Just do it."

The guarded expression didn't disappear, but she obeyed. Seth slipped his arms around her waist and hugged her. He didn't kiss her. Wanted to, but knew he couldn't trust himself right now. He did allow his hands to tangle in her hair. Took in her scent.

She pulled back. "What did you do that for?"

"To thank you."

"For telling you to tick people off?"

"No, for kicking me in the butt."

A wry grin appeared. "You are a strange man."

He dropped a quick kiss on her forehead. "And I think you were the answer to a prayer tonight."

Chapter Sixteen

Whoever said living in a small town made a person feel more relaxed was nuts. Julia felt so wound up she felt like the proverbial long-tailed cat in a room full of rocking chairs. Now, on top of a killer headache, thanks to another sleepless night, she had to work with Miss Mary I'm-so-out-your-league Sunshine.

Amy Vining was another thing Julia could blame on her stepsister, so she called Sarah the next morning on the way to work to complain. The phone rang so many times she was about ready to call the police to rush over to the apartment.

Finally, Sarah picked up.

"It's about time," Julia snapped. "Why didn't you answer the phone?"

A snuffling sound emerged, followed by a shaky, half-sob. "Hi, Julia."

Alarm bells clanged in Julia's head. "Sarah? What's going on? Is something wrong with—"

"His mother is in jail!"

"Huh?"

"She was only trying to protect her baby after they all

made fun of his ears, and then they put her in jail, and now she can't see her baby," Sarah wailed. "And that song!"

Awareness dawned as Julia pulled into a spot in front of Marry Me. "Wait a minute. Are you crying over a movie?"

"*Yes*! Someone gave me a whole DVD set for the baby, and I got bored, so I put one in. It's horrible! Poor baby."

With her panic subsiding, Julia released a shaky breath of her own. "Sounds rough," she said, staring at the window display of the angry mob chasing the bride.

Another sob. "Oh, my goodness! What if my baby has huge ears, too? Then I'll go berserk and get put in jail, and I'll never see my baby again!"

Julia wondered if she hadn't gone a bit too far with the bride in peril. "Do me a favor, Sarah. Find a comedy and watch that instead."

"Okay," Sarah said, though her voice still sounded frail and weepy. "Sorry. I think I'm going stir crazy. It's so good to hear your voice."

"Wait till you find out why I called."

"Why?"

"What on earth possessed you to tell Amy Vining I needed help? Don't you think I have enough on my plate without foisting her on me?"

"What are you talking about?"

"You told Amy Vining how overwhelmed I was, so she volunteered to help at Marry Me."

"I only told her how hard you've been working," Sarah said. "Are you saying she showed up and offered her services?"

"Yes. She was sitting at my desk when I got back with Mrs. Manning, and wouldn't you know the Dragon Lady adores her? Now, I'm stuck with Miss Perky Perkiness."

"I had no idea she'd show up there."

"I think she wants to spy on me. Make sure I'm not doing anything unsavory with Seth."

"Have you been doing anything unsavory with Seth?" Sarah asked, in a teasing voice.

"No."

"Well, why not?"

Julia was in no mood to be prodded about Seth. "Didn't I tell you to stop matchmaking?" she asked. "Besides, I've got a serious problem here. I'm being invaded. I half expect Amy's mother will show up and offer to help, too. Mrs. Vining has already warned me off."

"When?"

"A couple days ago. Not that there's anything she needs to worry about," Julia was quick to point out. "There's nothing going on between Seth and me."

"Well, except for the kiss."

Julia glared at her phone. "Remind me never to tell you anything important ever again."

"Are you sure nothing else has happened?" Sarah asked, like a dog refusing to give up a juicy bone. "Amy must be suspicious if she showed up and volunteered."

"Well, she might have gotten the wrong idea at the wedding last week. One of the guests got a little tipsy so Seth and I helped him get a cab home. We were talking in the courtyard, and Amy found us."

"Just talking?"

"Pretty much," Julia said, through gritted teeth.

Sarah giggled. "You kissed again."

"No. Then Seth showed up last night because he was upset about red soap dishes and a Session meeting to oust Meredith Vining."

"Who wants to get rid of Meredith?" Sarah asked on an outraged gasp. "And why didn't anyone tell me?"

"Because it just happened, and because you shouldn't be worrying about church politics right now."

"So, you're saying Seth came to you for advice and comfort?"

Julia squirmed at the notion of being any kind of confidante to Seth, which implied a deeper connection than she wanted to admit. "Don't go making a big deal out of one conversation. I think he likes talking to me because I can offer a different perspective."

"I think you protest too much," Sarah said, clucking her tongue.

"I'm hanging up now."

"Oh, don't go yet," Sarah said. "I am going crazy."

"I'll come by later. Right now I've got to go meet my new employee."

Sarah made a little sound, and Julia didn't need to see her stepsister to know she was pouting. "Okay."

"And no more sad movies."

"They're officially off limits," Sarah said. "You do me a favor, too."

"What?"

"The next time you're in a courtyard or an office alone with Seth, take advantage of it."

The little manipulator hung up before Julia could protest.

Still fuming, she got out of the car and trudged up to the shop. Amy had ensconced herself at the desk again, and her head popped up at the sound of the bell. Her smile was brighter than the sun reflecting off the water, and Julia felt the sudden need to put her sunglasses back on.

"What are you doing?" Julia asked.

Amy leapt up from the desk. "Hi. I hope you don't mind, but I saw your to-do list and started making calls. I've already called Karen Collier to set up the final dress fitting for the Morrison wedding. You also had a note about looking for a tent for the Creek wedding. Stewart's Outdoor Venues always supplies tents for the annual Covington Falls Carnival, so I called them. Got a great deal on a tent that accommodates one hundred people."

Julia couldn't help but be impressed. Amy could teach

the military a thing or two. "Aren't you the busy bee? Where's Betsy?"

"She has class this morning."

"She's going to school?"

"Mm hmm. She's getting her GED."

That stopped Julia in her tracks. "Betsy never finished high school?"

Amy's blond waves bounced as she shook her head. "Her mother got sick when she was fourteen. Betsy stayed home a lot to take care of her, so she didn't have the credits to graduate."

"Why didn't I know that?"

Amy gave a graceful lift of her shoulders. Everything the younger woman did seemed graceful, which was so annoying.

"I guess she's a little embarrassed about it," Amy said.

"She could have told me."

"You're new in town. She might not have known how you'd react."

Another reminder of her outsider status. Even with Betsy. The knowledge stung.

"It looks like you don't even need me here," Julia said.

"I went too far, didn't I?" Amy's smile faded. "I'm sorry. I should have waited for you to get here."

Julia didn't know what to say. She hadn't expected her new assistant to be so contrite and... *nice.*

"I'm always doing that," Amy said, working her way up to tears. "I push too much."

Great. "No, it's all right," Julia said, feeling as though she'd kicked a puppy. "I'm sure you're much more efficient than I am. I'm just jealous."

"Then we're even," Amy said, in a conspiratorial tone. "I've been insane with jealousy of you."

"Why?"

"Because you live so close to Seth, and you get to see him everyday. I couldn't help noticing you two seem closer."

Oh, man, what had Amy seen at the wedding? Did she know about Seth dropping by Marry Me last night? "We get along, but there's nothing romantic between us."

"Are you sure?" Amy asked, biting her lip. "When I saw you at Angela Jerome's wedding, you looked pretty cozy."

"We're friends," Julia insisted. "That's all."

Amy sighed in relief.

Julia decided to probe. "You've got a thing for him, right?"

A lovely flush of color stained Amy's cheeks. "Is it that obvious?"

"A little bit."

The blush deepened. "I'm such a fool. I've always been a complete idiot where he's concerned. It's just—"

"Just what?"

"I love him. I always have."

"Always?"

"It seems like it anyway."

Julia leaned against the corner of the desk. "I remember him being a nerd."

"Oh, no! He was so sweet and shy. And kind."

"He's a bit older than you."

"That was the problem. I was too young for him to notice me. Then he went away to school, and I grew up. I had these grand dreams that he'd come home one day, take one look at me, and fall instantly in love."

"Instead he brought someone else home."

Amy's pretty, sky-blue eyes misted. "Right. So, I stuffed all those dreams down and tried to get over him. When Beth got sick, I prayed for her like everyone else. I hated the thought of Seth suffering."

"You really love him?" Julia asked. "It's not a leftover schoolgirl crush?"

"I wish. Don't you think I'd rather be married with kids of my own, than pining for a man who's never even looked at me?" Amy asked, eyes wide-eyed and innocent. "That's why I got worried when I heard you were going to be living at Grace's house. Then when I saw you at that wedding, I thought my worst fears were realized."

"What fears?"

"That Seth would finally come out of mourning, only to fall in love with someone else."

A shiver ran up Julia's spine like an icy finger. "I don't think you have to worry about that."

"Oh, I realize how silly I was being now," Amy said, with a dismissive laugh. "You two are so different."

That hurt. It was nothing more than Julia had said to herself over and over again, but having the truth confirmed was not pleasant. "Right."

"In any case, maybe now we can be friends," Amy said.

Friends with Amy Vining? Oh, yeah, it was a banner day for sure.

****

Amy turned out to be something of a miracle worker. Her resources were endless. Someone needed an ice sculpture? She knew who made them. Needed two dozen, one-hundred-foot-long velvet sashes to drape down an aisle? She could find them. Or make them. Oh, yeah, she made the sashes. In under forty-eight hours.

Plus, everyone loved her. Women, men, even little kids lit up when they saw her, like she was some fairy princess come to life. It was enough to make a person feel like the proverbial redheaded stepchild. If Amy wasn't so nice all the time, Julia could have easily hated her. There hadn't been evidence of the earlier hostility, either. In fact, ever since Amy had made the big confession about Seth, she'd acted like they were best friends.

In any case, Amy's competence came in handy as Julia

and the crew made the final preparations for their next wedding on Saturday. Amy and Betsy were dispatched to the florist while Julia headed to Seth's church to meet with the wedding coordinator. The rehearsal was tomorrow, and there were a million details to go over. At least it seemed that way.

By the time Julia finished with the meeting, her brain was fried. Leaving the cramped broom closet that passed for the wedding coordinator's office, she made her way through the silent hallways. Seth's voice caught her attention near the open doors of the sanctuary. She stopped and looked inside, watching the figure on the stage for a moment before slipping into a pew in the back.

He was mesmerizing. Almost like a different man. He was practicing his sermon, and from what she could tell, Seth was not the type of preacher who liked to stand in one place and orate. He paced and then paused for dramatic effect. He used his arms to punctuate an important point. He was forceful and passionate, and there was a power in him that was absolutely transfixing.

And sexy as all get out.

Which had to be the most un-pure thought to be having while sitting in a church. She shouldn't be thinking about how all that passion could be transferred to other things.

To keep the lightning bolt from striking her where she sat, Julia tried to focus on the words.

"It's a simple story. I know most of you have heard it a thousand times, but some of you have forgotten or refused to listen," Seth said. "God created man, and he gave them everything they could ever want, but like greedy children they wanted more. They chose sin. But instead of turning his back, he embarked on the greatest rescue mission ever devised. A mission to rescue *you*.

"He sent a Son. His only Son. To be tortured and killed for you. He sent in the cavalry, by sending his Son to the Cross. For God so loved the world. For God so loved *you*, and all you have to do is accept that love. You don't have to do anything. Be anything. Just believe."

The tears that seemed to come much more freely in the last few weeks threatened to erupt again. Julia was filled with awe that the kid she once knew had grown into a man who could paint such a beautiful picture and touch hearts with a gesture. A look. A word. No matter how frustrated he got with certain members of his church, he'd clearly been born to preach.

As if sensing a presence, Seth turned toward her. "Julia—"

Her skin heated at his regard. "Please don't stop on my account."

After a moment's hesitation, he shook his head, almost as if he was coming out of a trance, and started walking down the aisle. "What are you doing here?"

"I had to meet with your wedding coordinator. I heard you, so I came in."

"How long have you been here?" he asked, leaning back against the pew in front of her.

"Long enough to know you've got an amazing gift. It's a beautiful sermon."

A smile touched his lips. "Thank you."

"I've never heard you preach before," Julia said, wishing she had the words to express her admiration. "You're a different person. It's like something powerful is pouring out from inside you."

"It is in a way, but it doesn't come from me. I only speak the words. God puts them in the hearts of those who need to hear them the most."

"I think God would be proud of the words you speak."

"I think that's the nicest compliment anyone has ever given me," he said, his voice rough with emotion.

The corner of her mouth kicked up. "You don't get compliments too often?"

"Remember the red soap dishes?" he asked, with a shake of his head. "And my music director? No, it's always easy to complain."

"Of course it is."

"Actually, I have you to thank for my sermon," he said, stuffing his hands in the pocket of his jeans.

She blinked in astonishment. "Me?"

"I imagined what I would say to get you to see."

"See what?"

A brief hesitation followed as he searched her face. "Just see."

Julia's finger traced the edge of the pew. "What if I can't see what you do?"

The unspoken question hung in the charged air. How could they ever have a relationship if she couldn't believe what he did?

"I don't know," he said, sounding wistful.

There had to be some way to back away from the cliff they were approaching. Maybe shock would work.

"What you do is incredible," she said. "It blows my mind, and frankly, it gets me hot."

The breath left his body so fast he nearly choked.

Mission accomplished. "I know, it's pretty twisted, let me tell you." She grinned at his stunned expression.

It took a few more attempts before he could speak clearly. "Who knew preaching was an aphrodisiac?"

"It is when you do it," she said, bending down to kiss his cheek.

He turned his head at the last second, and their lips met. It was soft. Not like the more frantic kiss on the balcony, but somehow every bit as devastating.

Julia jolted back, as if stung by a live wire. "Okay, that was—"

"Yeah."

"I have to go," she said, shaking her head to clear the fog.

"I've got to wrap boutonnières."

"Huh?"

"You take the flower and this green fern-like stuff and wrap the stems with green tape. Then you stick a pin through it and attach it to the men's tuxedos. It's a delicate procedure, but Amy Vining seems to be an expert at it, so we're doing it. It'll save the client a lot of money by not having the florist do it."

"Amy Vining is working for you?"

"Yes, and she's been a godsend, too. She's amazing. She could probably host her own show on one of those home decorating networks."

"I'm glad you have some extra help."

"Yeah, if only she wasn't so perky," Julia grumbled. "Between Amy and Betsy I feel like a clumsy, redheaded giant."

He looped a red curl around his finger. "You've got quite a complex about petite blondes."

"Try not being one in this town."

"I thought we'd established you're drop-dead gorgeous."

Oh, man a little heart pitter-pat. She almost fluttered her lashes like one of those cartoon characters when they spotted the handsome boy. "Did we establish that?"

"I did anyway."

There it is again. Step away from the preacher, Julia!

"I have to go," she said again, taking a step back. "I hope you knock 'em dead with that sermon. It's beautiful."

"Thank you. You should come hear the whole thing in person."

"We'll see."

A brow lifted as determination lit his features. "One of these days I'll get you here."

"One can always dream," she said, before hurrying away from temptation.

Chapter Seventeen

The day of Noelle Robinson's wedding turned out to be picture perfect, with a sky so blue it almost hurt to look at it. Only a few puffy, white clouds marred the perfection. Julia took this as a good sign.

Julia had spent a lovely morning with Roger at the country club. This time she'd brought Amy along, and sure enough, the stiff-necked manager melted like a wax candle under her cavity-producing sweetness.

Once things looked well in hand, Julia left Amy in charge and headed over to Seth's church, where Betsy was herding the wedding party. Julia hadn't heard about any catastrophes from that end, so she could only assume everything was going according to plan. At least she hoped so. She knew for a fact that every groomsman and bridesmaid had been present and accounted for at the rehearsal last night.

At the church, she found a parking space, jumped out and sprinted for the stairs. She had a hand on the door when someone called her name. She turned and saw a dark-haired man hurrying up the steps behind her. She recognized him as the brother of the groom. He was dressed in boxer shorts and a tuxedo shirt. Something about the odd attire caused her whole body to tense.

"Hi," Julia said. "Michael, right? Groom's brother?"

"Yeah, but right now I wish he wasn't," he said through clenched teeth.

Oh, that look is not good. Not good at all. "Why?"

Instead of answering, he held out a folded piece of paper. Julia stared at the sheet as if it were a rattlesnake coiled and waiting to strike. "What's that?"

Michael's eyes turned black with rage. "It's the reason I'm ready to disown my baby brother."

Every organ in her entire body constricted. "Please tell me that's not what I think it is."

"Sorry."

Her hands started shaking. "He's not coming, is he?"

"No."

I'm gonna' pass out. "What happened? He seemed fine last night. Nervous, but okay."

"He took off while I was in the shower. I came out and found this on the dresser."

"Where's he gone?"

"To find himself apparently," Michael said, lips compressing into a thin, white line. "He claims he doesn't love Noelle anymore, and that he's not ready to settle down."

A bitter laugh escaped her. "Right. That's always a good excuse. Did he take someone with him on this journey of exploration?"

Michael winced in answer.

"At least tell me it's not a friend or relative."

After another long hesitation, he cleared his throat. "One of the bridesmaids."

Unbelievable. "Typical. And no one knows yet?"

"No."

"Great," she said, through gritted teeth. "Do you want to do the honors?"

Now *he* looked ready to pass out. "I don't think—"

"Never mind," she said, grabbing the note. "I'll go, but I need you to call the country club and get Amy Vining on the phone. Tell her to stop everything and get over here. I'm going to need her to start making phone calls."

Michael looked like he was about throw up, but he nodded. "All right."

The walk to the bride's room was the longest of her life. As Julia entered the church, the first person she saw was Seth coming out of the sanctuary.

"Hi, Julia." He took one look at her face and stopped dead. "Are you all right?"

"No."

"What's wrong?" he asked, reaching her side in two steps.

The words wouldn't even come yet. "Could you come with me?" she asked. "I have a feeling you might be needed."

Alarm flitted across his face. "Has someone been hurt? Doug?"

Wordlessly, she waved the piece of paper in her hand.

A harsh breath hissed through his teeth. "Oh…"

They both started down the hall.

Betsy spotted them first, and her face lit up. "Hi, Julia! Everything is right on schedule. Noelle is almost dressed. Everything fits, by the way. The photographer should be ready to go in about fifteen minutes."

Julia held up a hand. "Betsy, I need you to do something."

"What?"

"Start calling people and tell them not to come. There's not going to be a wedding today."

"What? But why?"

Julia waved the little white flag again.

The color instantly drained from Betsy's face. "Oh, no. Oh, poor Noelle."

"Yeah, and I've got to go in there and tell her."

"I'll go start making calls," Betsy said.

The bride's room was once again a scene of chaos and confusion. Five women in maroon halter dresses performed a madcap ballet as they finished preparations. Noelle Robinson was today's prima ballerina. She was already in her wedding gown. The pure, white dress had little, puffy sleeves, a demure, sweetheart neckline, a fitted waist and a full skirt embellished with what looked like a million tiny pearls.

She looked like one of those figurines you'd see on top of the wedding cake. All at once Julia realized she was about to dash this young woman's dreams.

Seth stepped closer and settled his hands on her shoulders. "Do you want me to tell them?"

"No, I'll do it." She took a deep breath and cleared her throat. "I need to speak to Noelle. Alone."

Noelle giggled. "What? Has my father forgotten to pay a bill?"

Julia searched the room until she found Noelle's mother and silently pleaded for help. Mrs. Robinson took one look at Julia's face and immediately started herding everyone else out.

Once the room was clear, Mrs. Robinson turned. "Okay. Why don't you tell us what's going on?"

For the first time Noelle started to look concerned. "Has something happened to Doug?" Her eyes widened. "There's been an accident! Has he been hurt?"

"Not exactly."

Mrs. Robinson was no dummy. Her jaw tightened, and a mother-bear expression entered her eyes. "Where is Doug?"

Julia started to sweat. Why, oh why had she let herself get stuck with this job? "I don't know how to tell you this other than to just say it. Doug won't be coming today."

"What do you mean, he's not coming?" Noelle asked.

"He's left town. I'm sorry."

"That can't be," Noelle said, shaking her head, as if she

couldn't have heard right. "He said last night... he told me how happy he was. There must be some mistake."

"I wish there was."

Julia held out Doug's note, but Noelle only stared at it.

Mrs. Robinson wasn't so reticent. She snatched the paper, unfolded it and quickly skimmed over the words. Her lips pursed. "It's true honey. He's decided he can't get married right now."

Noelle giggled with relief. "Oh, so it's cold feet. If that's all, we can wait."

"I don't think waiting will help," Mrs. Robinson said.

Noelle's cheeks paled. "Is there something else in his note? Something besides him having cold feet?"

Mrs. Robinson raised anguished eyes to her daughter. "Oh, Noelle..."

What remained of the softness disappeared from Noelle's face. "Let me see."

"Honey, trust me. It's best if you let it go."

"Mother, give it to me," Noelle said, holding out her hand.

Without another word, Mrs. Robinson handed over the paper.

"He's run away," Noelle said in disbelief. "With Carrie. He ran away with my best friend. How can that be? She's been here all day."

"Actually, she forgot her necklace at home, so she left to go get it," Mrs. Robinson said. "That must have been about forty minutes ago. I didn't even notice she hadn't come back."

Noelle folded the note again in precise lines, focusing on the task rather than the occupants of the room. "How could Carrie do this? And Doug? Why didn't he tell me?"

Mrs. Robinson choked back tears. "I don't know."

Noelle finally looked up at Julia, with an almost unnatural calm "What do we do now?"

"I've already told Betsy and Amy to start calling the

guests," Julia said. "Amy will tell the country club staff and the caterer to hold off."

"But what should I do?"

"I think you should take all the time you need in here to let this sink in. I'll tell everyone outside to go home, so you don't have to answer any questions right now."

"All right." Noelle released a long, slow exhale. "Do you think I could be alone?"

Mrs. Robinson was crying openly now. "Noelle, I don't think that's a good idea."

"Just for a minute, Mom," Noelle said, keeping her eyes trained on Julia.

Mrs. Robinson sighed. "Okay, honey. I need to call your father and tell him what's happened."

Seth gave Noelle a hug before he left. "I'm here if you need to talk to someone."

"Thank you, Pastor Graham."

Julia started to follow Seth out of the room, but Noelle called out. "Miss Richardson?"

"Yes?"

"Could you stay with me?"

"Wouldn't you be better off with your mother or a friend?" Julia asked. "Or I can call Seth back?"

"My best friend ran off with my fiancé. I'm not too keen on friends right now," Noelle said. "Or men. Even ones who are ministers. Plus, I think if I look at my mother right now, I'll lose it completely."

Julia shut the door and stood in front of it, unsure what to do.

"Could you help me out of this dress?" Noelle asked, her voice still sounding calm. "I can't bear to wear it another minute."

"Of course."

Despite the row of tiny pearl buttons, the gown had a zipper. Julia lowered the fastening, and the dress slid to the floor in a silken heap. Underneath was a bustle. She untied the string at the waist, and yards of crinoline landed on top of the gown. Noelle stepped out of the garments and walked across the room.

Julia leaned over to pick everything up, but Noelle waved a hand. "Leave everything there for now."

Noelle grabbed a canvas bag from the corner and pulled out jeans and a button down shirt. After she was dressed, she sank onto the settee with a weary sigh. "Carrie and Doug. How could I have missed that?"

Julia chose a chair next to the door and sat down. "I'm sure you didn't want to see it. You loved Doug and trusted him. You trusted them both."

"Carrie dated Doug in high school. They were even king and queen of the prom, but she broke it off when they went away to college. She wanted to date other guys, you know?"

"That's not unusual."

"I never looked at Doug until a couple years ago. Even then I felt guilty somehow. Like I was betraying Carrie."

"How did she feel about you dating her ex-boyfriend?"

"She made good on her vow to date other guys. She stayed away after college. Got a job in Dallas. I talked to her about Doug, and she said she was happy for me. Then she moved back six months ago."

"Did she come home for him?"

"She told me no. She just wanted to reconnect to her small-town roots." Noelle blew out a harsh breath. "Stupid me."

"You're not stupid, Noelle. You trusted them, and they let you down. People do that all the time unfortunately."

The tears Noelle has held back earlier filled her eyes. "I feel like such a fool."

"You're not a fool either."

"I was. A fool to think someone as wonderful as Doug could ever love me."

"Okay, first off, Doug wouldn't rate as wonderful in my book. He's a jerk. A cowardly one at that. He let you prepare for this day, knowing he wasn't going to go through with it. He arranged it so you would have to face this humiliation on your own."

"I guess you're rig—"

"I'm not done yet."

Noelle blinked at the blunt tone. "Okay."

Julia got up and started pacing. "Where was I? Oh, right. Secondly, you're better off knowing this now, rather than figuring it out years from now when you're stuck with a husband who doesn't love you and kids to disappoint. This may hurt, but trust me, ending a marriage — or staying in one that's a lie — is the most painful thing you can imagine."

"Have you been divorced or something?"

"No, but I lived through my parents' endless string of marriages. I know what can happen when you marry the wrong person and then have to tear the marriage apart. It leaves scars that never quite heal."

Noelle wiped a hand across her cheek as a wobbly chuckle escaped. "So, you're saying I should be thanking him?"

Julia's mouth curved. "Maybe not today. Right now he's an unmitigated — uhh, jerk."

"It still hurts though."

"Of course it does."

"I had so many dreams. I already knew what our kids would look like."

"You can still have dreams. They'll be different than what you imagined, that's all."

"Do you think I'll find the one for me?"

How do I answer that, when I'm not sure "the one" concept has any basis in reality?

"I'm probably not the best person to ask," Julia said. "I'm a cynic myself. All those scars, you know. The longest relationship I ever had lasted all of six months."

"Oh," she whispered.

I'm the worst counselor of all time. I should have lied. "Look, I assume you're a churchgoer, right? You wouldn't be getting married in one if you weren't."

"I grew up in this church."

"If there's one thing I've heard since I got here, it's that everything happens for a reason. Do you believe that?"

"Yes, of course."

"Well, then you've got to believe that He has a purpose for this. He has a plan for you, and if you're meant to have a husband and family, He'll bring them to you when the time is right."

Noelle took a deep breath and managed a real smile. "Thank you for reminding me of that."

"You mean that worked?"

"Why are you so surprised?" Noelle asked, with a burst of genuine laughter.

Because I'm not sure I believe a word I just said. "Don't ask."

Noelle sighed and stood up. "I suppose I have to face everyone sometime."

"We can probably get you out of here without having to see anyone. Take you out the back."

"Call me a coward, but that sounds like a good idea," Noelle said without hesitation.

"I'll go out and speak to Seth and Betsy. We'll clear everybody out of the area."

Noelle leaned over to pick up the canvas bag. "Oh, my dress!"

"I'll have it packed up and sent back to your house later."

"Thanks."

"You're welcome."

Noelle touched Julia's arm. "No, I mean it… thank you."

"You'll be fine, Noelle," Julia said, leaning in to give the other woman a hug.

"I hope so," Noelle whispered.

A few minutes later, Noelle and her mother were on their way home, and the bridal party had dispersed. Julia went about the business of canceling a wedding. It was hours before everything was settled. By then, she was about ready to collapse. Everything ached. Including her heart.

The sun was starting to set as Julia walked outside and sank onto the front steps. She stared at the glowing orange orb as streaks of pink, purple, and blue darted across the sky. As the sun dipped below the horizon, the colors started to fade. Julia wanted to burst into tears. The disappearing sun seemed to be a metaphor for her heart. Right when she was starting to believe that perhaps love wasn't just a word used in songs, the bright colors faded, and she was left with darkness.

****

Seth opened the door and stepped out into cool air. God willing, he'd never have to go through something like that again. The faces of Doug's parents would stay in his nightmares for a long time. He gazed at the setting sun. Usually, he loved dusk. Loved the colors and the promise of a new day coming. Tonight there was no comfort.

Movement caught his eye, and he turned to see Julia sitting on the top step. Talk about having a bad day. Throughout the afternoon he'd glimpsed Julia off and on. Each time her face had been pinched and her cheeks hollow with tension.

Since misery loved company, he walked over and sat down next to her. "Well, that was awful. I've been on the phone, talking to relatives. Doug's parents are grief-stricken. They can't believe their son did this."

"I guess you don't get many brides left at the altar here."

"Not that I can recall." He reached for her hand and squeezed, his thumb drawing a soothing pattern along her palm. "How are you holding up?"

She glanced down at their intertwined fingers, then back up at him. In that brief instant her eyes shuttered. Retreat... they screamed. Julia swallowed, as if preparing to speak, and Seth fought the urge to clamp a hand over her mouth. Whatever she planned to say, he wasn't going to like it.

"This isn't going to be easy to do with you being so sweet," she said, pulling her hand back.

A vise clamped his heart. "Do what?"

"Doug hurt Noelle because he couldn't face the truth. I don't want to be like him."

"Julia, don't—"

Two fingers pressed against his mouth. "I couldn't live with myself if I hurt you," she said, utter devastation reflected in her blue eyes.

With an impatient flick, he grasped her hand. "What if you didn't hurt me?"

"I'm not sure I could help it."

"When are you going to learn to have faith in yourself?"

Julia laughed, but the sound held no amusement. "Isn't that the issue? My lack of faith? In love, in God, in practically everything you believe? I want—" She took a deep breath, as if trying to hold her emotions in check. "I want you to be happy. You deserve that after everything you've been through. You deserve to have someone who shares your faith and who believes in happily ever after."

"I know you're upset about what happened today."

"No. Well, of course it upset me. I've never had to break someone's heart before, but mainly it reminded me of things I'd let myself forget. It reminded me why it would be such a bad idea to let this thing between us go any further."

"What if I don't agree?"

"I think you should go out with Amy," Julia said in a rush, as if he hadn't even spoken.

Since Seth had been working up to an argument, it took a

second for his brain to catch up. Confusion crowded out his growing panic. "What?"

"You should date Amy."

Shock robbed him of any intelligent thought. "Amy?"

"Amy Vining. You know, the tiny blonde with the habit of dressing like she's going to a sock hop?"

Anger ripped through him as he realized Julia was foisting him off on someone else. "Of *course* I know who Amy is."

"Well, do you know she loves you? That she's wanted to be Mrs. Seth Graham practically since she was born?"

Amy wanted to marry him? "No."

"How could you not know?" she asked in astonishment. "If the girl had a glowing, neon sign that said "I love Seth" blinking on her forehead, she couldn't be more obvious."

"I guess I missed it."

"Clueless, is what you are," she muttered.

Seth bounced up from the step. "Why does it matter?"

"Because I think she'd make a perfect wife for you."

Oh, this got better and better. "You want me to marry her, not just date her?"

"She's beautiful, smart, a great homemaker. Everyone in town loves her. She also shares your faith. That's important. And did I mention she loves you? I mean totally adores and worships you?"

"I think you mentioned that, yes. So, you're saying you want me to date someone else? Marry someone else?"

"I think it's for the best."

Something in the defeated slump of her shoulders told him she was hurting. In her own strange way she was trying to protect him. He tamped down the urge to shake her and instead hunkered down again so he could look her in the eye. "Are you saying this because you're scared?"

"No, I'm saying it because I think it's the right thing to do. Don't you?"

Did he? Hadn't he been telling himself it was foolish to think he and Julia could ever have a relationship? "I don't know. I've never looked at Amy that way."

"Try. Maybe it's time for you to make a fresh start, and I think we both know that isn't with me."

"Are you sure we know that?"

"We should."

If this was so right, why did he want to scream? He bowed his head and rested his cheek on her upraised knees.

Finally, he rocked back on his heels. "You must be exhausted."

A tiny lift of her shoulders was her only answer. He stood up and held out a hand. After a moment's hesitation, she took it. He helped her to her feet. She wouldn't look at him, but stared somewhere over his right shoulder. "I'll see you around, I guess."

A fist lodged in his windpipe. "Right."

"Bye." She turned and walked off toward the parking lot without looking back. Without suddenly changing her mind.

"Bye," he echoed back.

Chapter Eighteen

There's something about hearing about another person's tragedy that makes your own problems seem like mere speed bumps, Julia thought. As she stared at the patch of grass where a man had almost lost his life, Julia told herself she shouldn't feel like every organ in her body had been taken out and pounded into the dust with a sledgehammer. She should be grateful she was whole and healthy.

"So, this is where you want your ceremony?" Julia asked.

Annie Truman turned from her contemplation of the road and smiled. "You still think we're crazy."

"I won't pretend to understand why you'd want to get married where you had your car accident, but if it's what you want—"

"It is."

A shudder worked its way down her spine as Julia surveyed the road again. "It looks so peaceful. I almost can't believe anything happened here."

"Sometimes it feels like it happened to someone else," Annie said. "Of course, in a way it did. Todd and I aren't the same people who drove around this curve that night."

"How did it happen?"

"We'd gone to my sister's birthday party. It had been raining most of the day. It started pouring as we left. My sister asked us to wait it out, but Todd had to be at work early the next morning, and I was tired. So, we started home." Annie pointed straight ahead. "We were coming around the curve here. We'd gone down this stretch of road a million times. Only this time we hit a patch of oil and water."

"That's all it took. A drop of oil." One drop and fates changed.

"Amazing, isn't it?" Annie said, as if reading Julia's mind. "I don't recall much, except looking at Todd and laughing about something that had happened at the party. Then a jolt. The next thing I knew I was coming to in the car, upside down."

"The car flipped over?"

"The police said it looked like we went into a skid, and when the car hit the grass, it flipped. We ended up right where I'm standing." She wrapped her arms around herself, as if to ward off a chill. "I don't remember much else, until I woke up. I do remember looking at Todd. There was so much blood gushing from his head. It was like one of those horror movies."

Julia stared at the grass under her feet, trying to picture the twisted steel. "What about you?"

"I was fine. Barely a scratch on me. I managed to get unhooked from the seatbelt and out of the car. I was trying to get to Todd, when I heard sirens. The person in the car behind us had a cell phone, and he called 911."

"It was lucky help got to you so quickly."

"It was a miracle that other car was out on the road. Anyway, the paramedics cut him out of the car, and they took us to the hospital. Todd went into surgery. He'd sustained pretty massive head injuries."

"He came out of it okay, though?"

"He survived it. Then we had to wait for him to wake up. He was in a coma for over a week. I don't think I moved from his bed the entire time. His doctors kept telling me they didn't know if he would ever wake up or what condition he'd be in if he did."

"I can't imagine."

Annie's lips trembled a little. "I've never felt so helpless. Then one morning I looked over, and he was staring at me. I started screaming, and everyone came running. His parents, my parents, the doctors."

"When did you realize he didn't remember you?"

"A few days later. At first it seemed like everything was fine. He was quiet, especially with me, but we all thought he was in shock. Finally, he asked if I used to sit behind him in biology. He wanted to know why I was always in his room."

"He didn't remember anything?"

Tears formed in Annie's eyes. "He remembered some things. His childhood. His parents and his brother and sister. In fact, the only thing that seemed to be affected was the last few years. All the years we'd been together. He didn't remember dating, falling in love, getting engaged. It was like I'd been extracted from his mind."

"Yet you stayed with him."

"I didn't have a choice," Annie said, with a soft smile. "I still loved Todd. I told him I was his fiancée, and he seemed to accept it. He asked endless questions. He wanted to know how we'd met, where we'd gone on dates. The food I liked, the books I read. We went on dates, and I took him to every place we'd ever been to together."

"Were you hoping he'd improve?"

"Maybe at first, but nothing sparked a memory. Pretty soon I decided we would have to make new ones. We literally had to fall in love all over again."

"Just like that?" Julia asked in amazement. "Snap your fingers and hope magic strikes twice? Weren't you angry? You had this incredible relationship. Your future was bright. Then in an instant it was gone."

"I could have been angry, I guess. In the end, I figured this was the first big test in our relationship. I was going to make a lifelong commitment in front of God. "In sickness and in health". Seemed like we'd gotten a head start on that part."

"You're amazing."

Annie held up a hand and laughed. "Don't go giving me any medals. Trust me, there were moments when I despaired. When I looked in Todd's eyes and saw that empty stare, I wanted to scream and cry."

"What kept you hanging on?"

"Faith. I knew that everything would turn out the way it was supposed to."

"Even if it meant Todd never learned to love you again?"

"Even then. Thank God I never had to find out, though. Pretty soon, our outings weren't history lessons. They became real dates. About nine months later, Todd asked me to take him to the place where he'd proposed."

"Which was?"

"It was at the spring carnival, which didn't happen to be up and running that night." Annie laughed at the memory. "I told him it would be an empty field of grass, but he didn't care. When we got there, he'd had a table-for-two set up. We ate dinner under the moonlight while a string quartet played."

Julia got goose bumps. "Nice touch."

A dreamy smile swept over Annie's face. A couple months ago such an expression would have made Julia cringe. Now she felt like going all dreamy, too.

"It was better than nice," Annie said. "And when we were finishing dessert, he reached over and took my hand. He told me he didn't remember what he'd said or what he'd felt the last time he asked me to marry him. He only knew I'd become the center of his new world. Then he tugged the engagement ring from my finger and asked if I'd accept it again."

That settled it. Julia had officially become a watering pot. She wiped a tear from her cheek. "That may be the best proposal I've ever heard."

Annie looked over and chuckled. "Sorry. I always forget my story makes people go weepy."

"No, it's fine. I'm starting to think I'm overdue for some emotion in my life."

Annie regarded Julia with an intense stare. "Why do I get the feeling you've got a good story, too?"

"It's far from good," Julia said, with a dismissive wave. "In fact, it would only depress you, and right now we need to concentrate on your wedding day and the life you're going have after it."

The mention of the wedding was more than enough to distract Annie from probing further. Almost enough to distract Julia from a certain minister who had turned her whole world upside down.

Chapter Nineteen

Had Julia known pinning down the final decisions on the flowers for the wedding-that-would-destroy-her-sanity was going to be so painful, she would've stabbed herself in the eye with a thorn and begged out of the appointment altogether.

The wedding date for Laurel Manning's nuptials was sliding ever closer, and that meant Mrs. Manning was becoming more belligerent than usual, which was saying something. At any moment Julia expected the woman to start shouting "off with their heads."

Compounding her misery was the fact that Julia was so lost when it came to flowers. And again, that was saying something. Colors she could fake her way through. Food was a piece of cake. Flowers left her in a state of utter confusion, which was depressing because after all, it was *flowers*.

Julia could identify roses and daisies, and if pressed, she was pretty sure she would recognize baby's breath. Beyond those basics, forget it.

There are like a million different kinds of bouquets. Not just flowers, but the way they were arranged. Julia recognized a regular old classic bouquet. Her boss's daughter had one of the flowing, waterfall-looking ones, which the florist had called a cascade. There was something called a beidermeier, which Julia could barely pronounce, let alone figure out what it was, plus composites and nosegays. Each one of those has about fifty million varieties.

And that was only for the bride's bouquet.

They also needed bouquets for the bridesmaids and three flower girls, corsages for the moms, boutonnieres for the groomsmen, and centerpieces for thirty-one guest tables, the cake table, and the buffet tables. The fun didn't stop there, either. They also needed huge arrangements for the dais where the ceremony would take place, as well as the aisles and the reception area. The list went on and on. Julia suspected the Manning wedding was using every flower in the entire state of Georgia for the occasion.

The monumental task of choosing flowers had gotten off the ground with Sarah's help, but now it was up to Julia to take the planning the last forty yards to the end zone. After what seemed like hours of bruising combat, Julia managed to get Mrs. Manning to decide what *she* thought Laurel would like for the wedding.

After that endless bit of fun, Julia raced across town for a fitting, followed by a visit to the zoo to check out a site for another wedding. Apparently the couple met while gazing at the monkeys, and it was love at first sight. Then a trip to the printer to correct an invitation that asked guests to witness the union of *Horror* James and Brent Carlson.

By the end of the day, Julia had reached and surpassed her capacity for dealing with nuptial bliss. So, when the phone rang at her desk in the cave Betsy liked to call an office, Julia's whole body tensed.

"Hello," she said, hoping it was a heavy breather or someone asking if her refrigerator was running. Anything but a hysterical bride… or her equally hysterical mother.

"Julia?"

"Yes?"

"It's Meredith Vining."

Relief flooded through her. "Meredith… hi. What's up?"

"My fiancé had to go out of town, and I hope you won't be offended that I'm calling because I'm lonely and don't feel like eating alone."

"I'm not offended, and I could use a night out," Julia said. "My life seems to consist solely of endless lists and vegging in front of the TV at the end of the day in a stupor."

Laughter flooded across the line. "Great. Why don't we splurge and go for something a little more fancy than The Old Diner?" Meredith said. "Meet me at *Bon Appétit* at seven."

An hour later Julia pulled into the parking lot of the restaurant. Covington Falls wasn't terribly original, so they'd named their one and only French restaurant *Bon Appétit*. The food was good, even if the name made Julia want to roll her eyes. She'd only eaten here once, when her father took the whole family to dinner for Grace's birthday.

Of course he'd left two months later, so maybe the grand gesture had been more out of guilt than affection.

The restaurant was intimate, with linen-covered tables, delicate white floral centerpieces, and tall white candles. The walls were covered in silk tapestries, painted with what she guessed were supposed to be bucolic scenes of the French countryside.

Meredith was already seated at the table. She jumped up, and they hugged. "I feel like one of those girls who only deigns to acknowledge her friends when she's between boyfriends."

"I hope that's not a telling sign of your relationship," Julia said, as she sat down.

"No, Brian and I are fine. Although, I'm a little amazed at myself because apparently I can no longer function when we're apart."

"I can't imagine being that dependent on a man."

Meredith's voice lowered. "Truthfully, I'm starting to like it."

Julia shuddered at the thought. "You like losing your independence?"

"I'm not losing anything. It's safe in a way, needing someone. Knowing I don't have to do it all alone anymore. I may have found that in a faith sort-of-way, but it's nice to have found it in another person, too."

"Whatever you say." Julia unfolded her napkin with a snap and spread it across her lap.

Meredith grinned. "Wow, you are a tough nut. I had no idea your cynicism ran so deep. I—" She froze and her mouth dropped open like a fish after it had been caught.

"What—" Julia asked, even as she swiveled her head around to see what had caused such a strange reaction.

Her gaze collided with Seth's. He looked a lot like the fish Meredith was currently portraying, eyes wide, mouth slightly agape. Julia's insides twisted as she looked to the left and focused on the person with him. The *woman* with him. Seems he'd taken her advice, because clinging to his arm was none other than Amy Vining. She looked like she'd been named queen for the day. Her smile could've led ships to shore on a stormy night.

Amy had spotted them, too, and her smile grew even wider. She turned and touched Seth's shoulder before drifting across the dining room, her feet barely touching the floor. Seth watched the progression like a man witnessing a horrific accident.

Meredith still hadn't recovered the power of speech so it was up to Julia to make intelligent conversation.

Fortunately for all of them, Amy had all her faculties under control. "I can not believe we ran into you two like this."

"You're here on a date?" Meredith managed to gasp out.

"I know. Our first," Amy said, her peal of laughter

sounding like delicate wind chimes. "I was starting to despair that Seth would ever see me, but I think he does now." She threw a look over her shoulder and waggled her fingers.

Seth waved back, but his expression remained frozen.

"Well, that's nice," Julia said, hoping she would recover some brain function soon.

Back at ground zero, the hostess approached Seth. Amy flipped her hair behind her shoulder. "I think our table's ready. See you later."

Julia forced herself to watch the hostess lead the happy couple to a table no more than twenty feet away. Told herself she should be happy he had asked Amy out.

The waiter appeared and placed a basket of warm rolls on the table. "Can I get you something to drink?"

"Something strong," Meredith muttered.

The waiter inclined his head. "Excuse me, Ma'am?"

"We'll have iced tea for now," Julia said.

As soon as the waiter left, Meredith grabbed one of the rolls and tore it into two thick chunks. "I'm not sure I'll ever recover from this."

"What's so bad about it?" Julia asked, watching her new friend mutilate the bread.

"Are you kidding?" Meredith shoved a bite into her mouth and chomped aggressively. "I'll never hear the end of it now. Amy and my mother will be picking out china patterns within the week."

China patterns? They'd have to be flowery.

"It's only one date," Julia said.

Meredith tore the roll again. "No, no, no. It's the hand of destiny."

"I thought God was the one in charge of destiny?"

"God. Destiny. Whatever," Meredith said, waving the roll in the air. "It's happening, and now I'll have to listen to my mother trumpet how the great dynasty is about to come to fruition every waking hour of the day."

Julia started playing with her silverware, swirling the fork in a figure eight pattern on the tablecloth. "It might not be so bad."

"Trust me, it'll be bad."

"She might make him happy."

Meredith paused mid-chew. "You actually seem in favor of this. Why? I didn't think you liked my sister."

"I don't *dislike* her," Julia said, doing her best to remain completely logical and unemotional. "Amy's been helping out at Marry Me, and she's a dynamo. She knows how to make boutonnieres with that green tape. She knows where to find a guy who makes ice sculptures. She even knows where to find doves."

Meredith's nose wrinkled. "Doves?"

"Catherine Manning wants doves for Laurel's wedding. Amy found a guy who wrangles them."

"I didn't know there was such a thing as a dove wrangler."

"Me either, but your sister did."

Meredith started on a second roll. "Okay, so my sister can plan a wedding, but I'm not sure that translates to her being good for Seth."

"Why wouldn't she be?" Julia asked, hoping her new friend could supply the answer. "Amy's a born homemaker. She shares Seth's faith. She runs the Sunday school program."

"There's more to marriage than being Susie Homemaker."

"I know, but she seems like a good match for him."

"You actually believe that?"

"I hope so, especially since I suggested he should ask her out."

The gaping fish mouth returned. "You did what?"

Julia wished she could plunge a knife in her chest. "I told him she'd been in love with him forever, and he should ask her out because she'd make a much better minister's wife than—" She snapped her mouth shut before she revealed too much.

Meredith noticed the hesitation. "Better than whom?"

"Anyone."

"Is there a specific anyone, or just anyone in general?"

Julia twirled her water glass, making the ice clink against the side. "Okay, hypothetically speaking, what if the anyone was me?"

It took a moment for her meaning to sink in. When it did, Meredith practically fell out of her chair. "You and Seth?"

"I said hypothetically."

"Fine, hypothetically," Meredith said, willing to allow Julia a last vestige of subterfuge if it meant getting to the meat of the story. "But you and Seth?"

Perhaps *she* could fall out her chair and disappear. "Maybe."

Meredith leaned across the table, like a white-haired, old biddy gossiping over the fence. "Since when?"

"Since I came back."

Ever since that day in the park when an orchestra had started playing as Seth was walking across the softball field.

Shock reflected on Meredith's face as she sat back. "I can't believe it."

"Look, it's nothing," Julia said, trying to dismiss the whole subject. "It's a weird attraction that neither of us expected, but we both know it would be a mistake to let it become anything else."

"I'm not so sure you and Seth getting together would be the worst thing that could ever happen."

"Have you ever thought of him in a romantic sense?"

An expression of abject horror passed over Meredith's face. "It'd be too much like dating my brother."

"Exactly, and I'm pretty sure it would end badly."

"Is that why you threw my sister at him?"

"It wasn't *throwing*. It was a suggestion. I honestly think she would make a better wife for him."

"I'm not so sure. Amy's acting based on a crush that she developed as a kid. She doesn't love Seth. She's in love with the *idea* of him, and the perfect version she's created in her mind. She'll smother him with those expectations."

Julia's eyes drifted across the room, and her gaze collided with Seth's again. Of course the waiter would sit them directly in her line of sight. She couldn't look away, and he sent her a little quirky smile, as if to say, *this was your idea.*

Julia tore her gaze away. "I hope you're wrong," she told Meredith. "In any case, it's too late now."

****

"Seth, did you hear me?"

Seth jerked his gaze away from the copper-colored curls across the room. He tried to focus on his... date. He stifled a groan. Great, he couldn't even *think* the word without his brain stumbling. A date. He was out on a date. For the first time since college. With Amy Vining of all people. How had this happened?

"Seth?"

"Yes?" he said, coming to attention.

Amy's eyes widened at his sharp tone. "I asked what looked good to you?"

Take a deep breath and calm down. "Oh. Umm... I don't know yet."

Grateful for any excuse to gather his wildly scattered thoughts, Seth escaped into the menu. Words swam in front of his eyes. He had to concentrate... and not on the woman across the way. He had to do this. The dating thing. With someone he might actually have a future with. Just his luck to pick the same restaurant where Julia was also having dinner. And to have her seated within his line of sight. All he had to do was let his eyes drift a little to the left and...

Stop it, Seth. Date. Amy. Try.

The waitress appeared and took their orders. Amy then launched into a recital about her day.

"So I called about a thirty different florists all over the state looking for purple daffodils…" Amy gabbed.

Julia had been hunting for purple daffodils the other night when he'd surprised her.

"…finally found one that specializes in special crossbred flowers, and they had them…"

Julia in a temper was something else.

"You wouldn't believe how demanding people can be. I'm sure I'll never be like that when I finally get married, now that I know what it's like on the other side."

Seth was glad to see her with Meredith, though. Julia could use a real friend.

"Don't you think so?" Amy asked, tapping his hand.

There he went again. "Hmm? Oh, right. I agree."

"Of course you do," Amy said, with a pleased smiled. "How could you not?"

What was she talking about? Why couldn't he stay focused? Here he was having dinner with a beautiful, intelligent, sweet woman. A woman like Beth in a lot of ways, which is why he'd finally worked up the courage to call Amy. They had things in common. Similar backgrounds. Shared values. A devotion to the Lord. *Blah, blah, blah.*

Stop it.

Shared beliefs were important in a relationship. He counseled couples in crisis. He'd seen the problems that erupted between people who had different core beliefs. Not just about religion, but about how to handle money, raise kids, family traditions the other didn't understand. Things that started out as little annoyances could escalate into World War III.

He'd finally faced the fact that he wasn't buried in the ground with Beth, though there'd been days when he'd wished he was. He couldn't hole himself up in Grace's garage apartment forever. He needed companionship. A physical connection to a woman. He needed a wife.

Amy seemed willing to step into the role. More than willing. In fact, he had the feeling that if he asked her to marry him right now she'd say yes and call someone to perform the ceremony within the hour. That kind of eagerness was a little daunting for a guy who was only testing the dating waters again. He was content to stick a toe in, while Amy seemed ready to go scuba diving.

Regardless, Seth owed it to himself to make an effort. He needed to stop putting up roadblocks before he'd given Amy a chance. Before giving himself a chance to find out if shared values trumped sizzling chemistry. To see if any woman would have lit the spark of his long-deprived love life.

Or if only the flame-haired woman across the restaurant could.

Chapter Twenty

After spending a few nights tossing and turning because of images of Seth and Amy cuddling in front of a fire dancing through her brain, Julia needed a distraction. Any distraction. Since weddings were the only thing in her life, one of those would have to do. Two weddings answered the need even better.

Yeah, some demented soul had gone and scheduled two weddings in one day. The knowledge that she had the power to screw up *two* couples' nuptials served to wipe all thoughts of pesky romantic entanglements from Julia's mind.

Compounding the anxiety for the day was the fact that she'd managed to lose both folders containing the information on the weddings. No more little diagrams with the squares and circles and the little yellow triangles. So, she was literally flying blind in a hailstorm.

Couple #1. Robin Sutcliff and Joe Bremmer. About the only thing Julia remembered from the missing file was the wedding was taking place out by Lake Rice. There was a picturesque pagoda on the north shore, a popular spot for weddings she'd been told.

The other fact lodged in her memory was that the ceremony started at eleven. Bleary-eyed from lack of sleep, Julia arrived at the lake as the sun began to peak over the horizon. Someone had beaten her to the venue, however. Amy was already standing in front of the pagoda directing the set up of chairs for the ceremony. Today, she'd exchanged her usual flowery dress with a decidedly feminine, but professional powder-blue suit.

"We need twelve rows, ten chairs across, five on each side of the aisle," Amy said, directing the guy who'd delivered the chairs. "Don't forget, there should be exactly eighteen inches between each chair."

Julia saluted with her free hand. "Good morning, General Vining."

Amy spun around, her mouth forming a perfect "O" of surprise, like a five-year-old who'd gotten caught with her hand in the cookie jar.

"Are you going to take out a ruler and make sure they follow the 18-inch guidelines?" Julia asked.

Amy flushed and Julia had to admire how truly adorable General Dynamo looked doing it. On the rare occasions when Julia blushed, she got all mottled and blotchy like she'd developed some sort of communicable disease.

"I've done it again, haven't I?" Amy asked. "I got here, and no one was around. Then the workers arrived, and it seemed—"

"I'm not mad," Julia said, holding up her hand to forestall the sputtering explanation.

Amy sighed in relief. "Oh, good."

"Is Betsy here yet?"

A delicate, blond eyebrow arched. "She's at the second site, meeting the caterers. We talked about this on Thursday. Since we have so little time between the two weddings, we decided to send her over to get things started."

Right. The clue helped jog her memory somewhat. "Of

course, I'm so out of whack this morning. I somehow misplaced both files for the weddings today."

"You lost the files?"

"I didn't *lose* them," Julia said through clenched teeth. "I'm sure they're somewhere in the back office. It'll be fine, though. I'm pretty sure I can remember enough to get by."

Amy patted Julia on the back. "You don't have to worry. I've got the plans."

Don't maim the assistant. "You have the files? Why didn't you say so?"

"I don't have them physically, but I read through them the other day," Amy said. "I know what they said."

"You know all the plans off the top of your head? Do you have a photographic memory or something?"

Amy flashed a no-irony-whatsoever smile and nodded. "Yes, so you rest easy. I'll take care of everything."

"Of course you will," Julia muttered, thinking she might have been better served to play hooky and go to a movie.

She's a robot, Julia thought. A cute, smart, perky, robot.

Amy beamed. "All you have to do is follow my lead, boss."

True to her word, Amy remembered every single detail about Wedding #1. Wedding #2, as well.

Before long the pretty lakeside vista had been transformed, and people were starting to arrive. The ushers were seating the guests, while the groom stayed out of sight behind some bushes. Since dressing rooms were not part of the lakeside décor, the bridal party planned to arrive in limos right before the ceremony. A fact Amy had reminded Julia about after she panicked because the bride hadn't arrived yet, and had a horrible flashback of the last disastrous wedding with the cold-feet groom.

Exactly fifteen minutes before the ceremony was to begin, two limos pulled up. Girls started pouring out, like overdressed clowns spilling out of a circus car. The bride emerged last. In the morning sun her white dress gleamed bright enough hurt your eyes.

Amy had gone with the caterer to supervise the final setup of the reception area, so Julia greeted the new arrivals.

The bride's smile flashed almost as brilliant as her dress. "Julia, is everything ready? Is Joe here?"

"Hi, Robin. Everything is perfect, and yes, Joe's here. He's waiting behind those bushes over there," she said, pointing across the way.

"I can't believe this is happening," Robin let out a tremulous giggle.

Frankly, Julia couldn't believe it either. Robin and Joe looked like they shouldn't even be driving on their own, let alone be getting married. They were, in fact, nineteen, which didn't seem much better. Julia supposed the trend of putting off marriage till later in life hadn't swept through Covington Falls the way it had in the rest of the country.

Julia didn't have time to dwell on Robin and Joe's youth because the string quartet started processional music. Julia remembered this part from the rehearsal at least. The mothers were seated. Then the bridesmaids made their way down the aisle.

Finally, only Robin and her father were left. "You ready, Robin?"

Robin beamed and nodded.

"Umm… you're not allergic to bees are you?" Julia asked.

"No, why?" Robin asked, with a puzzled frown.

"It's something I feel I should ask for an outdoor wedding."

"Oh, right, because of what happened at Lisa's wedding," Robin said, with an amused huff. "No worries. I'm not allergic to anything."

"Okay then, let's get you hitched."

The processional began, and Robin floated down the aisle on her father's arm. Julia breathed a sigh of relief. Another successful launch. Of course, they weren't out of the woods yet, but at this point she considered both parties showing up on the big day a success. Almost any other problem could be solved.

The minister went right to the vows. Julia drifted closer so she could hear their soft replies. Rings were exchanged, and the minister asked everyone to bow their heads. Prayer commenced. Julia kept her eyes open, mostly because she had an irrational fear that something disastrous might occur if she looked away for even a second.

She glanced toward the groom and something about him made her pause. He looked strange. Then he began to sway in a slow circle. Before Julia had a chance to move, Joe's legs buckled, and he fell in an ungraceful heap, pulling Robin to the ground with him.

Instantly, the guests surged to their feet. Julia started running and managed to push her way through the crowd.

Robin lay in a heap on top of Joe, her wedding dress billowing around them. "Joe! Joe!" she cried, shaking him like a rag doll.

"I think he's fainted," one of the groomsman said. "I told him not to close his eyes when we prayed."

Julia reared around to look at him. "You're not supposed to close your eyes? I thought that was one of the rules of prayer."

"Not when you're standing up. You start swaying and boom."

"Boom?"

"Boom. Happened to a buddy of mine at his wedding."

This was a new one to her. "Who knew praying could be a hazard to your health?"

Now that Julia felt sure she wouldn't need to treat anaphylactic shock again, she took a deep breath.

"Robin, you have to get up," Julia said, tugging on the bride's arm. The girl hung on like a baby monkey clinging to its mamma. "Someone help her."

Hands reached out and lifted the panicked bride off the ground. Julia knelt down next to Joe. By now he'd started to groan a little. She slapped his cheeks to get him to come around. If Betsy were here she would've already produced some smelling salts. Someone else lifted his legs. It was the groomsman who'd warned against eyes-closed praying.

"This will get the blood flowing back," the groomsman explained. "He'll come around in a sec."

"Are you a doctor?" Julia asked.

He shook his head. "No, but there was a nurse at my friend's wedding, and this is what she did."

Whether it was the slapping or the raised legs, the groom seemed to be coming around. Joe looked up in confusion.

"Hey, Joe," Julia said. "Welcome back."

"Where am I?"

Robin wrenched free from whoever had pulled her away. "Joe! Joe! Are you all right? Talk to me."

"Robin, give him a little room to breathe," Julia said, holding the bride back. "He just fainted."

Joe blinked. "I did?"

"Afraid so," Julia said. "Can you stand up?"

An embarrassed groan escaped him. "Can't I stay right here?"

Julia grinned down at him. "While I sympathize, no. I've got a busy schedule. Besides, Robin is here in the dress, and think of all the deposits you'll forfeit if you lie here all day."

"You're heartless," he said, eyes narrowing.

"No, I'm a realist. Just pretend you got knocked out playing football, and when you stand up everyone will clap and cheer."

"Let me try," Robin said. She leaned toward him and stroked his cheek. "Joe, sweetie, please get up. You're scaring me."

Joe popped up to a sitting position in an instant. "All

right, honey."

Robin beamed, and Joe gave a sheepish smile.

"I guess sweet does work on occasion," Julia said, acknowledging Robin's supremacy in groom handling.

Several groomsmen helped Joe to his feet. Julia looked around at the crowd of anxious faces. "Okay, everyone, drama's over. We've got a wedding to finish. Reverend, I think you were right at the part where he gets to kiss the bride?"

The minister took the hint and nodded. The guests returned to their seats, and Robin and Joe took their places again.

Julia went back to her position. Amy had returned, and she looked shaken and pale.

"You look worse than the groom," Julia said.

Amy's curls practically quivered with horror. "I don't deal well with illness."

Ah ha! A kink in Amy's armor! The cute robot fell apart in a crisis.

"You don't?" Julia asked, hoping the question came out curious and not gleeful.

"I fell off a swing when I was six and got this huge gash in my forehead. Blood everywhere," Amy said, as sweat broke out on her upper lip. "Now I can't stand the sight of it."

Julia managed not to pump her fists in the air in triumph. Instead, she patted Amy on the shoulder. "Don't worry, Amy, you let me take of everything."

****

With the threat of blood loss over, Amy returned to her normal self, so Julia felt safe leaving her assistant in charge while she went to help Betsy with the preparations for the next wedding.

Couple #2. Kelly Brown and Kevin McCormack. This ceremony would take place at Christ Memorial Church, which boasted a façade of grey stone with stately, stone columns and a huge set of oak double doors. A tall steeple reached high into the sky, and inside bells chimed out hymns at noon and six.

Thankfully for Julia's sanity, the reception would be held in the fellowship hall behind the sanctuary. Speaking of the sanctuary, her second miracle worker, Betsy, had already managed to finish the preparations in there. So, Julia made her way over to the fellowship hall, where Betsy stood directing half a dozen people as they scurried about.

Two women were draping yards of pale peach and white satin cloth around the perimeter of the room. Potted trees filled with a million little white lights twinkled merrily. Round tables with white tablecloths were complemented by chairs covered in white satin. Several longer tables were set up for a buffet, and in the corner Julia spotted Audrey Sampson assembling the wedding cake.

Julia put her arm around Betsy's shoulder. "I'm not sure I'm needed here at all."

"Hi." Betsy said, smiling in her enthusiastic way. "How did it go with Robin and Joe?"

"Did you know you're not supposed to close your eyes if you're standing up while the prayer is going on?"

Of course Betsy nodded. "Sure, you get disoriented and faint."

"Well, clearly our groom didn't get the memo on that rule."

Betsy's eyes nearly bugged out of her head. "No. He didn't?"

"Two sways and over he went. Took Robin down with him, which was probably a good thing because I think the dress cushioned the fall."

"Julia, you're terrible," Betsy said, with a light chuckle. "Where is Amy?"

"She'll be here soon. I left her in charge of wrapping things up. She was a lifesaver today. Somehow I managed to misplace the folders for today's weddings, but Amy memorized them in one read-through. You didn't happen to see the files, did you?"

Betsy's nose wrinkled in consternation as she shook her head. "Not since before the rehearsal."

"How did you know what to do here then?"

"I read the files."

"Don't tell me you have a photographic memory, too? If so, I may as well hand the business over to you and Amy and be done with it."

"I read the file, and *then* made notes." Betsy held up a sheet of paper, on which she had covered every available surface with scribbles, notes and little diagrams.

Julia stared at the paper in wonder. "You got all the information for the entire wedding on one sheet?"

"It's easier than carrying that big file folder around all day," Betsy said. "I know Sarah swears by them, but I usually can't make head or tails of all the notes she puts in there."

"You don't happen to know what those little yellow triangles mean, do you?"

Betsy's nose crinkled again. "Huh?"

"Never mind," Julia said, on a sigh. "Let's get this party started."

****

An hour later, Julia stood at the back of the church organizing the second procession down the aisle. Betsy, taking a break from the action in the fellowship hall, had come over to witness the ceremony. Amy stood by to help supervise... *Julia.*

Kelly Brown had to be the least agitated bride-to-be Julia had ever met. Calm made for a nice change of course, but the nothing-phases-me vibe struck Julia as weird. Unless it was chemically induced. Julia didn't have much experience in matrimonial matters, but it seemed unnatural to be so calm and collected when you were about to shackle yourself to someone for the rest of your life.

"You ready?" Julia asked, as she adjusted Kelly's veil one more time.

Kelly flashed an earthquake-could-strike-and-I-wouldn't-panic smile. "I've been ready all my life."

"Just don't close your eyes when the minister prays."

"Huh?"

Julia patted Kelly's cheek. "Eyes open at all times. Trust me."

One more askance look. "O… kay."

"Right then, let's go."

Kelly took her father's arm, and they were off. Julia held her breath the entire ceremony, alert for any signs of swaying or falling. She had just started to relax when she realized Kelly had begun to fidget. Anyone else, and Julia wouldn't have noticed, but Miss Self-Possessed didn't fidget.

Suddenly, Kelly squealed and whipped off her veil. "My nose! Not now!"

Julia had no idea what "my nose" meant, but she started running anyway, with Amy and Betsy not far behind. By now, Kelly had her head tipped back, while the groom held her up.

"What's wrong?" Julia asked.

"Nose bleed," Kelly answered, only her words came out sounding like "ose weed" since her fingers were pinching the aforementioned nose.

"What did she say?" Amy asked, hovering over Julia's right shoulder.

"I think she's got a nose bleed," Julia said.

"Blood? Oh, dear…"

Before Julia could move, Amy pulled a *Joe* and fainted dead away. For a moment Julia stared down at her fallen assistant. Seemed Amy's phobia about blood was real after all. Everyone screamed. Correction, one scream pierced through the confusion.

"Amy! Oh, darling! Amy, talk to me!"

Julia recognized the shrill tone, and in the next moment, Mrs. Vining emerged from the crowd and knelt on the floor next to her prostrate daughter. Meanwhile, the leaking bride continued pinching her nose.

Mrs. Vining looked around, her eyes wild with panic. "Someone call an ambulance!"

She could not be serious. "Ma'am, I think Amy fainted," Julia said, in her most reasonable manner.

"Are you a doctor now, as well as an incompetent wedding planner?" Mrs. Vining asked, eyes blazing with fury.

Well, now Julia knew where Amy had learned that laser-of-death stare. Julia touched a hand to her forehead, feeling for a giant, gaping hole. "No, but I think she fainted because of Kelly's nose bleed."

"Amy hates blood."

"Hence the fainting," Julia said, not even attempting to soften her sarcasm any longer.

"You can't leave her here like this," Mrs. Vining cried.

Control urge to throttle assistant's mother. "I wouldn't dream of it. Someone get a glass of water for my assistant!" Julia called out to the crowd in general. "And a towel before the bride drips all over her dress!"

Kelly squealed again. "My wess!"

Like magic, a cup and a towel appeared. Julia didn't have to look to know the magician was Betsy.

"Betsy, you get two gold stars today," Julia said. "No, make that three."

"This is unbelievable," Betsy said, swiping the hair back from her forehead.

"No kidding."

Betsy replaced Kelly's fingers with the towel, while Mrs. Brown held a second towel under her daughter's chin to make sure nothing got on her gown.

"Keep her head back," Mrs. Brown said. "The bleeding usually stops in a few minutes."

"Usually?" Julia asked. "You mean this has happened before?"

"I abways get ose weeds en I'm nerbous," Kelly mumbled around the towel.

Julia looked at the bride's Mom in confusion. "My baby is unflappable, but when she does get nervous or stressed out, it shows up in her nose," Mrs. Brown explained. "Or drips out of it."

"Bom!" Kelly howled in outraged embarrassment.

Mrs. Brown shrugged. "It's not like it's a big secret now, dear. Hush and keep your head back."

"I think I need to get a medical degree to do this job," Julia muttered.

"An EMT license at the very least," Betsy said, as she fanned their fallen comrade.

The two women looked at each other, laughter gleaming in their eyes.

Still chuckling, Julia glanced back down at Kelly. Then she froze as a new thought entered her mind.

A crazy, are-you-kidding-me, can't-be-possible thought.

Because somehow, in the midst of all the disasters and the craziness, Julia had actually started having fun.

Chapter Twenty-One

Seth tried not to flinch as the next person in the greeting line grasped his hand and squeezed like he was trying to juice an orange. George Benson came from the firm-handshake-shows-them-you're-a-man school of thought.

"Good sermon today, Reverend," George murmured.

Mr. Benson lumbered past, and Seth flexed his fingers in an attempt to get circulation back. He reached for the hand of the woman behind George and shivered. Did Mrs. Collinski stick her hand in a bucket of ice before she came to church?

Rupert Brown's beefy palm never failed to offer up clammy sweat. And Seth had seen little Leslie Peterson swipe a hand across her runny nose before she took *his* hand.

Ah, the hazards of the reception line. He wouldn't give up the moment, though. Often these short exchanges were the only time he spoke to many in his congregation.

A finger jabbed into his shoulder. He turned to find Meredith Vining behind him, with her arms folded.

"Ouch," he said.

Meredith's expression didn't lighten one bit. "Were you planning on telling me about the Session meeting?"

His smile dipped. "How did you find out?"

"Seriously? With the way gossip flies around here?" Meredith asked, with a delicate snort. "My mother found out from Mrs. Kramer, who found out from Mrs. Williams, who was told by Mrs. Donaldson, whose husband told her there was a meeting to discuss me."

"Let's not add more kindling to the gossip fire," Seth said as he glanced around the foyer. "I'm almost done here. Why don't you wait for me in my office?"

"Fine." At least Meredith seemed willing to hold off killing him.

A few minutes later Seth walked into his office and found Meredith and Brian waiting for him.

"Thought I'd keep you two company," Brian said, holding out a hand. "No need to start a different kind of rumor for the biddies."

Seth acknowledged his friend's wisdom with a quick bow. "Right."

Meredith didn't want to talk about gossipmongers anymore. "So? Were you going to tell me what's been happening? Or was I supposed to find out after I'd lost my job?"

"Do you two want to sit?" Seth gestured to the two leather-backed chairs.

"No thanks," Meredith said. "I'd like to stand so I can see the knife coming at my back."

"That's pretty harsh, Mer," Brian said. "I'm sure Seth is doing what he can."

Seth was grateful for his friend's cooler head. Especially when Meredith let out a gust of air and sank into a chair. "I know, sorry," she said. "I'm just upset."

Brian lowered himself into the one next to her. "Seth knows that."

A warning glance from Meredith's beloved told Seth he'd better understand. Since he liked seeing two of his oldest friends display such obvious devotion after a long struggle back to one another, Seth didn't take offense.

"I do know," Seth said, leaning against the corner of his desk. "It's okay, and I'm sorry you had to find out about this through the grapevine. The meeting only became official last night. I kept hoping I could head off a confrontation."

"You still should have said something," Meredith said.

"Perhaps, but I didn't want to upset you if there was no cause."

A single dark brow flew up in astonishment. "No cause? A group of people in my church wants to get rid of me. That's cause enough, even without an official meeting. How do you think it makes me feel knowing half the people out there want me banished?"

"It's not half."

"How many is it?"

"I'm not sure. I do know there are just as many who love what you've brought to the service."

"Are they counted among the Session?" Meredith asked doubtfully. "Most of them have been around forever. They're pretty old-school."

"I think they're split on the issue. Which is why we're having the meeting."

Meredith's eyes filled. "This is all my fault. If I hadn't been such a know-it-all hothead, running off with the first guy to strum a guitar they wouldn't—"

Brian reached for her hand. "You made mistakes. We've all done stupid things in our past. You've made your peace with God now."

"Brian's right," Seth said. "None of us are perfect. You've turned everything around. If I didn't have complete faith in you, I never would have hired you. I know where your heart is."

Meredith turned watery eyes his way. "You went out on a limb for me, and now you're in trouble. I never wanted you to catch heat for my sake."

"I can take it."

"But you shouldn't have to. You could lose your job." She took a deep breath, planted her hands on her knees, and stood up. "I'll quit."

Despite the tense situation, Seth couldn't help but chuckle at her willingness to martyr herself on his behalf. "Take it easy. You don't need to throw yourself on the pyre just yet. I don't intend for either of us to lose our jobs."

"How do you plan on pulling off this feat?" Meredith asked, fists braced on her hips.

"As a wise woman suggested, I'm going to knock some heads together," Seth said. "Remind them about the dangers of throwing stones."

"I like that idea," Brian said.

"Go on the offensive?" Meredith asked, eying him with curiosity. "That's not like you. Who suggested it?"

Why had he mentioned that? "No one in particular."

Meredith sniffed. "I know Amy would never give that advice. My dear sister would probably tell you to do the firing yourself."

"It was Julia, all right?"

"You told *her*?" Meredith asked, eyes wide in astonishment.

"Now don't get offended," Seth said. "I didn't plan on telling her. I went for a walk after I found out about the push to oust you, and I ended up at Marry Me."

Brian waggled his eyebrows. "By accident, huh?"

"Yes as a matter of fact."

Meredith wasn't the least offended. In fact, she flashed a huge grin. "And ended up telling her by accident, too?"

"Yes. I think I just needed an outside perspective. Someone who wasn't so close to the situation."

Meredith and Brian looked at each other and chuckled like they had a big secret. Brian rose to his feet. "Of course you did."

"Makes sense to me," Meredith said.

Seth glared at them both. "The two of you can stop with those grins. I know what you're thinking. So what if I confided in Julia. We *are* friends, you know."

"We didn't say anything," Brian said.

"I think it's nice you have someone to confide in," Meredith said. Then she sobered. "I also think it's nice that you want to defend me. You don't have to. I won't die if I can't have this job. If it's going to cause a rift in the church I'll go."

"No. I'm going to take care of this. We need you here. Some people need to be reminded about the power of grace. I plan to make them remember."

Meredith shook her head and let out another sputtering laugh. "Okay, Sir Knight. Thank you," she said, throwing her arms around his neck.

"We'll both be fine," Seth said, hoping it was true.

Drawing back, Meredith patted his cheek. "Go get 'em tiger."

They all shook hands, and Brian turned to leave, but Meredith hesitated.

"Something else on your mind?" Seth asked.

Meredith looked at the floor, and then back at him. "Have you told Amy about my situation?"

"No," he said, wondering what one thing had to do with the other.

An intense stare followed as she shook her head. "I see."

That boy-are-you-blind look set off warning bells. "You see what?"

"Have you asked yourself why you sought out Julia?" Meredith asked, still regarding him as if seeking an answer to a different question.

A spark of temper lit within him. "I didn't seek her out—"

"I know, I know," Meredith said, cutting off his

argument. "It was an *accident*. Fine by me if that's the way you want to play it. But Seth, have you asked yourself why you confided in Julia and *not* the woman you're dating?"

Chapter Twenty-Two

Julia left for work on Monday feeling indestructible. After dealing with Falling Down Groom and Nosebleedgate she figured she could handle any chaos. Unfortunately, all good vibes vanished the moment she walked into Marry Me to find Laurel and Mrs. Manning sitting at the desk with Amy.

Amy popped up from her chair like a little blonde jackrabbit, her smile brighter than bright. "Hi, Julia… how did your meeting with the caterers go?"

Caterers?

Amy winked, and Julia, not being a fool, decided to play along until she could solve the puzzle. "Fine?"

"Great. I told Mrs. Manning you were meeting with Devon about the wedding and got held up."

Good grief, she'd missed an appointment? "Thank you for covering for me, Amy. I hope I didn't miss anything important."

"We had the final fitting for Laurel's gown, which is going to be stunning by the way, and actually we're about done for today," Amy said.

Mrs. Manning glanced over. "I hope you will be prompt

for all our other appointments, Miss Richardson. The wedding is in three weeks, and there's so much to be done."

"Everything is right on schedule, Mrs. Manning, and I can assure you, nothing will go wrong," Julia said, keeping her smile firmly in place.

Mrs. Manning gave a little *hmph* indicating that Julia would probably screw up everything. Julia wasn't altogether certain she disagreed with the assessment, but the *hmph* stuck in her craw.

And since when did I start thinking hackneyed phrases like 'stuck in her craw' anyway?

Mrs. Manning turned back to Amy. "Thank you for all your help, dear. I hope Miss Richardson knows what an asset she has in you."

Julia clenched her teeth so hard her jaws ached from the pressure. "We think she walks on water around here."

Mrs. Manning's red-hot glare could have melted the polar ice caps. "You shouldn't be flippant when referring to a miracle of our Lord."

"Sorry," Julia said, lowering her head in what she hoped was a submissive gesture.

With another little *hmph,* Mrs. Manning gathered her daughter and swept out the door.

The minute they were gone, Julia hurried over to the desk to look at the calendar. "I checked this blasted book Friday, and there was no—" She glared down at the page, where the very clear notation 'Final Fitting: Manning' resided in black ink. "Where did that come from?"

"Maybe you looked at the wrong date?" Amy suggested.

"I may be clueless about the wedding business, but I can usually figure out the date."

"I saw the notation when I came in this morning. I would have called, but I figured you already knew about it. Then they got here, and it was too late."

Julia plopped down into the chair and started flipping

through the book in case she'd missed any other important appointments. "Thank you for covering for me. Did the fitting go all right?"

"Of course. The dress is exquisite. Karen Collier outdid herself."

Julia looked up from the schedule. "How in the world do you deal with Mrs. Manning and stay so chipper?"

Amy gave a humble little shrug in response.

"It's just another one of your many gifts?" Julia pressed. "Like the photographic memory?"

"Mrs. Manning isn't that difficult."

Since when? "Are we talking about the same person?"

"She's used to being catered to, that's all. So I cater. I suppose you could say that's my gift."

"Coddling massive egos?"

Amy giggled.

Julia flipped a couple more pages, making a mental note of everything she needed to do today. She stopped trying at the hundredth "to do" when a shooting pain streaked from the back of her skull to her forehead, indicating a coming brain explosion brought on by information overload. She lifted a hand to rub her eyes and squeaked in surprise when she realized Amy still hovered by the desk.

"Did you need something?" she asked.

Amy bit her lip. "I was wondering… about Seth?"

The ice pick to the brain lodged in her shoulders. "What about him?"

"I guess you know we're dating now."

Do not flinch, Julia. "Is it officially dating?"

"We've become quite close. In fact, I have a feeling—" Amy broke off with an adorable blush and looked away.

"It sounds serious. You haven't been going out long."

"Sometimes it doesn't take long. The way he looks at me, I just know."

I said, don't flinch. "That's great."

Amy let out a deep breath. "You mean you don't mind?"

"That you and Seth are—"

"Probably going to get married."

How did they get from a couple dates to marriage? Bile rose in Julia's throat, but she fought off the sudden wave of nausea. "Why would I mind?"

"I know you and Seth are only friends, but you didn't look very happy to see us together at the restaurant the other night."

Gee, and I thought I'd hidden my reaction so well. "I guess I was surprised, but I'm fine with it."

"You're sure?"

"Positive. I wish you both the best."

"Thank you. I'm so happy we have your blessing."

"Of course you do."

"That's such a relief," Amy said, a wide smile transforming her face. "I want us to be close, you know? After all, someday we'll be practically sisters."

Julia flinched.

Chapter Twenty-Three

"This is such a beautiful street, don't you think?" Amy asked, her body practically quivering in anticipation.

Since Amy was regarding him with the rapt attention of a dog eyeing a perfectly cooked steak, Seth answered the only way he could.

"Yes, of course," he said. "It's very beautiful."

Truthfully, Seth had never given much thought to the relative beauty of West Magnolia before. It was a nice, tree-lined avenue, with two rows of elegant houses. Not unlike most of the other tree-lined streets in Covington Falls.

Amy let out the breath she'd obviously been holding and favored him with a blinding smile. "I knew you would think so. I've always loved it, too. When I was a little girl I used to ride my bike over here and ride up and down."

"Really?" What an odd creature. Did all girls case their favorite street or just Amy?

"Mmm hmm." She pointed to a pretty, white, two-story home with the requisite wrap-around porch and blue shutters on the upper windows. "I especially loved this house here."

Seth studied the house in question and tried to drum up

the same enthusiasm. Yes, it was nice. Sweet even. Someplace he could see raising a family in—

Whoa.

The sudden, blinding truth hit him like a two-by-four as he realized the purpose of Amy's little field trip. A cold sweat broke out all over his body.

"Can't you just see eating around the dining room table at Christmas?" Amy gazed at the clapboard home in complete adoration. "Tucking the kids into bed right up there in that room?"

Good grief. Amy had been dreaming of living in this house since she was a child. Had he been the husband in question even then? The chills running down Seth's back answered a resounding yes. What had he gotten himself into? Amy had about twenty years worth of dreams stored up in her pretty blonde head.

And he didn't know if he could ever live up to the fantasy she'd created in her mind.

Chapter Twenty-Four

Saturday dawned, and where else would Julia be but at a wedding? She pulled into the parking lot at the Rotary Club, marveling that it had been a pretty good day so far. Joy Bennett and Matt Nichols had managed to get through their wedding ceremony without any fainting or blood spurting. All clothing had fit as intended, and there had been no wildlife in sight.

Julia considered this a huge triumph.

Her cell rang, and she answered assuming the caller had to be Amy or Betsy.

"What's this I hear about Seth dating Amy Vining?"

Shoot. The Inquisitor. "Hello Sarah," Julia said. "How are you?"

"I asked you a question," Sarah said, obviously not in the mood for small talk today.

"Which I'm ignoring. I'm in the middle of a wedding."

"I can't believe I had to find out Seth has been seeing Amy from my neighbor," Sarah continued as if Julia hadn't spoken. "I assume you do know about her."

"Yes. Actually, I was having dinner with Meredith at *Bon*

Appétit, and they came in together."

"Why didn't you tell me?"

"I've been busy, and anyway, it's none of my business who Seth dates."

"Are you kidding? Weren't you the one pacing my bedroom not so long ago, telling me about kisses?"

"I still regret telling you that."

"As I remember, you were also making up all kinds of reasons why you shouldn't date Seth."

Julia rolled her neck in an effort to ease the knot that had formed. "We both realized there was no sense in pursuing something that would never work."

"Of course. So, what did you do? Tell him to date Amy instead?"

Why did Sarah have to know her so well? "Oops. Sorry, Sarah, you're breaking up. Bad reception. Gotta go."

"Don't you dare hang up—"

"Talk to you later."

No more than a second passed before Julia's phone rang again. She knew her stepsister would only call back a million times until she answered.

"I can't talk now," Julia said.

"Fine, but you're not getting out of this."

"Can you grill me later? Please?"

"Okay," Sarah said, on a gusty sigh. "Come over here when you're done."

"I'll do my best. Bye now."

"Julia—"

Pushing the looming unease over Seth and Amy from her mind, Julia rushed into the Rotary Club. Of course she spotted one of the people currently making her life crazy right off. Amy had assumed total control as usual. Julia surveyed the room, assessing the progress. Two buffet tables were lined up to her right, and the caterers were busy putting out the food. A dozen other tables were scattered around, waiting for the guests to arrive.

"Everything looks great here," Julia said.

Amy preened, though she did her best to still look humble. "Everything has come together very nicely. How did the ceremony go?"

"No injuries to report. Betsy is helping to oversee the pictures, and I suspect guests will be showing up any minute. Can I help you with anything?"

"I've got it covered, boss," Amy said, with a breezy smile. "This has been one of the least painful receptions. Simple and easy."

Meanwhile, Julia would have been going out of her mind. "You're inhuman."

The first of the guests started arriving, and about forty-five minutes after that, the wedding party made their appearance. Julia started to relax. Dumb move on her part because dropping her guard meant Murphy's Law kicking. The law in this case took the form of Assistant #1. Julia was helping to supervise the cake cutting when Betsy walked up.

"This is the best wedding *ever*!" Betsy declared.

Julia chuckled at her enthusiasm. "It's gone well."

"Look at them," Betsy said, in full gush mode. "Everyone is so *happy*. Joy and Matt look so *happy*. And everyone is so *happy* for them."

Betsy flung out her arms as if to take in the entire room, nearly clubbing Julia in the ear. She managed to duck just in time, and stared at her assistant in bemusement. Sure Betsy resided in a land named Cheerful, but her current blissful state seemed too much even for her. The "happy, happy, happy" spelled scary, scary, scary.

Julia took a better look, noting the flushed cheeks and over-bright eyes. If she didn't know better, she'd swear… No way.

"You're feeling pretty good, huh?"

Betsy offered a wide-eyed grin. "I am *so* happy."

Yeah, a happy drunk. Prickles of alarm snaked along Julia's skin. She scanned the room again and noticed the noise level has increased tenfold. People were laughing, but now they seemed more out-of-control. The dancing seemed a little wilder too. In fact, things were beginning to look more like a college party than a wedding reception of an Elder's daughter.

"Betsy, what have you been drinking?"

"Only punch," she answered, blinking several times. "Why?"

Without another word, Julia bolted across the room, with Betsy close behind. There were two smaller tables set up with punch bowls and glasses. Julia hit the closest table, praying she was wrong. The law of averages, and her luck with these weddings, told her she wasn't.

She poured a small amount into a glass and took a sip.

"Is something wrong?" Betsy asked.

The punch had a definite kick not created by Ginger Ale. "Oh, I'm pretty sure something is very wrong."

Betsy's eyes widened in apprehension. "With the punch?"

"This stuff is lethal."

Julia looked around and noticed the tablecloth was bunched up on the bottom. The skin prickles returned full force as she leaned over and lifted the cloth.

"Is that what I think it is?" Betsy clapped a hand over her mouth.

Julia grabbed one of the empty liquor bottles. "Spiked punch. I thought these games only went on at school dances."

A scream pierced the air and Julia's senses. She and Betsy popped up, searching for the cause of the commotion.

"Henry!" a woman across the room cried. "Oh, Lord! Somebody call an ambulance."

"Call 911!" Julia yelled as she sprinted toward the commotion.

A crowd had gathered around, and Julia had to push her

way through. At the center of the mass of people stood a middle-aged woman, with a head of tight, graying curls. The object of her concern proved to be an older man who was slumped over in a chair. The woman shook him frantically, but he didn't come to.

Julia knelt down by the man's chair and checked his pulse. Pulled up an eyelid to look at his pupils.

"Do you know what you're doing?" his wife asked.

"No, but they always do this on TV. His pulse seems strong, and his eyes reacted to the light."

Julia leaned closer, slapping his cheeks. He stirred and let out a distinct snore. With the puff of air she also got a whiff of his breath.

This could not be happening.

"Has he had any punch today?" Julia asked.

"He drank a gallon of the stuff," his wife answered. "He loves it, even though he shouldn't have that much because it's loaded with sugar."

"Not today," she said under her breath.

"Where's the ambulance?" the woman screamed again.

Julia stood and tried to calm the older woman down. "Ma'am, I think he passed out."

"Then it *is* serious."

"No, Ma'am. I think he's drunk."

"That's impossible," the woman sputtered. "Henry hasn't touched alcohol in thirty years."

"Well—"

Betsy ran up at that moment, with Amy on her heels. "Amy was already on the phone. The ambulance is on its way. What's wrong with him?"

"I think he drank too much punch."

Betsy's mouth dropped open. "Oh, no."

"Oh, no?" The woman gripped Julia's arm hard enough to leave bruises. "What do you mean, oh no? What's wrong with the punch? Has it gone bad? Are we all going to be sick?"

"More like hungover."

"Julia? What's that in your hand?" Amy asked in the sudden silence.

Julia realized she still held one of the empty liquor bottles. *En masse* the crowd looked down as well.

"Is that vodka?" the older woman asked.

"It was," Julia answered.

A mottled flush crept up the woman's cheeks. "You put alcohol in the punch?"

There was a chorus of angry buzzing now.

"Unbelievable."

"How could she?"

"I knew we shouldn't trust her."

And the best one…

"Well, with a father like that, what can you expect?"

Julia faced them without flinching. "I did not spike the punch. I just discovered the bottles. I don't know how this happened. It was probably a prank. Amy, did you see anyone near the tables when you were setting up?"

Amy shook her head. "I'm sorry," she whispered, as tears started to form.

"I hope you're not trying to blame Amy for this travesty," the older woman said. "She would never do something like this. What about my husband? Do you know how much damage alcohol could do to a man his age?"

"I doubt he'd—"

Julia was saved by the welcome sound of a siren. The paramedics rushed in, and within minutes, Henry had been being hoisted on a stretcher and was being wheeled out of the room. His frantic wife followed behind, wailing about alcohol poisoning and asking if Henry's stomach would have to be pumped.

The party mood seemed to evaporate then. Some of the guests started leaving. Others conveniently began complaining about headaches and nausea.

Julia turned to her assistants. "Get lots of coffee made. Make sure everyone who drank the punch gets some. Watch the guests. Don't let anyone leave if they look tipsy. I'm going to the hospital."

They both nodded and rushed off toward the kitchen. Julia headed for the door.

Julia was about to hop into her car when her phone rang again. "Sarah, it's not a good time," she said, before her stepsister could launch into another tirade. "I'm headed to the hospital."

"That's convenient," Sarah answered. "So am I."

Julia froze with her key in the ignition. "You are?"

"Mary is on her way," Sarah said.

"Now?" White dots swam before Julia's eyes, and she clasped the steering wheel. "Isn't it too soon? Are you all right? Is someone with you?"

"Eric is here. And mom was visiting. We're on our way to the hospital now. It's early, but we pray not too early."

"I'll be there in a few minutes."

****

The drive to the hospital seemed to take forever. A quick inquiry directed Julia to the third floor.

Grace stood in the waiting room. "Julia. Thank goodness you made it," she said, opening her arms.

"Have you heard anything?" Julia asked. "Are they giving Sarah something to stop the contractions? How is she?"

Grace smoothed the hair back from Julia's face. "Sarah is fine right now. The labor has already progressed so it's too late for medication. The baby's coming."

"Is it too early?"

"She's at thirty-three weeks, which isn't too bad. Her doctor told me most babies do fairly well at this stage. We have to pray there won't be too many complications."

Julia didn't like the sound of that. "What kind of complications?"

Grace put an arm around Julia's shoulders. "Let's not even talk about that. If we start picturing horrible things, we'll make ourselves crazy."

"How can you not think horrible things?"

Rather than answer, Grace steered them toward a row of chairs. "Why don't we sit?"

"I can't," Julia said. "Actually, I was already on my way to the hospital, but for another reason."

"What's going on?"

"More proof that I don't belong in the wedding business, as if I didn't already know."

"Surely it can't be that bad."

What Julia wouldn't give for Grace's optimism. "Oh, it can. I'll be back soon."

It wasn't hard to find Henry. Or rather his family. There were about a thousand people gathered in the waiting room, and they all looked alike. Henry's hysterical wife sat in a chair wringing her hands, while another woman tried to comfort her.

"Mercy, calm down," the calm one said. "Henry will be fine. It's not like he drank the whole bowl, you know. He'll sleep it off and most likely wake up with a headache tomorrow."

Mercy stopped wringing her hands long enough to gasp in outrage. "Oh, Lydia, how can you be so uncaring? Henry could be dying in there, and you—" she stopped when she spotted Julia hovering in the doorway.

Julia tried to shrink back into the hospital-brand blue painted walls without apparent success.

"That woman tried to poison my husband," Mercy declared, pointing a bony finger in accusation. Julia half expected flying monkeys to swoop down and cart her off at any second.

"Oh, for land's sake," the other woman said. "It was vodka, not arsenic."

It may only have been alcohol, but most of the occupants of the room still seemed to think Julia had added the secret ingredient to the punch. An army of angry relatives stared her down with various shades of contempt. Except for one friendly and familiar face.

"Nicole Rivers," Julia said in shock, as her old friend from school waded through the crowd.

"Hi, Julia."

A horrible thought seized her. "Please tell me the guy who passed out isn't your father," Julia said.

"Uncle. Aunt Mercy is my mother's sister."

"Which one is your mother?"

"The one trying to keep Aunt Mercy from going off the deep end," Nicole said with a wry grin.

"Your uncle is going to be all right, isn't he?"

"I'm sure he is. We haven't seen the doctor yet, but it's pretty rare for someone to have serious complications from a few glasses of spiked punch."

"What about your aunt? Is she going to be all right?"

"Oh sure. Aunt Mercy's always been this way," Nicole said, with a flick of her hand. "She gets a headache and immediately imagines it's a brain tumor. My mom and the rest of the family spend most of their waking hours calming her down."

Julia looked around the room. "Are all these people related to you?"

"Yeah. My mother had five brothers and sisters. They all married and had kids. And so on and so on."

"Are they all ready to haul me off to jail right now?"

"Of course not." Nicole grinned. "I must say you do lead an exciting life. Malfunctioning dresses, malfunctioning noses, killer bees, grooms with cold feet."

"You know about my misfortunes?"

"Everyone knows about them. Most of us wait with baited breath to find out what will happen next."

Julia buried her face in her hands. "Fabulous, so I've become fodder for gossipy old biddies at the beauty parlor."

"And the country club, the Botanical Gardens, and now the Rotary Club I guess. You've become a legend."

"Well, now we can add contributing to the delinquency of senior citizens to my list of accomplishments. Should I expect lawsuits?"

"No one is going to sue you." Nicole put a hand on Julia's shoulder. "It'll blow over in a few days."

"I'm not sure serving spiked punch at an Elder's daughter's wedding is the way to win friends and influence people."

Nicole laughed again. "Oh, Julia, you certainly haven't lost that rapier wit. I always loved that about you. I've missed it and you."

Julia felt a silly sting of tears, which she fought back. "I don't think I've ever been missed before."

"That's not true. Grace missed you something fierce. So did Sarah."

They were interrupted when Nicole's mother walked over.

"Hello, Mrs. Coleman," Julia said.

"Hello, Julia," Mrs. Coleman said, with genuine warmth. "It's good to see you again. It's been a long time so I'm not even sure you remember me."

"I do now," Julia said. "I didn't realize the man I put into a stupor was Nicole's uncle, though. I'm so sorry about this. When I found the bottles under the table, I couldn't believe it."

"Do you know what happened?" Mrs. Coleman asked.

"Not a clue. I can only assume it was a prank of some kind. Of course, most of the guests think I was the one who doctored the punch."

"No one believes that," Nicole said.

"You obviously didn't hear the people around me."

"Julia—"

There was a stir at the other end of the room as the doctor appeared. Everyone came to attention as he surveyed the room. His mouth quirked as he took in the anxious faces.

"Henry is going to be fine," the doctor said. "Nothing a little nap and a couple aspirin won't cure."

"You're sure he doesn't have alcohol poisoning?" Henry's wife asked. "Did you have to pump his stomach?"

"I'm sure, and there was no need for stomach pumping. He didn't actually drink that much, but his tolerance level was low because it's been so long since he's had any alcohol."

"When can he go home?"

"We'll keep him here until he sobers up. Don't want him driving in his condition."

"Oh, thank goodness. My poor nerves can't take this." Mercy looked over at Julia. "I hope you're happy, young lady."

"I didn't—" Julia broke off. Why bother? They'd never believe her. "I'm glad to hear your husband is going to be fine."

"No thanks to you."

Julia couldn't stop the wince. She shouldn't care if the miserable old lady believed her, but the knowledge still stung.

"Mercy, stop it," Mrs. Coleman said in exasperation. "Julia had nothing to do with this."

Mrs. Coleman's show of support did a lot to soothe Julia's bruised psyche. *"Thank you"*, she mouthed back before turning to Nicole. "Listen, I only came down to make sure everything was all right, but I have to hurry back upstairs."

"What's going on?" Nicole asked.

"Sarah is here. The baby is coming."

Both Nicole and her mother looked concerned.

"It's still a few weeks early, isn't it?" Mrs. Coleman asked.

"Sarah is thirty-three weeks, which Grace tells me is good."

"Go, go," Nicole said, urging Julia toward the door. "I can't believe you came down here at all. We'll go to the chapel and say a prayer before we leave."

"And I'll call my prayer circle and let them know," Mrs. Coleman added.

"Thank you," Julia said, giving them both a hug.

The waiting room was a lot more crowded by the time Julia made it back. Seth had arrived with his father, and Eric's parents were there as well.

Grace raised her head from John's shoulder. "Is everything all right, dear?"

Julia didn't bother trying to explain her situation now. They could all dissect her latest disaster after the current crisis had been dealt with. "Any word on Sarah and the baby?"

"Not yet," Grace said.

Double doors opened behind them, and Eric strode out. Everyone froze as they waited for news. He smiled, though he still seemed tense. "I came out to tell you everything is going well. The labor is progressing nicely. The doctor thinks it'll only be a few more hours."

"Thank you, Eric," Grace said.

"I think Sarah could use a visit from her mother," Eric said. "She's worried."

Grace sprang out of her seat. "Of course I'll come."

They disappeared through the double doors. John leaned his head against the chair and closed his eyes, while Seth paced along the far wall. Eric's parents decided to take a walk. Spent, Julia sank down into a nearby chair.

Seth dropped into the seat next to her a moment later. "I hear you're spiking punch these days."

Her eyes flew open. "My growing infamy is out already?"

"Amy called me. How'd you do it anyway?"

The old Julia would have given a pithy response. The new, and currently unraveling Julia, couldn't manage to get any words out. The stupid tears she'd been holding back most of the day erupted.

Panic flashed across Seth's face. "Hey, what's this?"

"I didn't... put... anything... in the... punch," she managed to blubber.

"Aw, Jules, I know that," Seth said. "I was joking."

Julia gulped in a shuddering breath. "Oh... Okay."

"You have to stop crying. It tears me up." He ran a finger across her cheek, wiping away her tears. "What's going on?"

"Don't look at me like that." She swiped his hand away, unable to handle having him touch her right now. "I'm probably having a nervous breakdown. I'll be fine in a minute."

"You don't really think people blame you for the spiked punch?" he asked, relaxing into the chair again.

"I *know* they do."

"When did you start caring what all those people think anyway?"

"I'm not sure, but it's starting to tick me off," Julia said, with a shaky sigh. "Caring is so messy."

"Sometimes caring can also be incredibly rewarding."

Julia swiped the heel of her hand across her face. "Uh huh, and I'm sure you're going to tell me why it's so great."

"Of course I am." Seth pulled a handkerchief from his pocket and used it to clean her up. "Try this. Caring takes you beyond yourself. It makes you think of more than your needs."

There was too much intimacy in the act of him stroking her face, so Julia snatched the bit of white cloth before she did something stupid. Like cry on his shoulder again. Or kiss him.

"You carry real handkerchiefs around all the time?" she asked.

A corner of his mouth lifted. "Tools of the trade. People are always bursting into tears around me."

"Another one of the hazards of your profession, I suppose."

"No, one of the rewards. Easing people's pain is one of the best parts of my job."

"You are so strange," she said. No. He was wonderful and kind, which was such an inconvenience when she was trying so hard not to like him. Why couldn't he be insufferable and boring? Or forgettable?

He gave her a salute. "Thank you."

"Thank *you* for not carting me off to the funny farm."

"I told you, you're not crazy. Realizing you care for people is a good thing. It's growth."

"So these are growing pains?"

"Unfortunately."

"Hmm... still ticks me off."

Whatever Seth might have said in reply was cut off when Amy burst into the waiting room. She paused when she saw them huddled in the corner. With almost comical precision, Julia and Seth put a healthy amount of distance between themselves.

Seth widened the gap by rising to greet Amy.

"Darling, I came as soon as I could get away from the wedding," Amy said. "Is there any news?"

"Nothing yet. It could be several more hours."

"Oh, poor Sarah. She must be so worried."

Seth put an arm around her. "We all are."

For a moment they all went silent. Finally, Seth cleared his throat. "I think I'm going to hunt up some coffee. Anyone else want a cup?"

"I could use one," Julia said.

Seth went in search of sustenance. Julia glanced over at John and saw he'd dozed off. Which left her alone with Amy. The two women stared at each other in strained silence.

Amy launched the first salvo. "How is our unfortunate wedding guest?"

"Sleeping it off," Julia said, keeping her expression blank. "He should be fine."

"That's a relief."

"Are you sure you didn't see anyone near the punch table when you were setting up this morning?" Julia asked, searching for any explanation.

"No, I'm sorry," Amy said, fisting her hands together. "I feel so awful, like it's my fault somehow. I should have been paying closer attention. And I only made things worse by pointing out the empty bottle in your hand."

"Yes, thanks for that," Julia said dryly.

Amy managed a perfect little blush. "I hope the family isn't too angry with you... er... *us*."

"As it turns out Henry's niece is a friend from school."

"You have friends here?" Amy blurted out. "I mean, people you still keep in contact with?"

Julia suspected the first question hadn't been an accident. "Nicole Coleman. Nicole Rivers now. We hung out."

"Of course, I know Nicole. Her aunt is a nervous sort."

No kidding. "I noticed. Anyway, I'm sure things will blow over in a few days."

"Of course they will, and I'll help any way I can."

Why did that suddenly sound like a warning?

****

Four hours later, Mary Grace Austin greeted the world with what the doctor described as a lusty cry. The baby was immediately whisked away to the Neonatal Intensive Care Unit. When Julia finally got to see Sarah, the new mom was sitting up in bed, looking tired, but happy.

"Hi, you," Julia said, from the doorway.

Sarah tried to smile, but didn't succeed. "Hi. Have you seen Mary yet? I told Eric to go down and stay with her. I don't want her to be alone."

"I came here first," Julia said. "I think the doctors are working on her now."

Tears filled Sarah's eyes. "She's so tiny. Barely bigger than Eric's hand. They said there's a small hole in her heart. They're giving her medication, hoping it will close on its own. They said it's common for preemies—"

A shuddering sob escaped, and Sarah covered her face. Panic-stricken, Julia hurried over to the bed and climbed in next to her stepsister.

"I just want to hold my baby," Sarah cried. "She needs me."

"You will, I promise," Julia crooned. "You need to rest so you can get strong."

Sarah's hands clenched the sheets, as if she might rip them to shreds. "I tried so hard. I stayed in that blasted bed for months. I watched TV till I thought I'd go mad. I even peed into a cup, and it wasn't enough."

"Listen to me." Julia framed Sarah's face. "You did everything right. This wasn't your fault. Mary's impatient, that's all. You know she comes from strong stock. Besides, she's going to cure cancer and save my life some day. She has a destiny."

A soft chuckle took the place of weeping. "I'm such a brat."

"Yes, you are, but I love you anyway," Julia said, stroking Sarah's hair.

"Julia, did you hear what you just said?" Sarah asked on a shocked breath. "You used the "L" word."

Used the word and lightning hadn't struck. A few months ago, Julia would never have been able to utter them. "I did. I can't help it. You're impossible to hate."

"I love you, too," Sarah said.

How long had it been since anyone had truly loved her? Like a convict who'd been let out jail, the portion of Julia's heart that had been encased in a hard shell cracked open to touch freedom. If Sarah hadn't been in the room, Julia might have wept, too.

"Even though I'm hard to love?" Julia asked.

"It's not hard to love you," Sarah said. "Getting you to accept love is the difficult part. Making you believe someone could love you is nearly impossible."

"I guess I believe it now."

"Well, it's about time."

They both looked toward the door, where Grace now stood. Tears shimmered in her eyes.

"About time for what?" Julia asked.

Grace's smile was luminous. "To see my girls together again."

"Have you seen my baby, Mom?" Sarah asked, pulling herself up in the bed.

"I have." Grace walked over and stroked Sarah's hair. "Mary is beautiful and holding her own."

"Speaking of Mary, I need to go see the little savior myself," Julia said, easing off the bed to make room for Grace. "I'll be back."

The nurse warned her, but Julia could never have been prepared for the sight of the tiny baby hooked up to a million tubes. Mary looked like she was in some sort of lab experiment. Julia's insides clenched like an accordion. She stepped closer, resting her hands on top of the incubator, wishing there was a way to scoop the helpless infant up and run. Get Mary away from all those needles and wires.

"Hi, little girl," she whispered. "I'm your Auntie Julia."

The baby squirmed and opened her eyes. Of course, Mary probably hadn't heard, but if she could arrive weeks early and have a chance, anything was possible.

Julia sank down to her knees, until she was level with the baby's head. Their eyes met through the glass. "Listen, you're going to be fine. There are so many people who love you. Your parents are amazing. You have no idea how lucky you are there. I don't know your other grandparents well, but I do know your Grandma Grace is the coolest person in the world. And your Uncle Seth is the best man I've ever known. He's going to spoil you rotten. I can tell. Plus, I have it on good authority that you're supposed to save my life, so you're just going to have to stick it out."

The baby stared, unblinking for a moment, and Julia had the oddest sensation *she* was the one being reassured. A moment later Mary closed her eyes. Julia stood up, shaking from the intense encounter.

The door opened behind her, and she didn't have to look to know who'd arrived. She didn't object when Seth wrapped his arms around her waist. Maybe she should have, but for now she couldn't make herself pull away. Anyway, he only offered a comforting embrace.

Right, Julia?

Right…

Since it was only comfort, she let herself lean against his chest. He had a remarkably strong chest for someone who sat around writing sermons all day.

"I don't even know how they find enough skin on someone that small to shove all those tubes in," she said.

His lips brushed her temple. "I keep telling myself those tubes are what's keeping her alive until she can do it on her own."

"Mary looked at me. She opened her eyes and looked at me."

"I saw."

Fierce love rose up, and Julia knew she'd do anything to ensure this little girl lived and never had a worry for the rest of her life. "What happens if she doesn't make it?"

"We can only pray she does. The doctors seem to think she has a very good chance."

Prayer seemed the least she could do. "Teach me how to do it."

"Do what?"

"Pray."

"You don't need anyone to teach you," he said, with a gentle smile. "Just close your eyes, and say what's in your heart. God doesn't care how eloquent you are. He only wants to listen."

"Okay." She closed her eyes. "God, please let Mary live. We need her."

"Amen," Seth echoed.

To her shock, Seth had tears in his eyes. Reaching out, Julia wiped them away, like he'd done earlier to her. He caught her hand and touched his mouth to the tender skin on the inside of her wrist.

It would be so wrong to make out with a man over an incubator, wouldn't it?

Yes, absolutely wrong.

"Seth?"

Especially when he was dating the perfect woman… who happened to be standing right behind them.

Seth stepped back as Amy drifted closer. Her face revealed nothing, so Julia wasn't sure if she'd seen what Seth had been doing. Not that they'd been doing anything. Nothing they could be arrested for anyway.

"I came to see the baby," Amy said.

"I'll leave you two alone," Julia said, edging toward the door. "I'm going to sit with Sarah again."

As the door closed, she saw Amy take Seth's hand, and rest her head on his shoulder. They both turned to gaze down into the incubator.

Slowly, Julia let the door shut.

Chapter Twenty-Five

A grassy curve next to the road didn't seem romantic, but somehow the spot was the most beautiful place in the world. Mostly because it was where one life had ended, and where today, a new one would begin as Annie Truman became Mrs. Todd Baldwin. Annie had to be the loveliest bride Julia had ever seen. Not physical beauty, but a quiet loveliness born of loss and ultimate triumph. Molded by tragedy and complete joy.

Annie hadn't even changed yet, but her ratty jeans and T-shirt might as well have been silk and lace. Her tennis shoes satin slippers.

"I can't believe this is really happening," Annie said. "I feel like I'll wake up at any moment and realize I've been dreaming."

"If you're dreaming, I'm having the same one," Julia said.

She placed a dainty, white folding chair at the end of a row and stepped back to survey her handiwork. Four more rows of chairs were arranged in front of a trellis festooned with pink roses. About a hundred feet away were tables draped with fine linen. Devon and her crew were arranging long tables for the food to come, and a parquet dance floor had been set up.

Not bad.

"This is amazing," Annie said, a soft smile on her face. "It looks like a slice of paradise."

"Hard to believe, isn't it? I'm rather pleased with the results myself."

"You should be. Julia, it's perfect."

"I was worried about the weather last night. The storm had me wishing I'd insisted on tents, or an alternate inside venue."

"I think you worried for nothing." Annie's gaze tracked upward. "There isn't a cloud in the sky. God must be smiling today."

"He should, after all you've been through. I'd say perfect weather is the least He could do."

"Did you tell Him that last night while it was pouring?" Annie asked.

"Nearly. I didn't want to be too demanding, in case He got ticked off. I haven't had the best of luck with weddings so far. Between marauding wildlife, wardrobe malfunctions, and drunken sprees I'm crossing my fingers that the trellis doesn't collapse or that a giant gust of wind doesn't come through and carry off all these fragile-looking chairs."

Annie laughed in earnest and gave Julia a hug. "All right then, I'm going to get dressed."

"I'm amazed you took the time to come out here at all."

"I wanted a moment to see everything before the wedding. Banish all the horrible images of this place once and for all."

"I can't believe how calm you are when you're about to pledge yourself to someone for the rest of your life."

"Considering that the alternative is Todd not being here at all, I can only thank God I'm able to pledge myself to him."

How could Julia disagree with such a statement? "Put

like that, getting married seems almost trivial."

"Maybe not trivial, but I'm vowing to be grateful even for the difficult times."

"I'll call and remind you of that ten years from now."

Annie rolled her eyes. "Listen, I haven't even told you how grateful I am that you've managed to put this whole thing together in such a short time."

"I didn't do that much."

"You don't take compliments very well, do you?" Annie said, shaking her head in exasperation. "Would you please just accept my thanks?"

Julia stepped back and made an I-surrender gesture. "Okay, okay. You're welcome."

"There, that wasn't so hard, was it?"

"Not too bad."

"Then my work here is done. I'm off to make myself glamorous."

Hours later Annie returned with the bridal party. If she'd been beautiful before, there were no words to describe her now. She looked almost ethereal. This time she was dressed in a sleek column of white silk. A riot of curls fell about her head, with long spirals bouncing around her neck and shoulders. Dainty white baby's breath had been woven in among the curls. Three young women in wine-colored gowns trailed behind her, and bringing up the rear was Annie's mother. They all looked like they'd stepped out of a wedding magazine.

A long length of lattice had been erected behind the rows of chairs to hide the arrival of the bride. Even now Julia could hear the string quartet warming up on the other side of the barrier.

The only thing they needed now was the bride. Annie smiled as Julia approached. "Everything ready?"

"Guests. Check. Musicians. Check. Food. Check. One very impatient groom. Check," Julia said.

A delighted chuckled escaped, and Annie kissed Julia's cheek. "This is why I love you. If it wasn't for you, I'd probably be a blubbering mess by now."

"Oh, I can guarantee you won't get through this ceremony without major blubbering. It's that kind of day."

Everyone joined in the laughter, and from the looks of things, a few of them were on the verge of tears already.

Julia took Annie's hand. "Let's do this. I think you've waited long enough."

Mrs. Truman beamed before wrapping her daughter in a hug and then going to take her place down front.

Annie's father appeared to walk his little girl down the aisle, while Julia slipped around the lattice wall to cue the quartet to start the processional. The bridesmaids, including Annie's sister, her college roommate, and a friend from her first day in kindergarten, floated down the aisle.

Julia sent the maid of honor down the aisle and turned back to Annie. "Okay, Miss Truman, this is it."

"Miss Truman?"

"It's probably the last time you're going to hear that. I thought you might appreciate it."

Miss Truman immediately started to tear up. "That is so sweet."

"Oh, gosh, don't start that now," Julia said, waving her hands in panic. "You haven't even seen Todd yet."

"Well, you started it," Annie complained. "Bad, bad girl."

The tears were contagious, and Julia rolled her eyes, mainly to keep from losing it herself. "Come on now, get going."

One more cue, and the music began. Annie and her father turned the corner, emerging from behind the lattice wall. Two pairs of eyes met. Todd took a deep breath. Even from where she stood Julia could see his eyes fill.

Floodgates opened up all around because it was simply that kind of day.

Seth was officiating the service. He smiled at Annie and Todd, and then turned to address the guests. "Friends, loved ones, we are gathered here to witness more than a union of two people," he began. "We are gathered here to celebrate the triumph of love over tragedy. We live in a cynical world that doesn't make it easy to believe in love of any kind. I'm often asked to read *1 Corinthians 13* at weddings, but the sad truth is we have made a mockery of those verses. In our society, love is impatient, and often unkind. It envies and boasts and is filled with unseemly pride. It is rude, selfish, easily angered, and keeps a record of every wrong. It delights in things evil and rejects the truth. It fails to protect, abuses trust, dashes hope, and walks away rather than persevere."

Seth's eyes moved over the crowd, pausing when he reached Julia. For a moment everyone else disappeared. Somehow she knew his words were not meant for Annie and Todd alone.

He broke the contact and returned to his message. "Forgive me if that seems a bit out of place considering the occasion, but my friends, I'm here to tell you today that Annie and Todd have shown us all that these verses can and do exist beyond the pages of the Bible. They have lived them. Of course, Annie, you have an advantage in that Todd can't remember most of your wrongs."

A startled chuckle rippled through the crowd.

"The vows say for better or for worse, but you two have already lived worse and come out stronger," Seth continued. "Now, you get to live for better. Not that there won't be challenges ahead, but now you know you can handle those lows, and I know you, above anyone else, will praise God for the highs. So now, it is with the greatest pleasure, that I get to ask you, Todd Rodger Baldwin, to repeat after me…"

Wedding vows had never meant much to Julia before. They were pretty words wrapped up in grandiose promises, which were never kept in her experience.

Until today. Her heart ached, and she fought to take in a breath as the vows continued. The rest of the ceremony went by in a haze. Her chest tightened, and her mind thrummed with the idea that maybe… just maybe… she was wrong about the whole love thing.

Shaken, she escaped to the reception area where Betsy was helping to oversee the arrangements. Amy had the day off and was attending the wedding as a guest.

Betsy paused as she finished arranging flowers around the edge of the wedding cake. "Hey, boss, how's…" Her voice trailed off. "What's wrong?"

"Huh?"

"You're pale." The flowers hit the ground as Betsy reached for Julia. "Is something wrong? Has the trellis fallen over? Have we finally killed someone?"

Her assistant's panic snapped Julia back to reality. "No falling anything," she said, patting Betsy's arm. "Everyone is still hale and hearty. I think I'm tired, what with Sarah and the baby and all."

Betsy's eyes lit up, and she nearly jumped up and down like a five-year-old on Christmas morning. "I went by the hospital yesterday. Mary is so *precious,* and so *tiny*. It's *unbelievable.*"

Julia couldn't help but laugh at Betsy's enthusiasm. "Yes, she is, and yes it is. Now, what can I do to help?"

****

With his ministerial duties officially over for the day, Seth was able to relax and enjoy the evening. In theory at least. He *should* have been enjoying the evening. The moment Meredith's band launched into a medley of love songs, Amy had dragged him onto the dance floor. What was there to complain about when he held a beautiful, sweet, intelligent woman in his arms?

As Meredith launched into the climax of the song, Seth spun Amy in a circle and dipped her over his arm. She giggled her approval. Amy approved of everything he did. She hung on his every word. Agreed with them, too. If he told her the sky was purple she'd probably nod and tell him how observant he was for noticing.

Seth had never been the object of such constant attention. It was flattering, of course, but also daunting. Being perfect put a lot of pressure on a guy.

The last note faded, and Amy pulled back. A little. She never seemed to drift more than a few feet away.

"Who taught you to dance so well?" she asked.

"My mother, actually."

Amy arranged her bow-shaped mouth into a cute little pout and hummed her sympathy. "She would be so proud of the way you took to her lessons. She'd be proud of everything you've accomplished. The way you run the church. How you're so admired and such a great example for the community."

There. Such over-the-top comments made him itch.

"I'm completely parched," Amy said, fanning herself with an elegant twist of her wrist.

"Would you like me to get you a drink?"

"Oh no, I can get my own." She smiled and trailed two fingers up his arm. "You just relax and think about me while I'm gone. I'll be right back."

He cricked his neck one way and then the other and tried not to sigh in relief. At least not out loud.

When had dating become so hard and uncomfortable?

A flash of red caught his attention, and like a magnet Seth's head turned. Julia had stopped to speak to the caterer. She gestured toward the tables across the way and laughed at something Devon said. A trill skated down his spine, and he tamped down his instinctive reaction.

Seth wished he knew how to shut off the electricity she

sparked. Mostly, he wished he had never witnessed the tender moment between an innocent baby and a woman who'd made a vow not to care about anyone. Stepping into the NICU had been a big mistake. Touching Julia had been an even bigger one.

Someone tapped him on the shoulder, jolting him out of his daydream.

"Wanna' dance, Rev?" Meredith asked, grinning up at him. "I saw those fancy moves a few minutes ago."

Out of the corner of his eye, Seth caught Amy watching them like a hawk zoning in on a mouse. Her glare proclaimed silent outrage at seeing him with her sister.

"Uh… I'm not sure…" he mumbled.

Meredith followed his trajectory, flashed a *hello dear* smile at her baby sister and turned back. "Let her stew. She'll be fine. It's only one dance."

Across the way, a thundercloud passed over Amy's face. Seth suspected if they hadn't been in public, Amy would've stomped across the grass and ripped the hair from her sister's head.

Said sister didn't act offended by the murderous glance. In fact, she seemed amused by it. "I do love ruffling her feathers," Meredith said, proving his theory. "She puffs up so beautifully."

"You shouldn't tease her. She admires you a lot."

A *who are you kidding* expression flashed across Meredith's face. "Since when?"

"Since always, I think. You're her older sister. Of course she looks up to you. Besides that you're so confident and talented. She feels like she can't measure up so she over compensates."

"It sounds like you've gotten to know her well."

"We've spent some time together," he said, trying to sound vague.

"I know." Meredith tilted her head closer. "I hear she

showed you the house."

Seth stumbled and nicked her toe. "Sorry. What house?"

"Watch your feet, Rev," Meredith said, giving him another *come-on* look. She also wasn't giving up. "The house on West Magnolia. I heard Amy telling our mother all about your trip down Destiny Lane."

Was that a noose tightening around his neck? "Right. That one. Yes, we saw a house. Very nice."

"And that didn't make you the least bit uncomfortable?"

He twirled her out to the side. "No."

"It's a good thing you became a minister because you're a terrible liar," Meredith said as he pulled her back in.

"Why would I lie about a house?"

"Maybe because you flinch every time Amy looks at you. Or compliments you. Or touches you."

"I do not."

"Didn't I just say you don't lie well?"

Fancy dance moves and denial weren't working so Seth cut to the chase. "Is there a point to your interrogation?"

"Yes. Mainly the fact that while my sister is clinging to you like a leech, your eyes keep drifting toward someone else."

Seth knew better than to duck and dodge again. "I'm trying to do the right thing here, Meredith."

"How noble, but are you doing the right thing for you? For Julia? More to the point, are you doing the right thing for Amy?"

He stopped moving. "What?"

Meredith stared him down without blinking. "I won't pretend Amy and I are close, but she is my baby sister, and she's vulnerable where you're concerned. If you're dating her as some sort of experiment or using her to try and ignore what's going on with Julia I'll be upset with you."

"I don't plan on hurting Amy."

"You won't have to plan it," she said. "My sister will

have your wedding planned in her head within a month, and my mom will be right there cheering her on."

A lead fist slammed into his gut "A wedding?"

"Mmm hmm... think pink. Everywhere."

The noose constricted even more.

A pale, slim arm clamped around Seth's elbow. "Meredith, I think the band is trying to get your attention," Amy said.

"I have a few more minutes of my break left," Meredith said.

Amy's smile turned ugly. "Still, you should go check in with them. You are working tonight, you know. Annie and Todd paid you to entertain the guests, not dance with them."

"Your sister isn't a slave," Seth said, shocked by the snide comment and wondered how he'd never seen such darkness in her before. He'd never known Amy to be deliberately cruel.

Meredith let the rudeness roll off her back, however. In fact, she laughed in her sister's face. "Okay, Ames, I'll slink off and leave you to your boyfriend."

Meredith backed away a couple steps, rolling her eyes when Amy wedged herself against Seth's side.

"Hope you like pink," Meredith muttered before turning and walking toward the stage.

Chapter Twenty-Six

As a rule Julia didn't believe in miracles. Maybe they'd happened back in the Bible days, but she figured the era of seas parting and angels coming to announce a pregnancy had ended a couple millenniums ago.

That is, until the day Sarah and Eric walked through the door of their apartment with a tiny bundle in a pink blanket.

The entire family had come over to celebrate the homecoming. Grace and John, Eric's parents, Seth. Amy had come, too, and the ever-resourceful girl had made a giant "Welcome Home Mary!" banner. She'd also put together a gorgeous flower arrangement festooned with pink carnations, pink roses and a giant pink ribbon. The creation had been topped off with a bunch of balloons.

Julia had brought a bottle of sparkling grape juice.

It's the thought that counts, right?

Everyone clapped and cheered as Eric opened the door. Sarah's face lit up when she saw the crowd in her living room.

"Oh, my goodness!"

Seth snapped a picture, and the party commenced. Grace began slicing pieces of cake, which Amy had also made, while

Julia poured glasses of the juice.

Sarah brought the baby over to Grace, who had finally ceded to everyone's command to take a break. Sarah lowered the tiny bundle into her mother's arms, and sat down. Three generations all together.

"Ladies, look up here," Seth called out.

They glanced up from their adoration of the baby and smiled as Seth took more shots. Grace touched little Mary's cheek.

"Have you ever seen anything so incredible?" Sarah asked.

Grace smoothed a lock of hair behind her daughter's ear. "Once."

The two shared a knowing look that Julia assumed only mothers understood. Sarah put her head on Grace's shoulder. They might have been posing for a magazine cover.

A jagged knife sliced through Julia's ribs and pierced her heart. Her vision blurred, and she turned away before anyone else noticed. Connection. Those three women were connected in a way Julia couldn't begin to fathom. By blood, by experience, even by their faith. She'd never felt connected to anyone like that. Frankly, it had been years since she'd wanted to be.

How ironic. Julia finally got around to deciding she might be able to handle being part of a family, and her time in Covington Falls was up. Now that baby Mary was here, Julia would no longer be needed.

Shaken, Julia escaped to the kitchen.

A couple hours later the party broke up. Eric's parents were the first to depart. Seth and Amy left to have dinner with her mother soon after. Then Grace took John home. Eric began cleaning up in kitchen, while Julia and Sarah cooed over the baby in the bedroom. Julia felt guilty about leaving Sarah's husband to clean up on his own, but not enough to give up her first chance to hold Mary.

"I think this is the most beautiful baby I've ever seen," Julia said.

Sarah leaned close, as if she couldn't bear to be more than a few inches from her daughter. "How many babies have you seen?"

"I see them all the time. In malls, grocery stores, in parks."

"When was the last time you actually held one?"

"I might have been ten. Does it matter? Can't I simply believe she's the most amazing baby in the world?"

An unabashed grin lit up Sarah's face. "No, especially when I agree."

Julia gazed down at the slumbering baby. "I think this is the best thing you've ever done."

A soft hum of agreement floated from the other side of the bed, and Sarah shifted to lounge back against a pillow. "So, things seem to be moving quickly with Amy and Seth."

"That's right," Julia said, with a wry shake of her head. "Wait till I'm pinned down with a baby in my arms to start grilling me."

Sarah tried her patented innocent look, but Julia no longer bought such tactics. Sarah seemed to realize she'd lost the *"who me?"* advantage and gave up after a second. "It's your fault. You won't talk to me otherwise."

"Maybe because there's nothing to talk about."

"Amy has plenty to say," Sarah said, with a low grumble. "Did you know she sat in my living room, lamenting the fact that Mary will be too young to be a flower girl in their wedding?"

Contemplation of the baby's perfectly formed lips ceased. "What?"

Sarah grinned. "Gotcha."

Julia swatted the closest part she could reach. "Evil, evil girl. Even Amy isn't forward enough to start talking about wedding plans. At least outside her own family."

"I bet Mrs. Vining has the seating chart for the reception drawn up already," Sarah said.

"No doubt."

"And that doesn't bother you?" Sarah asked, bounding off the bed.

"No," Julia said with conviction, even as she fought the urge to check her nose to ensure it hadn't started growing.

"You're going to let some other woman steal him out from under you?"

"Steal him?" Julia echoed in disbelief. "When did we wind up in a soap opera?"

"You're not going to joke your way out of this one, Julia."

"Sorry, but I think you're overreacting."

Issuing a sound of disgust, Sarah threw her hands up in the air. "Because you're not reacting at all! I don't get it."

Julia rocked the baby as she watched Sarah pace. "Amy can't steal something that was never mine."

"What if he could be?" Sarah asked, planting her fists on her hips. "What if you let fear destroy the best thing that might ever happen to you?"

Julia couldn't do the "hands on hips" thing with the baby in her arms, but she thought it. "What if I did the right thing by ending it before things went too far, and one of us got hurt? What if Amy is the best thing to ever happen to Seth? I know you don't like her that much. Shoot, at this point I'm still not sure *I* like her, but if she's good for Seth and makes him happy, that's all that matters."

The logical argument caused Sarah to shove her bottom lip out in a mighty pout and flop back on the bed in a huff. "When did you have to go and start making sense?"

"It's a byproduct of living with Grace." She squeezed Sarah's hand. "I'm sorry I'm ruining all your romantic fantasies."

Sarah sniffled, as tears filled her eyes. "It's not your fault."

"Please don't start crying."

"Oh, don't pay attention to those," Sarah said, scrubbing her cheeks with the back of her hand. "I'm hormonal."

"I thought that was a pregnancy thing."

A droll eye roll helped dry up the last of Sarah's tears. "Apparently, there are postnatal hormones, too. Baby blues."

"Sounds pleasant."

"I don't mean to keep harping at you. I just want you to be happy."

"Aw, sweetie, I am happy."

Yep. Happy.

****

Deep, emotional conversations made for restless nights. Around two in the morning Julia gave up on sleep and went down to the kitchen for a snack. An inventory of the shelves turned up some leftover soup. As she was spooning some into a bowl to heat up in the microwave she heard a sound out in the hallway. A few seconds later, Grace shuffled into the kitchen.

"Hi, can't sleep either?" Julia asked.

Grace offered up a tired smile. "Too excited."

"Can I get you anything?"

"Oh, no, I heard you in here and wanted to check on you."

Julia couldn't help a small chuckle. "You think I need help? I'm only using the microwave, so you shouldn't worry I'll burn the place down."

"I'm not concerned about your cooking. I'm worried about you."

Concentrating on food preparation meant Julia didn't have to look her stepmother in the eye. She turned and put the bowl in the microwave and set the time. "Me? I'm fine."

"I saw your face at Sarah's today when I was holding the

baby. You looked devastated."

Grace always saw too much. "Are you kidding? This has been an amazing day, " Julia said, trying to head off another confession session.

"But you don't feel like you're a part of it."

Julia watched the bowl turn around and around, wondering how one was supposed to dodge sticky questions when dealing with a mind reader.

"I wish you'd tell me why you're so afraid to let us love you," Grace said.

"I'm not afraid," Julia tried once more.

Grace shook her head, stopping Julia with a knowing look. "You always were. When you lived here as a child, I'd catch you looking at Sarah and me with such longing. You wanted so badly to reach out, but it was as if you were afraid we'd disappear if you did."

There seemed to be no point in continuing to deny something Grace had already figured out. "Everyone always did disappear," Julia said.

"Yes, they did. I understand why you were so frightened then, but Julia you're not a child anymore. Isn't it time you took a chance and reached out?"

"I don't know if I can." The words were ripped from Julia's throat before she could stop them.

Then tears came. Julia wasn't even aware of Grace moving, but strong arms brought her close. They stood in the dark kitchen, while Julia sobbed and Grace cooed nonsense words she'd probably used when Sarah was a baby.

Finally, Julia pulled back, but she couldn't meet Grace's eyes. "If I tell you something, will you promise not to hate me?"

"You could never say anything that would make me stop loving you, Julia."

"Sometimes I couldn't stand Sarah," Julia said, disgusted with her own selfishness.

"Why?"

Amazement flooded through her at the matter-of-fact question. Why wasn't Grace shocked or angry? "Because she had you," Julia said. "She had a real mother. I had the woman who gave birth to me, but she wasn't my mother. She never tucked me in at night or read me a bedtime story. She never in her life baked cookies. She rarely hugged me, and she looked the other way when her creepy husband—"

Julia broke off and bit her lip. No need to get into the issue of Charles' underage preferences.

Grace sighed. "You know, your parents weren't quite the unfeeling monsters you imagine. Your mother did her best to protect you. Your father, too."

"What are you talking about?"

"Your mother never wanted me to tell you, but maybe now you're old enough to hear it and understand."

Confusion piled on confusion. "Understand what?"

Grace reached over and removed the bowl from the microwave. "Why don't we sit?"

They sat, but now soup was the last thing on Julia's mind. "What do you think I need to understand?"

"The reason you were sent here to live in the first place."

"I always thought it was because my mother didn't want me around."

"No, she sent you here to get you away from Charles."

Every cell in Julia's body froze. "What do you know about Charles?"

"I know he apparently liked to look at young girls," Grace said. "That is all he did, right?"

Grace suddenly looked fierce, and judging from her expression Julia thought it was a good thing Charles wasn't in the room right now.

"He never touched me, if that's what you're asking," Julia said. "How did you know about him?"

"Because your mother told me."

The admission felt like a slap in the face. "She *knew* what he was doing?"

"Apparently Charles made a few comments about your appearance. At first she was proud he thought you were so pretty. Then he said something about the way you looked in a bathing suit."

Chills broke out all over Julia's body. "I can't remember wearing a bathing suit around him. I wouldn't have dared."

"I don't think you knew he was home."

The soup lodged in Julia's throat like a lump of clay. She dropped the spoon and rubbed her arms, trying to get rid of the goose bumps.

"Your mother became alarmed and called here," Grace continued. "She asked for me specifically. She explained the situation and asked if you could come live with us."

"Why did she want to talk with you and not my father?"

"I think she knew I would understand. From one mother to another, she said."

Tears stung Julia's eyes. "I don't get it. If she knew, why did she stay with him?" The betrayal cut to the quick even after all these years. "Why keep him and send me away?"

"I never said your mother's maternal instincts were fully developed," Grace said, with a droll roll of her eyes. "She wasn't strong enough to leave him, but she did her best to protect you."

"Did my father know about Charles?"

Grace nodded. "He was ready to fly out there and tear the man limb from limb. So was I, for that matter."

"You didn't even know me."

"I knew you were a young, innocent girl, and the thought of that man going further than looking made me crazy. Your father demanded you be put on a plane and sent here immediately."

"I always wondered why it happened so suddenly," Julia said. "I thought she didn't want me around because having a teenage daughter made her look older."

"Oh, honey, no. And when your father and I divorced, your mother was still married to Charles, so he decided—"

"To send me to boarding school. Shuffled off again. This time onto strangers. I guess it would have been too much to ask that he keep me with him."

Even Grace couldn't find an excuse for that. So, yes Julia's parents had done their best, but their concept of "best" was limited to say the least.

Grace reached for Julia's hand, an expression of deep sadness reflected in her eyes. "Now I've made you feel worse."

"Don't feel guilty," Julia said. "As you said, at least my mother cared enough to get me away from Charles. That's something. And my father cared enough to get protective over it. It's more than I expected."

"Do you keep in contact with them at all?"

"I get a call on my birthday from my mother and a random gift certificate for some obscene amount at Christmas. My father will call out-of-the-blue a couple times a year. We never have anything to say. His current wife is younger than me. It's always awkward and stiff."

Grace rubbed Julia's arm, as if trying to banish the coldness in her veins. "Julia, I know it's hard, but maybe it's time you find a way to forgive them. They're a couple of selfish, flawed people, but they do love you."

"Sarah said that, too."

"You should take her advice. This bitterness is only going to eat you up. It's already left its mark. Here you are a beautiful, smart, successful woman, and you're stuck in this pit of fear, afraid to let anyone close to you. That's no way to live."

Julia didn't see a way to move past her anger. "How am I supposed to forgive them?"

"You pray about it. Ask for guidance. That the burden be lifted. God knows something about forgiveness. He forgave us when we certainly didn't deserve it. If you want to be set free from the chains of your childhood you will find a way."

"How can you be so sure?"

"Because I know you," Grace said, caressing Julia's cheek. "I know how strong you are. How caring, even though you try to hide it. I also know how much God loves you. That's all you need to do anything."

Julia couldn't stop a grin. "Have you ever thought about getting your own talk show?"

A startled bark of laughter escaped. "Good grief, no," Grace said. "Who would care what I have to say?"

"Plenty of people, I bet."

"I think I'll leave the talking to the professionals."

"You should consider it."

Grace stood up, still chuckling. "I'm going to bed. Are you going to be all right?"

"Me? I told you, I'm fine."

"I know." She pressed her lips to the top of Julia's head. "Goodnight."

Julia sighed and stared unseeing at the darkened kitchen. She was starting to think this whole issue of feelings was more trouble than it was worth.

Chapter Twenty-Seven

Julia woke up with a headache. Not surprising as tossing and turning all night did not leave one feeling refreshed come morning. As the sun peeked over the horizon, she gave up on sleep. A glance out the window revealed a glorious sunrise. Streaks of pink, purple, and orange stretched across the sky like fiery fingers. Against the azure blue sky, the sight was almost enough to make her cry.

Frustration gnawed at her gut. These crying jags had to stop... now... before she turned into one of those weepy women so often featured in Spanish *telenovelas*.

Forcibly shrugging off her melancholy, Julia showered and dressed before heading to Hadden Acres, where the wedding-that-would-steal-her-sanity would take place in forty-eight hours. First on the agenda was meeting with the plantation staff. As it was a designated historical sight, there were reams of permits to sign. Permits to set up chairs. Permits to bring in food. Permits to take pictures. Permits to park cars on the grounds. Permits to walk on the grass. Permits to breathe. Permits to blink.

Julia's wrist would never be the same.

When the paperwork was in order, she headed back outside to meet with the extra crew they'd hired to help pull off the monster wedding. Betsy would be the point woman for catering and entertainment. Amy had been charged with taking care of the wedding party. Julia wound up with grounds duty, and it became her task to make sure everything was set up for the ceremony and reception. After handing out task lists, the team dispersed, and the race began to see if they could pull it all off.

Chapter Twenty-Eight

Seth and sleep had become two things that did not go together. Everything seemed to be crowding in on him. The situation with Meredith at church, the snowball barreling downhill feeling whenever he got close to Amy, and of course thoughts of Julia. The latter concern seemed to crowd into his thoughts with a regularity that disturbed him.

He stumbled out of bed the morning after baby Mary's welcome home party and made his first unpleasant discovery of the day.

No coffee.

Which meant going down to Grace's kitchen. Which meant most likely running into Julia. He'd been avoiding the main house as much as possible. Call him a coward, but facing Julia before all his defenses were in place could only lead to disaster.

However, a lack of coffee trumped any misgivings he had about stopping the urge to reach out and twirl a strand of Julia's wild red hair around his finger. Seeing his dad at the table rather than Julia brought instant relief, along with a touch of disappointment he refused to acknowledge.

"Morning... son," John Graham said, the corner of his mouth kicking up as pleasure filled his eyes.

"Hey, Dad."

Guilt followed on the heels of relief. Seth had been so wrapped up in his own personal turmoil he hadn't visited with his dad as much. To be truthful, Seth had avoided his father because the old man knew him too well. Even a stroke wouldn't keep John Graham from seeing the turmoil in his son's eyes.

It was too late to run now, so Seth forced a relaxed smile and headed for the coffee pot. A bit of caffeine would help get his brain functioning.

"Where is everyone else?" Seth asked, wondering if he was going to get the double pleasure of looking at both his dad and Julia over the breakfast table.

Talk about an unsettling morning.

"Julia... left for work. Grace went... to see... Sarah and the... baby."

"Already?" Seth grinned at his dad over the coffee cup. "Looks like you're not going to be seeing your wife very much anymore."

John let out a wheezing chuckle. "No... it is good... to see her... so happy though."

"It's good to see you so happy."

Seth knew how hard things had been for his dad after his mother passed away. After losing Beth he understood his father's devastation even more. Yet, his dad had somehow been able to move on and find love again with Grace. Seth didn't know if that kind of peace was possible for him. Even now he woke up some mornings to find his pillow wet with tears.

"You never stop... missing them," his dad said. "Loving them."

Seth left off contemplating the depths of the black liquid he'd been nursing. "Who?"

"The one you lost," his dad said. "You don't have to... stop missing them... but you can... let another person in. A heart... expands to accept... love."

Talk about hitting the nail on the head. "How do you do that?" Seth asked, in sheer awe. "Mom used to be the one to read my mind."

"I had... to learn... on the job," said, with a wistful smile. "You are... so like... her."

Seth had heard people say that before. Before his stroke, John Graham had been a powder keg of energy. Always the one cracking jokes and entertaining everyone within earshot at parties. Susan Graham had been quieter, more introspective. She'd understood Seth better than anyone in the world. She'd been so good at looking inside a person and seeing the things they kept hidden from the world.

Like Julia did.

Seth's mind skittered over the thought like a stone skipping across the water. Julia was not like his mother. Sure, she could read people, but other than that the two couldn't be more different.

"You have a lot... on your... mind lately," his dad said. "You always seem... somewhere else."

Somewhere? Try a million places. "I've got a big meeting tonight at church. About Meredith Vining."

"I heard."

Surprise flooded through him. "You know?"

"The stroke... did not affect... my hearing," his dad said, pointing to his ears. "What are you... going to do?"

"Fight for Meredith. For what's right."

"That's good. She has... changed... settled down. Her music is... so full of worship. Others... see that, too."

"I hope so."

"Something else... is troubling you. Besides Meredith."

Seth scraped a hand across his cheek, wondering how much he should say. "How did you know Grace was the one?

Did you worry you were just lonely or wanted companionship? Do you love her the way you loved Mom?"

"Lots of questions," his dad rumbled.

"No kidding."

"Grace is… the woman who made me want… to live again."

Live again. Words Seth understood. He'd been experiencing the sensation of coming out of a deep sleep the last couple months.

His dad's expression turned earnest. "Son, love can be many things. Grace is not your mother. What I feel for her is different. Susan was my childhood sweetheart. We grew up together. Raised a son. But losing her changed me. I'm not the same man I was, and Grace is what I need now. Just like you are not the same man you were."

Seth was struck, both by the words and the fact that his father hadn't stumbled over them at all. "I'm not sure I know who I am without Beth."

"Beth answered a need in you. The needs of a young, inexperienced man," his dad said. "You are in a different place, and what you need has changed. When you meet the woman who meets them you will know. It won't make the love you feel for Beth any less. She'll still be there."

"But how did you know it was Grace?'

"Once I realized she was the first person I wanted to tell when something good happened. Or something bad. When I woke up and had her on my mind. That's how you'll know, too. Are you… asking because of… Amy? Do you think… she is what… you want?"

Seth chuckled inwardly. His father's speech had been perfectly clear when talking about Grace, but any other subject brought forth halting words. That had to mean something.

Unfortunately, Seth didn't have an answer. "I don't know."

His dad leaned back and folded his arms. "I didn't…

think so. So… who has you… tied in… knots?"

Another question he couldn't answer. "No one, Dad."

For a moment, Seth thought his father might press. Instead, John Graham shook his head. "Stubborn."

"How am I stubborn?"

"You get it… from me," his dad said, lips pulled down in a sort of half-frown. "Won't see… the truth… until it bites you… in the rear."

"What are you talking about?"

"You are not… ready to hear it. The answer to… all your questions is simple… but you will have to… take a leap of faith… to find it. You will have to… listen to your heart and… learn to let go."

"I'm not sure I can."

"You're my son," John Graham said clear as day. "Of course you can."

Chapter Twenty-Nine

"Miss Richardson, you've put Councilman Granger's wife next to Councilman Ingall's wife."

Julia's current job was to mark out where the chairs would go for the ceremony with little red flags. She'd been hunched over in a very uncomfortable position for far too long. A glance to her right revealed the tips of Mrs. Manning's navy blue pumps. Julia had been hoping to avoid the mayor's wife today to no avail. Mrs. Manning had interrupted six times already.

As she straightened, Julia had to remind herself that the flags were meant to go in the ground and not in someone's eyes.

"I'm sorry?" Julia asked.

"Isabelle Granger is seated next to Nadine Ingall."

"Okay?"

Had that come across as too flippant? Must have because Mrs. Manning's nostrils flared like a bull after spotting a red cape.

Mrs. Manning looked down her nose at Julia. Quite a feat as the mayor's wife stood a good six inches shorter. "Please reassign their seats."

"Why do they need to be separated?"

Madam Pain In My Rear stalked away before Julia could get an answer.

"Isabelle Granger and Nadine Ingall can't stand each other."

Julia spun around. Her erstwhile second assistant had appeared out of nowhere. "Hi, Amy. Did you finish up with the plantation manager?"

Of course, Amy nodded. "Yes, it was a successful meeting."

"That's good. What were you saying about the Granger and Ingall women?"

"They hate each other."

Oh, a small-town feud. Interesting. "Why?"

"They haven't spoken since Isabelle accused Nadine of cheating her out of the Miss Barley & Grain crown."

Well that seemed pretty tame. "A beauty pageant?"

"Our most prestigious beauty pageant," Amy said. "The winner goes on to the Miss Southern Jewel pageant."

"Oh, that does sound prestigious."

Was she flippant again? Julia imagined so. Amy's pretty blue eyes were shooting *ignorant Yankee infidel* vibes.

"One year the Miss Barley & Grain Queen went on to win Miss Southern Jewel and then to the Miss South Georgia Pageant," Amy said.

Julia decided to avoid a flippant comment so she could get to the real story. "Where does the feud come in?"

"Isabelle had won every local pageant in three counties, and she was the favorite, but Nadine ended up winning. Isabelle accused her of persuading one of the judges to vote for her."

Oh, juicier and juicier. "What kind of persuasion are we talking about? Did Nadine do favors for the judge?"

"She made a cake."

"A cake?" Julia asked in bemusement. "That's it?"

"Nadine always won the baking contest at the local county fair, and everyone knew Horace had a sweet tooth."

"Crowned by chocolate," Julia said. "Beautiful."

"After that they swore never to speak to each other again, and they haven't."

"How long ago was this pageant?"

"Twenty-two years."

"They haven't spoken to each other all this time because of a cake?" Julia asked in disbelief.

Amy seemed to grasp the silliness of the ancient feud and gave a rather embarrassed shrug. "Perhaps their egos won't allow them to be the first to apologize. If you don't need me here, I can head back to the office to redo the seating chart. I'll look it over to make sure there aren't more mistakes."

"I hardly think not knowing about a twenty-two-year-old cake war qualifies as a mistake."

Amy's eyes widened like a kewpie doll. "I wasn't accusing you of anything. It's just that you might not know these little details since you're not from here."

Taking a deep, calming breath, Julia fixed a pleased smile on her lips. "Sure, you go ahead and look over the list. Don't want any cat fights over the salmon cakes."

"Salmon *puffs*." So saying, Amy sashayed across the lawn. Julia watched the other woman go, wondering if a walk like that was learned or if came naturally from generations of Southern breeding.

"I'd like to puff her right in the mouth," Julia grumbled, bending down to try and finish her flag planting for the hundredth time, and vowed to shoot herself before ever agreeing to do a favor for Sarah again.

****

Near sundown, Julia dragged herself home. Her back

ached, her knees hurt, and her feet felt like an elephant had stomped on them. She literally hobbled up the stairs to her room.

Nice. She'd turned into a ninety-year-old woman.

Attempts to sleep proved fruitless. Closing her eyes brought images of Amy and Seth dancing yesterday. They'd looked so… right. So perfect. All that blonde sweetness next to his dark hotness.

"Agh!"

Forget it. Rolling out of bed, she grabbed the phone, and dialed Meredith's number.

Meredith picked up on the first ring. "Hello?"

"Do you run?" Julia asked.

"Not if I can help it."

"You can't help it today," Julia said. "Meet me at Lake Rice."

"Something wrong?"

"My whole life is wrong."

Meredith gave a little laugh. "I'll be there in half an hour."

Meredith stood waiting by the path when Julia ran up. "You came on foot?" she asked, her nose wrinkling in distaste.

"That's the point of going for a run," Julia said.

Julia insisted they stretch before they set off. In deference to Meredith's strenuous objection to real exercise, they walked. Silence enveloped them for several minutes, but Julia could feel Meredith glancing over every so often.

Finally, Meredith had apparently waited long enough. "You're going to have to give me a clue as to why we're here."

Something in her friend's gaze caused the floodgates to open, and Julia poured out the sad tale of her life. About her parents and the marriages. About the stepparents, the breakups, the shuttling back and forth, her brief stint in Covington Falls as a teenager, and all the years since when she'd decided to put her faith in building a career.

Meredith didn't say anything for the most part other than to offer an occasional, "no way" or "that's awful" when required.

When Julia finally wound down, Meredith shook her head. "At least now I understand why you sounded so wrecked on the phone. And why you've been so skittish about Seth. You're essentially surrounded on all fronts by the very things you've sworn to avoid in life. Weddings, love, and God."

They rounded the corner, and the entire lake came into view. The setting sun performed a miraculous ballet on the surface of the water, and Julia could almost feel those golden, shimmery flecks draining the tension from her body. At the next curve Covington Falls came into view.

Meredith slowed to take in the sight. "I've seen these falls more times than I can count, but I always forget how beautiful it is out here."

Julia left the path and reached down to trail a hand through the cool water. She turned to watch the falls flowing over the rocks, letting the sound soothe her soul.

"You look like you're ready to pass out," Meredith observed.

"I'm not very good at talking." Julia kicked at a small rock on the ground. "Not about feelings anyway. I don't do so well with those in general. They make me itchy."

"You say that as if you're trying to remind yourself about this apparent lack of character."

The rock came loose, and Julia reached down and picked it up. Ran her thumb over the water-smoothed surface. "I don't need reminding. I know this about myself."

Meredith grabbed the stone. "Well, I think it's a cover."

Julia's head snapped around. "A cover for what?"

"It makes it easier for you to keep your distance," Meredith said, tossing the rock in the air. "Tell yourself you're not capable of caring so you don't even have to put your foot in the water. From what you told me about the screwy way you grew up and the dysfunctional relationship you have with your parents, I'm not surprised. The thing is, Julia, you are not your parents."

"What's that mean?"

"Don't you realize you have successfully escaped the pattern they set?" Meredith asked, waving the rock in Julia's face. "The one you seem so sure you're going follow if you dare to try and have a relationship?"

"I don't even know what you just said."

"I'm saying I think your biggest fear is that you'll turn out like your parents. Unable to keep a commitment. Hurt people who've put their trust in you. Isn't that the root of all this angst?"

Julia had never had it put quite that way, but she realized with a start that her new friend was right. Her commitment phobia wasn't about not believing in love. It was about *her* not believing she could love someone without screwing it up. "I suppose so."

"You pushed Seth away, and even threw him at my sister, to protect him because you were sure you would end up hurting him."

"Right. Like I told Sarah, I only want Seth to be happy."

"Julia, don't you get it?" she asked, holding her arms out wide. "That's called *love*. Putting another person's happiness before your own. It's what your parents were never able to do, but you've done it."

"I have?"

Meredith laughed. "Don't look so stunned. If you'd ever stopped running from God long enough to open up a Bible, you'd understand."

"Why?"

"Because, it's exactly what Christ did for us. He sent His only Son to die for us because He loved us."

"You mean I'm not an emotional cripple?"

A wry smile was her answer. "Wounded maybe. That you can get over. I think you can have a very healthy relationship if you're brave enough to try."

"What if I try and it doesn't work? This family is all I have. If it ends badly, I'd lose not only Seth, but the rest of them as well."

"That's fear talking again," Meredith said, shaking her head. "More reasons to hold back. Turn the question around. What if it did work out, and you could make Seth happier than he's ever been? What if everything in your life has been leading to the two of you making a new life together?"

"Wait, I think I've heard this one." Julia put a finger to her temple, and then snapped her fingers. "This is all part of God's plan, right?"

Meredith ignored the sarcasm. "I would never presume to know God's plans for anyone. That has to come from your own heart."

"Copout."

Planting her fists on her hips, Meredith stood. "All right, you want an opinion? Six months ago, could you have imagined you'd reconnect with this family? That you'd run a wedding planning business and love doing it?"

"Who says I love it?"

"I do, and if you're honest you'll admit it, too," Meredith said, without even a crack of a smile. "Can I finish my point?"

Properly chastised, Julia nodded. "Sorry."

Meredith dropped her arms and gave a sheepish smile. "Actually, I think I already made it. Could you have imagined any of this? Realizing that you *do* belong to a family? Discovering that you're loved? That you are capable of loving someone?"

"No."

"So, don't you think it's possible that God brought you here for this purpose? To find Seth again? To heal him, and let him heal you?"

Julia stared, astounded someone who didn't know her that well had managed to explain her entire life in less than ten minutes. "I guess it's possible."

Meredith smiled as if Julia was a prized pupil. "I'd say it's very possible."

"You think I should tell Seth?"

"That's up to you. I think at the very least he deserves to know how you feel. That way he can make a real decision; not one based on something he thinks you want."

Julia couldn't help grinning. "I think I want to be you when I grow up."

Meredith laughed, but then sobered a little. "I'm not sure you'd like my life the way it's going right now."

"Why? What's going on?"

"There's a Session meeting in about a half hour from now, and my employment is the topic of discussion."

Julia gave a startled exclamation. "Oh, that's tonight? Seth told me about that a couple weeks ago. Are they really going to try and have you fired?"

"Some of them. Seth says there are plenty of people who support me, but I don't know..." Meredith bit her lip and pinched the bridge of her nose. "It's just a job, I know, but it feels so personal."

Julia put an arm around Meredith's shoulders. "Hey, aren't you the one who's always going on about plans from above?"

"It's easier to believe when it's someone other than me."

"Talk about a copout," Julia scoffed. "Listen, I'm still not exactly sure what I think about God's chess playing, but I do believe you will be fine no matter what happens. If God means for you to direct a church choir for the next thirty years, no roomful of pinched-faced, judgmental biddies will get in the way. Shoot, maybe He wants you to work in a bank or go pursue your music career again."

Meredith shook her head. "Wow, that was surprisingly

effective."

Julia clasped her hands in front of her chest and bowed. "You taught me well, Teacher."

"Now I want to be *you*."

"Oh no you don't. Then you'd have to deal with Catherine Manning."

Meredith screwed up her face in a grimace. "Right."

"Uh huh… bet a bunch of judgmental old men seem downright pleasant now. The way I see it, if I can handle Mrs. Manning and get Laurel safely hitched, I just might decide I can handle anything. Even a relationship."

Chapter Thirty

Seth couldn't remember the last time he'd been so nervous facing a group of men. Maybe when he'd gone before the Council for his final examination to become an ordained minister. Those men had held his future in their hands, and in a way so did the ones before him now.

He looked around the room at the fifteen men who made up the Session. They varied in age from early thirties to mid seventies. They were lawyers, doctors, businessmen, teachers, handymen, and a farmer. Some of them he knew well, like Ethan Thomas' brother Jake. Others he didn't. Some of them still looked at him as the skinny kid he'd once been and had trouble seeing him as their pastor.

Harris Matheson was one of those men. A tall, austere man with a perpetual scowl, he was a holdover from the James Markham days. Harris was fond of reminding everyone how long he'd been around and how everything had been run differently back then. Of course, *differently* was a code word for *better*. He also seemed to think it was his job to steer the young whelp in the right direction.

Harris had been the one to call the Session meeting in the

first place, and they'd barely gotten through the prayer before he stood to launch the first salvo.

"We're setting a dangerous precedent by allowing this young woman to assume such an important position," Harris stated. "She flaunted a lifestyle that goes against everything we believe, and now we're supposed to act like it doesn't matter?"

"Amen," the man to Harris' right said. Lawrence Bernhardt made up another third of the "Before Seth Graham" chorus. A prominent businessman, Lawrence had never been seen out in public in anything other than a three-piece suit to Seth's knowledge. "If we condone Meredith Vining's behavior, what kind of example are we setting for our youth?"

Emmitt Jackson, a pediatrician who'd moved to town about five years ago, cut in. "No one is saying we condone what Meredith did in her youth, but we all make mistakes. She deserves a chance to prove herself."

Lawrence rounded on the younger man. "Maybe you don't care if your children go down the path of unrighteousness, but others do."

A vein throbbed in Emmitt's temple, a clear sign he was trying to hold on to his temper. "I care what my children do. I've raised to them to know right from wrong, but if my son or daughter got into trouble, I'd hope that they wouldn't have to be condemned for it the rest of their lives."

"What if she tries to bring that rock music into this church?" the third member of the Before Seth Graham chorus chimed in. Bill Collingsworth, a lawyer with the county prosecutor's office, had remained silent for much of the meeting. Seth knew the balding, fifty-something man had merely been listening and gathering evidence to present his case. "What if she brings that poison into our midst? We don't want her type of music influencing our young people. I'm not sure we want *her* influencing them."

Jake Thomas jumped into the fray. "Oh, come on," he

said, with a impatient grumble. "You think Meredith Vining is going to be filling our kids' heads with thoughts of running off to be in a rock band or something? That's ridiculous. I have a teenage daughter, and let me tell you, I couldn't ask for a better role model. Who better to tell my daughter about the dangers of falling into temptation than someone who's been there?"

"I personally like what she's brought to the service, and the music," Joe Donaldson said. "Sure, it's different, but change is a good thing sometimes."

Seth looked over in surprise. Joe was a crusty old guy who owned the hardware store. Seth didn't know how old Joe actually was, but suspected he had to be nearing seventy. Having his support was shocking, but welcome.

"I still think having a young woman in that type of visible leadership role is a mistake," Harris interjected. "Especially as she has some questionable morals."

Rumblings went up around the room, some murmuring their agreement, others vehemently opposed. Tension rose thick enough to cut with a knife.

Seth had heard enough. He stood to face Harris and his two cohorts. "Gentlemen, I'm trying to be generous in understanding your concerns, but if we're going to travel down the path of questioning someone else's moral fitness it's time for me to take a stand. I have been struggling all week to contain my disappointment that my church could be so unwilling to forgive."

He paused and let his gaze rest on each man in the room. He had their attention. Now it was time to take Julia's advice and knock some heads together.

"A friend reminded me of the verse about throwing stones," Seth continued. "God has a lot to say about judging people. I look around this room, and I see friends. Many of you have sat in my office and confessed the struggles you've had with sin in your lives."

This time Seth was careful not to make specific eye contact, but names rolled through his head. One sobbing about his alcohol addiction. Another confessing of a one-night stand while on a business trip and wondering how on earth he was going to explain it to his wife. Another taking money from the company pension fund to cover a gambling debt.

All the men had stories they'd kept hidden from the world. Seth didn't know them all, but he knew enough.

"My heart has been so heavy," Seth said, struggling to contain his emotions. "Because what I don't understand, is how you who have been forgiven so much can attack someone else. Meredith has struggled with sin like all of us. She realized the path she was going down was the wrong one, and she changed course. She's made her peace with God, and He's the only one who matters."

"Amen," Jake murmured.

Seth nodded his thanks. "The Bible tells us of a story of a shepherd who goes in search of one lost sheep. He doesn't give up, and when he finds it, he rejoices. I know God rejoiced the day Meredith came home. Jesus himself told the parable of the Prodigal Son. The father welcomed his son with open arms and a celebration. It was the older son who protested. I ask you, are we going to be like that older son? Pointing out the speck in Meredith's eye while ignoring the plank in ours? I thought better of you. I thought better of this church, and this body of believers. I have to tell you, if we can't find a way to stop throwing stones we're going to bring the entire church down to the ground."

Drained and heartsick, Seth took his seat again and bowed his head. No one said anything for a while.

A voice to Seth's right cut through the stillness. "Thank you, Reverend, for reminding us about forgiveness."

Seth lifted his head. Grey eyes that had reflected despair over a moment of weakness swam with unshed tears. He looked around and saw several others were wiping their eyes.

A roomful of men stripped of their arrogance. In that moment, Seth knew a miracle had occurred. He didn't pride himself in thinking his words had turned the tide, but something powerful had happened.

Not all of them were happy, of course. The Before Seth Graham chorus sat with arms folded, their faces red with righteous fury. They had lost, and the defeat did not sit well with them. Seth figured he'd be short a few members come Sunday, but he could handle a slight exodus.

The meeting adjourned without taking a vote. None was needed. The men filed out, most without talking to anyone else.

Seth went to his office and prayed. Thanked God for averting the crisis and asked for strength and guidance. He even prayed for Bill, Harris, and Lawrence. By the time Seth walked outside, the moon had risen high in the sky. He paused to drink in the sight. No matter what madness human beings cooked up, the moon and stars stayed constant. To the naked eye at least.

He crossed the parking lot to his car but stopped when a voice called out. Jake Thomas loped toward him.

"I thought everyone was long gone," Seth said.

Jake shook Seth's hand and slapped him on the back. "A couple of us were out here talking. That was some thrashing, Reverend. Inspired even. I've never seen you so on fire. If I'd been in your place, I would have bashed some heads together."

Seth chuckled. "That's what my friend said."

"The same one who reminded you about throwing stones?"

"Right."

"Smart friend."

One more hand shake and Jake walked back to his car. Seth headed for home. Much of downtown was closed up tight. Devon's restaurant seemed to be doing a good business, though, and he could see several people milling around inside the bookstore. Main Street's one traffic light turned red, and Seth stopped.

He thought about Jake's parting comment. Julia had given him a good kick in the pants, and in the end she'd proven to be his inspiration. He should call and let her know what had happened. Better yet, he could go over and tell her in person. He couldn't wait to see her face when he told—

Somewhere in his mind a key turned. The drums he'd heard in the park on first seeing Julia started up again. Only this time they pounded like a thousand waves crashing into the shore. He wondered if this was what Paul had felt like on the road to Damascus. The clarity of vision. The utter certainty that his life had changed forever.

Who was the first person he wanted to tell good news and bad? Who had he come to for advice in the first place? Who had he been trying to *stop* thinking about for weeks now? It certainly wasn't Amy. His feet had taken him in the direction he needed to go before his heart had been willing to admit the truth. Meredith and Brian had recognized the truth, but he'd been too caught up in a memory. Too scared to let go.

A horn blared behind him, and he jerked back to the present. Seth waved a hand in apology, and after a slight hesitation he turned in the opposite direction from Grace's house.

A few minutes later, he made a left. He parked near the entrance and got out. Gravel crunched under his feet as he made his way past gravestones bathed in the silvery glow of the moon. Moist earth and the scent of dozens of different blooms filled his lungs. Crickets and his own breath were the only other sounds he could detect.

When he reached the magnolia tree he stopped. The words chiseled on the stone swam in front of his eyes, but he didn't need to see them.

ELIZABETH JOY GRAHAM

BELOVED WIFE AND DAUGHTER
ALIVE IN GLORY

Seth stared down at the grave marker. "Hey, BG," he choked and blew out a gust of air. A sweet-scented breeze slipped past his cheek, and he smiled. "Yeah, I guess you know why I'm here. You've probably been up there shaking your head, wondering when I'd get it. I'm stubborn, but then you know that, too. I didn't want to let you go when you were here, and I held tight even when you'd gone. But like my dad said, there's room in my heart for you... and Julia. It just took me a while to figure that out."

He squatted down, and touched the top of the gravestone. "Who would have ever thought? Prickly, bitter, keep-your-distance Julia Richardson. I guess she's had to be all those things to survive, though. I think you would have liked her. She's pretty special, BG. She'd kill me for saying this, but she's actually sweet and kind and loving. And she makes me glad I'm still alive. Dad was right about that, too. I think she *is* what I need now."

Pushing to his feet, Seth stood. A lump seemed to clamp around his throat as he stared down at the marker. Reaching into the vase of the grave next to him, he plucked a couple roses and placed them on the ground in front of Beth's tombstone.

The vise pressing down on his windpipe eased as fresh tears flowed. "Night, BG. Love you."

Without looking back, Seth walked away.

Chapter Thirty-One

"Get to the church, now."

Julia stared at the phone in confusion. She'd been focused on the million and one things that needed to be accomplished for Laurel Manning's wedding, including confirming final fittings, hair appointments, limousine service, catering, and delivery of everything from boutonnières to a mammoth ice sculpture of a swan about to take flight, to Hadden Acres. So, it took a moment to process both the identity of the voice and the disjointed comment.

"I'm sorry?" Julia asked.

"Unless you want to consign me to the fate of wearing a bubblegum pink Southern Belle number you'd better get yourself over to the church right now."

"Meredith?"

A distinct sigh of frustration floated through the phone. "Of course it's Meredith. Do you know anyone else with a sister who would force her to wear a hoop skirt and corset in the middle of summer?"

"I don't even know what you're talking about," Julia said as she read through her notes.

"Amy called to tell me Seth asked her to come by the church. To talk, she said. Amy has gone into blushing bride mode already. She's convinced he's going to pop the question today. She's on her way there."

The dire warning finally succeeded at getting Julia's full attention. "Where are you?"

"Giving a voice lesson," Meredith said. "I'd cancel, but I'm not sure thwarting my sister's engagement falls under the category of family emergency."

"Do you think he'd pop the question at the church? That doesn't seem very romantic to me."

"Amy seems to think it would be exactly the place he would pick. *Are you moving yet?*"

The last question was sharp enough to make Julia leap to her feet. She had her hand on the front door, her mind already wondering how on earth a person was supposed to stop an impending proposal. "Yes, I'm moving."

"You're going to bust it up?"

"I'm going to try."

Julia heard a little *whoop* on the other end of the phone. "Hallelujah! Go get him, sweetie," Meredith said.

Julia slipped into her car. "Shouldn't you be pulling for your sister at least a little?"

"Would you make me wear a skirt so wide I'd have to turn sideways to get through the door at your wedding?"

A shudder threaded down Julia's spine and a cold sweat broke out. "Don't mention a wedding yet. I'm still working up to the relationship part, but to answer your question, there would be no hoops or corsets."

"There you have my reason. Not to mention the fact that I think you and Seth make sense."

"Why?"

"You complete him."

"I'm hanging up now."

Meredith let out a delighted laugh. "Call and let me

know what happens. I'll be looking at wedding songs for you guys."

Julia hung up.

Despite her casual tone on the phone, Julia ended up breaking a few speed limits on the way to the church. Once there, she barely got the key out of the ignition before jumping from her car. Her mind raced. Where would Seth choose to propose? His office seemed way too formal.

Outside somewhere?

She wasted a few precious minutes circling the grounds, but the happy couple wasn't in the picturesque gardens or in the playground near the Sunday school rooms.

Sunday school. There was an idea. Amy was the director after all.

Julia slipped inside the building, paused to adjust to the darkness, and started off down the hallway. As she passed the open doors of the sanctuary, a flash of pink caught her eye. She skidded to a halt. Search over. Amy had dressed well for the occasion. Clad in a flowing, cotton candy-colored sundress, with a pink ribbon tied in her hair, she looked like a young 1950s starlet.

Julia took a step, ready to call out and stop the proposal, when it registered that Seth didn't look like a man who'd just declared his undying love. Furthermore, Amy definitely didn't look like undying love has been declared to her.

Amy's golden tresses swayed as she shook her head. "I don't understand. Everything was so perfect. We could be happy. *I* could make you happy."

Oh, bless the marvelous acoustics! Julia could hear every word loud and clear. She slipped into a pew in the back, careful to stay in the shadows.

"Amy, I didn't mean to lead you on," Seth said. "I never should have asked you out in the first place."

"It's your wife, isn't it? You can't get over her," Amy said. "I can help you do that. I can make you forget her."

"No one could ever make me forget Beth."

Amy must have sensed the rebuke and wisely backed off. "Of course not. I didn't mean it that way. I only meant—"

"Beth isn't the issue."

There was a moment of silence. "It's *her*, isn't it?"

Julia couldn't see it from the pew, but she somehow knew Amy's burn-your-face-off laser gaze had returned. Julia knew who "her" was too, and she sank lower in the pew in case there was another set of laser eyes in the back of Amy's head.

"Do you love her?" Amy asked.

Yeah, do you?

Seth didn't answer.

Come on. Answer her.

"She isn't worthy of you," Amy said. "She'll never make you happy the way Beth did. The way I can. She doesn't understand you and what you need."

"Actually, she does, probably better than anyone ever has," Seth said.

Okay, that wasn't exactly a passionate declaration, but it was a start.

"She's not like us, Seth," Amy said. "She doesn't believe the things we do."

Seth rubbed the back of his neck. "I never said it made sense. In any case, I don't know what God will do with her heart."

"What about your position here?" Amy asked. "Do you think the leaders of our church will approve?"

"I don't care."

Julia gasped.

"What was that?" Amy cried.

Julia ducked down in the pew as their heads turned. Her heart started pounding. Seth didn't care if people objected? If he faced criticism or even lost his position in the church because of her? Okay, so maybe it wasn't a big romantic gesture like a room full of roses or skywriting, but the declaration worked for her. A hot flush enveloped her whole body.

"I didn't hear anything," Seth said.

"Seth please—"

He held out a hand. "Amy, it's no good. I'm so sorry."

"She'll only hurt you—" Her voice cracked.

"I'm sorry."

Seth kissed her cheek, and Julia could tell by the stiffness in Amy's shoulders that she was trying to hold it together. Then she twirled around and hurried from the sanctuary. Julia barely had time to duck out of sight again, but Amy was in such a hurry she didn't even glance around.

Shoot, Julia thought, now she was stuck. It was one thing to stop a proposal, but to be caught listening in on a dumping was so immature.

An important question flashed through Julia's mind. How long would she have to wait for Seth to leave? Unless she could sneak out before he saw her?

Yeah. Apparently not happening, because when Julia glanced up Seth stood right… by… the… pew!

"Hide and seek?" he ventured.

Gathering her dignity, Julia sat up. "If it matters I didn't mean to eavesdrop."

"How much of that did you catch?"

"Some."

Seth's eyes narrowed. "Define some."

"I heard you."

A dispirited sigh escaped as he lowered himself onto the pew next to her. "What are you doing here anyway?"

"Meredith called me."

The answer brought forth a bemused glance. "Meredith?"

"She called to tell me Amy was in a state because you had asked her to come here."

A shake of his head indicated Seth still didn't

understand. Julia didn't blame him. She wasn't making any sense.

"Amy seemed to believe you were about to propose, and Meredith said I should get over here," Julia continued. "Meredith sort of knows about us."

A light seemed to dawn, and Seth turned more fully in the pew. "And you came to do what?" he asked, eyes growing sharper and more focused.

"To stop you."

"Why?"

His eyes twinkled, and Julia fought the urge to slug him. "Why what?"

Seth crowded closer. "Why did you want to stop me from proposing?"

Looking him in the eye was impossible right now. Instead, Julia covered her face. "You're going to make me say it, aren't you?"

"I'd like to hear it, yes. I did pour my heart out to you."

Such a bald statement earned a glare. "You poured your heart out to Amy."

The teasing disappeared, replaced with tenderness. "Is it so hard for you to say?"

"You know it is," she whispered.

"Were you going to race over here and *not* say it?"

Julia let out frustrated groan. "I don't know. I only wanted to tell you I ran because I was scared."

"I know that."

"No, you don't understand." Explaining seemed so hard. "I was afraid I was going to screw everything up and hurt you, and then I'd lose everyone. Grace, Sarah, baby Mary. Mostly, I couldn't hurt you."

"You could have let me make that choice."

"I know that now. That's why I ran over here. I wanted to tell you how I felt before you proposed to Amy, so you could choose. I didn't want you to marry her because I told you to."

"I wouldn't marry anyone because you told me to."

"You dated her because I told you to." Yes, the observation came out huffy, but she couldn't help it. Weeks of watching Amy and Seth coo at each other like a couple of morning doves had left her cranky.

"Because I was hoping—" he broke off.

This time Julia leaned closer. "Hoping what?"

"That what I was feeling was only a general need to love someone again. When Beth died, I thought that part of me died, too."

"Was it? A general thing I mean?"

"No. I missed you," he said, a smile playing about his lips. "I missed your sass and fire. Your sarcasm and your prickliness."

"What a romantic." Two fingers tapped against her chest. "Be still my heart."

Seth reached out and touched a strand of her hair. Wrapped it around his finger. "I missed this hair. The way it seems to sizzle like you do. I missed the way your eyes see right through me. I missed looking at you."

The man did have a way with words. Drawing in a shaky breath, Julia took his hand. "If we weren't in a church, I'd jump you right now."

The evil man chuckled and swooped closer. "Jump away."

"Forget it." She shoved a hand against his chest. "If I'm going to be dating the minister, I have to act like a proper lady. Making out in a church pew is not ladylike."

"Guess what?" Seth asked, hooking a hand behind her neck. "I don't feel very ministerial right now."

Okay, one kiss…

****

Didn't she say only one kiss? Julia gasped out a strangled

"enough" and shoved away from him. Strangled laughter bubbled up.

"What?" Seth asked, trailing a hand down her hair.

Catching his hand, Julia studied the grooves in his palm as if seeking an answer. "I'm wondering how we got here, that's all. There couldn't possibly be two more opposite people in the world. How did you know? I only figured it out last night."

An answering laugh rumbled up from his chest. "Then last night was one for discoveries. I was driving home from the Session meeting and—"

For a moment, all thoughts of their relationship disappeared. "The one about Meredith? What happened? Did you do what I said and knock some heads together?"

"Yeah. One of the guys said he'd never seen me so inspired. Meredith's job is safe."

Letting out a scream of joy, she wrapped her arms around his neck. "My hero. Tell me what you said. I hope you used the stones verse."

"Yes on that, too."

How could he keep information like that from her? Irritated, she socked him in the arm.

"Ow," he complained. "What was that for?"

"Why didn't you call me last night?" she asked, brows pulling down in a ferocious frown.

"I wanted to. I'd planned to come over and tell you in person."

"Did you get lost on the way home?"

A finger traced across the furrow between her brows. "No, I found myself," Seth said. "When I realized you were the first person I wanted to tell, I knew I'd been denying the truth for a long time. So, I had to make another stop."

"Where?"

"I went to Beth's grave."

Every fiber in her being froze at the mention of his wife.

"Why?"

"To tell her about you… and to say goodbye."

A lump rose in her throat. She pictured Seth standing in front of a grave marker that hadn't yet become discolored and aged by time. She knew how hard it must have been for him to take that final step and let go.

"I wonder if she'd be happy? I'm sure she wouldn't think anyone was good enough for you."

Seth's smile was full of relaxed confidence. "Beth would have liked you."

"Are you absolutely sure you want to get mixed up with me?" Julia asked, ready to give him one more out.

He waggled his eyebrows. "Didn't I just prove that a few minutes ago?"

"That could be a biological thing. Pheromones."

"I'm all for pheromones."

"Wicked, wicked man," Julia scolded. "But seriously. Amy probably is better suited—"

"Amy is like kudzu," Seth said.

"Huh?"

"It's a vine, like ivy, and it slowly engulfs everything in its path. Ends up killing all the other trees from lack of sunlight."

"Amy was engulfing you?"

"She was smothering me."

"Meredith said Amy had all these childhood hero-worship expectations."

"She had them all right. I could feel the weight of them every time she looked at me. She even took me to this house she'd fallen in love with as a child. The one she's always wanted to live in."

"One guess who she pictured as her husband in this fantasy."

A grimace twisted his mouth. "It took me a while to pick up on the clues. Then, when she showed up here today in that dress, I knew it was going to end badly."

"I think she picked it out because it would complement a ring."

"That's right. Shove the knife in deeper," Seth said, closing his eyes as if in pain. "I feel like I pulled the wings off a butterfly."

"If it helps, I don't think Amy's a butterfly," Julia said. "Far from it, actually. Would you have broken up with her anyway?"

"Yes."

"I wasn't a convenient excuse, was I?"

A look of great offense came her way. "There you go again. I thought I did a pretty fantastic job of convincing you."

"Pheromones."

He put his hands over his chest. "My heart. And body and soul."

Okay, that was awesome, but keep it together, Julia. "Did you mean what you said? The part about not caring what people thought here?"

"Amazing, isn't it?" he said, a smile returning to his lips.

"What about the faith part? What if I can't believe what you do?"

"I'll have to pray for you. *A lot,* and with great passion." He brushed her hair out of the way and nuzzled behind her ear. "Or I could come up with other enjoyable ways to convince you."

How was she supposed to concentrate when he was doing marvelous such things with his lips? "Is this an accepted method of persuasion?"

Hot puffs of air sent shivers down her neck as he laughed. "I don't know, but I'm seriously considering adopting it as a new form of conversion."

"Seth—"

"Julia, you talk too much," he said, as his lips covered hers.

Did she say only one kiss?

"Umm… Reverend Graham?"

The tentative question came from a discreetly dressed woman in her early fifties who seemed to have magically appeared by the pew.

The scream came from Julia.

Seth turned his head. "Hi, Gladys. Have you met Julia?"

If Gladys found anything unusual in finding the minister necking in a church pew, she didn't show it. "I haven't had the pleasure, no."

Julia studied the older woman, looking for outrage or scorn, but it was impossible to read anything in the other woman's expression.

"I'm so sorry to disturb you, but Ethan Thomas is here," Gladys said.

A reluctant sigh escaped Seth before he answered. "I'll be there in a minute."

Gladys nodded, and as she turned she caught Julia's eye and discreetly lowered one eyelid.

Julia gasped in surprise. "I think she just winked at me."

"She's probably thrilled to see me with another woman," Seth said. "Gladys has made no secret of the fact that she thinks I shouldn't be alone anymore."

"Who is she anyway?"

"My secretary and all around general of operations around here."

"Great, so I've already made a fine first impression on your staff."

He stroked her hair again. "I'm sorry to run off before we've talked."

"Whose fault is that?"

"Mine entirely," Seth said, with a smug grin. "The thing is, I do need to meet with Ethan."

"Who is he?"

"Old friend from school, but we meet every week. We

both lost our wives around the same time, and we sort of formed our own support group."

"Did she have cancer, too?"

"No, her death was sudden. An aneurism. Went to bed one night and never woke up."

Julia's heart clenched. "That's awful. At least you had time to say goodbye to Beth."

"Right. Now he's raising his two boys alone."

"That should be a comfort, though. At least he has a piece of his wife with him."

"I know," Seth said. "I envied him that for a long time."

An image popped into her mind, and Julia couldn't help but smile. "I can picture a dark-haired little boy with your eyes."

"Would you have cared? If I already had children?"

The thought made her heart flutter. "They'd be a part of you. How could I not love them?"

A hard stirring of emotion passed over his eyes. "You realize you almost used the 'L' word in reference to me?"

Julia's eyes closed, and she swallowed as sudden panic rose up. "I'm working up to it. I'll have to take baby steps, okay?"

"I'll hold your hand," he said, taking her hand and kissing each finger.

Laughing, she shoved against his chest. "Down boy. You have to go. I have to go."

With an exaggerated sigh, Seth held up his hands in surrender. "Okay, okay."

Seth helped Julia to her feet, and without breaking their hold they walked out to the foyer. Julia stared down at their joined hands, wondering how on earth she'd ever ended up in this situation.

"What are you thinking?" Seth asked, though she suspected he knew.

"I was wondering if we're crazy to think this could

work."

"I'd say we'd be crazy not to even try."

"What if I screw it up?"

In answer, he reached up and cradled her face with his hands. "You're worth taking a chance on. Who knows, you might decide I'm the one who's screwed up."

Okay. That deserved one more kiss.

"Whoa! Sorry!" a deep, male voice rang out.

This time the interrupter was a tall, blond man with devilish, green eyes. He was wearing dress slacks, a white shirt, and a blue tie.

"Gladys said I should make sure you hadn't gotten lost," the stranger said. He didn't bother to hide his curiosity as he looked at Julia.

Seth made the introductions. "Ethan Thomas, this is Julia Richardson."

A huge grin broke out across the newcomer's face, and Julia swore if she wasn't already hooked on Seth, she'd seriously think about attacking his friend.

"So, you're Julia," Ethan said. "It's nice to finally meet you."

Julia arched a brow in Seth's direction. "Finally?"

"Poor Seth has been out of sorts for weeks now," Ethan explained. "Mostly because of you. We considered dropping him from our weekly two-on-two basketball game, but in the end we were glad to see him coming back to the land of the living again."

Amazement filled her as Seth's cheeks turned ruddy. "My friends have no discretion," he said.

The thought that he'd been discussing their situation with his friends set her heart beating like the flutter of a hummingbird's wings. That still didn't completely erase her embarrassment at having been caught necking with the minister… twice.

"I'll let you two talk," she said, kissing Seth's cheek. "See you."

"Julia," Seth called.

The way he said her name made goose bumps race up her arm. She turned around. Seth smiled, and little fizzles of sensation streaked through her body. And for once, the sensation didn't frighten her.

Chapter Thirty-Two

Seth never knew he could miss someone after only a few hours apart. Couldn't remember ever being so edgy. He and Julia had so much they needed to talk about. They'd taken a first step, but Seth had no illusions their path would be easy. Baby steps, Julia had said. He had to hold on to that promise, otherwise she'd spook like a wild mare.

Oh, hang talking. They had plenty of time for talking. He wanted to hold her again. Now that he'd taken the chains off his heart, he'd become almost obsessed with seeing Julia. Touching her.

Man was he in trouble. Some might say he was whipped, but he couldn't think of a better woman to get twisted in knots over.

Watching television proved impossible, so Seth went out to the balcony for some air. At least that's what he told himself. Julia would be home soon, and he didn't want to miss her. She had a crazy schedule lately with the Manning wedding. With his luck she'd end up sleeping over at Marry Me.

A car door slammed in the distance, and he straightened.

A few seconds later, Julia rounded the corner at a brisk clip. She spotted him and came to a halt. Then she smiled, an expression filled with amusement and relief. He realized she'd been just as anxious to see him. The thought made his heart skip a beat.

Oh, yeah, he was in trouble.

"I was beginning to think our esteemed mayor's wife would keep you occupied all night," he said.

A clipped spat of laughter floated across the lawn. "I'm sure Mrs. Manning could come up with dozens of tasks to keep me occupied for the next year, but Betsy and I were too exhausted to do anything else, so we packed it in." She stopped right below him. "I should be furious with you, actually. Amy didn't come back to work after you dumped her. I think I've lost my second assistant."

"Should I have put it off for another few days?"

"Not on your life," Julia said, taking the stairs two at a time.

A burst of laughter bubbled up from her throat.

"What's so funny?" he asked.

"Me. I'm marveling that it's possible to miss a person after only a couple hours apart."

Great minds think alike. He opened his arms as Julia ran into them. He breathed in her scent and thought he could happily spend the rest of his life holding this woman. "Did you miss me?"

"Yes, and you can stop with that grin. I know you're pleased with yourself."

He touched the tip of her nose. "I'm smiling because I was thinking the same thing."

"Do you know what else I was thinking?"

"What?"

"That you have some making up to do. We kept getting interrupted after all."

Seth didn't need any more prompting, but quickly

captured her lips. The fervor with which she returned the kiss proved she'd been just as eager to see him.

"Umm... hmm."

They both jumped as someone cleared their throat below them.

Seth looked down and saw Grace standing below the garage apartment, hands on hips. Julia's cheeks went white, and he cursed his stepmother's timing.

Great.

"Hello," Grace said, her expression giving nothing away. "Why don't you two come inside, and I'll fix some tea?"

Without waiting to see if they followed her gently worded edict, Grace turned and walked inside the house.

Seth groaned in dismay.

"I'm guessing you haven't mentioned this to her yet," Julia said.

"No, I was hoping we would tell her together."

Fear rose in her eyes as Julia stared at the screen door. "Did she look angry to you?"

"I couldn't tell."

The sigh of a condemned criminal echoed in the night. "Let's get it over with then," Julia said.

Seth grabbed her hand, not about to let her run now. "Julia, it'll be all right."

"You don't know that," she said, pulling away.

Grace stood at the stove, waiting on the water to boil. "Have a seat," she said, without turning around.

Another soft and gentle order, and they knew better than to disobey. The teakettle began to whistle, and Grace poured water into three cups. She still hadn't said anything.

Julia glanced at him, and Seth winked. A little of the color returned to her cheeks, and she covered her mouth to hide a grin. When he turned back Grace was staring right at him.

Grace brought a tray with the teacups and took a seat across from them. "So, who'd like to volunteer to bring me up to date?"

"It was my fault—" Seth and Julia said almost in unison.

"Did I say there was blame to be assigned?" Grace asked, eyes widening. "I only want to know what's going on. I didn't imagine the two of you kissing."

"Grace, I love her," Seth said.

Both women gasped. Grace, probably from surprise, but Julia had to be flat out shocked. After all, they'd skirted around the love word all day. Seth was surprised at how easily the admission fell from his lips. Now that he'd said the words though, the truth of them flooded his being with a kind of peace he hadn't experienced since meeting Beth.

Gazing at Julia, Seth silently willed her not to freak out, and after a moment she took a deep breath and nodded. He could not have been more proud.

"I'm not sure how it happened," he said. "I was angry that Julia hadn't bothered to come back and visit you and Sarah in years. I wasn't very welcoming at first."

Julia jabbed a finger in his direction. "He was mean."

"You yelled at me."

"Because you jumped all over me."

A brow quirked. Were they going to get into a fight over who had been more obnoxious at their first meeting now?

"Okay, I guess I wasn't very nice either," Julia said.

Another quick glance at Grace revealed his stepmother was trying not to laugh. Of course, who wouldn't when he and Julia were squabbling like children?

"Anyway, we managed to put the past behind us, and we became friends," Seth continued. "Then something more."

Julia jumped in to add her own version of events. "Only I got scared and made him date Amy because I thought she'd make a better minister's wife."

"That was your doing?" Grace asked, not bothering to hide her amusement now. "I was very much afraid we were going to be stuck with that young woman as part of the family."

Seth choked at the thought. "Not on your life."

Julia chuckled at his quick-fire, gut response, and Seth glowered at her. After all, he'd gotten tangled up with Amy in the first place because of her. A rueful smile crept across her face, and then she mouthed a contrite, *"sorry"*.

Such cheekiness. "However I came to date Amy, she's no longer in the picture."

"I see," Grace said.

Did she? Probably more than most. Grace had lost a spouse, and had her heart broken by Julia's father. Now, she'd finally found love and contentment.

"I'm not proud of what happened with Amy," Seth said. "I hurt her a great deal, but I needed to see if what I felt for Julia was more than a first response to a woman after—" His throat closed. Surely Grace understood.

Her knowing look said she did.

Grace turned to Julia as if awaiting her side of things.

Taking a deep, bracing breath, Julia started talking. "Grace, this is the weirdest thing I could have ever imagined. I've been fighting it because I was afraid of hurting everyone, but the thing is I don't want to fight it anymore. Seth is the most amazing thing that could have happened to me. He looks at me and sees someone special, and for the first time I believe I might be."

Grace studied Julia for a moment and then looked back at Seth. "I think maybe it's time you moved back into your house."

Surprised laughter bubbled up. "Definitely," he said.

Tears filled Grace's eyes. "I was wondering when the two of you would stop being so stubborn and admit how you feel."

Julia's mouth fell open. "What? You knew?"

"I thought we were pretty discreet," Seth said.

"I'm not blind." Grace laughed and wiped a hand across her cheek. "Do you think I couldn't see the fireworks that threatened to erupt anytime you two were in a room together? Anyone who knew you well could see them."

"So you don't mind if I'm involved with Seth?" Julia asked, worry clouding her features as she sat forward.

Seth could see he'd have to go extra slow. Julia still didn't fully understand how much Grace loved her.

Ever patient, Grace took Julia's hand. "Honey, I know how much you need someone to love you unconditionally. I have no doubt Seth can do that."

"I can, and I do," he seconded.

"And, my dear, I hope you never have to watch someone you love lose a spouse," Grace continued. "Seth may not be my son by blood, but I would have done anything to prevent his pain. You've made him smile again. Made him whole. How can I not give my blessing to that?"

Julia blinked and her eyes filled, too. "Thank you."

The two women jumped up and held each other for a long moment. Then Grace pulled back and framed Julia's face, seeming to search for something. Suddenly, Grace smiled.

"What?" Julia asked.

"I needed to see it," Grace said, her smile widening.

"What?"

"Happiness. It suits you."

"Yes, I think it does."

Seth came around the table to hug his stepmother. "Thank you for giving us your blessing, Grace."

Grace touched his cheek. "I want all my children to be happy, no matter how they came to be part of this family." The gentle touch turned into a light tap. "I meant it about the living arrangements, though."

"I'll be out of your hair by the end of the week," Seth said.

"Well, then, I think I've had all the excitement I can stand for one night," Grace said. "Besides, I can't wait to tell John. We had a friendly wager going."

"Grace," he and Julia said in unison.

A rueful shrug lifted her shoulders. "You really didn't do a very good job of hiding your attraction."

"Goodnight, Grace," Seth said, giving her a kiss on the cheek.

"Don't stay down here too long, all right?" Grace said, before gliding from the room

Seth longed to take Julia back in his arms, but he refrained for the moment. "I should probably let you go to bed. You've got the wedding tomorrow."

"I don't think I could sleep a wink."

"Me neither."

"Do you feel like going out?"

"What? Now?" he said in surprise.

A conspiratorial grin lit Julia's face. "There's someone else we should tell, and since her baby led us to this predicament, I think Sarah deserves to know before the whole town finds out. I almost dread telling her. I'm not looking forward to the big I-told-you-so."

"Why? What does she know?"

"I had to keep her occupied while she was cooped up. So we talked."

Julia had been discussing him? "About what?"

"I may have mentioned the kiss," Julia said, cheeks matching her hair. "Both of them, actually. Plus, the Amy business, of course."

Better and better. Seth grinned, even as he recognized the impulse to beat his chest could only be labeled immature. "You talked about me?"

"Male ego. Doesn't matter what occupation." She took his arm and turned him in the direction of the door. "Come on, Romeo, let's go tell Sarah."

"Wait. I want to know," Seth said, following her outside. "Was this a comparative thing or—"

Chapter Thirty-Three

Today, Julia thought. After today the mayor's entire family would be out of her hair forever. She'd be rejoicing if not for the terrifying notion that something might go wrong. Plus, she still had to work on making the transition from dedicated single woman to one-half of a functioning couple.

Rejoicing could happen later. Same with figuring out the relationship thing. Right now she had two hours to get ten impossibly spoiled wannabe debutantes dressed, coiffed, and transferred to Hadden Acres in time for the grand nuptials.

Sadly, the impossibly spoiled wannabe debs weren't half as annoying their mothers. All of them seemed to be hovering like a bunch of ticked-off bears, and in the middle of it all was the Grand Poobah of angry bear-ness. Julia had spent more time catering to Mrs. Manning's needs than the bride and all her attendants combined. Between fetching bottles of water to buying grapes for her mid-morning repast, Julia hadn't stopped running all day. She envied Betsy and Amy because they got to spend the day at the plantation overseeing the setup on that end.

Julia shook her head, still amazed that her second

assistant had shown up for duty. Right on time, too. She couldn't help but be impressed. It took gumption to put on a brave face and pretend one hadn't been dumped. Perhaps Julia had pegged Amy wrong after all.

"Julia, my Laurel needs crackers."

Julia shifted her eyes toward Mrs. Manning as she worked to pin an errant curl back into submission on bridesmaid number six's head.

"Excuse me?" Julia asked, eyeing the tray of crackers she'd brought over from her last trip to the store… fifteen minutes ago.

Catherine Manning didn't even glance at the offering. "The gourmet crackers from Rice's Emporium."

So, clearly regular old crackers wouldn't do for Princess Manning. Julia reached for her ever-present cell phone. "I can call over there and have someone bring—"

La Manning's nostrils flared. Julia feared the woman's head might explode at any moment. Over crackers. No, *gourmet* crackers.

So, not getting around yet another trip to the store. "I'll be right back."

Grabbing her purse, Julia hurried out, but not before catching the flicker of triumph that flashed in the other woman's eyes.

Julia fought the urge to stuff those gourmet crackers right up Queen Manning's nose.

One hour and forty-five minutes later Laurel and all ten bridesmaids stood in their places, ready to go. A string quartet was playing. Guests had filled the impossibly elegant white chairs on the lawn. A white runner stretched from where the bridal party waited, to the arbor where the groom would be standing. A real, but temporary, hardwood floor had been put in place.

An ice sculpture of a swan about to take flight resided in a portable freezer, ready to be wheeled out in time for the reception. Three dozen round tables with the finest Egyptian tablecloths were waiting for hungry guests who would dine on their choice of prime rib, grilled salmon, or Cornish hens. Another table held the most incredible five-tiered wedding cake Julia had ever seen.

And in three little cages behind the arbor, rested three dozen white doves. Yes, she'd found the doves. Or rather Amy had.

Everything looked perfect, but nothing could quell Julia's fear. "I think I'm going to throw up."

"Me too," Amy seconded.

Without a word, Betsy produced two brown paper bags and handed them over.

Betsy's resources were endless. "Why aren't you running Marry Me?" Julia asked in amazement.

"Someday," Betsy said, flashing a sly grin.

Meanwhile, Amy stared down into her paper bag as if she might actually be thinking about using it.

"It took a lot of guts for you to show up here today," Julia said.

Amy looked up then, tears shimmering in her baby-blue eyes. "If you hurt him you'll have me to answer to."

Wow, Little Miss Perfect had just grown up, Julia thought. Who knew getting dumped would turn Amy Vining into a real human being?

"Thank you for helping me," Julia said. "I don't think I could have done any of this without you."

"I didn't do that much," Amy said, crinkling the bag in her hands.

"That's not true—" An alarm went off, and Julia jumped.

Betsy reached under her jacket and took out a tiny little device. "That's the signal. I'll get the groom and send the ushers back to escort the mothers."

"Where did you get that?" Julia asked.

"Online," Betsy said with a grin, and then hurried off to

herd the men to their places.

"That girl is going to run the world someday," Amy said.

"No doubt," Julia said. "Okay, will you see to the mothers? I'll track down the mayor and get the girls in place."

For the first time all day, Amy grinned. "Are you trying to avoid Mrs. Manning?"

"Unless we want bloodstains all over this nice white runner, I think it's best."

They parted company. Getting all the girls ready to go down the aisle was like getting ten baby chicks to run in a straight line. She managed the task, though. Mayor Manning proved to be a docile sort, following along behind the group as if he were taking a Sunday stroll in the park. Julia wondered if some sort of medicinal enhancement allowed him to be so calm in the middle of the chaos. Not to mention the roiling storm cloud that was his wife.

Julia looked down the runway and saw that the mothers were seated. She caught sight of Grace and next to her Sarah, who'd managed to pry herself away from the baby to attend. Sarah waved hello.

Chuckling, Julia waggled her fingers in return and then got back to business. She signaled Betsy, who sent the groom and his entourage out. Seth appeared behind them, and as he took his place, he looked right at Julia and winked.

Julia forced herself to concentrate as the quartet began the processional. She nudged the first duckling to get her going.

Bridesmaid number two… number three… number four… five.

Finally, they were all on their way, and Julia turned toward Laurel to adjust her veil one last time. The girl let out a tremulous sigh.

"Everything okay?" Julia asked, not really expecting an answer.

"Yes, thank you."

"You're welcome."

Laurel reached up and snagged Julia's hand. "No really… *thank you*. I realize my mother is—" the young bride glanced at her father, who playfully covered his ears. "—a pain, and you've been great."

Julia's mouth dropped open.

Laurel laughed, and Mayor Manning chuckled, though he tried to hide it by coughing behind his hand. Julia about fainted, but managed to pull herself together long enough to send father and daughter down the aisle. The quartet reached its climax as Laurel reached her groom, and Betsy signaled a thumbs-up from her corner.

Relief nearly brought Julia to her knees. However, she'd barely released the breath when a strange hum erupted behind her. Then a spitting sound. Followed by… water.

Lots and lots of water.

Streaks of it arched across the lawn from what seemed like a hundred sprinklers. And not little water-your-daisies drops of water, either. Huge, cannon fire streams of it. Going right over the guests.

Screams erupted, and everyone started running for cover.

"Where did these sprinklers come from?" Julia asked, unable to move.

"I'll go find the groundskeeper," Amy shouted, and took off across the grass.

The comment shook Julia out of her stupor, and she sprinted for the plantation house. Surely someone there knew what to do.

The plantation manager, perhaps alerted by the screams, met her at the door. The woman froze, gazing in horror at the chaotic scene. "What in the world?"

Julia grabbed the woman's arm. "We've got a Noah's Ark situation going on. How do we turn the sprinklers off?"

"The grounds crew," the manager said.

A call was made. Several blessed minutes later the water went off, but not before the guests had been soaked. The bridesmaids were standing in a pathetic knot, hair sprayed up-dos now hanging down around their shoulders like dead animals. Make that *wet* dead animals.

Laurel huddled against her fiancé, her beautiful white gown covered with mud and grass stains. In the distance, Julia could see Devon and her crew frantically trying to save any food they could.

Amy ran up with Betsy hot on her heels.

"I found the groundskeeper," Amy said.

"And I found the plantation manager," Julia said. "How did this happen?"

Amy gazed around, her face pale and scared. "The timers."

"What?"

"The sprinklers come on at the same time every day, unless the timer is switched off."

Heart sinking, Julia glanced at Betsy. "Did we have sprinklers on the list?"

Betsy gave a jerky nod. "It was checked off, too."

"But we didn't double check today," Amy said, keeping her voice low.

From somewhere to Julia's right a voice rang out. An outraged voice. "I'll sue! That incompetent fool ruined my baby's wedding!"

Julia's lungs threatened to collapse. "Okay, my mind has officially shut off. What do we do?"

For once even the unflappable Betsy seemed to be out of ideas, and she shrugged helplessly.

Taking a deep breath, Amy took charge. "Betsy, my car is unlocked. I've got some towels in the trunk. Go get them. I'll try and head off Mrs. Manning. See if I can get her to calm down."

"What should I do?" Julia asked, as Betsy took off for the parking lot.

"Stay as far away from Mrs. Manning as possible," Amy

said. "Hide if you have to."

Oh, this was bad. Disaster movie of the week bad.

"Julia!"

Could this day get any worse? Julia stifled a groan as Grace and Sarah approached, with Meredith close behind them. How could Julia face her sister now?

"Sarah, I'm so sorry. The timer on the sprinkler system went off," Julia said. "It was on our list of things to check, but I don't know—"

Meredith touched Julia's arm. "You couldn't have known."

"I should have, and now the wedding is ruined. I'm trying to stay out of sight until the mayor's wife calms down, which might be sometime next century."

Seth hurried up, grabbing Julia by the shoulders. "Hey, are you all right?"

With a strangled sob, Julia fell into his arms. "I'm hiding out from Mrs. Manning."

"She's not going to kill you over a little water," he said.

"A little water?" she echoed in astonishment. "Did you see what happened? It was like dozens of Old Faithfuls going up all over the lawn. Everyone's soaked. The wedding is washed out. Literally. The mayor's wife is humiliated, and it's my fault. I'll be lucky if I don't wind up in jail over this."

Seth kissed her forehead. "No one is going to jail."

"At the very least she'll sue and bankrupt the business."

There were no reassuring words from anyone to deny this claim.

"I never should have agreed to help," Julia said. "I knew I'd screw up."

"You didn't screw up," Sarah protested.

"Oh, yes, young lady, she most certainly did."

Julia jumped. *Shoot. Mrs. Manning.* Amy trailed behind the charging bull so her efforts at keeping the woman at bay had obviously failed.

There was only one choice, and she couldn't let some self-important, small-town tyrant cow her. Fighting the urge to turn and run, Julia instead stiffened her spine and prepared for battle.

Mrs. Manning never had a chance to do anything because someone else stepped in her way. "Grace, get out of my way," Mrs. Manning said, eyes narrowed to slits.

In that moment, Grace grew about ten feet. "No. If this is to be discussed, it will be done without your rants and threats."

Mrs. Manning looked as if she was about to have a stroke. Obviously she wasn't used to being challenged. "Fine. We'll discuss this professionally. My lawyer will be calling tomorrow."

"Julia!"

What now? Julia thought as Betsy ran up the steps. She didn't have any towels, but she did have an empty liquor bottle, which she held aloft. "Look what I found in Amy's trunk."

Julia took the bottle. "Her trunk?"

"When I went to look for towels." Betsy held out several folders. "I found these, too."

"These are the files I thought I'd lost."

Julia turned to look at her second assistant, as all the clues fell into place. "Amy."

Dozens of witnesses turned to stare at the resident golden girl, who'd gone deathly white. "I— "

Meredith looked horrified. "Amy, you didn't."

"It was you all along," Julia said. "All the mishaps and errors. The missed appointments. The spiked punch."

Fat tears started rolling down Amy's cheeks. "I thought I'd gotten all the bottles out of the car."

"You sabotaged Marry Me?" Julia asked. "Why?"

"I wanted you to go away," Amy said. "I thought if things went wrong, you'd realize you couldn't handle the business and go home, and then—"

A light bulb went off. "Wait, wait. I know," Julia said. "You could have Seth to yourself."

"I saw the way he looked at you. I'd waited all those years for him to notice me, and then you showed up."

A murmur of confusion and outrage was buzzing around her as people realized what Amy had been up to.

"And today? Was that revenge because he chose me over you?" Julia asked, gesturing to the soaked guests.

"I had nothing to do with the sprinklers. I swear."

Julia folded her arms. "Right. Why not let me get blamed for Sprinklergate as well?"

Choking back a sob, Amy shook her head. "No. I was angry and hurt, but I told you before, I want Seth to be happy, and if you're that person then—"

Meredith took her sister's arm. "Give it up, Amy. You're only making things worse."

"I didn't do this. I wouldn't," Amy said.

It was clear from the narrow-eyed stares all around that no one believed her.

Laurel Manning looked near tears again. "You ruined my wedding to try and chase Julia away? How could you do that? We went to school together. We were friends."

"Amy, I can't tell you how disappointed I am in you," Mrs. Manning said, unable to resist getting in her own jab. "I could believe such behavior from Miss Richardson, but your mother raised you better than this."

Julia opened her mouth to protest the injustice of that statement, but one look from Her Highness' gimlet eye changed her mind.

Mrs. Vining stepped through the knot of guests. "Her mother raised her to fight for what she wants."

What now? "I'm sorry?" Julia asked.

"I cannot allow my daughter to take the blame for this," Mrs. Vining said.

Like heads at a tennis match, the audience looked back and forth between mother and daughter and Julia.

The new player in this drama didn't pay any attention to the guests. She kept her eyes on Julia. For the first time, Mrs. Vining's habitually sour expression had disappeared. Instead, she looked almost forlorn.

"*You* did something to the timer?" Julia asked in shock.

"I've been on the board of Hadden Acres for years," Mrs. Vining said. "We approved the funds to put the sprinkler system in."

Amy looked as stunned as the rest of the crowd must feel. "Mother, why in the world would you sabotage Laurel's wedding?"

"For the same reason as you."

"You wanted to get rid of me, too?" Julia asked.

Mrs. Vining gave a faint nod.

"What is this?" Julia said, her voice rising along with her temper. "Some sort of mother-daughter tag team? You two have got to find a better way to secure a boyfriend."

Mrs. Vining scanned Julia's face. "You remind me so much of Thomas," she said, in a near whisper.

Hearing her father's name stopped Julia's heart in an instant. Knowing Thomas Richardson's predilections, she had a sick feeling about what was coming.

"Mrs. Vining, we should go somewhere private," Julia said.

"No, I'm tired of pretending."

Grace seemed to sense the worst as well, because she stepped forward. "Sylvia."

"You should hear this too, Grace," Mrs. Vining said, her chin wobbling. "You should know how I betrayed you."

Grace's shoulders slumped, and her head dropped. "Oh, Sylvia."

In the yawning silence, Seth stepped into the fray. "All right everyone. The drama is over. All of you go on home and dry off."

"But my daughter's wedding!" Mrs. Manning cried.

At long last, Mayor Manning stepped forward. "We'll reschedule the wedding. Obviously this family has some pressing personal matters to attend to."

"What about Laurel?"

He took his wife's arm. "Now, Catherine."

****

The Mannings took themselves off, and the rest of the guests dispersed as well, though most looked like they would rather stay and watch.

Seth went in search of the plantation manager, who found an empty office. He'd seen enough in Sylvia Vining's face to know they were in for a terrible confession. Bad enough to find out Amy had been sabotaging Julia, but now Mrs. Vining was about to change everything. Seth followed everyone into the room, wishing to be anywhere else. The truth could set you free, he knew, but the telling of it could leave devastation in its wake.

Everyone else must have felt the same way. Grace and Sarah were huddled together on a small couch. As if sensing impending doom, Amy had stationed herself inside the doorway, with Meredith propping up the other side.

Meanwhile, Julia had strolled over to the window and was staring outside. He studied her, trying to get a read on what she was feeling, but she'd closed up tight as a drum. He doubted the view had captured her attention.

No one said anything, so finally Seth strode to the center of the room and took control. "Sylvia, you're obviously very troubled."

Amy couldn't stand the suspense anymore. "Mother, what is going on?"

Mrs. Vining gazed at Grace with deep sorrow.

"Something I should have confessed long ago."

"Confessed?" Amy repeated. "What are you talking about, and who is Thomas?"

"That would be my father," Julia said, without turning from the window.

"What does he have to do with anything?"

"We had an affair," Mrs. Vining said.

The words might have been dynamite going off. Even though Seth had sensed the truth, he still wasn't prepared for the blow. Neither was anyone else. Julia's shoulders jerked a little, but otherwise she barely reacted. It was as if she'd known all along, though how could she not? Julia knew Thomas Richardson better than anyone. The other occupants of the room didn't have the benefit of Julia's experience though, and they gasped in shock. Sarah put a hand to her mouth, and Meredith and Amy turned white.

Tears formed in Mrs. Vining's eyes. "I don't know how it happened. He was so charming. So different from other men." She turned to Grace. "You understand."

Grace seemed to have aged ten years in the last few minutes. "I know."

"If it makes you feel any better, it wasn't a fling. At least not for me. I loved him."

Grace's hand trembled as she brushed a lock of hair back from her face. "Were you carrying on an affair our entire marriage?"

"No. Oh, Grace, I wish I could make you understand."

Julia finally spun away from the window, her lips curling in a furious snarl. "Good luck with that. Weren't you the one who went on and on about being the moral compass in this town?"

Sylvia turned, her face stripped of its arrogance. "Your father came into my life at a very vulnerable time. I married very young. I was only nineteen and madly in love with my husband, but it didn't take me long to realize the feeling wasn't mutual."

"Your husband didn't love you?" Julia asked.

"More to the point, Steven married me for a position in my father's company," Mrs. Vining said. "I'd been offered up as the price for promotion as it were."

Meredith shifted in the doorway. "You never told us any of this."

"It's not the sort of thing you talk about with your children," Mrs. Vining said. "But you knew, Grace. Maybe it was never said out loud, but I'm sure you guessed."

"I wondered," Grace said, looking down at her lap.

"In public Steven played the role of the perfect husband, but at home it was as if I didn't exist. My only purpose was to entertain his clients, and of course produce sons to carry on the name. I couldn't even manage that. He was terribly disappointed when I had two girls."

Julia threw up her hands, as if her patience had run out. "Your story is sad and tragic, but can we skip to the part where you betrayed Grace with her husband?"

"Julia, let her speak," Grace said, in a gentle reprimand.

Julia pinched her lips together and faced the window again. Everything in him cried out to go to her, but Seth sensed she'd rebuff him right now. Instead, he tried to listen with as much compassion as he could. Tried to contain his own anger and frustration as he watched Sylvia Vining rip his future apart.

"Thank you," Sylvia said. "Julia is right, though. A sob story doesn't explain my behavior or excuse it. However, I hope you will find it in yourself to understand when I tell you that I found out Steven had been keeping another woman on the side throughout our entire marriage. I didn't know, until I saw them together one evening when he was supposed to be working."

Amy looked near tears. "You never said a word."

"Again, not something you tell your children," Mrs.

Vining said, clucking her tongue. "In any case, finding out I'd been a fool for my entire marriage was devastating."

"Yes, I can imagine." Grace's words were seeped in irony.

Sylvia flushed at the pointed barb. "It was right after I found out that I ran into Thomas. I was sitting in the park crying, and he walked up and sat beside me."

"And gave you a shoulder to cry on?" Julia ventured.

Mrs. Vining absorbed the sarcasm with a level look. "As a matter of fact, that's exactly what he offered. He let me cry and talk. I told him about everything. My farce of a marriage, the other woman, how I'd never felt loved in all my life. He understood."

"He should have," Julia said. "My father was always on a never ending quest to find the love of his life. Too bad for him that his soul mate was never the woman he was married to."

"Julia!" Seth barked out, throwing a warning glance in Grace's direction. Lord knew, he was furious too, but Julia was going to say something she'd regret if she didn't get control of her temper.

At his harsh tone, Julia flinched and her cheeks flushed. "Grace, I'm sorry."

Grace smiled, but it didn't reach her eyes.

"I'm the one who owes apologies," Mrs. Vining said. "I responded to my grief by betraying one of my dearest friends. The thing is, Thomas understood me. At first all we did was talk. He was the only person I *could* talk to. I didn't have to pretend my life was perfect with him. There was no image to uphold, no standard I needed to live up to. Then somehow it became more. I knew it was wrong. That I was going against everything I believed."

"How long did it last?" Meredith asked.

Amy seemed incapable of speaking at this point. She couldn't even look at her mother, keeping her gaze focused on a dark knot in the wooden floor.

"Six months," Mrs. Vining answered. "Until I found out I

was pregnant."

This time Julia gasped. "Pregnant? Was it my father's baby?"

"I knew it wasn't Steven's. He hadn't touched me in years."

"What did you do?" Meredith asked.

"I told Thomas. I suppose in some corner of my mind I hoped he'd declare his love for me and—"

"Let me guess," Julia said. "He'd whisk you away, and the two of you would live out your days in some kind of fairytale romance?"

Mrs. Vining chuckled, but it wasn't a happy sound. "Sadly, I did have some notion of that. He did no such thing, of course. He was horrified, both at the thought of a baby and the realization that I'd fallen in love with him. Turns out I was only another conquest for him. I was furious. At him and at myself. There was a terrible scene, and I threatened him. I told him I would go to Grace and confess everything."

"If he didn't claim your baby?" Julia asked.

"No, the scales were lifted from my eyes by then. I told him he had to leave and never come back because you deserved better, Grace. I couldn't do anything about my marriage, but I could do something about yours."

"Wait a minute." Julia finally left her post by the window. "Are you saying my father left because of you? He didn't leave to be with another woman, he left to get *away* from one?"

"That's right."

"I don't understand," Meredith said. "You never had another baby."

Sylvia's eyes filled. "No, I didn't. I lost the baby only a couple weeks after Thomas left. Punishment for my sins, I always imagined. I never said a word to anyone until today."

"Steven never knew?" Grace asked.

"No, he wouldn't have noticed. Now that he's passed it

hardly matters. I don't care what happens to me. I only wanted happiness for Amy. The kind I never found."

At the mention of her name, Amy finally came out of her shock-induced state. "Well, how do you think I'll find that happiness now?" she shouted, her face flushed with anger. "The news will be all over town within hours. Who could ever want me knowing what you did?"

Meredith shifted in the doorway. "Amy—"

Amy spun around. "What? Don't get angry? Don't feel betrayed because the woman who raised me is nothing but a fake and a liar?"

"Just calm down," Meredith said.

"No. I'm through being calm. And I'm through listening to *her*!" Amy cried, pointing an accusing finger at her mother.

Pushing past her sister, Amy flung the door open and ran out.

After a long moment, Meredith went and knelt at her mother's feet. "Come on, I'll drive you home."

Sylvia nodded and stood up, pausing by the love seat where Grace was seated. "I know I did a terrible thing, but I hope some day you'll find it in your heart to forgive me."

When Grace didn't respond, Sylvia quietly left the room.

Meredith hesitated. She opened her mouth, but couldn't seem to find the words to say.

Julia didn't have the same trouble. "Why aren't you angry with her?"

"Maybe because I know a little something about betraying everything you believe in," Meredith said, with a sad smile. "Seems my mother and I aren't so different after all."

With one last apologetic glance, Meredith followed her mother out of the room. Everyone else sat in stunned silence, unsure what to say or do.

Seth tried to gather his emotions. If Thomas Richardson were here right now he'd beat him to a bloody pulp. He had to hold it together, though. Couldn't afford to let loose and punch a hole in the wall like he wanted.

Instead, Seth walked over to Grace. "I think it's time we went home."

Grace nodded. He could tell she was trying to act normal, but it was a failed effort. Her face reflected utter defeat.

Taking his outstretched hand, she stood, swaying a little. "I thought I was done being hurt by him."

"He only has that power if you let him," Seth said, slipping an arm around her waist. "Remember, you went on to have a wonderful life after he left, with a husband who adores you."

Grace leaned against his side, as if unable to hold herself upright anymore. "I know, but how do I put something like this aside? It shouldn't matter, but it does."

"Put *him* aside. Don't waste one moment thinking about Thomas Richardson. He's a miserable man who continues to seek happiness in ways that are doomed to fail. All we can do is feel sorry for him and pray his heart will be opened to the truth."

"You're right. I just don't know how I'll ever—" Grace broke off with a gasp as she remembered Julia. "Oh, honey, I'm so sorry."

"What do you have to feel sorry about?" Julia asked.

"You must be upset as well."

Julia's shrug of dismissal didn't fool Seth for a second. He knew her heart had to be splintered into a million pieces. "Surprised maybe. Like you, I thought I was done being hurt by my father. Seems it's a skill he'll always possess."

Sarah rose to her feat. "Maybe we shouldn't get into this now. We're all upset. We need to regroup, and then we'll figure out what to do."

"She's right," Seth said. "Nothing good will come about today."

They all filed out of the room, he and Sarah bracketing

Grace like bookends. As they crossed the threshold, Seth glanced over his shoulder. Julia stared back at him with eyes hollowed by sadness. Her throat worked as she swallowed. She didn't cry, though. Perhaps there were no more tears left in her to shed over her father.

Then she turned her back on him.

Chapter Thirty-Four

"Julia, we need to talk."

That's how Thomas Richardson had always started the it's-time-for-me-to-move-on conversation. By the time Julia was a teenager the phrase hadn't been too much of a surprise. But that day, as she'd sat at the desk in her fairy bedroom doing homework, the words had pierced Julia's heart like an ice pick. In the back of her mind she'd always known her time here would end, but she'd hoped the dream would last longer.

"Who is she?" Julia asked, not even lifting her head.

Her father's hands drifted into his pockets, a clear sign he was uncomfortable. "I'm sorry it has to be this way."

"If you were sorry you wouldn't keep doing it."

"That's enough, young lady."

"I could stay here."

"No."

"Why not?" Julia asked. "Or will I live with you?"

A long hesitation served as her answer. "I don't think that would—"

"Work out," Julia said, with a smirk. "I know. So, why can't I stay with Grace and Sarah?"

"Because you can't. It's best for everyone if we make a clean break."

"Best for you anyway."

A vessel flexed in his temple. "I said that's enough, Julia. It's been decided."

Julia had never understood her father's insistence on making a clean break. Until today. Now that she knew the subtext surrounding his sudden decision to leave she could even appreciate how, in his own way, he'd tried to protect Grace and Sarah. She didn't doubt Sylvia Vining would have made good on her threat to tell everyone about the affair. In leaving he'd spared Grace and Sarah that humiliation at least.

Julia looked out the window of the bedroom that had once been her sanctuary. The morning was dark and dreary with heavy clouds promising storms. Seemed even the heavens were in mourning.

If things didn't look brighter in the daylight, they were clearer. At least Julia's resolve was clear, which was why her bags were packed and sitting by the door. She'd been so stupid. Fooling herself into thinking her past with this family didn't matter and that the specter of her father wouldn't taint any relationship she had with them now.

Seeing Grace's face yesterday had proven what a foolish hope that had been. Seth had said it. The only way Grace could heal was to put Thomas Richardson out of her mind, and there was no way she could do that with a living reminder right under her nose.

Amy was right, too. The news of Sylvia Vining's betrayal would be all over town soon, if it wasn't already. Everyone would know why Julia's father had left, and her presence would enflame the firestorm. Plus, she didn't like to think of the disapproval Seth would face when people learned about them. He might not care if he lost his position, but she did.

So, a clean break it would be.

As Julia shut the last bag, a gentle tap sounded at her

door.

A moment later, Grace appeared. "Julia, I've made—" Her eyes fell on the suitcases. "What are you doing?"

"It's time I went back where I belong."

The door swung open wide. "You belong here."

"Where I can be a constant reminder of what my father did? How can you even look at me and not feel the sting every time?"

"I was overwhelmed yesterday," Grace said, hands fluttering. "We all were."

Not exactly an answer to the question.

"Honey, no one blames you for what your father did," Grace said. "I certainly don't. I just have to pray I can learn to forgive him. For my sake, I have to."

"You can't do that if I'm here. Even you aren't that much of a saint. It's best for everyone if I go."

"What about Seth? Is it best for him, when you were only starting to discover what you could have?"

Despair threatened to drown her. "That was another foolish dream," Julia said.

"It's never foolish to love."

"It feels that way."

Grace's eyes filled with tears. "Julia, please don't go."

"I have to."

"No, you don't have to run away."

Julia couldn't take tears anymore. "This is for the best," she said, kissing Grace's cheek.

Before Grace could respond, Julia slipped out of the room.

"Where are you going?"

"Out."

"Julia."

Julia kept going. She pushed through the screen door and stood on the porch, her lungs burning with regret and shame. She couldn't even process where to go. After a few deep breaths her gaze fell on Seth's apartment.

Without thinking, her footsteps took her up the narrow stairs. The knob turned easily, and the door swung open. Julia flashed back to the first time she'd come up here. The quilt caught her eye, and she drifted toward across the room. No one would ever make a quilt like this for her.

She spotted the framed picture on the dresser, and walked over. "I'm sorry I couldn't be the one he needed," Julia said, tracing the image of the pretty blonde woman.

There was a Bible open next to the picture. Words swam through a veil of tears.

"For I have plans for you. Plans to make you prosper and…"

She flipped the page.

"I can do all things through Christ Jesus who strengthens me."

Another page.

"For God so loved the world, that He gave his only Son, that whoever believes in Him shall not die, but have everlasting life."

Julia picked up the worn, leather-bound book and kept reading. Exactly when the tears streaming down her cheeks turned to something more profound than sadness, she didn't know. Many of the verses were familiar, but for the first time they were more than words. They filled spaces she hadn't even realized were empty.

"Ask and you shall receive. Seek and you shall find. Knock and the door shall be opened."

With a racing heart, she closed her eyes. "God, I don't know why you would even want me in heaven for all eternity. I'm sarcastic, cynical, and hardheaded. I'll probably drive you crazy. I thought I was fine on my own. I didn't need anyone, certainly not you. I was wrong. I'm a mess on my own. I'm probably not doing this right, but I need your love and your forgiveness, so I'm asking for it."

Taking a deep breath, Julia waited. If she'd expected a heavenly acknowledgment, like a crack of thunder or angelic chorus, it didn't come. A profound sense of peace flooded though her anyway.

"God, if I could ask one thing, then I'll leave you alone," she continued. "Please be with Seth and help him understand why I have to go. He's such a wonderful, loving man, and he deserves happiness. I don't know why you would offer us a glimpse of something amazing, only to yank it away, but I guess you have plans. Please help him accept this, and please bring him the perfect wife. Amen."

"He already did."

Julia's startled scream echoed through the small apartment.

Seth held up his hands. "Whoa. Sorry."

"You have got to stop doing that," Julia said, putting a hand to her chest. "How long have you been standing there?"

"Long enough." He stepped closer. "I guess you missed what I said, since you were too busy screaming."

A flicker of impossible hope rose up in her as he approached. "I may have. Run it by me again."

"You were praying that God would bring me the perfect wife, and I answered that He already had. He brought you. As for understanding and accepting why you have to leave, that will never happen."

"Seth, I wish I could believe it would work," Julia said, dropping to the bed.

"You could believe in me," Seth said, kneeling in front of her. "You could believe that I love everything about you, even the things that are messy and painful. That we can get through anything if we put God first and trust Him to guide us."

"What about Grace? I can't stay if my presence is going to be a constant reminder of my father's betrayal."

"Why don't you ask me why I'm here?"

"Okay, why are you here?"

"Because Grace called me in a panic. Said I needed to find you before it was too late."

"She did?"

He nodded. "Does that sound like a woman who wants you gone from her life?"

Julia laced her fingers through his. "Do you think we can make it?"

"Not if you keep running. I can't promise what the future will bring. Only God knows that. All I can tell you, is that I knew my life was going to change the first time I saw you on that softball field."

Something in her heart shifted. "Music."

"Hmm?" he said, eyes crinkling in confusion.

"Like in a movie. The first time the star-crossed couple meets. There are always strings and drums."

A startled expression passed behind his eyes, and then he chuckled. "I would have described it as a symphony."

"You heard it, too?"

"Yeah. About knocked me on my butt. Prickly, bitter, keep-your-distance, Julia Richardson."

The description rankled. "Prickly? Bitter? Is that how you saw me?"

"I'd much rather talk about how I see you now," Seth said. "And I'd like to know what you think this moment would garner on our soundtrack."

The faint hope turned to a blazing sense of certainty, and Julia pulled her hand away, but only so she could draw him closer. "I'm thinking a choir, some brass, and the *Hallelujah Chorus*."

"Amen," Seth said before lowering his head.

About the Author

Growing up Kristin devoured books like bags of Dove Dark Chocolate. Her first Golden Book led to Laura Ingalls Wilder, Nancy Drew, Encyclopedia Brown, C.S. Lewis and the Sweet Valley High series. Later, she discovered romance novels and fell in love all over again. It's no surprise then that Kristin would one day try her hand at writing them. She writes inspirational romance and women's fiction filled with love, laughter and a leap of faith. When she's not writing her next novel, Kristin works as an advertising copywriter. She also enjoys singing in the church choir and worship team and playing flute in a community orchestra.

You can connect with Kristin at
www.KristinWallaceAuthor.com on Facebook:
facebook.com/KristinWallaceAuthor and Twitter:
@KWallaceAuthor

Astraea Press
Pure. Fiction.
www.astraeapress.com

CPSIA information can be obtained at www.ICGtesting.com
Printed in the USA
LVOW11s1809040214

372305LV00005B/427/P

9 781494 298159